Time & Tide

A Hew Cullan Mystery

~

Shirley McKay

This edition published in Great Britain in 2011 by
Polygon, an imprint of Birlinn Ltd
West Newington House
10 Newington Road
Edinburgh
EH9 1QS

www.birlinn.co.uk

9 8 7 6 5 4 3 2 1

ISBN 978 1 84697 194 5

British Library Cataloguing-in-Publication Data
A catalogue record for this book is available on
request from the British Library

The publisher acknowledges investment from

towards the publication of this volume

Typeset in Arno Pro by Palimpsest Book Production Limited,
Falkirk, Stirlingshire
Printed in Great Britain by Clays Ltd, St Ives plc

Acknowledgement

With grateful acknowledgement to James Watson of Culross, the Scotland–Veere Organisation, Esther van Engelen of the Romantik Auberge de Campveerse Toren (open as an inn for the last 500 years); and especially to Peter Blom, municipal archivist of Veere and Paul Veenhuijzen of Earlshall, for keeping alive the spirit of the old *entente*.

Thanking thame maist hertfullie of their gude ancient lufe . . . Beseking thame that they will continew thair gude will towart us . . . the maist mutual ancient lufing affection quhilkis we haif born aither towartis utheris of auld tymes.

Campfeir [to] *the gude tounes of Scotland, 1578*

Prologue

St Andrews, Scotland
October 1582

Before he learned his letters, Jacob read the wind. He could not recall a time when its patterns made no sense to him, clearer than his catechism, whispered as a child.

– *What is thy only comfort, in life and in death?*

– *That I, with body and soul, both in life and in death, am not my own.*

Jacob read the wind, and cursed it when it dropped to lank and irksome stillness. When it turned against him, he was unprepared. It was not as if he had not understood. He knew precisely what this wind required of him, yet he could not rise to it. The waters came at last to blast upon the quietness, and Jacob knew, for certain, he was not his own.

– *I am not my own, but belong to my saviour, the Lord Jesus Christ.*

He had no hope of Christ in the bowels of the black ocean. It caught the little bark and tossed it like a winnower, blowing dust and thundering, threshing out the storm.

Joachim had been the last to die. He had died before the storm broke. And Jacob had stitched Joachim into a folded sheet of sail-cloth, weighed down with lead shot, before tipping the dead boy into the sea. Jacob's hands were thick and woolly, like a pair of gloves. He had struggled to sew up the seam. It was a blessing that the boy had died before the storm. Jacob saw his mother still, weeping by the river Leie in Ghent. He knew the family well, and had given her his handkerchief. But Joachim's mind had turned, like all the rest.

1

Jacob had restrained him in the hold, and all through the night had listened to his howls. The pity was it was not Joachim's fault. Jacob had allowed the boy to gorge himself on sweetmeats, leavening his last hours with the captain's bread. He heard him howling still, though Joachim had been dead for several days.

Jacob had acquired the captain's cabin, where he wrote to Beatrix after Joachim died. It took a little time, but he had time enough. *Tell Joachim's mother that,* he wrote, and crossed it out. He knew that Beatrix would make sure that Lotte learned to read, and so he wrote the child a letter of her own, and sealed them both with wax from the captain's candle stub. He found a wooden pepper pot, and placed the scripts inside, together with his book. The letter of its creed he had by heart. He let the candle drip to make it tight around the bung, carving the direction on the surface with his pocketknife, Beatrix van der Straeten, begijnhof sint Elisabeth te Gent. He considered for a moment whether he should set the casket on the open sea, or keep it in the stronghold of the ship, closed in the ocean's grasp. In the end, he kept it there, knowing it was all the same. He placed it in the captain's kist among the listless instruments, and lying on the captain's blanket, Jacob closed his eyes. Better to die quiet, and the ship might let him shelter for a while. He thought of Joachim sleeping on the seabed, where the little fish swam silver through the slack seams of his shroud, making streams of water from his eyes. He thought of Beatrix, fearless, with no breath of hope. He cursed the airless ocean, weeping for the sands. Yet when the wind picked up, he was not prepared for it. He climbed up on the half deck and cried out, choked and raging, not ready yet to yield so easily to death.

Jacob found the wheel, with little hope of turning it. Tobias was dead, and Jacob on his own could not hope to guide the vessel through the storm. Though he read the wind as clearly as a book, he had never been a mariner. He could not take in the spret sail, lower the foresail, bear up the helm or haul the tack aboard, or any of the things he had heard the first mate cry. He no longer felt his fingers in the wrenching wind. Vast waters bellowed, engulfing the deck, and Jacob was knocked from his feet. He clung to the mizzen mast, sodden and blind. He could neither veer nor steer her, rocking through the storm. She was cradled in a trough, where she drank in sheets of water, lapping up from either side. Jacob, drenched and sobbing, sought to scoop them out. He could not clear the decks as fast as she could fill them; and so at last he climbed, exhausted, to the stern, preferring not to drown inside the body of the ship. Yet he found he could not drop into the blackness of the sea. He turned the wheel again, and prayed his old adversary the wind to be a little kind to him. And for a moment, God – or was it yet the wind? – appeared to hear his prayer; the hull began to roll and the fickle gusts rebounded, taking up the sail. The ship was blasted on the waves and blown about its course, with a sudden list and lurching that washed the water out. Jacob gave thanks; to God, after all. And it was Christ his saviour, as Jacob understood, who lit the castle ramparts shadowed on the rock. Far off in the distance, he was coming in to land.

It took a while before he realised what the shadows meant. He came to shallow waters, in the darkness of the storm. The landing craft had long ago been lowered to the sea. Before the early fish-ermen set out to cast their lines, Jacob would be washed up on the strand, wrung out in the wreckage of the ship. He belonged to his saviour, the Lord Jesus Christ, for he had no spirit left in him to fight. He looked back at the mizzen mast, and felt it sag and spring. The bark began to fracture as she bore down on the rocks. And then he saw his cargo, braced above the hold, and understood at last what he should do. He found her fixed and fast, unflustered by the wind, though high above her flank the topsails flapped and furled. Jacob crept inside to listen for the crack.

And she was still and dark inside, quite dry, and so familiar in her warmth that when he closed his eyes he almost could forget the lurching of the ship, the howling of the wind he had often sought for her. And though she yawned and creaked a little, still she did not stir. She smelled of grease and timmermen when Jacob closed his eyes, so that when at last it came he almost did not mind.

Chapter 1

An Ill Wind

*The twa extraordinar professouris affirmis . . . they ar not subject
to live collegialiter to eat and ly within the college.*
Commission of Enquiry, St Andrews University, 1588

Hew Cullan kicked aside the broken slates as he turned briskly
through the entrance to St Salvator's, his hat and gown dishevelled
in the wind. He crossed the college courtyard and hurried to the hall,
setting straight his cap. He was, he was aware, a little late; and yet he
knew the hall would wait for him. The scholars rose expectantly to
see him take his place. They would have gaped like louns to catch
him at the chase, darting through the tennis courts in primrose-
stirruped slops. Masters, they well knew, could have no other lives.

And for the regents in their midst, who had the daily care and
teaching of these boys, this was true enough, reflected Hew. His
own place was a sinecure: *magister extraordinar* in law, in a college
that could boast no legal faculty. He played little part in its domestic
life or discipline. The appointment of professors in the laws and
mathematics had left no impression on the core curriculum,
grounded in philosophy and arts. Hew gave lectures to the college
once or twice a year. As second master, he was sometimes called
on to officiate, in the absence of the principal, anatomist Giles
Locke. When, as often happened, they were both engaged, on some
more pressing business of the Crown, the third professor, grumbling
gently, set aside his sums to step in to the breach.

This third professor, standing at Hew's side, reached across to nudge

5

him, breaking through his dreams. He plucked a withered fragment from Hew's sleeve. 'Acer maius, or, to many, platanus,' he commented. 'The greater maple, commonly, and falsely, called the plane tree or the sycamore.' The mathematician opened out his palm, showing Hew the seed, the winged fruit of the sycamore. 'You are sprouting wings. What as a bairn I chased round dizzy in the wind. We called them *locks and keys*, or *whirlijacks*.'

Hew suppressed a smile, which old Professor Groat, with his rheumy, washed-out eyes, was quick enough to see. 'I understand you well. You do not think that I could ever be a child; or else this fledging plane tree harks back to the ark.'

'Ah, no, not at all,' protested Hew, who had indeed been thinking something of the sort. How old, after all, was Bartholomew Groat? Sixty years? Eighty? Or, as Giles asserted, nearer fifty-three, of phlegmatic disposition, prone to windy gout.

The professor blew his nose. ''Tis true enough, that when I was a boy this maple was a novelty, which now is thought a scourge, and counted as a weed.'

He did not give up the seed, but wrapped it in his handkerchief to put it in his pocket; whether to preserve the ghost of little Bartie Groat, giddy as the wind, or to prevent its spread, Hew could not be sure. 'The winds were wild last night,' he remarked more diplomatically.

This observation had a sobering effect. 'Foul spirits stir up tempests,' Groat imparted gloomily. 'The milk kine startled in the fields, the storm has soured the milk. The priory trees are torn up by their roots; the shore mill lade is flooded. Tis providential, Hew.'

'Stuff and superstition,' Hew retorted. 'I do not believe in it.'

Bartie cast his eyes to heaven, sending up a prayer. 'The young are always quick to scorn. And yet the wind has one effect that cannot fail to move you. I heard there was a ship wrecked in the bay. All the crew were lost.'

'Dear God, rest them!' whispered Hew. 'Were the poor men Scots?'

'Zeelanders or Flemish, judging from the load. I wonder that you did not see it, on your way to town,' murmured Bartie Groat.

Hew shook his head. 'I lay at the West Port last night,' he explained. 'My horse does not care for the wind.' Dun Scottis cared for little that upset his regimen. He baulked at wind and water, with perfect equilibrium.

'You ought to take up lodgings, as I've said before. I confess myself perplexed that you will not consider it,' Bartie answered peevishly.

It was a well-worn argument, and one to which Hew struggled to respond. He had declined the rooms that came with his election, preferring to remain at home at Kenly Green. The house stood four miles south, an hour on foot upon a winter's day, and a little less in summer, on his sluggish horse. Returning to the college for a second year, he already felt the cloisters closing in, the hallowed kirk and walkways a conspiracy of spires. It was not a feeling he could share with Bartie Groat, who took his dinners daily at the college mess, and brightened when the cook doled out a second slop of neaps. Hew did not care to end his days *collegialiter*. He changed the subject quickly. 'I see the doors have closed. So we are all assembled, and ready to begin.'

One by one, the names were called, and the students swore allegiance to the university. The youngest scholar stumbled at the stand. In awe at the proceedings, he clean forgot his oath. Hew Cullan winked at him, and saw the boy's astonishment collapse into a grin. A regent hurried forward and retreated with his charge, who, to Hew's amusement, was named as *George Buchanan*. He saw nothing in the boy that stuck him as remarkable. It seemed unlikely that their paths would cross again.

Bartie had withdrawn, like a tortoise to his shell, where for the last half hour he had appeared to be asleep. When Hew was least expecting it, he blinked, thrusting out: 'It is not like our principal to miss matriculation.'

Hew answered stiffly, 'Indeed, not.' He cursed both God and

7

Bartie Groat. In a few more minutes' time, enrolment would be done, and he could take his worries out into the street. For now, he must stay resolute, civil and in place. He did his best to look discouraging.

'Perhaps he has been called out to a patient,' Bartie droned, relentlessly. Giles was a physician, as well as an anatomist, with a thriving practice in the town.

'Aye, perhaps.'

'Or on business of the Crown.'

'Tis very likely,' Hew agreed.

'Though on business of the Crown, you also are most frequently invoked. Therefore it may be inferred, since you are here, and he is not, it is not business of the Crown.'

Groat was penetrating, gazing once again with his colourless, damp eyes, no less clear and piercing through the film of age. Hew saw no escape. The ceremony drawing to a close, the boys were ushered out, to lecture rooms and lodging houses. Hew was left behind with Professor Groat. He did not dislike the man. Groat was a fine astronomer, and lyrical upon the motions of the spheres. But he remained inclined to gloom, his prognostics seldom ending happily. On this subject, at this time, Hew had no wish to talk to him.

'His young wife is with child, of course,' Bartie reached his pinnacle.

'She is,' admitted Hew.

'Pray pardon – I had quite forgotten – he is married to your sister, is he not? Who has the falling sickness?'

'I commend you on your powers of recollection,' Hew returned abruptly.

Groat persisted, undeterred. 'Doubtless, there are dangers there. Please tell Giles, they are in my prayers.'

'Doubtless, he will thank you. I will tell him straight away.'

Professor Groat was right. It was unthinkable that Giles would miss matriculation, without a word of explanation or apology to

Hew. If he was not in college, then he must be at home, and if he was at home, that could only mean one thing. Hew abandoned Bartie at the door and hurried down the North Street towards the Fisher Gait.

The streets beyond the college were deserted, as though the wind had swept them clear, and left behind its footprints in a scattering of leaves. The fisherwives had dropped their cries of codlings and late crabs, their empty crates and buckets littering the steps. A bare-legged child stood watchman, rushing at the gulls. Hew called out in passing, 'Are the markets done? The clock has just struck twelve.'

The child stopped to consider this, sucking on a thumb. It offered up at last, 'All gaun, tae the wreck.'

'And left you on your own? Good bairn,' Hew answered vaguely. He could not discern, from the whisper thick with thumb, whether he was talking to a girl or boy. He found himself unsettled by the queerness of the child, and by the empty thoroughfares that led to the cathedral, the town and markets suddenly bereft, upended by the storm. He hurried past the fishing quarter to the castle on its rock, towards the little house that overlooked the cliff. The wind had dropped back, the sea a sheet of glass, where a hazy sunshine skittered, bouncing back and lighting up the stones.

The house was battened fast against the wind and sunlight, doors and shutters closed. Hew's knock was answered by the servant, Paul. 'I kent it was yersel,' he yawned, 'by dint of a' the din. The master is asleep. I'll tell him that you called.'

'How so, asleep? Has your mistress had her child?' demanded Hew.

'She hasna' started with her labours yet. No doubt you will be telt, when her time is due.' The servant had retreated, pulling back the door. Hew stopped it with his foot. 'I think you know me better, Paul,' he warned. 'Since I am not the blacksmith, nor the barker with his bill, you do not close the door to me. It seems you have forgotten it.'

The reprimand struck home. Paul began to stutter and to blush.

'Tis only that . . . your pardon, sir, but do not tell the doctor. He is fair forfochten.'

'Do not tell him what?' a sleepy voice inquired, and Giles himself came rumbling through the hall, squinting at the light. 'If that is Master Hew, then bid him wait until I'm dressed.'

'By your leave,' muttered Hew to the servant, who allowed him to pass with a hiss. 'Do not say, sir, that I did not prepare you.'

'Prepare me for what?' Hew hissed back.

'Why is it so dark in here?' Giles had opened up the shutters, letting in the air, and blinking as the sunlight filtered through the room. 'How comes the sun so bright?' he pondered paradoxically.

'How comes it that your household is asleep?' retorted Hew.

'I know not . . . What? What time is it?' Giles rubbed his eyes.

Paul answered, disingenuously, 'Mebbe eight, or nine? I cannot rightly say, for I havna' heard the clock.'

'It is a little after twelve,' corrected Hew. 'And yet it is no matter, Giles.'

Giles looked baffled, like a man disturbed from walking in his sleep, to find out he has trodden on his spectacles. 'Of course it matters!' He made sense of it at last. 'I have missed matriculation.'

'No matter, that,' said Hew. 'Professor Groat and I have managed it between us. And save for my solicitude, and Bartie's speculation, we managed it quite well.'

'I've no doubt that you *managed* it,' protested Giles. 'That is not the point. The point is in the principle; that is, I am the principal. Did I not tell you to wake me?' he rounded on Paul. 'Did I not tell you, *expressly*?'

The servant stood his ground. 'I do not recall it, sir. Now, I was looking for your hat, when Master Hew came chappin' at the door; I'll go and find it now, and by your leave. I doubt you must have left it at the college.' He slunk off down the passage, with a backward glance at Hew, which plainly spoke, '*You* stirred it; now you settle it.'

Giles looked hopelessly at Hew. 'Much good my hat will do

me now! I must be severe with him, for he has gone too far. He always goes too far. Does he? Has he? Has he gone too far?' he flustered.

'He does, and has, and always goes too far,' acknowledged Hew. 'And yet, on this occasion, he must be commended, for clearly he holds your best interests at heart.'

The doctor groaned. 'Then he is above himself, and ought to be dismissed!'

'I cannot think that that will help. What is the matter, Giles? This is not like you,' said Hew.

'I am not quite myself,' admitted Giles. 'My world stands on its end. It is the helter-skelter of a dizzy heart.'

'Indeed, that does sound serious,' Hew answered with a smile.

'It is serious. The matter is your sister Meg. She spent last night in thrall to the falling sickness.'

'I feared it,' Hew exclaimed, 'though am loath to hear it. How does she now?'

'Sleeping like a child. The worst of it has passed; the nurse has come to sit with her. I closed my eyes a moment . . .'

'Then Paul is right and I am to be blamed for waking you,' Hew declared emphatically. 'The crisis point is over, rest assured.'

'*Rest assured?*' Giles cried. 'If I could rest assured . . .! I am helpless to help her, Hew. *Helpless.*'

It was the closest he had come to frank despair, and Hew felt at a loss. 'You are too much in the dark,' he tried at last, 'and want a little sun, to show this prospect in a fairer light. Come, then, walk with me. The air will do you good.'

The doctor shook his head. 'I cannot leave the house.'

'And yet, a moment past, you were all for setting out, to see the boys matriculate,' Hew reminded him. 'You are disordered, Giles, and have lost your balance. Come, I insist. We'll keep the house in sight.'

They settled on the path above the castle beach, and walked along the cliff top to the summit of Kirk Hill, that led down to the harbour and the shore.

11

'I am right sorry,' ventured Hew at last, 'to hear that Meg has taken fits again, at this close stage of her confinement. I cannot comprehend it, for I thought the sickness well controlled.'

'For that,' Giles returned, 'you had not reckoned with the wind.'

'What has the wind to do with it? You sound like Bartie Groat!' objected Hew.

Giles looked small and cowed in the shadow of the cliffs, his towering bulk diminished by the water and the sky. 'Do you not see it?' he urged.

Hew resisted stubbornly. 'I do not see at all.'

'Then I shall explain it,' Giles answered with a sigh. 'You are my dearest friend, and know me well enough to know I do not sink to superstition, like Professor Groat.'

'I thank God for that,' snorted Hew.

'And yet it is a fact that the wind effects disturbances,' the doctor went on earnestly. 'It sets the world on edge. The master at the lector-schule remarks it in his bairns, running wild and shrieking when the gusts blow high. It has no less effect upon your sister Meg, and one well fraught with danger, in agitating sickness, and precipitating fits. I can no more control it than the raging seas.

'The sailors with their quadrants cannot make the compass of the ocean's toss and turn, where chance clouds overlap the constant flux of tides. We draw the moon and oceans, the heavens and the stars, and shape their folds of darkness to our little worlds, yet for all our charts, we cannot map the surface of one fragment of the whole. We think ourselves ay at the centre, at its very heart, that somehow we have harnessed nature, bending wind and water to our will, yet all the while we are as nothing, specks and motes caught in the breeze, that nature taunts and tosses like the frigate in a storm.'

'I know you do not think that,' remonstrated Hew, 'who own the finest sets of instruments that I have ever seen.'

'They are but trinkets, toys. I thought to make a horoscope!' Giles contested bitterly, 'But think of that! I thought to mark his coming on a *chart*. And would that smooth his passage, do you think? Would such calculations help the bairn?'

'Well, I do confess, I have never made much sense of your prognostications; I make a poor astronomer,' reflected Hew. 'Yet I will affirm your measure over nature, your medicine and your physic over its disease. As I have seen Meg, with her potions and simples, mop out corruptions and clear up the cough.'

'Meg is a special case,' conceded Giles. 'She turns nature in upon itself, and bends it to her will. Then nature is become an art, and sickness makes the cure.'

'Well then, trust in her. She proves it can be done. And when your courage fails you, put your trust in God.'

'Amen to that.' The doctor fumbled in his pockets, drawing out a string of beads. Awkwardly, Hew turned away, allowing Giles the quietness of prayer. He watched a young girl clamber over rocks, throwing pebbles on the beach below. The girl glanced up and caught his eye. Then, to his astonishment, she ran across the sand to turn a perfect cartwheel, white limbs whirling naked in the shadow of Kirk Hill.

'Look there!' Hew exclaimed. 'And you might find your thesis proved: the world turns upside down!'

Giles looked up and frowned. He slipped the rosary into his pocket. 'That is Lilias Begg, who should not be out alone. She is an innocent; a natural fool. The louns unkindly cry her, daft quene of the shore. Come up, Lilias Begg!' he called out to the child, while Hew gave thanks to God for the distraction.

The girl smoothed down her dress, and climbed the steps carved in the cliff, her bare legs flecked with sand.

'If she is seen as lewd and loose, the kirk will hold her mother to account,' Giles asserted anxiously.

Hew objected, 'Surely, she is just a child!'

'She is seventeen. Lilias Begg!' Giles called out again, 'Where is your mother? Does she know you're gone?'

'You do not need to shout,' said Lilias sweetly. 'For, I am here.'

13

She turned a somersault. 'I can coup the lundie,' she announced.
'So I see,' Giles tutted. 'Lilias Begg, this will not do.'

Lilias Begg had skin like milk, paler than a swaddling bairn's, that never saw the sun. She had brittle, flaxen hair, fairer than the smallest child's, and fey, elfin features, like a faun from faerie land. She stared at Hew with solemn eyes, and did not return his smile.

'Where on earth has she come from?' Hew whispered to Giles.

'She is the daughter of Maude Benet, that keeps the haven inn, and of Ranald Begg. A drunkard and a sot,' Giles declared contemptuously. 'He drank himself into an early grave, and left the world a better place once he had gone to Hell. He beat Maude Benet senseless, when she was with child. For which he put a shilling in the poor box, and escaped a fortnight in the jougs.'

It was rare for Giles to speak so unequivocally, and rarer still to hear him damn a man. The damage to an unborn child had cut the doctor deep. Nonetheless, he qualified, 'Or so I have been told.'

Lilias said suddenly, 'I am the whirlijack.'

'And what is that?' demanded Giles.

'The *whirlijack.*' Lilias began to spin like a whirlwind, perilously close to the edge of the cliff.

The doctor caught her hands. 'Be still; you will dance us all giddy! Whatever do you mean?'

'I am the whirligig, that spins the world.'

'The seed pods from the sycamore,' suggested Hew. 'The leaves and fruits are blown all over town.'

'Aye, but spins the world?' Giles fretted. Something had unsettled him, returning him to gloom. He was already looking back towards the house.

Lilias said helpfully, 'It came here on a ship.'

'Some trinket she has picked up at a fair,' Doctor Locke concluded. 'A trick to catch the wind. This is Master Hew,' he turned again to Lilias, 'who will take you home.'

Hew spluttered, 'I will *what?*'

''Tis plain enough,' insisted Giles. 'She will not go alone.'

'Ah, but surely, Paul . . .' said Hew.

'Paul would prove no match for her,' Giles argued. 'For all she is an innocent, she's cunning, in her way. She will lead a man a dance if he allows her to. Now she has come of age, it is her natural instinct. If Lilias is taken by a man, then it must be someone who can give a good account of himself.'

Lilias smiled knowingly. 'I saw a man, in my Mammie's bed. I saw a man, and his hands were all black,' she confided.

'Dear God!' muttered Hew. 'I take your point,' he said to Giles, 'though it is scarcely reassuring.'

The doctor hesitated. 'I would go myself . . .'

'Peace, I'm on my way. Lilias, take my hand!' Hew addressed the girl perhaps more brusquely than he had intended, for her lip began to quiver. 'I want Mistress Meg.'

'So that is it,' Giles sighed. 'Meg has ay been kind to her, and gives her sugar suckets for the cough. I will have some suckets sent to you,' he promised, 'but you cannot see her now. Mistress Meg is not well.'

Lilias asked brightly, 'Will she die?'

Hew said, 'Hush, for pity's sake!' as the girl began to sing, 'Mistress Meg is dead and gone, poor dead sailors all are gone.'

Giles cleared his throat. 'No one here is dead and gone. Yet I must leave you to it. In the temporal sense,' he excused himself to Hew, 'I have been gone too long.'

'Aye, for certain, go,' his friend assured him. 'I will see her home.' He turned to Lilias Begg. '*You* are trouble, as I think.'

Lilias smiled. 'Come see!' She took his hand and ran, down Kirk Heugh and through the harbour, turning south along the shore, past the priory and the Sea Port, past the fishing boats and mill. The boatmen stared at Hew, in his scholar's drabs. 'This is not the way,' he panted, 'to your mother's house.'

Lilias giggled, stopping short. 'Look! Look there!' She pointed to the rocks at the far side of the bay at Kinkell Braes, across the damp dark sands, flattened by the ebb and flowing of the sea. The tide was coming in, and a thinly straggled crowd came scrambling up the beach, retreating from the wreck. Four horses were backed up from the bulkhead of the ship, straining at the water's edge. Lilias stood pointing, laughing in delight, 'Look! There it is, the *whirlijack!*'

And there it was, the whirlijack, a perfect wooden windmill, braced against the foremast, high up on the deck. It was painted blue and white, and cross-sailed like the saltire on a summer's day. And flanking both its sides were ropes and stiff machinery. The town had summoned all its arts in salvaging this toy, bright above the wreckage in St Andrews Bay.

Chapter 2

The Hidden Catch

The crowds receding from the ship had settled in the harbour inn, trailing sand and silt. Some took their dinner with them out onto the pier, which overlooked the wreck, to gossip over bowls of soup and sops. Others crammed round trestle tables in the common hall. The air was sweet with onions, melting into broth, and bitter with the fog of candle light. A tapster lassie flitted to and fro with tankers full of ale, batting back the banter of the drinkers at the bar. Lilias clung tightly to Hew's hand. 'Mammie will gie us dennar, ben the hinner house,' she promised, tugging past the drinkers, through a narrow door.

They came out in the kitchen, where a girl of about fifteen stood squinting at the pottage in a vast iron pot, furrowing the surface with a wooden spoon. The boards were lined with rows of bannocks, yellow slabs of bacon fat and collops of salt beef. An offal pie stood centrepiece, spilling out its gizzards in a scattering of mace. The paunch and udder filling had acquired a greenish tinge.

The young pot stirrer started at the sight of Hew. 'Where have you been, wee *lurdan*?' she confronted Lilias. 'A'body's gang speiring for you.'

'Where's my *Mammie*?' Lilias answered blithely.

'Doun the ladder.' The girl retreated to a little hatch, open to the wine cellar. 'Lillie is come hame,' she shouted through the floor.

'Aye, I hear you, Elspet,' wafted from the vaults. 'There is no sense in flyting with her, for she does not understand you.'

'Likely,' muttered Elspet, 'she will understand a skelp.'

17

'I heard that too,' the cellar warned. 'And you ken well enough what I will answer, if I hear you speak it once again. Send Archie down, to help me lug the cask, and gie the bairn her dinner.'

'Archie isnae up here,' Elspet called back down.

'Where is he, then? The louns will drink us dry. I cannot shift they barrels on my own.'

'He has not come back,' Elspet replied. 'But Lilias has fetched up with a paramour.'

Lilias gave an unexpected show of wit, in poking out her tongue at her. Hew removed his cap and gown, and set them neatly on a stool, before rolling up his sleeves.

'God save us, sir, what are you doing?' Elspet shrieked.

He answered with a wink, 'Helping with the cask.'

'Take it!' cried the voice. The head and shoulders of a flask of wine emerged above the hatch. Hew knelt down to catch it, and dragged the flagon up onto the earthen floor.

Lilias announced, 'Tis Mammie!' as Maude herself appeared, dusting down her skirts, to gaze at Hew appraisingly. 'I thank you, sir, but who are you?'

'He is Master Hew!' Lilias clapped her hands. 'Come here for his dennar.'

'I am Hew Cullan, master at St Salvator's. I brought your daughter home,' Hew explained. 'I found her on the cliff beside my sister's house. My sister is married to Giles Locke.'

'The doctor? Aye, they are good people,' Maude approved. 'Your sister has been kind to her, and Lilias does not forget. She is like the little bird that comes back for its crumbs. Where she takes a liking, she is quickly tamed, and that is rare enough.'

Maude Benet had the look of Lilias, withering with age. Her lightness and fragility had fused to wiry strength, the froth of blonde hair grizzled and grown coarse, the pale skin weathered to a motley red. After years of flyting sailors from their drunken fights, there was little shy or subtle left in Maude. And yet she spoke more gently than the common tapster wife. She had an air of comeliness, and simple commonsense. 'I thank you for it, sir. She is a silly bairn, that has no understanding. I hope she has not caused you trouble?' she went on.

'None at all,' said Hew. 'She has been showing me the windmill.'

'That is some sight, is it no!' marvelled Maude. 'The whole town is astuned at it, and it was in the hubble that the lass gave us the slip. It will take something to shift it, right enough.'

Lilias tugged her skirt. 'Mammie, we are come for *dennar!*' she repeated patiently.

Her mother smiled. 'It is a thing when we must ken our manners from a silly child. Come sir, what will you eat?'

'Madam, you are kind.' Hew shook his head emphatically, and moved a little downwind of the udder pie, gently warmed and pungent in the close heat of the fire.

'I ken what you are thinking, sir,' intercepted Maude.

He muttered indistinctly, 'Truly, I hope not.'

'We will not keep you long,' Maude went on, oblivious. 'What is that you do there at the university?'

'I am a professor,' Hew admitted, 'in the civil laws.'

'You do not say?' She looked impressed. 'Yet even a professor must have his dinner hour. Let go the gudeman's hand,' – this latter was to Lilias – 'and he shall have a fish.'

'I thank you mistress, but I must be gone.'

'I do not hear you. Elspet, gie the bairn her broth,' instructed Maude.

Elspet ladled pottage in a bowl, and placed a piece of buttered bannock on the side. Lilias began to cram the bread into her mouth, broth and barley seeping down her chin, while Elspet rolled her eyes, reaching for a cloth.

Lilias whimpered, 'Master Hew!'

'The bairn will not be settled, till you have your dinner too,' her mother pointed out. 'I pray you, sir, sit down!'

Hew gave in reluctantly, caught between the two, as Maude produced a haddock from a pail. 'Here he is, fresh from this morning's boat. You shall have him fried in butter, for he will not keep till fish day.' She slapped down the fish and slit it with a knife, spilling paunch and pudding on the wooden slab. 'See how fresh he is! His heart is beating still!' The sliver sat, still pulsing, in the circle of her palm.

Lilias looked up, 'I want his beating heart,' she mumbled, through a mouth of crumbs. Elspet gave a shudder of disgust.

Maude Benet frowned. 'Why would you want his heart, my pet?'

'For Gib.'

'I have *telt* you, poppet, that your must not feed the cat. For what use is Gib Hunter, if he will not make his dinner on the mice?' her mother told her fondly.

Lilias set her lip. 'He likes the fish heart better.'

'Then he has no business to.' Maude scraped out the innards of the fish, and scooped the debris up into the pottage pot. Elspet pulled a face. 'And you need not girn like that,' her mistress scolded. 'When were you so proud? Take out the wine and pottage for the baxters.' Hew felt his stomach lurch as Elspet poked the fish eye to the bottom of a bowl.

'Your pardon, sir,' she asked him, passing with the tray, 'But what are *civil laws*? Do you teach the lads their manners?'

He smiled at her. 'Not quite.'

'A pity, for they want them,' she retorted.

'It is the law of persons, not the kirk. But do the students come down here?' asked Hew.

Maude Benet answered tartly, 'Aye, it has been known. For they are not so delicate as you.' She poured oil and butter in a pan, and placed it on the flame. 'We shall leave it there until it smokes, and you shall have a cup of wine to wash it down. You will not make a better banquet, anywhere in town.'

The pan began to sizzle and the scent of melted butter filled the room. Maude had carved the haddock into four white gleaming fillets, when the kitchen door flew open, and an anxious voice demanded, 'Is it true, what Elspet said?'

20

Maude continued with her cooking, unperturbed. 'James Edie, you are come into our kitchen, not the common drinking room. I doubt you missed your way. If you want the quiet house, then go out in the yard.'

James Edie growled, 'Why must ye be so hindersome? Ye ken what I'm about. Elspet said the lass ran off, and came back with a man of law? Is it true, sir?' he appealed to Hew, as to a man, of better sense.

'You need not answer,' countered Maude. 'It is not his business.'

James Edie's beard and hands were neat and trim, suggesting some clean trade. He wore well-fitting workday clothes, of decent, woollen cloth, in shades of russet, grey and blue that matched his woollen cap, and on his cap a little pin, a wheat sheaf wrought of yellow gold, suggested he did well from it. A baxter, Hew inferred. He put the baxter's age at forty-three or four, older than Maude Benet by a year or two at most, though more kindly treated by the passing of the years. The little grey that flecked his hair and beard, the few light lines that creased his eyes, had mellowed and improved his looks, and lifted him above the commonplace.

Hew answered, civilly. 'I am professor at the college, in the civil law. I found Lilias lost, outside the doctor's house, and brought her home, at his request. My interest in this matter starts and ends there, sir.'

'Then I am grateful to you.' James Edie looked relieved. 'Maude kens well enough, that it is my business, though I wish it were not, if she allows her daughter to run riot through the streets. The kirk will not condone it, for they cannot thole such wantonness.'

'The bairn does not run wanton in the streets,' contradicted Maude. 'No more do I allow her to. She slipped away, this once. You ken yourself what rare events have happened here today.'

'I grant it, that the day is quite extraordinary. Yet you will admit it happened once before. And if it should again . . .'

'I swear that it will not,' said Maude.

'God keep you to your promise then.' James Edie glanced about the room, and found another cause for discontent. 'This bannock is not baxters' bread,' he noticed, picking up a loaf.

'That bannock is for private use,' said Maude. 'We do not sell it.'

James Edie tutted. 'Tell that to Patrick Honeyman, when he demands your penalty.'

'I will not have to,' Maude retorted. 'He will never see it. It is for private use, and in our private kitchen. *Out!*'

'Peace, for I am gone! And welcome to your bannock, and to her, for both are hard and coarse!' James Edie turned to Hew. 'Yet Maude mistakes my better nature, if she thinks I won't tell Honeyman.'

'Your better nature, James, and what is that?' scoffed Maude. 'I ken you will not tell him.'

'Do not count on it. Take care, and keep her safe,' the baxter warned.

Maude softened. 'Aye, I hear ye. I will keep her close. We all have been unsettled by the day's events. She will not wander off again.'

'Who was that?' asked Hew, as Edie closed the door.

'James Edie, the baxter.'

'Aye, but what to Lilias?'

'He is some distant cousin of her father,' Maude explained, 'my late husband, Ranald Begg. For which he seems to think he has the keeping of her. Some months ago, she strayed out on the street, and was had up by the kirk, for lewd and loose demeanour, as they like to cry it. Wherefore they found her wanting, as a silly bairn, they count the puir lass innocent of shame. James Edie claims they put her in his charge, that he must lock her up, as lunatic and furious, if she is caught again.'

'Is he her closest agnate?' questioned Hew.

'Her closest *what*?' gawped Maude.

'Her nearest kinsman,' Hew explained, 'upon her father's side.'

'I suppose he is.'

'Then I am afraid he spoke the truth,' he told her seriously. 'For it is his duty and his right to see her locked away, if the kirk requires it.'

'Truly?' wondered Maude. 'I thocht it was a tale he put about, to fright us into thinking that he has some purpose here.'

'Why would he do that?'

'No matter. It is like him. Yet, you say, he has the power to lock her up?'

'More than that, he *must*, if she offends the kirk. Else he himself must bear the burden of her punishment.'

'Then I have mebbe misjudged him.' Maude reflected, 'for I did not know it. I am in his debt.'

'I should tell you, perhaps,' Hew went on, 'that when I saw your daughter on the beach, she was playing coup the lundie.'

'What on earth is that?'

Hew floundered for a moment, scuppered by the phrase he had repeated word for word, not knowing what it meant. He was rescued by Elspet, returning with the tray. 'She was turning somersaults! Bad girl!' she answered with a grin.

'And who has taught her that? Elspet, was it you?' demanded Maude.

'Mary, more like.' The girl said self-righteously.

'I made the whirlijack,' Lilias translated, scrambling from her cushion. 'Shall I do it now?'

All three of them cried, '*No!*'

Maude suggested, 'Go outside with Elspet, and pick parsley for the fish. I see, sir, I do see,' she said quietly to Hew. 'I must take better care of her.' She dropped the fish into the smoking pan, and placed a slice of bannock on a wooden plate.

'James Edie seems a decent man, at least,' Hew observed.

'A decent man,' repeated Maude. 'A baxter, and a bailie on the burgh council.' She grinned, unexpectedly. 'I'll tell you a thing I have noticed about baxters: the cleaner their hands, the blacker their bread. James Edie is the exception. His bread is as white as his hands.'

Hew could not tell if she liked the man or not. He suspected, both.

'Did you see the baxters huddled at the bar?' Maude continued scornfully. 'They are having one of their extraordinary meetings, as they cry them.'

'What, all of them? There must be fifty, sixty, in the gild,' objected Hew.

Maude conceded, 'So there are. They hold their convocations on the Gallows Hill. The four of them out there are keepers of the keys. Four locks, four keys; four keys, four men, that no man can unlock the baxters' box without the cunning of the rest.'

'And what is in the box?' asked Hew, amused at this.

'God knows, biscuit crumbs,' Maude shrugged. 'They four are come to batten on the wreck, without a thought for those puir sailors lost. Their eyes are fixed full on yon windmill.'

'I cannot think they have much hope of having it,' said Hew.

'Then plainly, you have not had many dealings with the baxters. Whisht now, here is Lilias coming back with Elspet, who both have wagging tongues. What have you there, my flower?'

'Marigolds. And parsley, for Master Hew his fish, because he is my *friend*,' Lilias said insistently.

Her mother smiled at her. 'I do believe he is. Now he shall have his haddock.'

Maude lifted out the fish, a translucent, steaming white, and set the fillets on their sops in a foaming butter sauce, freckled with the parsley and a sprinkling of verjuice.

By the time Hew returned to the bar, most of the drinkers were gone. The reclamation had been halted by the tides, and the rest of the town had drifted back to work. The baxters, though, were still entrenched, locked in weary battle lines, of empty stoups and cups. James Edie stumbled, bleary-eyed, to catch him as he passed. 'Your pardon, and your patience, sir. I hope my business with Maude Benet caused you no offence?'

'None at all,' Hew assured him, attempting to inch closer to the door.

24

'I have no liking for my charge,' persisted James. 'Yet I have been advised it is the law.'

Hew nodded. 'I explained as much to Maude. I think she understands it.'

'Then I am obliged to you. Will you have a drink with us?'

'No. I thank you,' Hew said firmly. 'I would not interfere in matters of the gild.' The baxters had a look of long drawn out campaign, which he was not prepared to join.

'The baxters' work is done. We are now convened on business of the town, and would welcome an opinion from the university.' The man was not so easily repelled. Before Hew could extract himself, he introduced his friends. 'Our spokesman, Patrick Honeyman, is deacon of the gild, and like myself, a bailie; this is Christie Boyd, town clerk and baxters' scribe, and this, his brother John.'

Christie had a minute book, in which he scribbled endlessly, scraping with his pen. His brother John was sullen, dour and taciturn. Hew knew the bailie Honeyman by sight, a fleshly man with beetle eyes, burrowed in his cheeks like currants in a bun. His flabby face and hands were scorched from constant close exposure to the fire. The bailies were town councillors, which made James Edie's offer harder to refuse. There was no love lost between them and the university; the council thought the colleges aloof and supercilious and the colleges in turn found them rude and superficial. Each resented bitterly the interests of the other.

'I am absent from my college, and in academic dress. I cannot stay to drink,' Hew hurried to excuse himself. As he had anticipated, refusal caused offence.

'What is it, then? Too proud?' bridled Patrick Honeyman. 'We are not fit for converse, with the un-i-var-sitt-ee!'

The Honeymans were baxters, born and bred. When Hew had first enrolled as a student in St Leonard's, it had been a Honeyman who baked the college loaves; some elder, poorer cousin to the deacon of the gild. At laureation feasts, or when fights broke out in hall, there was no surer weapon than the Honeyman bread roll. The order had been cancelled when a student lost an eye, and St Leonard's opted for a lighter bake. It helped explain, perhaps, the baxter's animosity.

'It is not pride, bur propriety dictates,' defended Hew. 'I must set an example to the students in my charge.' There was a little truth in his excuse.

The clerk, Christie Boyd, looked up from his notebook, at which he had been scratching all the while. 'They will not see you, sir,' he promised confidentially. 'For all of them are fled, save one who is sequestered in the lassies' sleeping loft, and dares not show his face till you are gone.'

'I thank you for the notice, though I wish I had not heard it,' Hew answered with a groan.

'Your students are a pestilence, a plague upon the town. I charge you, sir, to flesh him out, that we may see him whipped.' Honeyman revealed a cheerful prurience, which served to further strengthen Hew's resolve. 'His discipline is not my place. Yet I take note of your concern,' he replied dismissively.

The deacon stared at him. 'Not your place? Then what, sir, is your purpose here? I *ken* you, Master Cullan. You are assistant to Giles Locke, who is our town recorder of unnatural deaths. Are you come at Doctor Locke's request?'

Hew admitted, 'No . . . and yes . . . I came at his request, but not on business of the town.'

'I see that you prevaricate. Then let me ask you bluntly, what is your interest in the wreck?' demanded Honeyman.

'I have no interest in the wreck, saving for the common one, of pity at the loss of life, and vulgar curiosity,' asserted Hew.

Honeyman said rudely, 'I do not believe you, sir.'

'Do you say I'm lying?'

'I am a plain man. I speak in plain words.'

Hew said, '*Plainly*. Then let me tell you plainly once again, I have no interest in your wreck; now I will take my leave, and you will let it rest. There is a man of law, will serve you at the marketplace. He charges by the hour.'

'Ah, do not take offence, for we are not as sleekit in our words as you. We cannot all be orators,' the baxter smiled unpleasantly.

'Indeed,' retorted Hew. 'And yet we can be civil.'

'Aye, and that's the point,' James Edie interjected. 'Are you not professor of the civil laws?'

'That is the nomination,' Hew agreed.

'Then you can give us counsel, on a civil matter.'

'As willingly, I will, when you ask a civil question.'

'It is a question,' said James Edie, 'of the common good, and concerns the windmill. Will you not sit, sir, and consider it? It is a point of law.'

James Edie struck Hew as a decent man, although the same could not be said of Patrick Honeyman. By some secret notice, which had passed between the two, the deacon settled down and held his tongue.

'Aye, then, what's the matter?' Hew accepted with a sigh. He saw no option but to stay and hear the baxters out. James Edie answered gratefully, 'The matter here is this. As you must be aware, a windmill has been washed up in a broken ship. We four are come together here to help in her recovery.'

'Which aid you offer,' Hew suggested dryly, 'from the comfort of the inn.'

'We are convened, ye ken, in a consultative capacity,' corrected Patrick Honeyman, 'and call our privy council to oversee the rest. The mechanics of the task is as well left to the millers, for they have ingenuity, as well as the brute strength.'

'The work is skilled and delicate,' James Edie said, more tactfully, 'and wants a careful hand. The mill itself is of great interest to the baxters, and if we could acquire it, would greatly serve the town. There are five watermills at present, grinding all the corn, to which the town is thirlit and bound to for their bread. The mill lade runs the course of the Kinness Burn, westwards from the shore to the Law Mill on

27

the fringes of the town. The rents from the mills are split between the college and the ancient priory; though some are falling now to private hands. It has oftentimes been motioned, in our inner council, that if one or more of them were under our control, it would better serve the interests of the town.'

'The interests of the town, or of the baxters?' Hew inquired shrewdly.

'Since I cannot think those interests are in conflict, they may coincide,' admitted James.

'As you yourself are not impartial in this matter. I'm told that you own land, on the Kenly Water, where there is a mill. In which case, ye will ken that your tenants must be bound to it, while you draw profit from the rents.'

Hew sensed he had been well dissected, in his time with Maude. Doubtless he was written, with the details of the mill, black and double scored, in the baxters' secret book. He had small impact, and less interest, in the land at Kenly Green, and left it to his factor to collect the rents.

He was a landlord, nonetheless, in the eyes of Christie Boyd, who set aside his pen in a gesture of disgust. 'Then his advice may not be worth a fart, for ye cannot expect him to uphold the common good. Most likely, he will want the windmill for himsel',' he commented.

'That does not follow,' answered Hew. 'Yet you are free to judge it, as I hear your case. Is it that you want to have the mill?'

'That is our intent, sir,' James Edie said succinctly. 'A mill in common ownership, and managed by the baxters, could only serve to benefit the town.'

Hew had no quarrel with the common ownership. Yet he suspected that the baxters' plan would drive their prices up, ensuring the monopoly.

'We have these past few years,' James Edie said, 'been subject to long winters, of implacable severity, and when the mill lade freezes, all five mills are stopped. And likewise in the summertime, the burn is prone to drought, and oftentimes, for half the year, the waterwheels lie still. What the town lacks – what it has lacked for too long – is a *windmill*. For windmills are not common in these parts, and are hard to come by. The winds on our coasts are far too wild and forceful to make them worth investing in for common use. We lack the will to build them, and we lack the skills. A windmill in a storm, such as we saw yesterday, is of little use. And yet . . . and yet, as a supplement, through cold, still, winter months, it would profit greatly if one could be acquired. And so, when she appeared . . .'

'You might call it providential,' Hew suggested.

'Aye,' agreed the baxter. 'Like a gift from God.'

'The problem though,' Hew pointed out, 'is that she is not yours.'

'That is the rub,' James Edie said, 'for if we knew who owned her, we might buy her squarely, for the common good.'

'Or else,' said Patrick Honeyman, who lacked his colleague's subtlety, 'we might have control of her, in some other way.'

James Edie glanced at him, a quick and warning look. 'We do not flout the law, but seek to understand it,' he insisted. 'The windmill's place of origin remains a mystery. The ship is called the *Dolfin* – that is the porpoise, or the delfin fish, in Dutch, and not, as we suppose, the king of France. And yet she has not come here from our staple at Campvere. She was not expected, and no one in the town here kens aught about her fraught. Then since she is a wreck, we hoped that you might tell to us the process of the law. For some say that the town has title to the wreck, and others, that the whole is forfeit to the Crown. Pray, sir, which is true?'

'In a sense,' Hew considered, 'neither and both. The shipwrack law is clear enough. In principal, the admiral decides, for shipwrack must be brought before his court. One part of the profit falls to the admiral, another to the Crown, and the third to any heritor who comes to claim his share.'

'Then nothing to the town? But surely, when the town has gone to trouble and expense . . .' Honeyman objected.

Hew shook his head. 'I come to that. For often does the practice differ from the principle, and commonly the admiral will recompense the town. He is, in truth, quite likely to allow the town the windmill, since the cost of its recovery might well exceed its worth. However,' he went on, 'there is one provision. The law of shipwrack is reciprocal. Strangers wrecked upon our shores are treated here as they treat us, if we are lost to them. So if it comes from such a place, as returns our wrecks to us, then the cargo still belongs to the place from where it comes. If she is a Flemish ship, then they will have a claim on her. They have a year and a day in which to seek her out. If no one comes to claim her, then she will be shipwrack, and forfeit, as before.'

'A year and a day?' repeated Honeyman, incredulous. 'It is a traveller's tale!'

'It is, precisely, that,' conceded Hew. 'I should caution you, perhaps, that to cunningly conceal her, is against the law. There is, it seems to me, a further possibility, that she may be a casualty of the religious wars, and was taken from the Dutch, by Spanish hands, for that might well explain why she has drifted from her course. In which case, she is forfeit to the Crown.'

'And we might have some hope of her, by grace of the admiral?' suggested Patrick Honeyman.

Hew agreed, 'You might.'

Honeyman was satisfied. 'Then it is most likely that may prove the case. I'll warrant that the beggar had a swarthy look.'

'Blackish, right enough,' James Edie echoed doubtfully. 'And yet . . .'

'What beggar do you mean?' asked Hew.

'Yon Fleming, fishman, limmar, loun, they fetched aff fae the ship,' Honeyman expanded. 'A Spaniard, to be sure.'

'Your pardon,' Hew persisted. 'Do you say there was a sailor saved?'

'Of course there was,' said Honeyman, perplexed at his stupidity. 'Surely, ye must ken of it. The beggar that had crept into the windmill, that's lying now, forfochten, in Maude's feather bed. For that is why we wait here, in hopes he will wake up. Though little hope of that, afore the morrow's morn.'

'Ah! That changes everything,' Hew capitulated. 'For in that case, the law does not apply. If any living creature has survived the storm, the ship cannot be claimed as wreck. It need not be a man; the shipman's dog or cat is sufficient for the rule. And you are well advised to keep your salvage safe, for anything you take will count as theft.'

'Then we can have no hope of it?' the deacon answered heavily, a glower of disappointment shadowing his face.

'Your hope is that your sailor is owner of the windmill, and he may choose to sell it, for the cost of its recovery. Tis likely, though, he has already sold it, and it is expected somewhere else,' concluded Hew.

'Yet suppose,' said Patrick Honeyman, grasping still at straws, 'supposing that he does not last the night? Supposing that your man, or shipman's dog, or cat, is taken off alive and does not last the night? I pray you, sir, what happens in that case?'

Hew gave a little thought to this. 'In truth, I cannot say,' he allowed at last. 'In principle, the ship would not be shipwrack, even if he died, if he was taken living from the ship. Tis possible that nonetheless, the courts would claim it quietly, assuming that there was no notion of foul play. For such a case would call for closer scrutiny. It is a crime, I need not say, to leave a shipwrecked sailor to a lonely death.'

'I do not understand,' Christie Boyd complained, 'Will we have the mill? Or won't we have the mill?'

'I cannot rightly say.' Hew stood to take his leave. 'Nor can I help you more. These are strange events.'

'They are indeed,' James Edie answered thoughtfully. 'And we are much obliged to you. The waters here are deep. And time alone will show us up the catch.'

Chapter 3

A Miller's Tale

Hew arrived at Kenly Green as the light began to fade. He slipped down from Dun Scottis, coming to the trees, and wandered through the gardens to the house. Someone had begun to clear the broken branches, smoothing ragged edges and raking up the leaves. The hawthorn and the holly trees had suffered in the storm. In Meg's walled garden, too, the hands had stripped and trimmed; the gillyflowers tied back were oddly neat and desolate. The damp earth smelled of mushrooms. Hew thought of Meg returning, bairn in arms, for lavender and primroses, and blaeberries and plums, but found he could not picture them. An apple basket lay forgotten underneath the trees. He gathered up the windfalls and took the basket with him to the house. Servants flitted out like moths to meet him on the path; his horse and saddle blanket, boots and coat and hat were taken from him, taken care of, fed and watered, brushed and folded, stacked and hung on pegs, the lanterns in the doorway pricking out the gloom.

A kitchen lass retrieved the basket with a cry, 'You didna want to dae that, sir!' *I did not want you to,* was what she meant. The pippins would be pulped, in pottages and pies, conforming to a pattern that would shape the winter months, and according to a process he was not supposed to see.

'Will you want your supper now?' the kitchen lass inquired.

'I had a fish at dinnertime,' he said apologetically.

'A fish? But it is not a fish day!' It was a plainly a reproof, for a flouting of convention that caused the girl offence. It was bringing home the apple basket, on a grander scale.

'That was the least of the strangeness,' Hew told her, 'on what was the strangest of days.'

He felt a draught of loneliness when she responded blankly, 'Will you take your supper then with Master Nicholas?' He sensed a cool indifference in her lack of curiosity, her wish to be restricted to the business of the house.

'Aye, why not?' he sighed. 'How does he now?'

'No worse than when you saw him last. He is in the library.'

Hew nodded. 'That is good.'

'There is a pippin tart.'

'Even better,' he agreed.

He watched her as she disappeared, returning to the house an inner life, which did not belong to him.

Hew climbed the turnpike staircase to the place where he had come most often, since his father's death. He had not replaced the tapestries or carpets in the hall, which were left to Meg, and though the fire and lanterns were kept lit, he rarely used the room. Instead, he spent a little money on the library, on caquetoires of walnut wood and bolsters worked in silk, with patterned leaves in greens and gold and flowers of mauve and blue. There were matching walnut almories, or cabinets, for books, and a knotted table carpet, fringed in scarlet wool. In part, it was for Nicholas, who lived on as librarian, in quietness and solitude, through frail and failing health.

Hew found his old friend reading by the fire, curled up in a resting chair. Matthew Cullan's hunting hound lay napping at his side, twitching as it slept. Hew closed the shutters one by one, lighting all the candle wicks, that cast a honeyed shadow on the stone. The grey dog blinked, and yawned, showing yellow teeth. Nicholas set down his book. 'I did not hear you come in. How is Meg?'

'No news as yet,' said Hew, pulling up a chatter-chair, 'nor showing of the child. Meg is agitated, flustered in the wind, and Giles is out of sorts. The world is turned on end, and wild and strange today.'

Nicholas said quietly, 'I have felt it too.' He hesitated, searching for the words. 'You will think it foolish; I have had a premonition.'

Nicholas was not inclined to frantic fears. His close and clear precision in enforcing rational argument was something that his friend had come to trust. Hew wondered if it was the sickness, winding slick and sinuous, starting to infect his mind.

'Tell me.'

'I dreamt that you were dead. You were thrown from your horse and fallen from the cliff, like King Alexander, at Pettycur.' Nicholas had turned away, laying bare his heart, as he covered up his face.

Hew answered awkwardly, 'Then it was a dream, that has no place or business in your waking fears. You know my horse better than that, than to think he would venture abroad through the storm. We slept at the West Port last night. There was no way of sending word.'

'There was, of course, no need to,' Nicholas said quickly.

'No,' acknowledged Hew. He sensed his friend's embarrassment, and let the matter rest, picking up the book that Nicholas had dropped. 'What have you been reading?' he inquired.

Nicholas confessed, 'It is a nursery tale, about the daughter of a miller, who is ravished by a duke. Although it may be frivolous, it has a certain charm. The book is Painter's *Palace of Pleasure*, and belongs to Meg. It serves as a distraction in the quiet hours.' Nicholas did not sleep well, and suffered aches and tremors in his limbs.

'Then there is little wonder you are given to imaginings, for you have spent too long in Painter's pleasure house. A philippic of Cicero will prove a sharp phlebotomy, and cure you of these ills. I prescribe one, straight away, turned into Greek,' said Hew, with mock severity. His change of temper proved effective. Nicholas returned his smile. 'Your prescription has a sting.'

'No more than you deserve, for all your soft indulgences,' said Hew. 'Yet if that proves too poignant, whet your wits on this. I have an inquisition here to chase away your fantasies, if you will turn your mind to it. And, by some fate or fortune, it is a miller's tale.'

'What is it, then? A paradox?' asked Nicholas, intrigued.

'Of sorts. The pith of it is this. A man is in a windmill, and the

34

mill is on a ship, the one inside the other, like a grocer's nesting box. What does it signify?'

Nicholas considered this. 'A circle, I suppose. Or else the world,' he guessed.

'Your reason, if you will?' commanded Hew.

'For man is a circle, and the windmill turns a circle, and the ship is a windmill, that circles round the world,' his friend expounded, 'like the English pirate, Francis Drake.'

'I like that,' Hew approved. 'But why is man a circle?'

'Because he is a little world, a microcosm.'

'So he is. Ingenious. You have proved your wit, though you have not solved the problem.'

'Then I am perplexed. What is the answer to the riddle of the ship?' Nicholas asked curiously.

'There is no answer,' Hew admitted, 'for there is no paradox. The ship is not a riddle, but a wreck. It washed up in the storm last night, on the rocks by Kinkell Braes.' He told his friend the story, ending with his meeting with the baxters at the inn.

Nicholas said soberly, 'A strange and tragic tale. You say the wreck was found at Kinkell Braes? That's where I saw you falling in my dream.'

'Tis likely that some ghost of it came howling on the storm; the wind has many voices that reach to us in sleep. Yet I am here, and safe, so put it from your mind,' instructed Hew.

They sat in silence for a while, gazing at the fire, until the serving girl appeared with supper on a tray, and brought a busy brightness to the room, laying out the plate and pewter cups. She set a chafing dish of onions, leeks and cheese to toast upon the coals, with a wheaten loaf for dipping into it. The dish was closely followed by the tart of pulped green apples spiked with cloves, by white and claret wines, and a rose and almond cream.

Hew broke off a piece of bread. The loaf was fine white manchet, and bore the baxter's signature, a gathered sheaf of corn. 'Where do we buy our bread?' he asked the serving lass.

'This bread, sir? The manchet? The boy brings it from town.'

'Aye, but from which baxter?'

'From the bailie, James Edie, that bakes the best bread. That is his mark. Is it not to your liking, sir?' the girl returned, confused.

'I like it well enough,' he answered, buttering the crust and handing it to Nicholas. 'Does all the bread here come from James Edie?'

'Not all of it. The manchet is for you and Master Nicholas, when you are at home.'

'And when I'm not at home?'

'Then he makes do wi' bannock, same as a' the rest of us!' the girl became exasperated. 'I do not understand you, sir! Is anything the matter with the bread?'

'No, nothing,' Hew assured her, as she bustled out.

Nicholas advised, 'I think they will not thank you, if you meddle with the bread. The order was approved by your sister, Meg.'

'God help me, for I did not know they fed you bannocks,' Hew confessed.

Nicholas responded with a smile. 'And wherefore should they not? For I have eaten bannocks all my life. The grain is from your land, and ground here at the mill, more wholesome than the finest wheaten flour, that often has been coloured white with lead. I do prefer, it, Hew. Was James Edie among those brave baxters you met?'

'It seems he was the best of them, on more than one account,' considered Hew. 'The finer in his manners as the purer is his bread. I cannot say I took to his friend, bailie Honeyman. The Honeymans are bannocks of a coarser grain.' He dipped a chunk of bread into the melted cheese, and they sat in close companionship, mellowed by the warmth of food and drink. At last, when they had finished off the apple tart and cream, Hew judged the time was right to give voice to a plan which had been brewing gently since that afternoon. 'I have resolved to move into the college, for a while.'

'But you were set against it!' Nicholas exclaimed.

'Tis only for a week or two, until Meg's child is born,' his friend explained, 'For Giles is quite disordered and distraught. It will relieve his burden, in some little sense, if I can take his place. The students want a clearer jurisdiction, as it seems.'

Nicholas said wryly, 'I had not set you down to be their scourge.'

'God knows, I do not want to be,' said Hew. The notion was abhorrent to him. 'Do you think they are much worse, than we were at St Leonard's?'

'Worse in what way?' asked Nicholas.

'Drinking, brawling, and the rest. Irksome to the town,' expanded Hew.

'For myself, I never drank in taverns,' Nicholas reflected. 'I could not afford to. I did not jangle in the street. As for the rest, I kept quite clean and chaste. I cannot speak for you.'

'Of course you can! We lived and worked together. There was nothing much between us,' Hew objected.

'There was everything between us,' Nicholas demurred, 'because you were a gentleman, and I was not.'

Hew chose to ignore this. 'I never knew a woman, till I went to France.'

'Where you were led astray.'

'Where I had instruction, in the *gentle* arts,' corrected Hew. 'The students are unruly now, and more so than we ever were, even under Gilchrist's lewd and errant sway. We did not dare to riot under George Buchanan.'

'Everything grows worse with time,' Nicholas proposed.

'Or else grows better, Giles would say,' smiled Hew. 'I have not told him yet. I mean to use his rooms. To lodge with Bartie Groat would be a step too far.'

Nicholas looked sceptical. 'I should prefer his sniffs to Giles' strange collections. The flesher in his killing-cloths, against a room of rheums. It is an invidious choice.'

'Come with me,' Hew said suddenly. 'You understand the way a college works, far better than I ever will.'

His friend shook his head. 'Do not ask it, Hew.'

'What once was held against you has been long forgotten. You did nothing wrong,' insisted Hew, a sudden rush of pity showing in his face.

'The transgressions I have made are in my heart, and I have not forgotten them. You do not understand me, if you think I am afraid to die, or live my life, alone. Do not confound me with yourself, and imagine that I share your discontent,' Nicholas said quietly.

'What say you, I am discontented?' questioned Hew.

'Tis clear enough you are. This life does not yet satisfy you; you are not happy here, and you will not be happy there. You will not be content, until you have a cause to fight.'

'Am I so transparent?' Hew felt reluctant to own to the truth of the matter; he wanted still a purpose in the world.

Nicholas smiled sadly. 'As water in the burn. You must not mistake me, Hew. Our hopes and dreams can never be the same.'

'But once they were,' Hew argued. 'Once, when we boys, you had the keenest mind.'

'We never were the same. You will be careful, won't you?' Nicholas said suddenly. 'And not just on the cliffs?'

'You know me, and my horse, who is averse to risks,' Hew smiled.

'I'm serious, Hew. Yet promise me, that you will take great care.'

'You have my word,' said Hew, 'whatever that is worth.'

There was nothing more to say. Hew's mind was fixed upon the college and the town, his thoughts and prayers with Giles and Meg. And Nicholas, he knew, would end his days in solitude, fading out in quietness, alone among the books at Kenly Green. There was little, after all, that Hew could have to offer him. He rose before the dawn and saddled up his horse, setting out at daybreak for the town.

Maude preferred the quiet hours, before the town was properly awake. She opened up the windows, allowing pink-streaked sunlight to warm the polished wood, and sweeping the stale rushes out into the street. The wind, fresh and light, gave no hint of storm. The fishing boats had already put to sea at the first pale trace of dawn, and the cobles still remaining in the dock were beached; the tide had reached its lowest point, and turned, creeping back to lick against the pier. Across the bay, Maude could see an early party setting out to secure the windmill, horses, carts and ropes trawled across the sands, trailing slow and blearily into the morning light. She returned to the house and began to make her bread, baked upon a skillet on the tap room fire. The serving girl, Elspet, appeared, sleepy-eyed and fumbling with her cap. She shared a bed with Lilias, in the lassies' sleeping loft, accessed by a ladder in the common drinking hall.

'A braw fine day,' her mistress said, 'for scrubbing of the floors.'

'Aye?' the girl replied, distracted. She had wandered to the door, absorbed in the commotion.

'Come away,' scolded Maude.

'They're fetchin' aff the windmill. It looks unco heavy.'

'And so it will be. Come away. When the men are finished, they will have a thirst on them.'

Maude removed the bannock from the flames, breaking off a piece of it. She set the morsel on a tray, with a pat of yellow butter and a foaming cup of ale. 'Take this to our guest.'

'I will not,' said the girl, with unexpected spirit.

Maude glowered at her. 'What do you mean, you will not? You will do as you are telt.'

'I cannot!' and, to Maude's astonishment, the lass began to cry. 'There's sickness in that room,' she sobbed, 'and more, for Mary says the ship has had a curse on it.'

'Then Mary is a lurdan,' Maude informed her grimly. 'And you are not much better, if you gie her heed.'

'Ye manna mak me do it,' Elspet wept.

Maude sighed, 'Aye, very well. Look to Lilias.'

Her daughter had appeared, bare shod in a linen shift, pink like a bairn in the flush of sleep. She giggled as her mother kissed her. 'Bide awhile wi' Elspet! Do not let her stray,' Maude advised the

39

serving girl, 'or else . . .' The threat died away. Maude was never cruel, for all her cross complaints. She had been a victim far too long herself, for conscience to permit her to resort to that. A lassie should not have to live in fear.

Maude took up the tray and went back through the house. Her guests were lodged upon the second floor, accessed by a turnpike at the rear. There were two spare rooms, the larger of which slept as many men as it could hold, and was let for sixpence, without bed or board. A pallet, sheets and blankets could be had at extra cost. The small and dearer room was furnished with a standing bed and graced from time to time by a stout and sweaty kirkman from Dundee, who for a while had rented Mary too, till Maude had put a stop to it. Maude had bought the bed after her man had died, burning the old mattress in a bonfire in the yard, a conflagration visible for miles. She had thrown on Ranald's clothes and his possessions, one by one. Her husband's shoes had been the last to burn, the molten leather curling like a sneer.

The sailor had been put to rest in Maude's own feather bed, in a closet off the kitchen that stank of kale and slops. Though on this night there were no other guests, he had been too sick to climb the stairs. The closet room was dark and cramped, the only other furniture a stool and pissing pot, with a peg upon the door for hanging clothes. There was one small window, opening to the back. It looked over empty barrels and a rusted metal can, which served as the latrine, behind a wooden pale. Maude gave the door a warning tap, for fear her guest made water or was kneeling at his prayers, before she pushed it open with her foot. The man lay still in bed, and did not sit up. Elspet had been right, there was sickness in the room; not the usual sourness she was used to in the bar but a thickly sweet decay that made her stomach turn. Maude set down the tray and opened up the shutters, letting in the light and the savour of the sink-hole in the yard. She turned to see the stranger gazing back at her.

'Oh! You are waking, are you? You were sleeping like the dead.

Half a day and a night you have slept. Look there! They are lifting out your windmill. You will have to pay a fee to have it back,' she greeted him.

The stranger answered, '*Beatrix.*'

'Not Beatrix, Maude.' Maude picked up the tray again and approached the bed. 'I have brought you breakfast, though you must not expect it. As soon as you are well enough, then you will have to speir for it, and shift up to the lodging house. The board and beer costs tuppence, and a sixpence for the bed, with a penalty of fourpence, if we have to wash the sheets.' This was wishful thinking, right enough, for Maude had little hope of being paid. The stranger, she could see, followed her intently. She also was aware that he had barely understood. Yet this did not deter her; she was used to Lilias, and knew that comfort could be had from kindness in a voice.

'Ik niet mijn,' the stranger pleaded.

Maude had learned some Flemish from the sailors at the bar, bad words, in the main. She tried hard to make sense of this. 'That will not do. I do not understand you. *I am not my* . . . You are not your what?' She made her voice sound firm, for that was commonsense. Maude was seldom daunted by a foreign tongue.

'Ik niet mijn eigen ben.'

Maude puzzled at this, trying, 'You are not your *eyes*?'

Perhaps it was his eyes, for now the stranger closed them, whispering, 'Niet mijn.'

'*Not my*,' repeated Maude. 'Then do you mean that you are not yourself? Eek neet myself?' she guessed.

'Niet van mijzelf, mijn ben.'

'Who are you, then?' protested Maude, 'if you are not yourself?'

'*Beatrix.*'

'For sure, you are not Beatrix,' Maude replied indignantly. 'Beatrix is a lassie's name.' She pointed to herself. 'Naam. My naam is Maude. What is your naam?'

'Jacob . . . Ik ben . . . Jacob.'

41

'Yacob? That is a good name. It is the same as James,' Maude approved. She set the tray beside him on the bed. 'Eat.'

She could tell the man was famished. Yet he had trouble with his hands, and could not lift the cup. In the end, she had to feed him. She crumbled up the bread, and soaked it in the ale for him. He took it gratefully.

She judged him in his early twenties, not much older than her bairn, and strong enough, at least, to have survived the storm. The men who had brought him from the shore had stripped him to his shirt; his other clothes were draped upon the stool, still sopping wet, while Maude had lit a fire for fear he'd catch his death. The smoky embers filled the sunlit room. He was not a sailor, for he did not have the breeks. Nor was he a merchant, for his coat was plain and workmanlike. Maude sensed that he had once been clean and tidy, before he had been ravaged by the sea. Most alarming were his hands. His limbs were bruised and black, and he could not flex his fingers, his body like a drowned man's Maude had once seen on the beach, sluiced and puffed and blackened by the sea. To her dismay, Maude saw that he was crying; a rush of silent tears that soaked and streaked his face. She wiped them with her apron skirt. 'You manna greet,' she told him. 'You maun be a man.' Since Jacob did not answer her, she left him to his prayers.

Chapter 4

The Drowned Man

The baxters were like gulls, returning with the fishermen to scavenge for the catch, and Maude was not surprised to hear them chapping at her door. The windmill had been taken off the strand and trundled, inch by inch, towards the customs house, while the baxters trailed behind like birds around a boat. All fetched up together, at the harbour inn. Maude said, 'We are closed.'

'We are not come to drink,' said Patrick Honeyman.

'I think you do mistake us, then. This is an inn,' Maude pointed out.

'Do not be obstructive. Ye ken why we are here. Tis business of the council,' asserted Patrick Honeyman.

'Then pursue it at the tolbuith. This is not the council hall.'

'A brief word with yon mariner will see us on our way. *If* it is convenient,' Honeyman said heavily. Maude tried to stand her ground. 'It is not convenient. And he is asleep.'

'How now, asleep, still asleep?' said James Edie with a smile. James was one to watch, thought Maude, for he was not so easily put off. To prove the point, he added, 'Tis no matter, we can wait. The beauty of the baxters, Maude, is that we bake by night, which leaves us free to barter in the day.'

'Ye'll find no bargains here,' retorted Maude. 'We're closed.'

'But *not to us*,' said Honeyman. There was a touch of menace in his voice that Maude could not ignore. They were the burgh council after all. She conceded, 'Please yoursel', though it may little profit ye, who do not ken the Dutch. For he has not a word of Scots.'

'Then you have spoken with him, and he is awake,' James Edie said astutely. As always, he was sharp, and once again, too quick for her, thought Maude. He tempted her with friendship, breaking through her guard. And still, of all the baxters, she trusted him the most. *I will look out for you, Maude.* And he had, had he not, in his way?

'He was awake a while,' Maude admitted grudgingly, 'and now has gone to sleep again. He isna feeling well.'

'And *whit* is *wrang* with him?'

The baxter bully boys had somehow found their way into the common hall, more by insinuation than by force. Elspet was mopping down the trestles and the floor, while Lilias sat playing with the dice and knucklebones, kept in little boxes underneath the bar. The morning air had not yet cleared the chamber of its fug, the weary aftertaste of sour ale, sweat and soot.

'In truth, I cannot say,' shrugged Maude. 'Perhaps it is the plague.' It was a clever after shot, that scored a pleasing hit on bailie Honeyman, for all his bluff and bluster a coward through and through. 'Sweet Jesus Christ!' he swore. The rumour gathered force with Christie Boyd, who pointed out, 'There were no other bodies there, and that would seem to fit. For so the grievous sick are set adrift in ships, with neither port nor quarter, till the plague is spent.'

His brother echoed grimly, 'It is a ship of ghosts.'

James Edie quashed the rumour with a grin. 'Maude is sporting wi' us. She does not for a moment think it is the plague, or she would not have him in her bed. She'd turn away a man, wi' colick or the cauld, for fear of him infecting Lilias.'

'Lilias is prone to maladies of chokes,' Maude replied defensively. She had fallen, for a second time, into the baxter's trap. There was a little truth in what James Edie said, and Maude found herself surprised that she had not considered it. Somehow, in her pity, she had left it overlooked: she must be growing soft. 'I do not think,' she owned at last, 'that Jacob has the plague, only that you must allow, it is a possibility.'

'Jacob is it, now? Then you are quite close friends,' James Edie said, relentlessly.

She did not rise to it. 'Yet I can assure you, sir, that he is sick and frail. His hands and face are black; he cannot sit or stand.'

James Edie turned to Honeyman. 'I think it would be best,' he mused, 'to have the doctor called, and free ourselves from all fear of infection.'

Honeyman conceded, 'Aye, then, fair enough. The girl,' he waved at Elspet, 'can go for Doctor Locke, and likewise find a man that kens the Flemish tongue. And you can bring us breakfast, Maude,' he added, generously.

'And *you* can wait outside, and whistle for your breakfasts. This is not a cookshop. We are closed,' said Maude.

'You *will* be closed, right enough, if you dinna mind the bailies,' Honeyman declared.

'What do you mean? You cannot close us down!' Maude replied indignantly.

'For sickness in the house? You can have no doubt of it.'

Maude knew when she was beaten. 'You may sit up at the bar and sup a stoup of ale, and let that be your breakfast, for I offer nothing more.'

Elspet tugged her apron, anxious to set off. 'Where do I find a man, that speaks the Flemish tongue?'

James Edie pressed a penny in her hand. 'Try the customs master,' he advised. 'And for the doctor, you must fetch Professor Locke. You will find him at the college or his house upon the Swallow Gait. Ask for him by name.'

'Then will I fetch the minister, from the kirk of Holy Trinity?' Elspet wondered eagerly, warming to her task.

James Edie frowned. 'The minister? Why him?'

'For he can say a prayer,' the girl explained. 'Because the ship is cursed.'

'Dear God!' erupted Honeyman. 'I thought it was your daughter was the daftie, Maude? Tis we that have been cursed, with a witless shiftless villain of a wench! Away with you! Be gone!'

James Edie said, more reasonably, 'Elspet, you are young, and you have not worked here long, yet you must surely ken, that the minister is *never* wanted in this house.' Maude Benet glared and glowered at them, but chose to hold her tongue, pouring out the ale as Elspet scurried off. The baxters settled warily on stools around the bar, to wait for her return. Only James Edie appeared at his ease. When Maude slipped to the back room to attend her cooking pots he took the chance to follow her, begging for some bread. Maude resisted with a scowl. 'We have none. Since ye all are baxters, go and bake your ain,' she told him crossly.

'Ah, sweet Maude!' he pottered round her kitchen, peering into pans. 'Has anybody telt ye that your pottages are rank?'

'Feel free to take your leave of them, at any time you like,' Maude sniffed.

'If I had not been marrit, Maude, I swear . . .'

'What do you swear, James Edie? Aye, then, what?' She rounded on him.

Laughing, the baxter held up his hands. 'Peace, little bear, for I do not come to bait thee. Tell me why you do it, Maude?

'Why do I do what?'

'Go out of your way to flyt with Patrick Honeyman, when you know he has the power to shut you down? Why do you walk the hardest path, when you could take the gentle one?'

'I do not ken, James. Why do you? And why are you intent on coming to my kitchen? Are you not afeared of plague?' she answered scornfully.

James Edie shook his head. 'I do not for a moment think it is the plague. Confess it, Maude, he is not sick. Why won't you let us see him?'

'Because he is not well,' insisted Maude, 'and because . . . I ken that you will cheat him, James, and fleece him like a lamb. I could not bear to see him bullied by the bailies into giving up his mill. Tis like shining torchlight at the bandage of the blind, or like my wee lass Lilias, baffled by the kirk. There is an innocence, a tenderness in him.'

46

'Do you think that he has lost his wits?' James Edie pondered seriously.

'Not lost his wits. But he is somehow . . . *lost*,' said Maude. 'He is so very far from home.'

James Edie smiled at her. 'You are like a crab, Maude, soft and sweet inside, and on the outside . . . *crabbit*! You must know that we do not mean to put him to the test. We hope to have his windmill, that is all. And if he will not give it, so be it. Come,' he held out his hand to her. 'You know me, Maude. Though I am keen, I am not cruel. Then let us go and wait upon the doctor, whose proper care and counsel shall set your mind at rest.'

Maude nodded, and went back with him, leaving Jacob safely to his rest. She made a show of polishing the wood, and counting out for Lilias the bone and wooden dice; she did not trust the baxters, when her back was turned. Once or twice she opened up the door, but saw no sign of Elspet coming down the hill. The baxters were implacable, and seemed to her quite stubbornly entrenched, when a strange sound from the kitchen stopped them in their cups. It began as a low keening, rising to a howl that set Maude's teeth on edge. Lilias gave a little shriek, and dropped her knucklebones.

Jacob understood that men would come for him. He knew, when Maude had left him, that the time was near. He was not surprised. Tobias, Joachim and the rest had not died quietly, and would not lie quiet at the bottom of the sea. He took some consolation in the things around him, visible reflections of the commonplace: the stale scent of cooking fat, the scraping of the barrels in the cellar down below, whistling on the stairs. From the small shuttered window, he could see the sun, and told himself the time, as he had once been taught. He heard the pot boy clatter in the yard outside, a long, seamless pissing, streaming in the pail. He watched the ginger tomcat, arching from the window ledge, insinuate itself around the corners of the room, and settle on a patch of sunlight, filtered through the slats. The cat had greenish-yellow eyes, like the liquid centre of a wound. Although the room was stifling hot, he knew that he was lucid still. He listened to Maude talking to the man outside, and understood their purpose, though he did not know the words. He was aware they were not speaking Dutch. Yet all of these sensations were recovered thick and curved, as though he saw and heard them in a glass. They did not dull the pricking in his skin, the creeping of his flesh that began to spread, insidious, throughout. A dry fire had consumed him. His belly could not calm the swell of sops and ale, and Jacob vomited. Joachim and Tobias swam like fishes through his dreams, reflected in the water pot; Jacob heard a howling, and the tomcat's hackles rose.

Jacob knew that he would have to die. He had not known that it would hurt so much.

The baxters stood outside the door. They had gathered at the first unearthly note, but none of them had wanted to go in. The cry had pierced the stillness in the bar, and Christie Boyd had spilled his drink over the minute book, blotting out the record of the previous day. It was not a human sound. Now they stood and listened to the keening, perspiring in the close heat of the kitchen fire. It was Maude, in the end, who pushed open the door, James Edie the first man behind her.

'Oh!' called out Maude, 'it is only Gib Hunter, the cat!'

Gib Hunter backed against the kitchen wall, each white-lipped orange hair shaft startled to its tip, like a ginger porcupine. Lilias gave a giggle, 'Scaredy! Scaredy cat!'

'Aye, it was the cat. And yet we must be wary of the devils he has seen. What is he afeared of?' James Edie answered quietly. There was a low hush to his voice, as though he came across shy creatures in the fields, and did not want to startle them to flight. It made Maude think of night owls, fixed on little mice, their heartbeats in the darkness tiny pricks of fear. What fright had moved Gib Hunter, to his wild and frantic howls? James was staring straight at Jacob, holding up the candle he had taken from the wall, so that Jacob's eyes were captured in the flame. Jacob was sitting bolt upright, a terror tale of torment frozen on his face. His black lips blabbered wordlessly, his black hands clutched and fumbled, helpless at the air.

'Whisht, what is it?' Maude came soft and soothing, holding off the ghosts. Though doubtless, there were devils in the room, she felt only pity, and was not afraid. Jacob pointed wildly and began to sob.

'Hush, now, hush, for there is nothing there.' She took him in her arms and rocked him like a bairn. She felt his fear aflutter, through his solid chest, like the little mouse, or like the tiny fish heart, beating in her palm, from the writhing haddock she had cooked for Hew. 'Hush, you are safe now,' she whispered.

'De duivel,' Jacob moaned.

'There are no devils here.'

'*Ahhh.*' The wind had found its way at last, both through and out of him, as Jacob sighed. Maude felt him tense and slacken in her arms. She touched her fingers, briefly, to his lips.

'Tis well that you have calmed him,' Honeyman came blustering, as if the air from Jacob's lungs had blasted into him. 'I cannot thole they frenzied fits, that foreign folks are prone to. What do you think it was wrang wi him?'

Maude stared at him, aghast. 'Do you not see, you futless slump? You useless, feckless, hopeless, lourden of a limmar of a man, that he is dead?'

The bailie buckled at the torrent of her words. '*Deid?*' he replied at last. 'In which case, since you are distressed, we are prepared to overlook . . . we will go back precipitate, and look out for the doctor,' he concluded lamely. The brothers Boyd were quick to follow, leaving James alone with Maude and Lilias.

Maude whispered, 'Go, my petal, find Gib Hunter. He has had a fright.'

Lilias ran gaily, calling for the cat. Maude looked helplessly at James. 'He was well enough before, I swear it, James, in spite of what I said.'

James Edie answered sceptically, 'Perhaps.' He eased the dead man from Maude's arms, and let the body drop back on the bed. 'The corpus is decayed,' he pointed out.

'Tis what I said before. I swear to you, he spoke to me. He ate and drank.'

'So it would seem.' James was sniffing at the piss pot, looking at the tray. He picked up a piece of bannock. 'Someone here has breakfasted on bread.'

'So I did not give him baxter's bread. What can that matter now?'

'It will matter still, if Honeyman should come to hear of it. He will not let a death deflect him from the rules. It will mean a fine.' James Edie shook his head.

'James . . .' Maude pleaded.

'Do not fear.' He threw the crust into the embers of the fire, 'We will not tell him. Let us clear the tray, and the piss pot too, and tell them that he did not eat or drink. Then we will go and wait.'

When they came through to the tap room, Elspet had returned, with a doctor by her side, who was not Professor Locke. For that doctor could not come, as she explained to Patrick Honeyman; his wife was at that moment labouring with child. 'His servant said, he canna come today, nor yet tomorrow, as he thinks.'

She had expected thundering, a summer storm, at least, and was surprised when Honeyman said mildly, 'You did your best, I doubt. It is the barber-surgeon that ye brought?'

Elspet nodded, 'Aye . . . and sir, I couldna find a man that spoke the Flemish tongue,' she ventured timidly.

'What? No matter, lass. He is not wanted now.' Honeyman was thoughtful, and the bluster had gone out of him. Elspet was encouraged and astonished. She had feared his wrath, and worried what to do. And then she had remembered the barber surgeon's boy. His name was Gilbert Blair, and one night in his cups he had told to her his trick, and it had made her smile. The boy was not a prentice, or anything as grand, but acted as a lure, for Gilbert kept a pocket full of worn and broken teeth, to be hidden in his cheeks for the surgeon to draw out. When strangers came on market day, the boy would step up first, in painless exhibition of the surgeon's art. This small deception never failed to please, though Gilbert Blair had far more teeth than cavities, and the next brave man to follow soon saw through the fraud. This surgeon seemed to Elspet as good as any doctor, wearing his credentials spattered on his coat. And so she had resorted to his buith upon the market street, where she had had to wait while he drew out a tooth.

James Edie looked at Honeyman. 'I suppose this man can certify the death?'

The bailie nodded, 'Aye.' He showed the surgeon to the closet room. James Edie followed to the rear, while John and Christie Boyd hung back, and Maude remained with Elspet, Lilias and the cat, who had come in from the kitchen, none the worse for wear. 'Take Lilias out,' instructed Maude.

The kitchen lass stared at her, 'I am just back!'

'Go and tell Mary, we will not be open today.'

'Why won't we open?' Elspet asked, wide-eyed.

'For there is a death in the house.' Maude was clear now, and calm, which was how it should be. She did not understand why she had been so moved. For this was not the first death that had happened in her house. Or even, she reflected, in her bed.

James Edie and Patrick Honeyman stood watch over the surgeon, as he examined Jacob's body. They were bailies of the council, and they were rightly there, as arbiters of law to represent the town. Honeyman was sweating, sickly, in his handkerchief; James Edie stood by, sombre and composed.

'This body was recovered from the shipwreck?' asked the surgeon.

James Edie nodded, 'Aye, he was.'

'Then why has he been left so long?'

'We did not ken . . .' said Honeyman, and paused.

'For clearly,' said the surgeon, 'this man has been dead for several days.'

James Edie looked at Honeyman, but neither bailie spoke. They watched the surgeon turning Jacob's hands, resting puffed and blackened on Maude Benet's linen sheets.

James Edie ventured cautiously at last, 'And why do you say that?'

'Tis plain enough to see. This putrefaction in the limbs,' the surgeon pointed out, 'suggests he was long dead before he left the sea.'

'How long dead?' asked James.

The surgeon shrugged. 'Four days, mebbe five. You really ought to put him in the ground.'

'And I suppose,' James said, 'a man in your profession, must be used to death.'

'More used to it than not,' the surgeon smiled. 'I recommend, you move him from the kitchen, for his close proximity does not promote good health.'

'You are quite right; it shall be done at once,' Honeyman agreed. 'But can you signify for us the cause of death? It is not the plague?'

The surgeon shook his head. 'It is not the plague, man! He died by drowning, sure enough.'

'I see,' said Patrick Honeyman. 'Then we are much obliged to you. The burgh council will be pleased to meet your fee, if you will make a full report, and write it down. Come, now, let us show you out, and back to drawing teeth.'

They saw him quickly through the door, for fear that he might stop to take another look, and change his mind.

'What does it mean, James?' murmured Patrick Honeyman, once they were alone again. 'It makes no sense at all.'

'Some sort of witchcraft, perhaps?'

Honeyman shuddered. 'God help us, then! What do we do?'

'Since we have a duty to keep order in the town, there must be no talk of magic, whatever we may fear,' James Edie warned. 'The first thing we must do is to have the body dressed, and taken out from here. I think we must proceed with caution, for we do not know what happened to the crew. We only have his word that there is no infection. And his word cannot be trusted, since he told us that he drowned. Why, did you not tell him that he died here his morning?'

Honeyman retorted, 'Why didn't you?'

'For you are the first bailie,' James Edie smiled, 'I defer to you.'

Honeyman evaded this, proposing, 'Let us bury him at sea. His end in his beginning. He came here from the ocean, then let him be returned to it. For properly, he drowned. And he was dead already, when we took him from the sea.'

'He was not in the sea,' James reminded him. 'He was in the windmill, which was dry inside.'

'Yet he had been battered by the storm. Suppose then, that his lungs were filled with water. In his last gasping breath, he came to life, to drown again, as drowning men must do. It is a grasping death.'

'Then he returned to life, to die again?' James concluded thoughtfully.

'Precisely,' nodded Honeyman. 'And since he died before, we have the clear advantage, that the ship is wrack.'

'Maude Benet heard him speak, and will not have him drowned,' James Edie pointed out.

'Then you must talk to Maude. Go to it, James,' the bailie smiled. 'Of all of us, she likes you best.'

James found her in the kitchen, slicing neaps and onions into a bowl of broth. She had not wept, for Maude was not a woman prone to tears. James did not recall when he had seen her cry; not when her child was born, or when her man had died, though she had not been likely to have wept at that. A life with Ranald Begg had wiped the tears from Maude.

He placed a hand upon her shoulder.

'*Don't.*'

'Some women will come soon and dress the corpse. We will take it out to sea,' he told her. 'You may open up again, once it is gone.'

Maude continued slicing, with quick and angry strokes. She was unsure why she should feel such rage; she blamed it half on James, though he was not the cause. 'Is Jacob not to have a Christian burial?' she inquired.

'We shall say a psalm for him, perhaps. But since he died at sea, we think it right and just.'

'He did not die at sea,' Maude pointed out..

'I understand that it runs contrary to sense, and yet we must believe it, Maude. The surgeon says he died before he came here.'

Maude shook her head. 'A dead man cannot eat and drink. A dead man cannot talk,' she countered stubbornly.

'You said yourself, he had the semblance of a drowned man,' James reminded her.

'I felt him flesh and blood, his beating heart. He was not a ghost,' insisted Maude.

'He was a drowned man, Maude, that coming back to life by some strange quirk of nature, drowned again.'

'He spewed into the chamber pot.'

'Spillage of the sea. It shall be cleared away.'

He told it to her patiently, and afterwards, she thought, that when he was explaining it, it all made perfect sense, though on her own, it baffled her. Yet that did not surprise her, for so it often was, with James. He had a way with words.

The bailies sent three fisher wives to wash and dress the corpse, paying them a pittance from the common purse. They brought a clamour and a coarseness to the quiet of Maude's room, robbing Jacob's body of the decency of death. They broke into a tussle, fighting for a ring they had found fixed on his finger and could not pull off. At last it was dislodged, and flew across the room, where Maude came to recover it. Because it was not possible to keep it with the corpse, she placed it in a little box, high upon a shelf, and sent the thieving fishwives squabbling from her house. Left alone with Jacob now, she laid him out herself, and washed his bruised limbs tenderly in oils and scented soaps. She dressed him in his clothes that lay warming by the fire, and combed out his yellow hair, tearing up the bed sheets to serve him as a shroud and folding Jacob neatly in his winding cloths. The bailies came by presently, and took him out to sea, to the place where they had found him, somewhere far from home.

Professor Locke saw none of this, for he was on the Swallow Gait, advising his son Matthew on his entry to the world. He gave a barrage of instruction, which the midwife battled fiercely to ignore. The doctor's presence there offended her on every front. 'Be careful,' he had warned her, at the cutting of the cord, 'that the residue is not too long, and not too short. For according to the ancients, where you make your cut will determine the length of the infant's private member, or, as some would have it, of his tongue.'

The midwife sniffed. 'A thousand new boy babbies have I brocht into the world, and not one of them has ever made complaint I made his pizzle over lang or small.'

The nurse, who was a silly girl, remarked, 'They say the young king James' tongue is muckle for his mouth.'

'My point precisely,' nodded Giles. ''Tis likely, in the hopes of making sure the king's succession, he was overreached.'

'As to that, I cannot say,' the midwife answered sourly. 'For I did not deliver him.'

'Five fingers' width,' insisted Giles, 'as a rule of thumb.'

The midwife placed a square of linen on the floor, and laid Matthew Locke upon it, folding up the end to form a pocket for his feet. She tucked in the sides and began to bind them straight with narrow woollen bands. Meg called over anxiously, propped up on the bed, 'Must it be so tight?'

'You soon will have the knack of it.' The midwife slipped the baby's arms into his linen waistcoat, and wound the strips of linen round, fixing fast his hands. She attached a stay, holding firm his neck, and finished with a pair of little caps, one of linen, one of wool, tied beneath his chin. So life began and ended, in a strip of cloth.

Chapter 5

Sisters in Arms

The news of Matthew's birth was welcomed at St Salvator's, where Hew had settled in to Giles Locke's turret tower. The clear advantage of the tower was its location on the corner of Bow Butts, on the cusp between the college and the town. It looked out upon the North Street, and back upon the cloisters, allowing the illusion of belonging to both worlds, while it reserved the option of a quick escape. The occupants could come and go without the closer scrutiny of porters at the gate. The drawback was the inner space, where Hew now worked and slept. As Nicholas had noted, Giles kept strange collections in his rooms. He had borrowed from the fleshers' buith a small dissecting block, on which he did experiments, made drawings, or took notes. Often, there were seed pods, or the heads of flowers, examined under glass and cut into cross-sections, copied into books with coloured inks. He had recently acquired a human foot, perfectly embalmed and smooth as wax, the outer layers of which were slit and opened back, in an exquisite piece of butchery.

For all its eccentricities, or, perhaps, because of them, the turret tower reminded Hew of Giles, and he felt quite at home. More irksome to him were the college codes of discipline, which he was now expected to follow and enforce. Giles Locke had clear authority, for reasons he would not have understood, by virtue of his arguments, baffling in complexity, and his impressive bulk. In his absence, things began to slip, and Hew was soon required to step into the breach. The entrant boys were meek and cowed, fresh faced from the grammar schools, and rarely caused offence. The boldest

56

had begun to swagger by their second year. The tertians were the worst; lacking both the callowness of youth and the earnestness of magistrands, who realised that their college days were coming to an end. They were brash and quarrelsome, inclined to win by force, what they could not win by argument. Several were discovered with a savage range of weaponry, in flagrant violation of the college rules. Hew had spent a weary morning dealing with the renegades, one of whom now glowered at him across the turret tower.

The boy stood solid in the centre of the floor, resenting him. He was fifteen, or sixteen perhaps, with a sun-flecked, freckled face and hair the colour of wet sand. Hew caught a glimpse of metal, glinting at his belt. 'Your regent tells me you would not give up your dagger, and were uncivil to him. May I see the weapon?' he requested.

The boy produced it sulkily. 'It is a pocket knife, for meat.'

'That is not a pocket knife. It is a rapier. Put it on the pile there with the rest.'

'My father gave it to me. He wished me to be able to defend myself.'

'Who is your father?' questioned Hew.

'My father is the Earl of Gowrie. Who is yours?' the boy said rudely.

Hew said, very quietly, 'You garner no advantage by miscourtesy to me, for I am not the one who is diminished by it. You must be Ruthven's bastard, if you are his son; your name is entered in the roll as William Wishart, gentleman. Though *gentleman* is open to dispute.'

'I said I was Lord Gowrie's son. I did not claim he owned to it,' returned the youth.

'Then you dishonour both your parents, at a stroke. Lay down your sword, and make your peace, or I must write to' – Hew glanced down at the roll – 'Sir William Wishart, elder, at Craighall, to ask him to remove his weapon, and his son, before the end of term.'

'You cannot do that, sir. It is a first offence,' the boy objected.

'Your first offence *this year*, yet not, I think, your first. Then let it be your last. I would not have your fault corrected, publicly, in school.'

The boy conceded, nor would he.

'Then we are agreed on that,' said Hew. 'Give up your sword, and make your peace. Know if you offend again, then I will send you home.'

'I think you are quite wrong,' the student grumbled, setting down his sword, 'to take away our arms. What happens if the college is besieged?'

'When that happens,' Hew said dryly, 'you may have them back.'

'What is that?' the boy demanded, pointing at the foot. Hew had left it in full view, in the hope it might make an impression on the students. Some had been impressed, though not quite in the way that he had hoped.

'It is a human foot, belonging to Professor Locke.'

'That's *braw*!' admired the boy.

'In Latin,' Hew reminded him.

'*Bene,* then! Where did he get it?'

'From the last malefactor,' Hew replied severely, 'that came here with a sword.'

'S'trewth!' The boy let out a long, low whistle. 'Do you think he'll let me have it, when he's done?'

Once the student was dismissed, on promise of reform, the morning's confiscations were complete. The arms had made a mountain in the centre of the floor: six cuirasses, eight swords, four rapiers and an axe, with twelve assorted helmets and a buckled sheet of plate, of which the owner could not give a good account. Hew settled down to read a grammar of the sea. He was no further than the first few pages in – the duties of the shipmaster in making safe his freight – when he was interrupted by a rapping at the door. Groaning, he put on his sternest voice. '*Veni!*' he called loudly. There was a moment's silence, and then the knock again, if anything more tentative. Exasperated, Hew leapt to the door, and threw it open fiercely. 'I said *veni! Come!*' He imagined some delinquent, cowering on the stair, too fearful (as he hoped) or dull (as he supposed) to make the right response. Instead he found a grave young woman, of the gentle class, who gazed at him through curious blue eyes.

'Your pardon, sir, it seems that I disturb you. You are Doctor Locke.'

'Ah, no, not at all,' Hew stammered. 'That is, you have not disturbed me, and I am not Doctor Locke. I am Hew Cullan, his depute. Giles is on leave, at present. Can I be of help?'

'I do not know,' the woman seemed uncertain, and Hew felt himself grow hot. She was, he judged, no older than his sister Meg, and yet so poised and serious she had him blushing like a boy. She was immaculately dressed, in light grey watered silk, set off with little pearls.

'You are the second master here?' she asked.

He recovered his composure as he made his bow, answering, 'I am.'

'Forgive me; you seem young. No matter,' said the woman, 'I am grateful for your help. My brother is a student here, just recently enrolled. He left his Latin grammar at my house. I thought to leave it for him at the college gate, but was turned away precipitate. The man would not allow me to explain. And so I brought it here, to Doctor Locke.'

'The servant is officious here,' Hew groaned. 'The truth is, in his rudeness, he obeys a rule. He may not let a woman pass beyond the gate. Our porters are not used to converse with the gentle sex. It is our excuse, though scarcely a defence. I beg your pardon, humbly, if we have offended you.'

'There is no offence. In truth, I only meant to leave the book.'

'Come inside a moment,' offered Hew. He could hear the college servants on the stair below.

She said, a little hesitant, 'Would that be allowed?'

'Madam, I am quite sure it is not allowed,' he smiled, 'and yet I would not have you standing on the stair. I pray you, take a seat.'

He ushered her inside, plumping up the cushions on the doctor's favourite chair.

She sat down with perfect poise, smoothing out her dress. 'What a strange chamber this is,' she remarked, looking round.

'Yes. It is Doctor Locke's study. He uses it for . . . studying.'

'How extraordinary! What are those?' She pointed to the pile of weapons on the floor.

'That is the college armoury,' Hew improvised. 'In case of war. Not that we expect a war,' he added, sensing her alarm. 'Yet if there is a war, it were well to be prepared.'

'Indeed. And the armoury is kept in the professor's lodging house?'

'It is the safest place,' he assured her.

'I see. And what is *that*?' She pointed at the foot.

'That . . . that is a model of a foot,' he draped it quickly with a cloth, 'that Doctor Locke employs, in teaching of anatomy.'

''Tis very true to life,' the woman said politely. 'I will not keep you long. My brother's name is George Buchanan.'

'I know him!' Hew exclaimed, astonished and relieved, that it was not the boy that he had recently rebuked.

'Do you, sir?' she brightened.

'That is . . . I saw him take his oath,' he replied more honestly, 'and took a little notice of the name.'

She gave a little sigh, and owned, 'Ah, yes. It is a trial to him.'

'I will be glad,' Hew offered, 'to pass on the book.' He noticed that she held the grammar in her hand, and yet did not relinquish it.

'I suppose I had some hope of seeing George,' she confessed. 'You will think me foolish, as I know my husband does, but I cannot help but fear for him. My brother is not strong, and has never been a scholar. He is willing, but is not a subtle boy.'

The mention of a husband disappointed Hew, for reasons he could not have given, were he to be asked. It had been plain from the beginning she was someone else's wife; her manner and her clothes, the way she wore her hair, all gave the clear impression of the married state. His heart slumped further when he heard what she said next. 'I fear, sir, that you will be hard on him. He is a timid boy.'

The plea, he knew, was meant for him. 'Why would you fear that?' he asked.

'I thought perhaps I sensed it at the door. A certain want of *sympathy*.'

'Mistress, I assure you . . .' Hew was lost for words. For how had she construed him, to think he could be cruel?

'I do not blame you,' she said quickly, 'for I know the life is rigorous, and that you must be strict. You will think my poor brother is petted and spoiled. He is not strong, in spirit or in health. Yet he is not overindulged. I fear that what I say will turn your mind against him. I do not explain it well.'

'Madam,' he assured her, 'you have put his case most gently, and in no way is he disadvantaged by your coming here. You leave him in the safest hands. His regent is a conscientious man, who takes great care and interest in the students' education, and will set your brother kindly on the straightest path. And, if he falls sick, our principal Giles Locke is a most excellent physician, and the best of men. Besides, he has a young son of his own.'

She responded warmly. 'That is good to know, then. How old is his son?'

'He has lately ventured on his second day,' admitted Hew.

'That is young,' she acknowledged gravely, with the shadow of a smile.

'As for myself, I know not what to say, in my defence. You caught me off my guard, and found me cross, and yet you are mistaken if you think I am severe. In truth, I have the least authority, and am the last man that the students may have cause to fear,' he told her earnestly.

'I thank you for your kindness. You have set my mind at rest.'

Hew offered, 'If you still wish to see your brother, I can have him called.'

She hesitated. 'Is that done?'

'It could be done.'

'But then,' she said, with a rush of sensitivity, 'I think he may not like to be called out from his friends.'

'I think that more than likely,' Hew agreed.

'Then I am reassured. I will not be the cause of his embarrassment.' She handed Hew the grammar book. 'My husband will be waiting for me. I think you are mistaken, in that you lack authority. I think it very likely they look up to you.'

Suddenly, he blurted, loath to let her go, 'I too have a sister.'

She gazed at him a moment, astonished and amused, before she answered seriously, 'She is fortunate, then. Good day to you, sir.'

Hew watched her from the window, and scowled at his own foolishness, muttering, 'I too have a sister! What devil did induce me to say that?' Too long, he decided, in the company of men. He had not even thought to ask her for her name.

He also had a sister, nonetheless, who had been foremost on his mind the last few anxious hours. He could stay away no longer, but hurried to the Swallow Gait. He was delighted to find Giles recovered and restored, larger and more cheerful than his usual self. For once, the doctor spoke without equivocation. His professional verdict was that Matthew was the fairest, fattest, strongest, bravest, boldest infant ever seen, 'And how could it be otherwise, when he has such a mother?'

'In truth, I am right glad to see you,' he confided privately. 'The place is thrang with womenfolk, and you will have to vie with them, for audience with Meg. Go to, and tell them I insist on it, if they are to remain here in my house.'

This somehow lacked the courage of the doctor's sworn conviction, and Hew responded nervously, 'Go into the women's room? Alone?'

'Why not? She is your sister, Hew. Be certain to insist on it. And I will join you presently. I want a word with Paul.'

Hew had the sense that he was sent in as the vanguard, to distract the troops. The entrance to the birthing room was gated like St Salvator's, as if the college porters met their match in wives. The women were invincible, and would not let him pass, till Meg called out beseechingly, 'Pray let my brother in.' The sentries were disbanded and straggled through the hall, with a dagger-backward glance of murder towards Hew.

The room was dark and womb-like, and Hew felt a moment's panic, starting back for Giles, until he saw his sister, sitting up in bed. She was propped up on a pillow, with Matthew in her arms. Hew stood still and stared. He felt a sudden shyness that he did not understand. Meg held out her hand to him, whispering, 'Come see,' as though it were her brother, and not Matthew, was the bairn. 'Come, see Matthew Locke.'

Her voice was low and soft, and everything was closed and dark, to make a quiet cloister for the mother and her child. And the bairn himself was lapped up in his swaddling bands, a tiny human package staring stiff and strange, through two dark solemn pinpricks blinking up at Hew.

'You made him, Meg. How clever of you,' Hew observed at last. The lightness of his tone betrayed the tremor in his heart.

His sister smiled. 'I had a little help. Come, will you hold him? He is firmly wrapped.'

Hew peered back at the parcel, but did not pick it up. 'Do you think he likes it?' he asked her, critically.

'I had not thought,' considered Meg. 'For it is always done.'

'We do not ask him what he *likes*,' said Giles, appearing at the door, 'for fear he will grow up like you, to question everything. The muscaters are mustered in the kitchen, and will presently regroup,' he warned, 'so we do not have long.'

'You must not be unkind to them, when they have been so good to us,' objected Meg.

'It is unkindness, born of terror,' Giles assured her, 'and a wilful longing, to be left alone with you.'

'Patience. You will have us for a lifetime.'

'Amen to that,' said Giles, turning back to Hew. 'Paul has just informed me,' he mentioned with a frown, 'that there was a suspicious death, at Maude Benet's inn.'

'Was it the stranger?' wondered Hew.

'The man from the windmill,' said Meg.

They both of them gaped at her. 'How in the world can you know about that?'

'You think I am confined here? Yet the women have been coming in for days. There is no scrap of gossip that I have not heard.'

'Well, I had heard nothing, till now,' grumbled Giles. 'It seems I am the only person in the world who was not informed, until his servant thought it ripe to tell him, he was wanted there two days ago. We must go at once, and hope that we are not too late.'

'We are certainly too late,' Hew pointed out.

'I mean, too late to verify the cause of death.' Giles kissed his wife and child. 'Dearest,' he said briskly, 'I shall not be long.'

Chapter 6

A Glass Perspective

It had made sense, Maude protested, when the bailies told it to her. It was something she could not explain.

'Try,' insisted Giles. 'What happened to the corpse?'

'It was taken out to sea.'

'Why to the sea?'

'It had come from the sea, and so it was returned, to the place where he had drowned,' Maude recited, like a catechism. James Edie had instructed her and she had learned the drill. She realised now that it did not stand up to scrutiny. Though that was the way with a creed; you had it by heart, and did not question why, or else the whole world would be riven into shreds. She wondered that they did not see it.

The doctor said, 'As you must see, that cannot be so.'

Maude appealed to Hew, 'It was like the fish, sir. I felt his beating heart.'

'What does she mean?' inquired Giles.

'The fish heart went on beating, after it was dead,' remembered Hew.

'That happens with a fish, but rarely with a human heart. A man is either dead, or not,' the doctor insisted.

Hew advised her kindly, 'No one blames you, Maude. Yet you must talk us through it once again. What happened here, *exactly?*'

They were standing in Maude's bedchamber, adjacent to the kitchen. All trace of Jacob had been cleared away. The closet shared a chimney, and a fireplace, with the room next door, and the air was thick and claggy with the smell of frying fat. A recess in the wall looked out onto the yard, facing back upon the jakes, away from the direction of the sea. A blue flannel blanket lay folded on the bed, turned upon the sheets.

'Are those the sheets he died in?' questioned Giles.

Maude shook her head. 'The linen was cut up, to mak' his shroud.'

'What happened to his clothes?'

The clothes had gone too. Yet Maude recounted clearly, every hook and thread. She remembered his long coat, of dun-coloured wool, that the sea had matted, turning into felt, his white linen shirt, with lace around the cuffs, where a careful hand had stitched, his darned black breeks and salt-scuffed shoes. His hat, she supposed, had been lost in the storm.

'Then he was not a mariner?' persisted Hew.

Maude agreed that Jacob had not been a mariner. Sailors wore short coats, with wide, baggy breeks, and shoes soled with rope, for gripping to the decks. Sailors dressed like banderoles, in red and white and blue.

'Did he eat or drink, vomit, use the jakes?'

He had drunk and eaten, ale and bannock sops, and he had pissed and vomited, both into the water pot. The residue had gone into the jakes, the jakes a metal pail that emptied to the sink, the sink a narrow gutter-pipe that ran into the sea. The leakage had been washed away, with no trace left behind.

'You say he spoke to you. What were his words?'

He had said his name was Jacob, but that he was not himself. He spoke the words in Flemish; she had understood them. 'I am not my, he said, and I am not myself. In Flemish, Eek neet mine, Ik neet van Myzelf.'

What had she understood by that?

'I am not myself.'

What had she understood by *that*?

She had not understood.

'I am not myself,' Hew repeated carefully. He sounded out the Dutch, and wrote it down.

'And when he died, you say you heard a noise?'

'It was the cat, Gib Hunter.'

The cat was in the room with them. It wound its legs round Hew's, quivering its tail.

'He came in from the yard, and could not escape.'

Gib Hunter gave the lie to this, by leaping up on the window ledge and out into the yard, the way he had come in.

'Did Jacob speak again?'

He spoke out to a woman, Beatrix was her name. And he called to the devil, just before he died. She meant to say, before he died again. For he was dead already, and he brought the devil in his dreams.

'Tell us, how that works,' persisted Giles.

'The surgeon came and wrote it,' Maude reported stubbornly. 'It was death by drowning.'

'Is it possible, at all?' murmured Hew to Giles, 'That drowning was delayed? That water had collected in his lungs?'

'Possible, indeed,' Giles answered unequivocally. Hew had not expected him to answer straight and plain. 'And yet I do not think,' he added, true to form, 'that that was how he died. Besides which, if I understand you, Jacob was a corpse, some time before he drowned. He drowned not once, but twice. Is that not correct?'

Maude agreed unhappily. 'When I hear you say it now, it does not make much sense. But had you seen him when they brocht him from the sea, so swollen, blue and black, you might understand it, sir. The surgeon said that Jacob had been dead for days.'

'Yet you were not afraid, Maude,' Hew remarked astutely. 'A dead man in your closet sat and drank and talked with you, pissing in your water pot. You had him close at hand there, when you prepared my fish.' This was an unpleasant thought, he wished had not occurred to him. Yet he had proved his point. Maude had sheltered Jacob, and she had felt no fear.

'Tis true,' admitted Maude, herself surprised by this. 'I never was afeared at him. I cannot tell you why. Yet I had quite forgotten, sir,' she broke in suddenly, 'that there is something here, that I have kept to show you, that will make it plain.'

'Something left behind?' asked Hew.

Maude Benet answered oddly, 'Aye, sir, something left behind. It will help you understand. Tis what the surgeon saw.' She reached up for the little box, high up on the shelf, and handed it to Giles. 'Jacob wore a ring,' she said. 'And when the women came to dress the corpus, they fell to squabbling over it. They picked at him like crows, and found it firmly fixed. I took it from their grasp, and thought to keep it safe. It was the only part of him not given to the sea.'

Giles opened up the box, whooping with delight, 'Sweet, subtle Maude, you are an angel, Maude! Look at this, Hew! Is this not rare?'

'What is it? Oh, sweet Jesus Christ, what is that? Whatever did possess you to keep such a relic?' Hew cried in disgust. For Maude had kept the ring as it had come from Jacob's body, with the blackened stub of finger still attached.

'I did not have the heart,' she answered helplessly, 'to throw the remnant out.'

Giles marvelled, 'Look close at this putrefaction, Hew!'

'I have it in my scent. It must be two days old,' protested Hew.

The doctor countered, 'Ah, that is the point; it is far more than that. This ripeness and contusion makes the matter plain.'

'The ripeness of the matter is beyond dispute, the meaning far from plain. I wish you would explain.'

'So shall I, in due course. This ring was fast upon the poor man's finger, Maude?' pressed Giles.

Maude answered, 'Aye. In truth, the ring was buried in his flesh, his fingers were so black and puffed the first that I had seen it there, was when the fisher wifies pu'ed it off. You ken, sir, that I had no thought to have it to mysel?'she appealed to Hew.

He nodded. 'Aye, we know it, Maude. You keep an honest house.'

'Just so. What will you dae wi it, now?' wondered Maude.

'*Experiments*,' said Giles. 'In hope the ring will tell us, who its owner was, while from this ragged finger, we may learn how he died. I see now, why the surgeon has mistook the time of death. For Jacob was alive still, when this finger died.'

'What ever does that mean?' demanded Hew.

Giles beamed at him. 'I cannot say as yet.' He patted round his clothes. It seems that I have come without a pocket to my coat. Wrap it in your handkerchief, and slip it into yours.'

'Let in a little light,' instructed Giles, 'and we shall see, what we shall see.' He threw the shutters wide and allowed the day to force its way into the turret tower. The morning mists had cleared, and a cold shaft of sunshine settled on the astrolabe. Hew stood shivering in his shirt. He had barely been asleep, when Giles came with the dawn to start on their dissections.

'You are precipitate,' Hew groaned.

'And you are a slugabed. I rose up with the lark. Or to be precise, with the young Matthew Locke, whose piping woke the household,' Giles admitted cheerfully. 'There is something to be said for a separate set of chambers. Are you not yet dressed?'

'In a moment, by your leave.' Hew fumbled with his points. Giles rummaged through the bookshelves. 'Have you had my pinching-tenals?' he inquired.

'What would I with your pincers?' snorted Hew. The forceps, tongs and tweezers that informed his friend's anatomy surpassed the barber surgeon's, and their very mention left him feeling faint. He buttoned up his coat and felt round for his purse, in which the finger had been safely settled for the night.

'They have a multitude of uses,' Giles persisted peevishly. 'And you have left the chamber in a sad state of array.'

Hew did not deign to flatter with reply. The students' weapons had been cleared into the buttery, and now that Hew was up and dressed he made no other mark upon the cluttered room.

'Remind me how we lived together, in the Rue des Fosses?' the doctor asked, self-righteously.

'I wonder that myself.'

'Now, this is what I mean,' said Giles, pouncing on a book. 'You have left your Latin primer where I keep my cupping glass! Have you been teaching schoolboys while my back is turned? Or are you numbing them with gerunds, while you let their blood?'

'Neither,' Hew retrieved the grammar with a groan. 'It was left here for a student, and I fear I had forgotten it. I promised to his sister I would pass it on.'

'A sister? Ah! What sort of a sister?' Giles began to quiz. Hew replied repressively, 'The *married* sort. Your pincers are right there, behind the astrolabe,' he pointed out.

'Ah, yes, I do recall . . . there was a little matter of the rule, that wanted some adjusting. Yet I fear, tis broken now.'

'Perhaps it was the wind?' said Hew.

Giles coughed and cleared his throat. 'Go to, where is the finger? Set it in the light, and on the flesher's block. It will not be affected, by the taint of blood. You may move the foot.'

'*You* may move the foot,' corrected Hew.

Giles spread out a square of gauze upon the blank dissecting board, setting out his instruments. The sunlight dipped and flickered, bouncing off the blades. 'Make haste now, or the sun will damage it,' he warned.

'That seems a vain precaution,' Hew remarked, 'when this remnant is already so decayed.'

He untied the pouch and shook out the blackened contents. 'Here is a pocket that I will not want to fill again.'

'Do not stop to fret about the puddle in your handkerchief. Twill come out in the wash.'

'Twill come out in the furnace,' answered Hew.

'You are too meticulous,' his friend complained. 'Patience, if you will, and we will make this finger back into the man.'

'As in a puff of smoke.'

'We are philosophers, not conjurers,' Giles replied severely. 'I think you are not suited to the task.'

'I commend it, I assure you. Tis only that I find it rather grim,' admitted Hew.

'Then you shall turn your wits, to finding out the ring, and leave the rest to me.'

Giles held the putrid finger closely, teasing out the metal from the bone. He wiped the ring clean on his shirt sleeve, handing it to Hew. 'You want a *glass perspective*. Back there, on the shelf,' he gestured indistinctly, returning to his prize. 'This putrefaction came on by degrees,' he commented, 'and by degrees, in turn, gives up to us its secrets, that we may hope to learn from them.'

Hew searched among the book shelves that lined the turret tower, through almanacs and pickle jars, bones and broken clocks, until at last he found the hidden box of spectacles. He picked up a crystal, cut into a prism shape, and held it to the sun, captured in the colours he saw dancing in the glass.

The doctor grumbled mildly, 'Let the colours lie, Hew! Feckless as a bairn! We want a cunning optic glass, that shows the world writ large.'

'I am a bairn, distracted by the sunlight in the glass,' Hew admitted openly. He took the lenses from the box, and tried them one by one. 'I have not met with optics such as these.'

'They are of the most common kind,' said Giles dismissively. 'There are more special glasses I have not acquired and several others yet, that I never seen.'

'Such as what?' asked Hew.

'Hhm?' Giles was scraping at the relic on the gauze. 'There is a glass magicians use,' he mentioned thoughtfully, 'wherein a man may look and see an image not his own. That is the sort of looking glass that I have never seen, much as I would like to. I fear our optics here are of the simple kind. You want the glass that shows the world writ large. It is the plainest, at the back.'

'I see it,' Hew confirmed. He held the ring up to the light to scrutinise it through the glass. 'This is a costly piece, for a man in workday clothes, and something rich and rare. It is an Antwerp diamond, fashioned like a flower, they call the rose, or Holland cut.

71

Tis wrought of yellow gold, a little scratched and worn, which signifies a metal of the purest kind.'

Giles set down his scalpel in astonishment. 'In truth, I did not count your taste in diamonds so refined, that you might ken the setting from the stone,' he commented.

Hew said, a little poignantly, 'It is no great passion of mine. But when I was apprenticed to the bar with Richard Cunningham, I came to know a little of the goldsmith's craft, for Richard had a fondness for fine rings. His diamonds were reset to suit the king.'

Giles, from tact, said, 'Ah,' and refrained from further comment as his friend went on, 'And this is such a ring as Richard used to wear, his kid gloves finger-slashed, to show the diamonds off. Tis called the Antwerp rose, because it was invented there. Yet we must pause to ask ourselves, how Jacob came to have a ring, that sits a little oddly, among his modest clothes. This is a costly piece.'

'Do we know him by the ring, or better by his clothes?' considered Giles.

'That must be our question, as I think. He told us, Maude reported, he was *not himself*. Then we must look for subterfuge,' said Hew. 'Better then to know him by his hands. For there, at least, he cannot tell a lie.' He gave the glass to Giles.

'Now you expect too much. For since we do not have his hands, we must know him by his finger,' Giles objected. 'I hope to chance to hazard how he died; I cannot hope to tell you how he lived.'

'Then with his death,' conceded Hew, 'let us now begin.'

The doctor nodded. 'Why could the gudwives not remove the ring?' he asked.

'Because it was too tight.'

And why was it too tight?'

'Because it was not made for him,' suggested Hew.

'That is more than likely. Yet that remains another question, and concerns his life, when we are now turned to his death,' reminded Giles. 'So set that thought aside, and look to the discolouration. Do you see it, Hew?'

Hew swallowed down his squeamishness. 'I see it,' he confirmed.

'This is a dead finger,' said Giles. 'By which I do not mean it is a dead man's finger, but that the finger died before the man. Before that, it was swollen. The ring became too tight as the finger came distended. What then, was the cause?'

'Could not the cause have been the ring itself?' argued Hew. 'Because it was too tight, it cut the finger off?'

'Your thoughts are once again, drawn to the living man. And that is only natural,' said Giles. 'But concentrate on this. This was not the only finger blackened and distended, though it was the only one that bore a ring. Maude told us that his face was dark and blotted too.'

'They took him for a Spaniard,' Hew recalled. 'A black and swarthy creature, as the baxters said.'

'Swollen, blotched and putrid,' Giles summed up. 'So that the surgeon took him for long dead, which in a sense, he was. He suffered from a gangrene, of a dry pernicious kind.'

'Sweet lord!' whispered Hew. 'What was the cause?'

'I cannot tell you that. And yet I do suppose it died out on the ship. Dearly, I would love to know what happened to the crew.'

'Maude said,' Hew remarked, 'that Jacob called to demons as he died.'

'As I confess, that vexes me,' the doctor said, 'For Maude is not a woman given to wild tales.'

'That we must count as madness, or else something worse.'

'What had you in mind?'

'You said there was an occult glass,' said Hew, 'wherein a man might see another man, an image not his own. And Maude said, he reported, he was *not himself*. Do you think it likely Jacob was bewitched?'

'It is a possibility,' the doctor answered carefully. Plainly, he had thought of this, 'That I do not discount. Though, I prefer to be pragmatical . . .'

'You prefer to be equivocal,' interrupted Hew.

Giles went on regardless, impervious to the jibe. '. . . I count it less than likely, though I cannot say for sure. When a man dies seeing demons, I am more inclined to ask, what he last had to eat and drink. Your theory is provocative. I had you for a doubter, of the occult arts.'

'Though I do not fear their magic, I do not doubt its power to harm those that believe it,' answered Hew. 'If I am cursed, and told that I must die, that it is my believing it that kills me in the end. And for that reason, we must keep all hint of witchcraft secret from the town.'

Doctor Locke agreed. 'I shall make report, and send it to the coroner, that now is our new sheriff, Andrew Wood. Tis likely we shall hear from him, for he is most assiduous.'

'Then he serves as contrast to our old one,' remarked Hew.

'So it must be hoped. I met him only once, and cannot say I took to him. No matter, these are desperate times, and want a will of iron to make the measures straight. I have the feeling,' Giles reported gloomily, 'that we shall know him well before this year is out. For now, I have a little pot, in which this scrap of finger may safely be disposed, and keep its secrets closed. I hear the morning lecture bell, and have not had my breakfast yet. Will you come and join me, in a buttered egg?'

'Not for all the world,' said Hew emphatically.

They parted at the turret door, where Hew turned sharply back and through the college gates, George Buchanan's grammar in his hand. He caught the trail of students snaking to the hall.

'Which one of you,' he called, 'is George Buchanan?'

A thin and pale-faced stripling stepped up with a sigh. 'I am George Buchanan, sir,' he answered wretchedly, as though the very question were a burden to be borne, which Hew supposed it was. The boy bore no resemblance to the scholar.

'I have your *Rudimentia Grammatices*. Your sister left it for you,' Hew explained.

The student answered, 'Oh!' and blushed a livid puce, from the purple of his thropple to the pink tips of his ears. A reprimand, Hew sensed, was preferable to this. In kindness, he should turn away, and let the matter drop. Despite himself, he asked, 'Is your sister your tutrix, then, George?'

The boy blinked in surprise. 'Is she my what, sir?'

'Are you her ward?' Hew glossed.

'I have no tutor, sir, for I am come of age.'

'Of course you are,' Hew countered quickly. 'I only meant to ask, where is it that you live? Are you come here from her house?'

'I come here from my father, sir. I do not bide with Clare. I stayed with her a night. Tis only that her house is somewhat close to here, my father's at Linlithgow, somewhat far away, and that is where I live – that is where I lived,' George corrected poignantly, 'since now I must live here.'

Hew felt a prick of guilt.

'Why do you ask it, sir? Have I done something wrong?'

The boys behind them nudged and winked.

Hew sighed, 'Not at all.'

'I will be late, sir, for the lecture, and the regent will be vexed.' George took the book and stuffed it in his breeks, with a furtive backward glance towards his waiting friends.

'Your sister came in kindness. You need not feel ashamed,' admonished Hew.

George coloured once again. 'I am not ashamed of Clare. But for it is a *bairn's* book,' he blurted out, in Scots.

'It is a Latin grammar book, and it will serve you well. And God help him who laughs at it,' Hew threw out to the crowd, 'and does not know his verbs. Now, what must you say to me?'

'Benigne, magister . . . domine . . . professor, sir,' George responded awkwardly.

'Bene. Vive valeque,' Hew dismissed him with a nod. He watched him scuttle off, gaunt ghost of a child, following the rest into the lecture room. It had not been his intention to humiliate the boy. Why had he forced him to the inquisition? What matter, who his father was, or if he lived with Clare? *Clare Buchanan*, Hew reflected, trying out the name. Despite his twitch of conscience, he found it brought a smile.

Chapter 7

The Dolfin

Hew first met the sheriff late one afternoon, as he was packing up his saddlebags, preparing to return to Kenly Green. Meg and Matthew grew from strength to strength, and Giles was now restored to full command, though he retained a tendency to drift back to the Swallow Gait, at dull and quiet moments in the day. The coroner replied to Giles' letter, by bursting without warning into the turret tower, startling Hew to dropping all his books.

'Andrew Wood, of Largo,' he announced abruptly, 'looking for Giles Locke.'

Hew recovered quickly. 'Sir Andrew Wood, the coroner and sheriff?'

'One and the same.'

Hew rose to his feet to scrutinise his guest. Sir Andrew was appointed in the place of Michael Balfour. The Balfours had been sheriffs and coroners of Fife before the fall of Regent Morton, whose downfall had led to their disgrace. Hew had dealt with Michael in the past, and had found him weak and ineffectual. He had no preconceptions of the man's successor. As he stood before him, he seemed brusque and penetrating, severe in his expression and his dress. His eyes were clear and thoughtful, taking in the compass of the tower, and giving the impression that nothing small was missed. His clothes were cut from fine silk cloth, yet bore no jewel or ornament, sober as a clergyman's, with less resort to vanity. His beard and hair were dark and closely trimmed, with few white pepper flecks, to give away his age. His family fortune, Hew recalled, was built upon the back

of ships; he was the third in succession, though the fourth in genera-
tion, to Andrew Wood the admiral, scion of the sea, and master of
the fleet to James the Third. Since the time of Morton's downfall,
he had held the privy purse, as treasurer or comptroller within the
royal court, a position which brought scant reward, for huge respon-
sibility. The debts he had discharged in service to the king had
brought him to the brink of ruin, and were rumoured to have cost
him £7000. His offices in Fife, which he received in recompense,
did little to relieve him of the burden of his loss. All this Hew kept
in mind as he replied, 'Giles Locke is at home, with his wife and
child.'

Wood responded curtly. 'You, sir, are Hew Cullan, and professor
in the law, which is to the good, for I may have a use for you, and
that may serve as well. I do not have the time to wait on Doctor
Locke. He is, I'm told, much exercised, in this small matter of his
child. Does it affect his judgement, do you think?'

'Not one jot,' Hew answered, masking his surprise.

'But then, you would say that. You are his brother, as I think,'
suggested Andrew Wood.

'He is married to my sister,' Hew agreed. 'And yet to me, he is
much more than that.'

'Aye, then, fair enough. For I have sometimes thought,' conceded
Andrew Wood, 'to say I *love him like a brother* were a cunning form
of wit, since brothers may be profligate, envious, or cruel.'

'I have no brother to compare him,' answered Hew. 'But if I were
to have one, I should like it to be Giles.'

Sir Andrew sniffed. 'You are not pious, as I hope? More than the
proper, commonplace?'

'I do not think so,' Hew demurred.

'That is to the good. I do not want a pious man, for what I have
in mind. For that might prove impediment,' Andrew Wood said
thoughtfully.

This was his second mention of a use for Hew, and Hew felt
some excitement at the prospect of a task. He realised, looking at

the books now spilling from his saddle bags, that he was wearying of life, from Kenly Green to college, and from college back to Kenly Green.

Sir Andrew seemed to read his mind, for his glance followed Hew's. 'I see you pack your bag. Were you going on a journey?' he inquired.

'Home to Kenly Green,' said Hew. 'Now Giles resumes his place, I am not needed here.'

'In truth,' Sir Andrew commented, 'your aptitudes and interests have been wasted in the college, and tis high time they were put to better use. I have a proposition, that requires you to remain here for a while; therefore I suggest that you unpack your things.'

'What proposition?' queried Hew.

'You will hear it, in due course. You work with Doctor Locke, your brother and your friend, who also is our *visitor*, who makes report to us upon suspicious deaths. Then you must trust his judgement, I suppose?'

Hew assured him, 'With my life.'

'*With your life,*' Sir Andrew echoed him. Hew could not quite read his tone. Irony, perhaps, or frank intimidation? Or an echo, simply, to force the message home? The words had taken on peculiar significance. Hew did not regret them in the least. 'I would trust him,' he repeated, 'with my life.'

'Aye,' said Andrew Wood, somewhat more dismissively, 'but he is a physician, is he not? And that is what we do with our physicians; *we trust them with our lives.* I find it rather galling, I confess. We cannot have them charged with mis-selling us, like baxters, for promising to cure us, after we are dead. Your doctor keeps a strange collection,' he went on to observe. 'What is in those jars?'

'You do not wish to know,' Hew told him with a smile.

'No?' Sir Andrew snatched the stopper from a jar, sniffing at the contents. He did not recoil, as Hew had expected, but remarked appraisingly, 'Some sort of embalming spice.'

'He makes it to his own receipt,' acknowledged Hew.

'What does he with the entrails? Divinations?'

'Giles is no magician.'

'I am pleased to hear it.' Wood replaced the stopper and took up another jar. 'Is this relic human?'

'It is the finger of the shipwrecked Flemish sailor, who died at Benet's inn.'

Giles preserved his relics, almost lovingly, as Meg preserved the rosehips and the sloes at Kenly Green, bottled into jars and boiled in marmalades. The jar had been recorded in a ledger, with a clear note of the contents and the date.

'Is it now? Then that is apposite,' the coroner approved. 'For that is what I come to speak about.'

'Better then to speak to Giles. For I am no mediciner,' protested Hew.

'You are something else,' answered Andrew Wood. 'I have had report of you, from John Lundie of Strathairlie, an old friend of your father. He tells me you are wilful, reckless, rash and bold. You do not listen to good reason, and you overstep your place. You interfere in business that does not concern you, where your conscience moves you, upon some fickle whim.'

'That is . . . frank,' said Hew.

'You do not contradict it,' Andrew Wood observed.

'I do not pay an old man that discourtesy.'

Sir Andrew smiled. 'He is in his dotage, you imply.'

'That I leave to others, sir, to judge.'

'As we shall, be sure of it. It may well prove to your credit, that you choose not to gainsay it, for what he counts as fault in you, sits well enough with me. Such flaws and indiscretions, as are faults of youth, are curbed with careful management,' Andrew Wood said thoughtfully. He left Hew in no doubt, that he meant to manage him. The coroner went on, 'I heard you were a thorn in Michael Balfour's side. You sought the killer of a Largo fishing lass, when Balfour would have let the matter rest. I ask you, out of interest, was the case resolved?'

'In a manner,' Hew confessed, 'though not as I would wish. There was a boy – a fisher lad – that had some carnal knowledge of the lass, and though he was suspected of the crime, he could not be indicted, and the trail went cold.'

'For want of proof?' asked Andrew Wood.

'For want,' said Hew, 'of witnesses. The fishermen kept close, and would not break their ranks, in giving up their own. In their own way, they settled it. The fisher lad was sent out in a boat, with Rab, the dead girl's father, and only Rab returned.'

'A form of natural justice, then,' the coroner concluded.

'I did not think it so.'

'Then you are a man of fine distinctions. I ought perhaps to tell you, I am not Michael Balfour, content to let a matter rest for fear of awkward questioning. I would have had your fisher lad, and had him by the neck. Does that discomfort you?'

'It does,' admitted Hew. 'Because there was no proof.' He had begun to feel like one of Giles Locke's specimens, pinned out on the chopping board; his answers were stripped down and close inspected, in a glass of careful scrutiny. It seemed that he had passed the test, for Andrew Wood resumed, 'I wish you to investigate this Flemish sailor's death, of which I hear disturbing, and quite differing reports, from Giles Locke and the burghers of this town. Professor Locke has written he was brought ashore alive, and suffered some pernicious rot, a gangrene of extremities, the inner cause of which he cannot ascertain. According to the surgeon who certified the death, the man was dead before he landed, and had drowned at sea. I came here through the marketplace, where I heard strange reports, of dead men walking, and a man twice drowned, that starting back to life brought devils in his wake. I hear the people talk of witchcraft, and of plague, which terrors I am anxious to assuage.'

'They are rumours,' Hew assured him, 'that have no base in fact.'

'I do not doubt it, Hew,' the light use of the given name seemed oddly soft and intimate, a lure to draw him closer in to the intrigue. Unwarranted, as Hew reflected wryly, since he was already snared.

'Yet I am well aware,' the coroner went on, 'that rumour is more dangerous than truth. And I am vexed by these reports. Tis hard enough, to keep peace for the king, in these troubled times.'

'The king himself is not at peace, nor yet at liberty, as I have heard,' Hew answered recklessly. The sheriff's closer confidence had made him drop his guard.

'What have you heard?'

'That the king has been forced from his favourites, by the Earl of Gowrie, and is held against his will.'

'That,' said Andrew Wood, 'is what you have *inferred*. The king has made a public proclamation to dispel this rumour; he is not coerced in this, and nowhere held and forced against his will. And *that* is what you heard.'

It was impossible to tell where his allegiance lay. Hew continued unperturbed. 'And when a king makes such a public proclamation, that he is not held and forced against his will, the public draws its own conclusion. The candle snuffer fans the flame.'

Sir Andrew Wood said coldly, 'I charge you to dispense with rumour, not to play a part in its dissemination. If you are to work for me, then you must curb your tongue, and keep your close thoughts quiet from the crowd. Let us now return, to the matter of the wreck. I wish for you to search the ship, and find out what you can. Tis likely that some papers have remained as evidence.'

'Has that not been done?'

'In the scramble for the windmill,' Andrew Wood explained, 'it seems that such procedures, as are commonsense, were sadly over-looked. There is, besides, a small impediment, which I will come to in a while. I would have you seek out any document pertaining to the mill. The town council is most anxious that St Andrews should retain it, for the common good. The baxters have petitioned me to grant it to their gild. And then there is my brother, Robert Wood, with whom I understand you are acquainted?'

Hew shook his head. 'I do not know the name.'

'Now that surprises me. Your name was spoken to me at his house.

81

Unless . . . no matter, though,' the coroner broke off. 'My brother owns the Newmill on the Kinness Burn, and clamours for the windmill to be sited on his land. The millers, in their turn, are squabbling for the working of it. It would greatly please me, if you could find a way to prove our legal right to it, that all these men's petitions might be put before the admiral. At present, they want answers, that I cannot hope to give. The windmill sits secure upon the shore, and there must stay until we learn her fate.'

'Yet supposing it turns out that we have no legal right to it?' asked Hew.

'I do not ask for perjury. Find out what you can, beginning with the ship. Go to her tomorrow, at the break of light.'

'I can go right now,' said Hew, impatient for the chase.

Sir Andrew Wood replied, with the small ghost of a smile, 'That will not be possible. I mentioned, as you may recall, there was a slight impediment, or else I should have gone there first, and boarded her myself. The *Dolfin* is no longer beached upon the strand. The burgh council had her floated off, and towed back out to sea. She presently lies reeling in a trough, and neither sinks nor floats. She cannot last there long.'

Hew exclaimed, 'They launched a wreck! But why would they do that?'

'It is suspicious, is it not?' the coroner agreed. 'I questioned Bailie Honeyman, whose reasons were for one, a fear of hidden sickness, still lurking on the ship, for two, a fear of witchcraft, for that the wreck was cursed; and three; for fear of harm to children on the beach, for the town could not afford to mount a guard. All of which seemed plausible enough. I have hired a craft for you, tomorrow at first light, and men to help you board. Take care, and take Giles Locke. For last year, as I heard, when you came to cross the water, the boat was overturned, and you were almost drowned.'

'Who told you that?' Hew blushed. 'John Lundie, I suppose.'

Sir Andrew shook his head. 'John Lundie's sphere of influence does not extend so far,' he answered enigmatically.

'Perhaps it is my horse, that you have set to spy on me?'

'You are, I think, impertinent, which may require correction,' the coroner observed.

'I bow to your direction, sir,' Hew retorted dryly.

'It's clear that you do not. And that is why I want you,' the coroner replied.

They set out at for the harbour at first light, to find the lighter waiting on the shore, with an expert pilot to steer them to the ship, and a small fleet of fishing boats to follow in their wake. The *Dolfin* had drifted out north of the bay, listing badly to the stern.

'We will steer alongside her, as close as we may, and grasp at her with clips,' the pilot said.

'There is a hempen ledder at her side; tis fortunate they let it doon, for she is someway higher than the waterline. Do you reckon you can climb her?'

'Possibly,' said Hew, with a covert glance at Giles.

'I widna count your chances wi' yon burding at your back,' the pilot answered bluntly. 'I'll send a lad or twa to scale her from the side, and we can fix a timber board across. We'll hold her as we can; she is too great for us to steady her for long, or to tow her back to shore, yet we have ropes and hooks, if ye want to tighten her.'

'What does he say? Do we have to climb the ladder?' ventured Giles. He had taken off his cloak, and unbuttoned his vast britches at the knee to let the legs flow loose like sailors' slops.

'He will send a boy across to make a bridge.'

'Thank God for that. I feared I'd have to scale the rigging like a brigand, with my dagger clenched between my teeth.'

'You might stay below, and witness from the lichter craft,' suggested Hew. He felt a wave of warmth and affection for his friend, who stood willing in his makeshift slops to set aside his fears.

'And let you broach a sinking ship alone? I do not think so, Hew!' Giles scoffed. 'You suffer *mal de mer* in the ripples of a bath vat, and are already queasy from the bumping of the boat.'

Hew grimaced, for the charge was true enough, and he was trying not to notice it.

'Besides which,' Giles went on, 'I am intent as you in looking at the evidence.'

They climbed aboard the ship, between the sagging ropes, and crept into its carcase netted like a fish, that cracked its toothless maw against their bones.

'Tread soft,' the sailors warned, 'else she will rift.' To spit them out or swallow them, thought Hew, like Jonah in the swill. 'Is there no light?' he whispered.

Giles had brought a tinderbox, and lit the clutch of lanterns swinging from the rafts. He cut one with his pocketknife and handed it to Hew, casting yellow moonshine on the decks.

Hew found his way towards the capstan, gaping down into the innards of the ship.

'Ye canna go down there,' a sailor said. 'The hold is filled wi wattir.' And like a belly full of bilge, the swollen timbers groaned.

'Can it not be pumped?' asked Hew.

The sailor shook his head. 'Too much stir will sink her. There is a crack in the hull.'

Hew set the lantern down upon a plank and dropped down to the lower deck. He called to Giles, 'Let down the light!'

Giles passed the lantern through the hatch. 'Will I come down?'

'Not for a moment. Set lamps upon the ladder rungs,' instructed Hew. He moved towards the wooden door that opened to the hold. The water had begun to seep up through the joints, and the timbers were sodden and soft like a sponge. He felt the surface shift, a restlessness beneath his feet, that threatened to let loose the flood upon the upper decks. He hung his lantern on a hook above his head, where it flickered and dipped dangerously. Someone had done as he asked; from the ladder above shone pale strips of moonlight, marking out the path for his escape. Cautiously, he undid the catch, pulling at the ropes, and opened up the entrance to the hold. The waters seeped insidious, lapping round his feet. Hew peered into the void, where he saw nothing but a chasm of black bilge, slopping like the belly of a fish.

'Come away,' he heard cried faint above. 'You cannot go down there.'

Hew took down the light, and lay flat on his stomach at the entrance to the hatch. He lowered down the lantern to the water's edge, and allowed its light to flicker round the hold. He felt the timbers sagging, and a cold and creeping dampness leaking through his clothes. The darkness held its force, and Hew saw nothing but the yellow light repelled; then gradually, its brittle shards made holes, like pinprick moths in velvet, through which daylight showed. They caught the flash and flicker of a shoal of silver fish, that darted quick and seamless through the cracks, and Hew was startled by the scuttle of a crab, that had made a rusted barrel hoop its home. The ship had been stripped bare of its cargo; a fluid film of seaweed wrapping round its husk, barrels split and siphoned, strings of onions bobbing, woollens rank and shapeless, blotted by the sea.

Hew drew up the lantern, making fast the hatch. He called up to Giles. 'Come down, if you will. The lower deck is sound.'

The ladder creaked and swayed, and in a moment, Giles appeared. 'What lies down below?'

'Some ruined pelts and cloths,' said Hew. 'Apples, onions, little left of worth.'

'No clue to Jacob's death? And no sign of the rest?'

'None,' admitted Hew. 'However, it is plain to see, the *Dolfin* had both passengers and crew.'

The passengers were quartered on the lower deck, on which they stood. Some left behind only a blanket, some a thin straw mattress, tied into a roll, and one or two more practised, and of the merchant class, had pinned up sheets as curtains round the rafts, marking out their sleeping space, a cubicle no larger than the compass of a man. The sailors lay flat on the boards, with little else for comfort but the rocking of the sea. They left behind pouches and cups, lettered and carved with their names, knucklebones and dice, a second best shirt hung to dry in the sun, a battered pair of boots, streaked with salt. Giles moved among the blankets, sniffing at the cups.

'What is you are looking for?'

'I know not, liquor, spices, crumbs.'

'All is spoiled or spilled. The galley was below us, in the hold.'

'It is a pity,' answered Giles.

They cast the lanterns one last time upon the debris on the deck, the bric-a-brac of human life, that told them all, and nothing, that had gone before. Above their heads, a sailor called.

'The wind is getting up. We cannot stay for long.'

'There must be something,' Hew reflected, 'in the captain's cabin. 'Tis likely that the schippar kept a notice of his wares. Then let us look aloft.'

They climbed up to the captain's cabin, that was sectioned dry below the steerage deck, the only portion of the ship to be closed off from the waves. The room was barely bigger than the narrow wooden bunk, built into the corner of the bulkhead of the ship. Beside it were a chair, a table ledge and kist, in which Hew found the captain's books and instruments, together with a wooden pepper pot. He called out, 'Look at this!'

'Hhm?' Giles had been distracted by the captain's box of instruments, and was busy plotting out an imaginary course. 'What have you found? The purser's record sheet?'

'Letters, and a question-book, Lutheran, I think.' Hew unfolded the papers, breaking the seal. 'He made a fat fist, whoever he was. The letters are in Dutch, signed Papa and Copin, which is a name for Jacob, is it not? Then this could be our man, unless there was another Jacob on the ship.'

'It is a common name,' Giles cautioned.

Hew picked up the pepper pot. 'And here is written, Beatrix van der Straeten, begijnhof sint Elisabeth te Gent. I have heard of the begijnhof, which commonly in French is called the beguinage. It is a women's convent. Has the package come from there, or is it a direction, do you think?'

'To send reformers' text into a convent may seem contrary,' Giles observed.

'*You* may think so; I should count it pertinent,' said Hew. 'Though we may never know, unless we read the rest. I don't suppose you ken the Flemish tongue? You keep a high Dutch grammar in your rooms.' He had come across the book wedged in the cupboard door, where it appeared to be a prop to hold a broken catch.

'High Dutch, not low. Though to be frank . . .' said Giles.

''Tis not Frank, but Flemish,' Hew corrected with a grin.

'To speak *frankly*,' Giles continued, undeterred, 'I am a beginner. Some years ago, I met with Adam Lonicer, town physician at Frankfurt am Main. He is an herbistare of some renown. We have since corresponded, generally in Latin, and in recent months I consulted him on Meg. He was kind enough to send a copy of his *Kreuterbuch*, which last edition he has written in his vulgar tongue. And so I was resolved to learn the Dutch, though partly as a courtesy, in greater part because . . .'

'If Jacob was the captain, then he left his hat behind,' Hew was no longer listening. 'I cannot think that Jacob was the captain; for first of all, he was too young, and secondly, his clothes . . .'

'Masters, we can hold the ship no longer,' a voice called from the deck. 'We will have to loose the clips, or she will drag as down. Make haste, or else ye maun jump.'

Hew glanced across at Giles. 'Then we must set our hopes on what we found. Tis pity, that we cannot broach the steerage room.'

'Do not attempt it,' warned his friend. 'Meg will not forgive us if we go down with the ship. I dare not risk her wrath, in perpetuity.'

'Rest assured, I do not mean to. Stay the ropes, we're coming,' Hew called up. Taking pen and ink, he copied the direction from the wooden cask, and slipped the letters and the catechism close inside his shirt.

'Now why do you do that? Why not take the casket?' wondered Giles.

'For then it would be seen – aye my hearties, wait, we come!' – Hew cried aloud, and dropped his voice. 'Sir Andrew Wood has spies. And I would like to know what we have found, before we have to hand it to him.'

'What say you? You suspect the coroner?'

'Though I may not suspect him, I reserve my trust. The more we know of this, the better we may judge, and the harder it may be for him, to hide from us his hand. Meanwhile, we must find a man to read the letters.'

'That is no great task,' reflected Giles. 'We have one at St Salvator's. Professor Groat is fluent in the Dutch. His family came from Antwerp, where his father was de Groote.'

'Truly?' marvelled Hew. 'I did not know. Then he will serve us well, on all accounts. He will, of course, play puff and snuff, complaining he is put upon, while all the while this tragic tale will find him in his element.'

'He's too much in his element, and we will shake him out of it,' said Giles. 'Throw caution to the wind, and ask him out to supper!'

The boat gave a great lurch, and the cabin doors flew open. 'Master, come you now, or you will not come at all.'

They scrambled back up on the deck, and across the narrow timbers to the lighter, listing badly with the strain. 'Let loose the clips,' the schippar cried, and with the last uncoupling of the ships the *Dolfin* gave a shudder and a sigh, and then a mighty crack, that rippled through her decks, splitting her in two, as if some unseen hand had reached up through her bowels and dragged her slithered entrails through the bottom of her hull. She turned in upon herself, with a sickening wrench.

'God love us,' whispered Giles. 'But that was close.'

'Aye,' said the schippar, 'ye were cutting it fine. Did ye find out what you wanted?'

Hew sat ashen faced. 'I cannot say,' he stammered. 'We will tell it to the coroner.' He recovered his composure when he saw the schippar scowl.

As the boat turned back to land, Giles said a little shyly, 'It may not be the time to say . . . though in the face of death, and all, what better time to say? But Meg and I would like you to be gossop to the child . . . that is, to be Matthew's godfather.'

'I would like nothing better,' answered Hew. 'Forgive me, though, I thought . . . I saw you with the rosary,' he finished awkwardly.

'Ah. That was your father's,' Giles confessed. 'And has an old significance, to Meg. So we are returned, in darkness and extremity, to what has meant the most to us. Some call it superstition, Hew, and others call it faith. I trust that you were not offended?'

'Less offended, then afraid.'

'Then not for Matthew's soul, I hope?' the doctor smiled. 'He is to be baptised in the kirk of Holy Trinity. I should warn you, there are some provisos, set by Meg, that you must now fulfil, before she is persuaded to entrust him to your care.'

'And what are those?' inquired his friend.

'That you will not let him ride upon your horse, and that you will not take him out to sea in boats.'

Chapter 8

Copin

Meg had dismissed the midwives, and returning to the hall, had recovered her position at the centre of her world. She sat by the fireside in a loose kirtle gown, working yellow flowers upon a scarlet rug, the bright silks in a bundle by her side. The shutters were closed tight against the wind and all the lanterns lit. The bairn lay sleeping in a wicker basket, a little distant from the fire.

'You should not stitch by candlelight. You will hurt your eyes,' Giles cautioned fondly.

Meg set aside the work. 'It is a quilt for Matthew's bed, and a pattern for the one our mother made for Hew. I wish I had her touch,' she sighed. 'In truth, I am more practised at my herbs, and would rather tend my garden.'

'All in good time,' the doctor soothed. 'The work is very fine. I like this little horse.'

'It wants a thread of gold.'

'I will find one out,' Giles promised, as he laid another log upon the fire. They made a circle so complete that Hew felt shy of breaking it. His sister smiled at him. 'Has Giles asked you, Hew?'

'I caught him on the boat,' said Giles, 'when he was fearful for his life, and would say yea to anything. He is pleased to be his nephew's gossop, and is much relieved we do not mean to raise him in the Church of Rome.' He grinned at Hew, who answered with a blush. 'There is nothing, in my heart, could please me more,' he vowed to Meg. 'And I have wondered what to give him, for I cannot think he wants for silver cups.'

'Or spoons,' considered Giles. 'If ever he should want to crack an egg, he has a plenitude of spoons.'

'He wants for nothing,' answered Meg, 'save your good counsel, and your love.'

'Then both shall he have freely. Yet he must have a christening gift. I thought perhaps that he might like my horse . . .' Hew teased.

'You will *not* give him your horse.'

'. . . but I have since decided on the mill at Kenly Green, and all the land that follows on the south side of the burn. I'm told it has some worth. And though it will not suit him yet, I hope he may grow into it.'

'You cannot give him that!' cried Meg.

'I do not see why not. It need not be a burden, for the factor will continue in its closer management, while Matthew draws the profits from the rents. I am not proposing he should work the mill,' smiled Hew.

'I mean you cannot dispense with our father's estate. You must keep it for your own bairns, Hew!'

'Somehow I do not see it,' Hew said lightly. 'Yet that is provided for. Have no doubt, what I give Matthew is the meanest portion of our father's legacy, and leaves no deep impression on the whole. The rest he must wait for, until he comes of age. In truth, our father left me far too much, and it is right and proper some of it should be bestowed on him.'

Giles, who had spoken nothing all the while, now put in quietly. 'You do know that we cannot take this gift.'

'Indeed, you cannot,' Hew asserted, 'for it is not given to *you*.'

They were saved from further conflict by the timely entrance of Professor Groat.

'Dear me, quite a chill, and I am in my whitsun short hose, quite wrong for the time of year . . . God bless my soul,' he broke off, startled, catching sight of Meg, 'Professor Locke! I did not think to find your wife abroad!'

91

'She is not abroad,' Giles reasoned. 'She is safe at home, where she belongs.'

'I mean to say, up and about.'

'Even so,' answered Giles. 'Is there something here offends you?'

'Your wife is only lately deliverit of child,' Groat answered to the point. 'That cannot be thought natural.'

'Scarcely unnatural,' Giles pointed out.

'You are playing with me, sir,' Bartie said, affronted. 'I am tired and old, I do not ken your ways. It is not kind.'

'You are right, it is not kind,' interrupted Meg. 'Professor Groat, I'm sorry if my presence here offends you. The minister himself was here today. He had no qualms to sit, or drink a cup with me. In truth, he ate his fill, and crammed his pockets full with sugar biskit bread, for fear we meant to keep it for a christening feast. Matthew will be baptised in the kirk of Holy Trinity, in two or three weeks' time.'

'Which does remind me,' Bartie said, appeased, 'I brought the child a gift, that I have somewhere hidden in my cloak.' He felt among the folds of his long scholar's gown. 'I pray it may prove useful to him, in these desperate times.'

'What is it, then, a sword?' asked Hew.

Bartie blinked at him. 'It is a *book.*'

'Of which he cannot have too many,' Giles approved.

'Quite so.' Bartie cleared his throat. 'It is a book of common courtesies, *Stans puer ad mensam*, that will teach him not to fiddle with his knife. Such lessons are more pertinent than any Latin grammar. I daily see our students snivel up their sleeves, or wipe their greasy fingers on the table cloth. Not one of them, a napkin or a handkercher! Good families, too, and not poor beggar clerks, whose want of manners ought to be excused, for they may know no better. Some of them are orphans,' he confided sympathetically. 'And though I do not doubt you mean to teach him gentleness, this little tract will stand him in good stead, should some affliction carry off his parents at a stroke.'

Meg started at this, even as Hew smiled. 'In which sad case,' he answered solemnly, 'the poor orphan's education will depend on me. I pray you, let me see the book.' He snatched it from Groat's hand and read aloud, '*The book of nurture, or the school of good manners.* "Belch thou near no man's face, with a corrupt fumosity." Tis sound enough advice. Who is the author of this work? He does not say . . . but wait, the bookseller has writ it at the end, "compiled by Hewe Rodes, of the King's Chapell." Hew Rhodes, no less! A proper scholar!'

'It is an *English* name,' expounded Bartie Groat, 'which may explain the rift. I own, thou shalt not belch in someone else's face is a singular injunction. We must infer a nation of some savageness, and a peculiar fumosity.'

'I have not found the wind particular to Englishmen,' reflected Giles.

'I hear it passes largely to the Dutch,' Hew answered gravely, 'who turn their windmills with it.'

Professor Groat looked pained. 'I fear my little gift is ill received.'

'Piffle, tis a fine thing,' sniggered Hew.

Meg rose to her feet. 'It is a fine thing you might learn from,' she rebuked her brother. 'Clearly, you want manners. Professor Groat, it is a grand gift, and the kindest thought.'

To Bartie Groat's dismay, she kissed him on the cheek. He quite forgot his creed, together with his handkerchief, and spluttered in his cap. Hew gave way to laughter as Giles cleared his throat.

'Quite so. *Stans puer ad mensam.* That is, shall we eat?'

When they had had their supper, and were settled by the fireside with a second jug of wine, Hew brought out the letters. 'We hoped that you might read them for us,' he explained.

'Aye? Then there is something still I have to teach you.' Bartie sniffed.

'Professor, there is much that you can teach me. Forgive me my discourtesies, for I do repent of them. Tis no matter of your learning that I do dispute, only that you see it through a dark perspective glass,' Hew protested.

93

'Your spectacles are clear,' alleged Professor Groat, 'and your perspective, as you call it, shows a different hue. For you have health, and wit and wealth, and a place here in the college superior to mine, for all the folly of your youth. You can want for little in your life. Yet some of us are born from baser stock, and struggle to ascend our poor profession, lacking your advantages.'

'Bartholomew, I did not think . . .'

'You do not think. It is the failing of your rank, and of your age,' Bartie answered sadly.

Hew was stricken with remorse, until Giles pointed out, 'You are a frank imposter, Bartie Groat, for you are neither frail nor poor as you pretend to be. Your father was a man of means, and you are in your element. You have lived close and cloistered all your life.'

'That is what I like about the young,' chuckled Bartie Groat. 'They are so very green, and gullible.' He produced from his sleeve a pair of folding spectacles, and propped them on his nose, as he embarked upon the letters with a furrow and a frown, designed, at least in part, to prevent them slipping off. 'Tis hard to decipher such a crooked hand. Tis not so much unlettered, as ill-formed. Well now,' Bartie said, 'the letters have been written to a woman and a child – Beatrix, and Lotte, from a man called Jacob – Copin, as he calls himself, in this one to his wife, and *papa*, in the letter to the little girl. They are both lodged in the begijnhof at Ghent.'

'What is the be-hine-hoff?' queried Meg.

'It is a sort of convent, called in French, the beguinage. Common in the low lands, and some parts of France. Tis not a common nunnery, but rather like a commune, or a convent, where women live together, and may work in peace. They take no vows of chastity, and are free to leave to marry, or to have a child,' Hew explained.

'Then they must be blessed. Are they not papists, then?' asked Meg.

'Aye, they are papists, as I understand it. Though they are not devout.'

94

'It is, in truth, a way to manage women, when a surplus does abound,' put in Professor Groat, 'A convent, or a coven, for the meaning is the same. Tis not, you understand, to serve the gentle class, but rather for disposal of the low and common kind.'

Giles returned Meg's grimace. 'Professor Groat is antick in his ways.'

'The *letters*, now,' said Hew.

'Aye, tis pertinent you speak of papists, for he sends the child his creed,' Professor Groat resumed.

Hew nodded, handing him the text. 'There was a book.'

Bartie Groat examined it. 'This is the Heidelberg catechism, a tract of the Dutch reformed church. Then Jacob, it appears, was of a different faith. It is a proper missive, from a father to his child. Tis filled with hopes and prayers for her, that she should learn her letters, and live and love full well.'

'He must have been a man of rank and means, that taught a little lass to read and write,' reflected Meg.

Her brother shook his head. 'Not so, of necessity. The nuns will have a school. Tis common, in the low lands, for simple folk to read.'

'Truly? Then I like that place. It seems that he foresaw a life for her, outside the nunnery. God bless him for a fit and loving father,' Meg approved.

'He bids her well, commends her to her mother, and to God. Affecting, aye, but unremarkable. The letter to his mistress tells a darker tale.' Professor Groat looked up, his spectacles askew. 'I think there is no optick glass could colour it more brightly, except it were the prism of his tears.'

This was said with such simplicity, and so sincerely meant, that Hew and Giles both glanced at once at Meg, who shook her head emphatically. 'No matter, though, I want to hear.'

'A moment,' Giles requested, 'and a quill and paper. I will write it down.'

'*Dearest, my own, my beloved Beatrix,*' Professor Groat began, once

Giles was settled at his writing slope, 'and other such effusions of the sort.'

'You need not read the tender parts,' said Hew. 'The matter will suffice.'

'There is nothing less than seemly here, though there is a poignancy,' Professor Groat went on. 'He writes, *They all are gone; the captain, Henryk, young Joachim, that came with me from Ghent, so filled with spirit and with life. I close my eyes, and I can see his mother in the Vrijdagmarkt* – that is the Friday market – *selling flowers . . . scent of poppy heads and pinks; I hear the peal of bells, the wagons on the cobblestones, bright with copper pans. Tell Joachim's mother that . . .* – this last he has crossed out.'

'Does he not say what happened to them?' interrupted Giles.

'He comes to it; tis hard to make it out. *Fair stood the wind when we left Vlissingen.* Vlissingen, that is the place called Flushing, on the river Scheldt,' the professor glossed. '*I built my windmill on the upper deck, and painted her bright coat against the white-slopped blueness of a sailors' sky. The shipmaster was pleased, and took me on as timmerman. A windmill, strange to say, is very like a ship.*'

'Then it was Jacob made the windmill,' Hew concluded thoughtfully.

'So it would appear. *Then we came north to . . . to market where . . . the men had business, and took on fresh supplies. We sailed up coast to Rotterdam, for casks of Rhenish wine. The schippar and his friends ate well that night. The meat and bread were fresh, though shrivelled up and stale by the time they reached the crew. I made my small supper of biscuit and salt, counting that my debt to the shipmaster was spent. Then, with his death, the matter was discharged.*'

'Tis pertinent,' said Giles, 'he mentions what they ate. Yet meat and bread, I fear, are not specific.'

'Do you wish for the receipt?' Bartie Groat inquired.

'If he gives it, aye.'

'*The wind stood fair,*' Professor Groat went on, '*and all was well, and then the weather turned* . . . no, not the weather, something turned, *I know not what* . . .'

'A moment,' muttered Giles, scratching with his pen, 'You know not what, or Jacob knew not what?'

'*I know not* . . . *know not* something, for the writing is ill writ,' muttered Bartie Groat.

'That does not surprise me. Aye, go on.'

'By your leave, I try to. Tis very black and crabbed. *It began with Frans Hanssen, the wine merchant, who suffered flux and creeping of the flesh, and burning in his limbs. He loosened all the stoppers from the wine, saying that the casks were full of blood. It ran like rivers through the hold, spoiling Eyman's cloth, who told me that red gillyflowers had blossomed in his heart, the day before he died.* Now that is quite extraordinary!' Bartie Groat exclaimed. 'I have not mistaken it. Tis plain poor Copin was quite mad.'

'Is it, though? Let me see!' demanded Hew.

'What is it, now you ken the Flemish tongue?' Groat retorted crossly.

'I would see the hand.'

'You are an expert, too, in pothooks, I presume?'

Hew had seized the letters back from Bartie Groat and set them side by side, squinting in the candlelight.

'Your young subordinate is sudden and intemperate,' Groat complained to Giles. 'It is a fault in him I have observed before.'

Giles conceded cheerfully. 'It is his finest virtue, and his worst. I find it better, on the whole, to allow him his head. Are you done, Hew? Shall we now proceed?'

'I am done. Look here.' Hew drew the lantern close, so that the sullen lamplight fell across the page. 'Do you observe a difference in the hand?'

'No, none at all. Both are thick and crabbed. Which given what we know about poor Jacob's hands, is not to be remarked on,' Giles reasoned.

'Aye, but both the same,' reiterated Hew. 'And to the same degree then, the affliction, would ye say?'

'I should say so, aye,' his friend agreed.

'Then written at one time. And yet the letter to his child, by your own account,' Hew turned to Bartie Groat, 'is proper and right reasoned. Wherefore we may suppose the other is a clear account, of events that made no sense to him. It was not want of wit, that baffled understanding.'

'Ingenious,' admitted Giles. 'Now what more does he say?'

Groat took up the letters with a sideways jab at Hew, 'If I may, without fear of distraction? *The schippar was a stranger . . . was most strange, he suffered from the grips. He flew into a rage and beat the cook so savagely he had to be restrained. Henryk did not recover from the fright. The schippar was mistrusting, and his manner changed to us. I feared he had suspected me, and found out my intent* – what was that, I wonder? – *but in his franticness he came to hate us all, accusing all alike. His eyes and nose streamed black, like molten lead. All the venturers and more than half the crew were phrensied, mad or sick. Some died shrieking in their beds. Eyman thought he was on fire, and leapt into the sea; the rest we tethered in the hold, and daily flushed them out, the dying from the dead. Our one hope was the steersman, who had kept his wits. He set our course westwards, for Kingston on Hull.*

'*We tried to put ashore, those men who were sick, yet could we find no haven; they feared us like the plague . . .*' Groat faltered. 'This is very bad.'

'He says like the plague, he does not say the plague,' insisted Hew. 'Go on.'

'*. . . and saw us off with cannon shot. Tobias was persuaded to steer us further north. His hands were pale and mottled, and he could not peg the traverse board, yet I hoped that we might come to Scotland as I planned . . . Lucas and Tobias, myself, and young Joachim; Joachim was the strongest in heart and in limb. And in the hold we held a dozen raging men. We took them one by one. God forgive us what we did; the furies took the devil at his rest. God forgive us, but they would not let us land.*'

'What was it that they did?' Meg whispered fearfully.

98

Her brother shook his head. 'Who knows? They let the sick men die . . . or worse, perhaps. No port would give them harbour, that is clear. And Jacob had a conscience to the last.'

'Tis clear enough his fellows were possessed,' Bartie Groat affirmed. 'And Jacob was well rid of them.'

'*Nothing* yet is clear,' insisted Giles. 'Are we at the end?'

'The end is most affecting.' Bartie blew his nose.

'*Lucas and Tobias both are gone, and Joachim, too; the fury came upon him at the last. Tobias met a stranger fate; I dare not say a quiet one.*

'*The wind has dropped, the water now is still, and there is nothing but the sea and sky. I put my trust in God, yet find no answer in the wilderness of grey, as if the world is empty, disappeared. The stillness is a curse, but I am not afraid to die. I close my eyes and look upon your face, and I hear Lotte's laughter in my dreams.*

'*I fear you will not know me, for I cannot send your ring, as fixed upon my finger as your likeness on my heart. Sometimes, it grows hot, and burns me like a fire, and yet I will not mind it; tis a part of you. I do confess, it troubles me that I do not return it. How are you to know me, if I do not send the ring? But I remember then, that this will never reach you, unless the wind that took away my world takes pity on my soul and moves to seek you out.*

And how then should you know me, when I do not know myself?

The wind is still, and I am lost.

You will not hear.

Your Copin.

'Dear, dear,' said Bartie Groat. He became a little agitated, fumbling through his clothes for a clutch of pocket handkerchiefs, on which he wiped his spectacles, his hands and eyes and nose. A line from one of George Buchanan's psalms came fleeting to Hew's mind: *mens fraudis expers. Et manus innocens.* Like Pontius Pilate, Bartie washed his hands, or rather, blew his nose, of knowledge and of sin. 'Weak bairns and feckless wives would weep at such a tale,' said Bartie, and blew his nose again. 'Now the hour is late; the college gates will close. Tis time that this old man went homeward to his bed.'

Giles recovered quickly. 'I will walk with you.'

'Ah, no need, indeed,' the old man said. 'For I shall take a turn, to contemplate the moon, before the watchman tolls. The stars are bright tonight; I sense a frost.'

'Indeed, the air is cold. You must not stay out long. I will walk you home, I do insist,' said Giles. It was plain that Bartie was now anxious to be gone. Giles trailed him as he shuffled to the door and out into the night. The lanterns in the street were lit, the faintest flare of hornbeam from the castle gate and cookshop, a narrow yellow curvature beneath the quiet moon.

Inside the chamber, Matthew whimpered in his sleep. Meg scooped him up, and brushed her lips against his milkiness, breathing in the softness of his cheek. She brought the infant closer to the firelight, standing with her back to Hew. 'You could send the letters, could you not?'

Her brother answered softly. 'We could put them in a packet to Campvere, from where they might be taken to the beguinage in Ghent. Their passage there would not be safe assured, for the low lands are at war. And yet there is a chance; it could be done.' He pictured Beatrix, waiting, with her little daughter and wondered what a packet of this sort could mean to them, whether it were worse, or better, not to know.

'I wonder how old Lotte is?' Meg's whisper was half buried in the blanket of her child.

Her brother answered, '*Don't.*'

'Or you could send a letter with the ring, to say the ship was wrecked and all were lost, but Jacob died a gentle death, and peaceful in his bed,' Meg pleaded.

'I could do that, indeed,' said Hew. 'It is not so very different from the truth. But she would never know the words he wrote to her.' Hew imagined Jacob, scratching on the paper, the pained and slow progression of the blackened finger stubs, spurred on by thoughts of Beatrix and her child. 'If you were Beatrix, which you would prefer?' he asked.

'Oh, do not ask me that!' cried Meg.

'There is no crueller kindness than the truth,' said Hew. 'Perhaps we may do both, and send the letters in his hand, together with assurances, that Jacob died at peace.'

'That would be an answer,' Meg accepted tearfully. ''Tis almost as if Jacob had two different deaths.'

'It is,' allowed Hew, 'exactly like that.'

They were disturbed by Giles returning, with a worried frown. 'I fear we taxed an old man, more than he could spare,' he fretted. 'I confess, it vexes me, for I had not expected it of Bartie Groat. He babbled on, of conjurers and ghosts, his logic disappearing in a cloud of smoke. Such terrors are contagious. Pray God he does not spread them.'

'He has a small acquaintance,' Hew said reassuringly.

Giles was unconvinced. 'His fellowship is serving men, laundresses and boys. He has repercussions of a most pernicious kind. I fear that we were reckless, when we set him the task. I had not bargained he would take such fright at it, bolting like Gib Hunter from the hounds of Hell. I have enjoined him, most soberly, to keep the matter secret. Let's hope he does not prattle it.' He broke off to remark, 'You have been crying, Meg!'

Meg wiped her eyes. 'My wits are turned to water since the bairn was born,' she excused herself.

'It is not the bairn. It is this sad report, which does affect us all,' Giles answered soberly. 'Yet you are the one person in the world I can rely upon, when the whole wide world is lurching, from dizzy lack of sense. You are not thrawn by fears, like Bartie Groat. So set aside your tears, and look upon the matter in the harsh light of the day; be cold, and analytical; and tell me plainly, what do you make of this madness?'

'That it is a sickness,' Meg concluded.

'My thoughts, precisely.' Giles looked at his notes. 'The symptoms are distinct, and of two sorts. The one is madness plain, frantic and delusional. The other is a putrefaction, gangrene in the limbs. The one afflicts the body, and the other one the mind.'

'Jacob suffered both,' Hew pointed out.

'So it seems he did. Yet he was not deluded when he wrote the letter. The frensie came on quickly, and the rot was slow. Jacob's mind was sound, until the last. I do not think that Jacob's madness was the same as theirs. What causes such illusions, as Jacob has described? If we discount the devil, and the occult arts?' mused Giles.

'Something in their food or drink?' suggested Meg.

Giles nodded. 'As I think most likely.' He read out from his notes: *he said the casks were full of blood . . . he told me that red gillyflowers had blossomed in his heart.* I had a patient once, who thought his breast contained a flight of birds, and felt their flutter in his ribs, the scrapple of their beaks against his throat.'

'What happened to him?' Hew inquired.

'Unhappily, he died. We traced it, in the end, to a surfeit of nutmeg, of which he was inordinately fond. The only man I ever knew, who died of honeyed milk.'

'Yet dying of a posset often is the way,' said Hew.

'At someone else's hand,' his friend agreed.

'Then could it have been nutmeg?' wondered Meg.

'I do not think it likely,' Giles demurred. 'For he was most uncommon, and took it to extremes; he bought nutmeg by the pound. Among so large a crew, I cannot think a surfeit is to blame. Poison seems most likely, as it did it before, yet I can only hazard at the source.'

'You have seen these things before?' concluded Hew.

The doctor nodded. 'Once before, in France. The symptoms were delirium, and creeping of the flesh, sweeping through a village, like a flame. The cause was counted magic in that case, and the sickness known as *ignis sacer*, holy fire.'

They passed the letters on to Andrew Wood, who was not pleased to find they had been read. 'These letters must at all costs be kept secret from the town; the terrors they report would put the fear of God into an honest man,' he swore, 'and scare the wits and water from a wrong one. You are quite sure the sickness here is spent?'

'I have no doubt,' the doctor said, 'it died out on the ship. The sickness was a dry pernicious gangrene, known as holy fire, and I begin to have a notion of the cause.'

'It would oblige us greatly if you found that out.'

'I will explore my theory, and write to Adam Lonicer.'

'Write to whom you will,' said Andrew Wood impatiently, 'As long as you do not spread rumour through the town. You are quite sure,' he asked again, 'there is no present risk?'

'Quite sure,' answered Giles.

'Nor taint upon the windmill, where the man was found?'

'As I have implied,' said Giles, who rarely would commit himself to matter more direct.

'And you would stake your life on it?'

'My reputation, certainly,' the doctor answered huffily.

'Then that must suffice. Since Jacob was the owner of the mill, and he and all the other men are dead, I think we may declare the ship as wrack,' the coroner declared. 'The letters will be put before the admiral.'

'Not yet returned to Beatrix, who may still have a claim?' asked Hew.

'They may, in due course, be returned. I doubt she will pursue it from a convent house in Ghent. For myself, I had far rather burn them, for they bring nought but consternation, dread and fear. Yet keep the matter close. The brightness of the windmill is a clear, beguiling lure, and the people will forget the manner of its coming, at the prospect of its staying in the town,' decided Andrew Wood.

And so, indeed, they might have done, Hew soon came to reflect, had it not been for the death of Gavan Lang.

103

Chapter 9

Big Fish

The corn mills marked the southern edges of the town, built along the Kinness Burn, that split the leafy South Street from the mellow swathes of countryside beyond. Most of this land had belonged to the priory, now gradually reclaimed and squeezed into the coffers of the burgh or the Crown. Some was in the keeping of the college of St Leonard, and other parts had fallen into private hands, to local lairds and landowners, one of whom was brother to the coroner of Fife. Robert Wood owned land and waters westward of the town, on which the Newmill stood. The mill itself was feued out to the miller, Gavan Lang. Gavan was a modest, unambitious man, who took a simple pleasure in the daily grind. He liked the slow monotony and steady pace of work. He liked the flow of water, under his control, close measured to the fineness or the coarseness of the grain, carefully assessed through skill and long experience. He liked the scent of barley, roasted in the kiln, and the soft rub of the flour dust falling through his fingertips. He liked to share, particularly, these pleasures with his son. His son had already begun to acquire the broad, flattered thumb that came from rubbing flour to test it for its fineness. He also had acquired the miller's cough, a dry and rasping husk that kept the boy awake at night. He was eight years old.

The boy caught the flour that ran down from the millstones, and swept it into sacks. He was too small to lift the sacks of grain. When the bell rang, to alert the miller that the hoppers had run dry, he was the quickest on his feet, nipping up the ladder to refill them. This was essential, for if the stones ground dry they would be damaged, at the best, and at worst would spark a fire, that threatened to ignite the structure of the mill. The water drove the wheel, the wheel turned the stones, the hoppers fed the stones, and the stones ground the flour. Nothing pleased the miller more than to watch this happen smoothly, with Harry by his side.

The mill house was a meeting-place, where people stopped to chatter as they waited for their flour, as fine a place for tittle as the barber shop or kirk. In general, Gavan did not mind the thranging to and fro, and collected scraps of gossip to amuse his wife at suppertime, brightening up her day. He liked those moments, when the three of them were sitting round the fire and the rush of water on the paddles had been stilled, and she looked to him expectantly, for some snippet of a tale. But he liked better still the long hours at the mill, with no one but the boy, who watched him through a solid, concentrating frown, rolling up his sleeves and pulling out his shirt, rubbing with his thumbs, just as Gavan did.

On the day that Gavan died, his pleasure in his work was spoiled by Robert Wood, whose presence placed an obstacle between him and the boy. Robert had stood waiting for a customer to go – a baxter, who had quibbled over flour – before he gave expression to his thoughts. His close and silent scrutiny made Gavan feel uncomfortable. Finally, the baxter left, and Robert broke his silence to demand, 'Have ye been to look at her?'

'Aye,' admitted Gavan. He could not, in honesty, pretend he had not known what Robert meant. For Robert meant the windmill, and who in the whole town had not been down to peek at her? For certain, not one of the millers. Henry Cairns had had the measure of her, with his square and rule, and had made her picture, in a little book. Gavan Lang had never used a rule, though he could draw a pattern, from memory alone. He had a hand, and he knew by that hand the scale of anything, perfectly apportioned, from the fingers to the thumb. It could not be forgotten or misplaced. And if by some misfortune he should happen to be parted from it, as had happened to a wheelwright he had known, then he had a spare one, up the other sleeve. When Harry was a little older, he would teach him too, how to take a measure by a rule of thumb. At present, he could take the boy's whole fist, and enclose it in his own strong hand, which served to remind the miller how tenuous and small, was this one clear intimation of a perfect world.

'And?' Robert Wood was brusque, and Gavan Lang regretted this, knowing that his attitude would not be lost on Harry.

'She is beautifully wrought, sir, by a skilled engineer and a craftsman, and all of her joints are made true. If she is taken apart, for to move her, she will slip back like a tongue into a groove, every piece of her slid smoothly, fitting to perfection. She was made with an exquisite skill, and more than that, with love. However, she is not complete. She is a post mill, but lacking her post. Whoever takes her will need to found her on a solid base; the best is from a living tree, cut down and sunk again into high ground. Near to the coast will serve well.'

'I have land to the north of here,' Robert Wood said thoughtfully.

'The good thing is you do not need so much space on the ground for her, as for a watermill. But you do want a hill, or else to raise a mound, as high as you can make her. And you must brace her post with quarter beams, that you box in, if you will, with stones, to hold her resolute. Her sails must be removed, and then must be reset, and threaded through with cloths. And she will want millstones, of course.'

'We have land, and we have trees, and we have men to build her,' Robert Wood declared. 'Under your direction, she will be ours. Then you shall have the working of her, Gavan, think of that! Not only those who are in thirlage to the mill, but all the town will come to you – to us. They will come when the mills are stopped by frost and drought, in summer and in winter time, and when the rivers run, then they will come from choice, because they are not bound to us.'

'They will not come to me, sir.' Gavan shook his head.

'What say you, man? Of course they will! They know you for an honest man; an honest miller, too, and *that* is rare enough.' Robert Wood laughed mirthlessly.

'I mean I dinna want her, sir, for I am happy here. The working of the windmill will go to Henry Cairns. You ken it will. He already has the biggest share of business in the town, and the running of three mills. He and his sons, besides, are *ingineers*.'

'Henry Cairns is not the sheriff's brother,' Robert Wood declared. 'Well, do as you will. If you will not comply, I must take more in rent.'

'You canna do that, sir,' Gavan protested. 'For I already give you more than we can afford. The sluice gate is rotting, and wanting repair. What little I can make back from the multure barely meets the cost.'

'Then you know what to do,' Robert answered bluntly. 'The trouble with you is that you lack ambition. Do not irk me with your grumbling and complaints. If you are poor, you know how to mend it. Think of your boy, here. Harry, is it not?' He let his hand rest a fraction above the boy's head, almost, but not quite, ruffling through his hair. The boy looked up and smiled at Robert Wood, easily and guilelessly. Harry had a smudge of flour across his nose, and Robert Wood dislodged it, with a careless, callous flicking of his thumb. Gavan stiffened, hating him. 'What is it you are doing, Harry?' Robert asked.

'Shifting out the fine flour for the baxter's riddel,' the boy answered, rubbing it. 'The baxters then will sift it. Shifting for sifting.' He took a childish pleasure in the pattern of the words. And Gavan loved him then, even as he hated Robert Wood. Another cloud flew up, and settled in his hair, a scattering of dust. Robert said, 'You are a clever boy.' Gavan willed him not to touch. 'A boy like that,' Robert said, 'could go to the grammar school. He could go on to the college, at the university.'

'He is a miller's son,' Gavan Lang said simply. He imagined Harry, at the grammar school, and at the university, and at the pulpit, thundering, the great book in his hand. He wondered if it could come true, and hated Robert Wood.

Robert answered, 'Even so.' His interest had declined to milder irritation, as though he had grown bored. He no longer looked at Harry, though the boy was blinking up at him, anxious still to please. 'Think about it,' he advised. Gavan knew that he was angry, though he had not lost control. At the door he paused, to take a parting shot, 'Have you caught that fish?'

'Not yet.'

'I want her,' Robert warned.

'Tonight,' the miller promised. 'I have made new traps. Tonight, I shall have her, sir, I swear.'

'See that you do.' Robert Wood let the door slam behind him. He did not stay to chatter with the customers outside, the baxters and the tenants who were gathered on the bank, to gossip and to wait for the wheel to make their turn.

The boy asked, 'What's ambition, Dad?'

'Ambition is a sin. It is vanity and pride.'

'Oh.' The boy took a while to digest this information. He considered everything, always, and so carefully, that Gavan heard the questions turning in his mind. 'Does the laird have ambition, then?' he ventured at last.

'Aye. And he is not the laird,' Gavan answered shortly.

'He is to us. He is our landlord. And he seems to do well from it,' Harry pointed out. Gavan saw the boy was disappointed in him. He saw it in the boy's eyes, pricking at his heart, and it was more than he could bear.

'Robert Wood is cross,' he explained to Harry, 'because he kens full well he cannot hae the windmill. She will go to Henry Cairns.'

'But *you* could have it, if you would. Why to Henry Cairns?' the boy objected.

'Because he is the better miller,' Gavan Lang confessed. It hurt his heart to say it. The boy was close to tears.

'He *cannot* be.'

'You see, son, that sometimes . . .'

The boy shook his head. He said fiercely, 'He cannot be. Because I have telt them that you were the best. I telt them at the kirk, that you would have the windmill, that Robert Wood would have it, because you are the best, and his brother is Sir Andrew Wood the sheriff and the coroner.'

Gavan's heart was sick with dread. 'Who did you tell it to, son?'

'All of them. Tom Honeyman, George Cairns, and Wallie Brooke.'

The baxters' and the millers' sons, thought Gavan, miserably. 'You should not have done that, Harry,' he said gently. 'It was wrang of you.'

There were tears, now, and angry ones. The boy rose up to challenge him, '*Why*, then, was it wrang?'

'Because it was not the truth. And even if it were true, it was wrong to say it. It was boastful bragging, vain and proud.'

'Is there *nothing*,' asked the boy, 'that makes you proud?'

Gavan looked at him, at the fierce little face, so like his own, the tearful grey eyes, the light tuft of hair that Robert Wood had smudged. 'There is one thing,' he said quietly, and turned away.

'The water is flowing too fast. Come outside, and I will show you how to slow it with the sluice.' Instantly, the boy was at his side, eager and compliant. He had never been allowed to touch the gates. 'May I move the catch?'

'You may. But you must never, ever, touch it by yourself. The flow is fast, and if you lose your step, you will be swept away.' He lifted the boy up at the sluice, high above the torrent that raged down below, holding him so tightly that the boy began to squirm. Customers were watching them, waiting for their turn.

Someone called out mockingly, 'Have you not caught that eel yet, Gavan? I saw Robert Wood. And he was not best pleased with you. Outwitted by a fish!'

The boy answered quickly. 'He will catch the eel tonight. He has a plan.'

The baxter, James Edie, said, 'She is a wily one. Your Daddie will

109

outsmart her. He is a clever man.' Gavan nodded gratefully. James Edie bought imported wheat, and brought it to be ground; then Gavan had his share, which always pleased his wife. And though he was particular about the grade of flour, he was well-mannered with it. He did not, like Patrick Honeyman, accuse him of dishonesty, or demand to weigh the tithe the miller was entitled to, or feel beneath the runner stone, for secret ways the miller had of siphoning the flour. He baked white loaves and biscuit bread, and sometimes sugared buns, which he gave to Harry as a gift. Gavan did not know if James Edie had a boy, but he knew how to talk to one, and how to win him round.

The eel had lurked within the mill pond, for the past five months. Though it was more than likely she had lived for years there, hidden in the mud, she had only recently begun to be a nuisance, growing thick and fat, and feeding off the river trout, owned by Robert Wood. Gavan Lang had never understood how a man could come to own a fish, or own the stretch of water that the fish had made his home. It seemed to him like laying claim upon the sky, though Robert Wood would have that also, if he could. The last straw had been a clutch of ducklings, stolen by the eel in early spring, which Robert had expected to be fattened for his board, smothered in a sauce of gooseberry or plums. Try as he might, Gavan could not catch the fish. It was a source of some amusement to frequenters of the mill, and a constant disappointment to the boy. The Newmill was dammed from the Kinness Burn, and did not use the mill lade, which ran down to the harbour and emptied at the sea. The eel had found her way from sea to burn to dam, and had settled in the pond, becoming gross and fierce, cut off from the passage to the shore. She was visible at night, in the fullness of the moon, when she emerged from the bottom of the pool, a sleek and limpid yellow-bellied green, long and soft and sinuous. Sometimes she slid out onto the bank, and left a silver trail, snaking through the mud. Gavan had set traps, of various kinds, but always, the fish had eluded him. Once, he had almost had her in his grasp, when the boy had coughed; the sound had warned her off, and she had wriggled out of sight. It had not been Harry's fault. Yet Gavan all but wept with the force of his frustration.

When the day's work was done, Gavan closed off the sluice, allowing the boy to fasten the catch. He noted, once again, that the bottom rung was loose and in need of some repair. It affected the flow, and control of the wheel, which had vexed him; James Edie's flour had been coarser than he would have liked. Gavan made a note to begin the repair the next day.

He ate supper in the mill house with his wife and the boy. James Edie had left a loaf of white wheaten bread, and Sally had been pleased, even though he had no tales to tell. He did not care to speak of Robert Wood. The boy was brooding still, and Gavan was aware that he had disappointed him. It was a fault in the boy, he thought, although he knew, deep down, the fault was in himself. He was not the father that the boy deserved.

Sally said, 'The baxter telt me that ye mean to catch the fish tonight. The sky is clear and bright. Tis likely we will have a frost.'

Her husband nodded. 'Aye. Tonight will be the night. I am assured of it.'

Sally smiled. She had faith in him, and accepted his humility. He brought her white wheaten bread, and sometimes little almond cakes. And she was touched, and pleased, and did not ask for more. He did not disappoint her, as he did the boy. She helped him weave his traps, of supple willow wands. Gavan had tied the traps around the edges of the pond, before he had come in for supper, for the third hour after darkness was the most auspicious time to catch the eel. The traps were baited with small strips of flesh; the eel was a scavenger, and drawn to scent of blood.

The boy said, 'Can I come with you?'

'It is too late,' Gavan replied. 'You must go through to your bed.' He knew that this would hurt the boy, that he would mind it bitterly. In part, it was to punish Harry, for his lack of faith in him, and for having scared the eel away. But mostly, it was fear, that the boy would see him fail again. The boy dropped his eyes, the want of satisfaction clear upon his face.

'You shall have her fried in butter, on a bannock for your breakfast,' Gavan promised him. The boy did not reply. Robert would not want to eat the eel. The oily flesh disgusted him, coiled round like a serpent on his plate. He wanted fat pink perch, the muddy flesh of salmon trout, and duck eggs with their yellow yolks, all of which were robbed from him, stolen by the eel. She would feed the miller's family for a week, smoking in the ashes of the kiln. And the sweeter she would taste, because Gavan Lang had beaten her.

Once the boy had gone to bed, the miller left the house, and climbed down to the Kinness Burn. He had set his traps in stages along the river banks, pegged out in the earth, or trailing from the trees, so that they drifted with the current of the water, and were easily withdrawn. For often in the night the long fish heaved her heavy head and tail above the dam, slinking down the brae towards the moonlit stream. She left her silver shadow trailing in the grass, yearning for the sea. She never found her path, for in the morning light she crept back through the grey mud of the weir, returning to the pond. She had mellowed from the yellow of her youth to the colour of the mud. Gavan imagined her, crackled and charred, her skin scorched and split in the heat of the fire. He examined the traps methodically, working his way back to the dam. The traps were eel-shaped sheaths of wicker, closing at the top, and baited with a sweet, metallic scent. Too often he had found them bitten, by the sharp teeth of the fish, and the eel had slithered off, slick and sated with her heady feast of blood. The eel was sly and cunning, slipping from his grasp. Sometimes, in the cold light of the moon, she did not come at all, and for days he dared to hope that she had gone back to her spawning ground, before she reappeared, to snatch a frog or duckling from its mother's grasp.

The traps along the Kinness Burn still floated on the surface, empty and untouched. Gavan worked his way back to the weir, upstream of the mill. The millpond was the eel's habitual haunt,

112

buried in the silt or banked behind the sluice, where the heavy waters gathered for the moment they were drawn. The waters now were still and smooth, stifled by the closing of the gates. Between the millpond and the house were stretched a bank of trees, the willow and the holly bush, the rowan and the sycamore, and though there was no wind, Gavan saw a tremor in the leaves and heard the snap of twigs. He knew at once that it must be the boy. In a low voice, he called to him, 'I hear you, Harry. Go back to the house. Or I will cut a willow wand, and whip you to your bed.' There was a rustle in the trees, and then the woods were still. The miller nodded, satisfied the boy had gone. He knew that Harry knew, though it would bring them both to tears, that his father would not hesitate to act upon his word. He knew no other way to keep his child from harm. A boy could slip down in the darkness to the bottom of the weir. God could not be trusted, to keep the whole world safe.

One of Gavan's traps had broken from its strings, and floated in the centre of the pool. Gavan felt a quiver of excitement. In the thin trail of moonlight he could see the catch was closed. It was likely that the thrashing of the eel had pulled her from her bounds, yet she had not succeeded in biting through the trap. He had no doubt that she was safe enclosed. Enticing and frustrating him, she floated out of reach. He broke a slender willow branch, and tried to fish her gently, but the rod could find no purchase on the willow trap. He was fearful that her movements would release the catch, and she would escape to the bottom of the pond. Stripping to his shirt, he waded through the shallow edges of the pool, where the night hung shadowy and still. The coldness took his breath away. His feet trod thick and heavily through muddy banks of water; he leant across the surface, yearning for the eel. He looked up in the shadow of the moon, and saw a figure hunched above the bank. He called once for his boy, before his mouth was filled and stoppered by the flood.

Gavan Lang was not swept through the sluice, for the bottom of his shirt had snagged upon the wood, so that he rose up to the

113

surface with the gate, with his sark full blown and billowed like a ship in sail. It was clear that he had drowned while hunting for the fish. And when they brought him out, and laid him flat upon the bank above the lade, it turned out he had caught her after all, for the long eel slithered out from the inside of his shirt, twisting about his body with her serpent's tail. Because she was a scavenger, she had nibbled at his cheek, and left a small black puncture in the miller's face. Someone fetched a stick to spear her to the ground, but she slithered back into the bottom of the weir, where she rolled her yellow eyes towards the morning sun. Robert Wood called out Giles Locke, to certify the death. And since it was a miller's death, Giles arrived with Hew. The doctor and his lawyer friend found little to remark upon. The eel trap was recovered from the centre of the pond, and Hew paused to examine it. He noticed that the catch was closed, though no fish was inside, with little understanding, what that might have meant.

'A simple drowning, nothing more,' Giles reported sadly, as he closed the miller's eyes. 'And I have seen it often so, in millponds and in lakes, where waters may lie still, and people do mistake their deeper treachery. It seems that he went in to try and catch the eel, and found himself ensnared upon this rotten gate, whereupon he drowned.' He glanced at Robert Wood. 'The sluice is in a sad state of repair.'

'So he did say,' Robert Wood confirmed. 'Which sad dereliction has cost the man his life. Hopeless to the last. He did not even manage to bring home the fish.'

A small voice answered, 'You are wrong. He did.' Harry stood by watching, hidden in the crowd. Robert's conscience pricked, for he felt into his pocket and tossed the boy a coin. 'Take that to your mother. Tell her, I will come and see her by and by, and pass on my condolences. For now, I have to find a miller for my mill. And you will have to find another place to live.'

Hew stared at Robert long and hard, not much liking what he saw.

Chapter 10

A Miller and his Son

The death of Gavan Lang left Robert Wood without a miller for his mill. The first full shower of rain had caused the dam to flood, washing out the hay bales that lined the tenants' fields, and threatening to submerge the recently sown crops. Because the Newmill was not channelled from the lade, its stopping had no impact on the other mills in town, except, as Robert noted sourly, to increase their share of profits, since his tenants were now free to take their corn elsewhere. He eyed the mill sluice gloomily, spilling out its wastage on his land. The waters had grown thick and stagnant, choked with mud and silt from the bottom of the dam. The old grey eel lay puddled in the thick slime of the pond. There were no duck or plover eggs, no river carp or trout, as the waters settled down into a sallow winter's dearth.

Robert was resolved, and placed a notice in the market, and in every church, seeking for a miller to restore life to the mill. A wish to work the windmill was a clear advantage, for Robert made it plain he meant to manage both. The notice was pinned up on the kirk door of St Leonard's, where it was seen on Sunday by the miller Sandy Kintor, tenant of the mill at Kenly Green. The minister was kind enough to read the words aloud, and tell him what they meant. Hew Cullan read it too, for he preferred the quiet kirk, with its plain and simple service, to both the weekly rout and thunder of the kirk of Holy Trinity, and the claustrophobic closeness of the chapel of St Salvator. St Leonard's linked the college to the countryside, and the scholars in their gowns were flanked by cottagers and tenants, from the farms and scattered villages southwards of the town. The parish stretched as far as Kenly Green, connecting Hew's estates, and his father's former home, to the place where he had come to study as a boy. Though Matthew had remained a stranger to reform, his father had been buried here, and laid to quiet rest by scholars of St Leonard's in the distant shadow of the grey stone kirk. There was a doleful solace in the melancholy psalms, the dullness of the sermon and the lack of fire or flair, that Hew found oddly comforting, reassured, through tedium, that all lay still in place. He left the service settled and refreshed, to find Sandy Kintor waiting by the door.

'Good master, may I speak with you?' the miller asked.

'Of course you may,' said Hew. The miller, as it happened, had been closely on his mind, in the context of the gift he was about to make to young Matthew, and he was pleased enough to take the chance to talk to him.

'It is a privy matter,' Sandy said reluctantly. 'I would not care to have it overheard.'

'Then shall we walk a little?' Hew suggested. 'Since the streets are quiet at this time.' The sermons at St Leonard's were measured, grave and short, and for want of blaze and brimstone soon brought to a close, an hour before the snuffing of the flames at Holy Trinity. And in that quiet hour, the busy streets were stilled, and even God, it seemed, was occupied elsewhere.

They walked towards the castle, and the lonely cliffs, looking out to sea, till presently, the miller said, 'I wonder if you read that notice, sir, that Robert Wood put up in the kirk.'

Hew acknowledged that he had.

'He's speiring for a man, a man to work his mill.'

'So did I see,' said Hew.

Sandy blurted out, 'I wish to be that man.'

'Oh,' Hew answered foolishly, more than a little vexed. He had not known what it was he expected, but he had not expected this. 'You want to work for Robert Wood?' He felt a childish surge of

116

disappointment: *you wish to work for Robert Wood, rather than to work for me?* the voice spoke in his head. And yet he was aware he should not stand in Sandy's way. Besides which, he had meant to give the mill to Matthew, and had not yet had the courtesy to pass this message on.

'I want to work the windmill, sir,' the miller answered simply.

'So that is it,' Hew sighed. 'There is no guarantee, as you must be aware, that Robert Wood will have the windmill on his land.'

'No, sir. But Robert is the brother of Sir Andrew Wood, the coroner, who has it in his power to influence the admiral. And so it is supposed, among the millers in the town, that the windmill will be his.'

'I have met Sir Andrew Wood,' contended Hew, 'and he has shown no sign that he prefers his brother in this matter.'

'Nor is that much expected, sir, that he would speak it openly. Yet awbody here kens, that that must be the case. A brither is a brither, sir. Ye cannot blame a man, for that.'

'I daresay you are right,' Hew sighed. 'Then you are come to tell me I must seek a miller for the mill at Kenly Green?'

The miller hesitated. 'I came to ask you, sir, for letters testimonial, to take to Robert Wood. For since he has laid claim upon the wind-mill, there likely will be more contenders for the tenancy. My virtues are not known here in the town, as well as those of men like Henry Cairns.'

'Your virtues,' Hew repeated with a smile. 'Remind me, if you will then, what they are.' He knew the miller for a true and decent man, yet he felt inclined to cause some small discomfort to him, sorry as he was to let his tenant go.

'I hope, sir, you have found me honest. I have always paid the rent,' protested Sandy Kintor. Hew allowed begrudgingly that this, at least, was true.

'Yet other men might say the same. I hoped, sir, you might write that I had known a windmill, and knew how to work her. That, and

117

that it came from a man of your high standing, is likely to sit well with Robert Wood.'

'Now that,' Hew warned, 'I doubt I cannot write, for I do not know it for a fact.'

'But it is true, sir. You have my word on it,' answered Sandy Kintor, in a tone of such simplicity that Hew felt loath to have to let him down. 'But you must see, Sandy, that I cannot take your word for it,' he told the miller gently. 'I cannot put my name to it, unless I see the proof.'

'I have served you well as tenant to the mill, and served your father too,' the miller answered stubbornly.

'And that much will I put into the letter,' Hew agreed, 'that I write to Robert Wood. I cannot promise more.'

'Yet I can read the wind,' the miller said. 'There is an art to it, that many men may lack. I learned it from my uncle, that is miller at Dundee.'

'Then so much you must say to Robert Wood,' Hew suggested.

'But it will please him better, if it comes from you.'

'I am a lawman, Sandy, and I cannot put my name to what I do not know. There is no malice in it, as I find none in you, and yet I cannot grant you what you ask,' determined Hew. And he was sorry, nonetheless, and in spite of his dislike for Robert Wood, for Sandy Kintor seemed an honest man, and he had little cause to doubt his word.

'But I could show you, sir,' Sandy offered suddenly. 'We could go together now, and see her on the shore. And I could show to you the workings of the mill.'

Hew paused to consider this. Though he had passed the windmill several times, he had never seen inside. It struck him now that he should see the place where Jacob had sought refuge in his final, desperate hours, when he had sheltered from the storm. To look at her through expert eyes, and see inside the mind that made her, might throw another light upon the holy fire. He nodded. 'Aye, why not? The haven will be quiet at this time.'

The harbour inn was closed, for no one broke the Sabbath there except the cat, Gib Hunter, who went about his business sniffing out the gulls, with a hearty disregard for the threat against his soul. Maude obeyed the sanction of the kirk, and did not open up until the prayers were done. The windmill was unmanned.

'She is a beauty, sir,' the miller said admiringly.

'I understand,' reflected Hew, 'that she was built aboard the ship. But what I cannot understand is how they took her off the ship.'

Sandy Kintor smiled. 'It is a feat of ingenuity. Yet with enough horse power, and oxen, and men, there is no limit to the weight that man can lift. What a thing it is, to be in charge of men, and have that power. Did you never look at the cathedral, and wonder how those men could build it, lifting up those towers and arches carved in stone, so high and vast and awful, stretching to the sky?' For so it was he saw the world, through the careful bird's eye of the engineer.

'I have wondered, rather,' Hew said with a smile, 'how came it we dismantled her, in such a few short years, that she falls now in ruins, her glory and her grandeur bared and desolate. What men took several lifetimes to construct, the quiver of a heartbeat did destroy.'

'They had built her on a falsehood, and to a false religion,' affirmed the miller starkly.

'True enough,' said Hew. 'Yet it was their faith in it that gave to them the power.'

'So too with the windmill,' Sandy Kintor said. 'So men may move the earth, if they have the will. They wanted her; that was enough.'

'The whole town came together then, and lifted her as one,' reflected Hew. 'They brought her to the haven, by force of common bond, and now are in dispute, as to who has claim on her. I doubt there is a moral to be read in that, for no man on his own may shift her from this spot, and bear her heavy burden higher up the hill.'

'He cannot, as she stands. But she will be dismantled, and lifted bit and bit. And even as she stands, this mill is not complete. She wants her centre post, that is a great trunk taken from a living tree, set into the ground, on which she can be turned into the wind. Dare we go inside?' the miller ventured shyly, suddenly in awe of her.

'There is none here to gainsay it. And I do not see why not.'

The door was tied with rope, to form a weak deterrent, which Hew dispensed with swiftly, with one flick of his knife. He led the way inside. His voice came oddly echoed through the hollow wood. 'How long might a windmill like this take to build?'

'It need not take long, sir, for she could be up in a day,' the miller's voice returned. 'It is not time but skill, that makes her as she is. Look at the work in those joists!' And even Hew could see the beauty of her craft. A small framed timber house, she was built of ship-lap board, in horizontal stripes, painted white and blue. She had windows on all sides, letting in the light, and at her crown a little door and deck, that allowed the miller to adjust the sails. Her roof was pitched, and lined with board, to keep her dry and light. She was meant, the miller said, to balance and to turn upon a single pillar post, spun upon her axle to make best use of the breeze. She was built so that whichever way she turned she would not veer and topple in the wind. She bore the faint, sweet scent of freshly seasoned wood, of oil and tar and paint.

'Once she is on her post, and off the ground,' the miller said, 'then she will want a ladder, for ascending her. Then picture her as raised upon a stilt, with all her wings in flight, and all her bright machinery, turning through the sky upon a summer's day. And then, you see, here, which now is a shell, is where she will have set her stones.'

The windmill had a purity and symmetry that pleased, sailing like a ship against the pale blue sky. And like a ship, the miller went on to explain to Hew, she was at the mercy of the wind, now its master, now its slave, and she required a careful hand, to steer her through the storm. 'But when she starts to turn, she shivers into life, and there is nothing like her, sir, the air is warm and ripe with the scent of roasted corn, her floors turn white with dust, her great wings rise and fall; the miller has the wind in his command.'

Hew warmed to his enthusiasm. 'Though I confess, I do not see it quite, I think you prove your worth in taking on the mill. For that you show your love for her, I can have no doubt, and so much will I write to Robert Wood. And yet I am right vexed, for I shall want a miller for the mill at Kenly Green.'

'I pray that you may not, sir,' Sandy put in cautiously.

'Tis evident, I will. I have a duty to my tenants, to provide them with a place where they may grind their corn. You will allow, it is a little far for them to come to town,' Hew said with a smile.

'I hoped, sir,' said the miller, encouraged into confidence, 'that you might pass the tenancy to Alasdair, my son. For he is come of age, and is well placed to follow me.'

'That is fair enough,' considered Hew. 'Then am I persuaded, and answer with good grace. And I shall write a letter testimonial, and have it sent tonight, to Robert Wood. And as I think, the time is ready for the tenancy to change, for I have thought to pass the mill on to my sister's son, to be held in perpetuity – you need not fear for Alasdair,' he assured the miller quickly, 'for I have no doubt, the terms will stay the same. What I propose is this; that when your business is concluded here with Robert Wood, come to me in College, and bring your eldest son. We shall go together then to see my man of law, and draw up such a deed, as gives tenancy to Alasdair, and control to Matthew Locke.'

'I know not how to thank you, sir,' the miller answered gratefully.

'In truth, I am right glad the matter is resolved. I bid you, come on Thursday afternoon, which gives Robert Wood fair time to decide upon the matter.'

'I thank you. I will go precipitate, to see him at the mill.'

'Tomorrow, as I think,' Hew corrected gently. 'Though Robert is a man of business, tis likely even he may be inclined to keep the Sabbath.'

'Oh! I had forgotten!'

Hew was touched and amused at the man's eagerness. 'Go home,' he advised him, 'and share your fortune with your wife and bairns.'

'I will sir, for, in truth, I left them waiting at the kirk, and they will be wondering what can have become of me. Ellen sends her prayers for your sister and her bairn. I hope that they do well,' Sandy Kintor finished with a blush.

'I thank you, aye, they do.'

'We kent her when she was a little lass. Tis likely she does not remember. Ah, your pardon, sir! It is a poor man's foolishness. I take up your time.'

They had stepped outside the mill, and found themselves disturbed by the coming of a crowd, that had drifted straight from service to batten at the inn, thirsty from the day's recriminations in the kirk. Among them were the baxters, and the bailie Patrick Honeyman, come to spend his dinner hour in routing out sly drinkers who had not turned up in church.

'And *what* is this?' he thundered, scandalised and fierce enough to rival Reverend Trail. 'Wha dares to broach the windmill?'

'I do,' answered Hew, with a wink at Sandy Kintor.

'And on whose authority?' the bailie roared.

'On that of Andrew Wood; de facto, of the Crown.'

Hew sent letters testimonial to Robert Wood, and thought no more of the matter until Thursday afternoon, when he was sitting in the turret tower with Giles. They were both embarked upon their own researches, though Hew's were of a vague and desultory kind. 'What are you reading?' Giles asked with a sigh, conscious that his friend had not settled with his text.

'*Perkins' Profitable Book*,' Hew answered with a grimace, 'though I have not found it very profitable.'

'Aye? And what is that?' posed Giles, with half an eye still on the seed pod he had split upon the board. He sifted absentmindedly through a heap of grain.

'A profitable book of Mr John Perkins . . . treating of the Laws of England, and translated out of French. I have read it in the English, and I've read it in the French, and little profit both,' admitted Hew.

'Why would you read of English laws?' objected Giles.

'Because,' Hew answered crossly, 'I have nothing else to do.'

'Your trouble is, you never should have given up the law. At heart, you an advocate,' advocated Giles.

'At heart, I am a wanderer,' said Hew. He tossed aside his Perkins, and wandered round the tower. 'What is it you are doing?'

'Looking for the source of holy fire.'

'In a pile of seeds?' Hew demanded sceptically.

'Just so. The world may well be pictured, in a speck of grain.' Giles took up the seed, and held it to an optic glass. 'What means the word *zapfen*, in Dutch?'

'I have not the slightest idea.'

'Then make yourself useful, and flush out that grammar book. There is a wordbook written at the back.'

Hew retrieved the grammar from its station in the cabinet, setting loose the rattle in the catch.

'Zapfen is a pin, or else a core,' he read.

'Now is it? Very good,' Giles answered with a nod. He was working on the transcripts he had made of Jacob's letters, examining the words as closely as he had the blackened finger stub, stripped back to the bone. Propped open by its side was the German *Kreuterbuch*, with other works of physic, pharmacy and botany. From time to time he made a note, in careful Latin script. Hew envied him his art, and left him undisturbed, until they both were startled by a rapping at the door, and the unseemly entrance of Sandy Kintor's son. 'Have you seen my father, sirs?' he ventured breathlessly.

Hew replied, astonished, 'Not since Sunday last. Why, then, have you lost him?'

'He has not been seen, since Tuesday afternoon.' The miller's son burst into tears.

'Dear, dear,' tutted Giles. He set aside the *Kreuterbuch* to focus

123

on his patient, abandoning the quest to find the holy fire. 'Come, sir, and sit down. If you look there in the cupboard,' he instructed Hew, 'you will find a flask of brandy wine. Not that – that is embalming fluid. *Who is he?*' he hissed after, in a loud stage whisper.

'Alasdair, the son of Sandy Kintor, the tenant of the mill at Kenly Green.'

'Another miller? Ah,' Giles answered with a frown. 'Where was he seen last?'

Alasdair gulped down the brandy, struggling to compose himself. 'My name is Sandy, sir, for no one but my mither ever calls me Alasdair. Your pardon, but I knew not where to come. I knew he was expected here, and hoped . . .'

'Start at the beginning,' Hew advised. He felt a deep sense of foreboding, and sought for reassurances.

'Aye, sir, as you will,' Sandy answered miserably. 'What happened, sirs, was this. My faither went on Monday past, to speak with Robert Wood. And there was it appointed, that he should have the mill; for he had had your letters, sir,' he paused to glance at Hew, 'and he was right impressed, with the testimonial.' Giles looked askance at Hew, which Hew chose to ignore.

'My faither was right glad, sir, to have it there and then. That I had cause to wonder, if it went not to his head, though he is not, in truth, a vain or boastful man.'

'For certain, he is not,' Hew conceded quietly. He found he could not calm the heavy surge of dread.

'And he was set to drinking, in the haven inn, just to drink a toast, to you and Robert Wood. For Robert Wood said, with a man of such skill, he was sure of having the windmill. And whether it were Robert Wood, or else it were my faither, sir, the word at once got out, for nothing is kept secret round a mill. And it was spread abroad, that Robert Wood preferred a country miller, to a miller from the town. And the tenants of that mill were pleased and glad, that they should have their miller and a good and honest man, and they would drink his health, which for the sake of courtesy my dad could not refuse. So he came home that night a little worse for wear; in truth, he staggered home to Kenly Green. And on his way back home, he saw a boy, who brought to him a message from the miller Henry Cairns, congratulating him upon his deal with Robert Wood, and asking him to meet. My father was well pleased, for Cairns is his first rival for the mill, and he intimated that their interests might be joined.'

Giles said oddly, 'When was this?'

'Twas as I said, on Monday night. I ken, sir, what you want to say,' the miller's son said miserably, 'yet if I may go on?'

Giles nodded, 'Aye, go on.'

'The meeting was to be on Tuesday afternoon. And so my father set out for the town, on Tuesday morn. But he did not return. And all the day on Wednesday, I searched along the shore, for fear that he had fallen in his cups, yet found no sight nor sound of him. My mother sent me back into the town, to see if he had lodged with Robert Wood. Which, sir, he had not. But Robert Wood was pleased to hint, that he might lose the prospect of the mill, if he should prove a man that could not be relied upon. And so I came at last to visit Henry Cairns. And there I found . . .'

'What did you find?' demanded Hew, while Giles asserted gravely, 'I know what you found.'

Sandy looked back at them both, and answered in despair, 'That Henry Cairns is sick abed, and has been for the past few days. He had not seen my faither, and he did not seek to meet him, nor could he have been thought to, when he could not lift his head.'

Giles nodded. 'That I can confirm. For Henry Cairns has been my patient, at death's door since Sunday last. Though I am pleased to say, he makes a slow recovery. Whoever sent that message, it could not be him.'

'Nor yet his sons or pickmen,' the miller's son said wretchedly, 'who have had their hands full at the mill.'

'Then who did send the message?' wondered Hew.

125

'That I cannot find,' the miller's son replied. 'Nor did my father tell me, where they were to meet.'

'I suppose you did not think to look inside the windmill?' questioned Hew. He fought against the notion, that was foremost in his mind, that he had somehow sent the miller to his death.

'Strange enough, I did,' the miller's son replied. 'For that it was so dear to him. But I found nothing there.'

'I think that it is likely,' Hew considered, 'that whoever sent the message, knew that Henry Cairns was sick.'

'That is more than likely,' Giles agreed. 'And yet it does not help us much, for that is almost all the town.'

'It *cannot* be,' objected Hew. 'For I was not aware of it, and nor was Sandy Kintor, nor Alasdair, his son.'

'And that, Hew, is my point,' Giles replied emphatically. 'That you were unaware of it, because you were at service at the chapel of St Leonard's, and Henry Cairns was taken ill, on Sunday morning last, in the kirk of Holy Trinity. His vomiting and flux were really quite spectacular. The Reverend Traill was lost for words, for quarter of an hour.'

'Dear God!' started Hew. 'Then everybody knew?'

'Save you and Sandy Kintor? As it would appear.' Giles fished into his sleeve and found a pocket handkerchief, which he bestowed benignly upon the miller's son. 'Have courage,' he advised him, 'your father will show up.'

And so he did, that Friday afternoon, when Henry Cairns felt well enough to struggle out of bed.

Chapter 11

A Dry Drowning

Henry Cairns was fearful as he languished in his bed. He feared that he would fail in his bid to have the windmill, and he would lose his place among the millers in the town. He feared too that his bid might be accepted, and the windmill might blow over in a gust of wind, because he had no notion how to make her work. He feared that the baxters would make good their claim, and make him sell his birthright for the common good. He feared that the Lawmill would encroach upon his business while he lay sick in bed, and that his wife Effie would take off in a huff, refusing to empty the chamber pot. He fretted that he had not fixed the padlock on the granary, and someone might have broken in, stealing all the grain. But most of all, he feared that he had forfeited the sacrament, for his offence of boking in the kirk communion cup, the only vessel he had had to hand. The Reverend Geoffrey Traill had failed to reassure him on that point, for his promise of God's pardon had been notably lukewarm.

Henry discharged bitterly into the foaming pot, and took the foul black purgative the doctor recommended, however ill-conceived a remedy for flux. He was thankful enough when he could swallow some thin gruel, and venture weakly out into the brittle sunshine of an autumn afternoon. To his great joy and relief, he found that the world was much as he had left it, the sweeter for the days that he had suffered in the sickroom. The fallen leaves were crisp, and the air smelt pleasantly of mushrooms, wood and smoke. The mills at the both the shore and priory ground on in his absence, worked by the pickmen and his elder sons. The winds were brisk and fresh, the lade was running clear, and with a gladdened heart, he went to check the granary. The corn had not been turned for several weeks, and Henry felt the need for a little light exertion, to ease him back from indolence to a severer health.

The granary lay north-east of the abbey mill, close to the old holy well. It stood three storeys high, and broke the north-east wind, so that the new inn guest house stood shadowed in its lea, allowing royal visitors a quiet resting place. In latter days, it had become a grain store for the town, with sacks of flour and seed corn stored in bins. The surplus corn was banked against the failure of the crop. Kept clean and dry and cool, the grain stores lasted years, and saved the town from famine when the harvest failed. The corn was spread out thinly on the ground and sifted through and turned, once or twice a week, to free it from the chaff. And as it dried and cooled, it was shovelled into heaps, to depths of several feet, over months and years. The more frequent the turning, the longer it would last.

The corn upon the upper floor was more than six foot deep, and it required considerable exertion, to turn it to the sides from the centre of the room. A funnel in the centre channelled grains of barley to the floor below, where they were placed in sacks and carried to the mill. The oldest and the driest corn, according to the baxters' lore, produced the finest flour. The granary itself was raised and watertight, protected from the mice by its distance from the ground, and from weevils by the turning and a clean flow of dry air. The padlock at the door was rusted at the hinge, and Henry had intended to replace it. It no longer held the bolt intact, and swung open to the touch without call for the key, which had caused him, in his sickness, several sleepless nights. He was relieved to find the padlock still in place, and to all appearances safely closed and locked. The sacks of meal and flour, and the bins for seed, were ordered and untouched, just as he had left them the week before. The baxters kept a store of fine

128

imported wheat, a lure to any thief, which Henry saw at once was safely stacked and sealed. He liked the smell of corn, and the crispness of the husks, the clean and welcome coolness of the oats and barleycorn. Today there was a new, more pungent scent, which Henry had not noticed there before. He realised that his stomach still felt sour and raw, and climbed the ladder quickly, to settle it with exercise.

The taste and stench of sourness filled his belly and his mouth, and he suppressed it firmly. This was not the place. For a moment, on the upper floor, the pungency was worse, and Henry felt a sudden wave of sickness, dizzy at the summit of the steps. Yet he would not give in to it; he knew that it would pass, and taking up the shovel from its hook upon the wall, he begin to turn the corn, methodically and vigorously, working up a sweat. And soon he had convinced himself he was not sick at all, turning close and rhythmically, churning up the corn. Until at last his shovel, shearing through the grain, landed with a thud, and out fell Sandy Kintor, tumbling from the chaff, his mouth a gaping grimace sliced by Henry's spade. And Henry realised that he was not well at all, and fell into the chasm that had once been Sandy's face.

The corpse was taken out, and laid upon the green, beside the cowering form of Henry Cairns. His son had come to look for him, and found the broken padlock swinging on its hinge, and the front door opened wide upon the granary. Inside, he found his father, lifeless and prostrate. It had taken Giles some time to sort the living from the dead, while Henry Cairns was limp and ashen-faced. He was brought round in the end, by the sheriff, Andrew Wood, whose attentions were more pertinent, and harder to ignore. Henry now knelt quivering, at the sharp end of a sword.

'He must hang precipitate, for was caught redhand,' insisted Andrew Wood.

'Dear, oh dear,' sighed Giles. 'When will you cease this foolishness? Henry Cairns is innocent of any part in this.'

Henry could not calm his belly from its swell; from terror and revulsion, he could barely speak. They forced him to look down on Sandy Kintor's corpse, the frozen, grinning rictus he had carved into his face. Giles dipped his handkerchief into the miller's mouth, scooping out a pocketful of grain. A crowd had gathered, fronted by the baxters, who had been in council with Sir Andrew Wood. The siting of the windmill was the matter for discussion.

James Edie asked in horror, 'What has happened to his face?'

'Henry struck it with his spade. Yet it was not his fault,' Giles replied succinctly.

'Can we not close his eyes?' proposed Hew. He told himself that Sandy was long gone, and that seemed clear enough, the corpse bore scant resemblance now to any living thing. There was, he noticed, very little blood.

'In a moment,' Giles returned. The miller's face turned upwards, yearning for the light, had drained of life and blood before it met with Henry's spade. He had been struck upon the head, with a blunt and heavy force, before he had been buried in the grain. Yet even that, the doctor said, had not resulted in his death. His mouth and throat were choked, as hoppers in the mill. The miller had died gasping. He had drowned in corn.

'These little pricks of blood,' instructed Giles, 'that leaked into his eyes, are proof of how he died. A dry drowning, we may call it.' It was a choice of phrase he came later to regret. Giles closed the miller's eyes in one swift, decisive movement, and rose a little stiffly to his feet. 'The examination of the corpus is complete,' he said to Andrew Wood. 'Now you may take him to the kirk. And pray you, let this poor man back up from his knees, where the dampness of the grass can do him no great good.

'I will prescribe a vomiter,' he told Henry kindly.

The coroner withdrew his guard, allowing Henry Cairns to struggle to his feet. 'I pray you, sir, no womitar, I do not need a purge,' the miller moaned.

130

'You shall have one, nonetheless,' insisted Giles, 'So shall we purge this black bile from your belly, and its terror from your soul.'

'I thought you said the man was innocent,' objected Andrew Wood.

'That does not mean these horrors will not keep him from his sleep.'

Sir Andrew turned to Hew. 'I gather that you knew this man?'

Hew nodded shakily. 'He is Sandy Kintor, tenant of the mill at Kenly Green.'

'A miller, and your tenant?' Andrew Wood repeated. Foolishly, Hew blushed. 'Aye, but lately . . .'

'Lately? Aye, then, *lately*,' Andrew said ironically. 'That is beyond dispute.'

'I do not mean that he is dead. He recently gave up the mill, and took up work in town – he was to take up work – with your brother, Robert Wood,' retorted Hew.

'With Robert?' said the coroner. Hew saw his face turn thoughtful, yet could not read his mood.

'Aye, sir, with your brother,' Hew repeated boldly. 'I do not see him here among the crowd.' And that was strange, he thought. For almost all the worthies of the town, and many of the worthless, had gathered at the granary to heed the hue and cry.

Sir Andrew rubbed his beard. 'He attends to business, and is not in town,' he answered cryptically. 'Now, you are telling me that two men have been killed, and both of them were millers, at my brother's mill? Then this no longer seems to be an accident.'

'This man's death,' said Giles, rising from his feet, 'was not an accident. He has been first felled, by a blow to the head.'

'How came he to the grain store?' questioned Andrew Wood.

'According to his son,' said Hew, 'he came here to discourse with Henry Cairns. We know that for a subterfuge, for Henry has been sick, in no ways fit to make a tryst.'

'This defence stands true?' Sir Andrew Wood demanded.

131

'I can confirm it,' swore Giles.

'Then you are excusit, for the while,' Sir Andrew said magnanimously, 'and need not hang precipitate, without a chance of trial. We shall consider, in due course, the evidential facts.'

Henry thanked him humbly, if a little sceptically.

'I do wish,' grumbled Giles, 'that you would leave the man alone. For surely you can see, he isn't very well?'

'It is the windmill,' a voice shouted out from the crowd. 'Did I not tell you, the windmill was cursed? First the Flemish sailors, and now two millers drowned.'

'Speak plain, and show yourself!' ordered Andrew Wood.

'It is I, the baxter, Thomas Brooke,' the heckler countered bluntly. Hew recognised him as a most officious tyrant and an elder of the kirk. He had not made the inner council of his gild, no doubt because his piety had made him much disliked.

'What is that you say? This man has not been drowned.'

'It was a dry drowning, as the doctor said.' Thomas Brooke reminded them. A murmuring began to echo through the crowd. 'And this man lying dead now, I saw last at the windmill. He was there with *him*.' He pointed straight at Hew.

'You were at the windmill?' Andrew Wood demanded.

Hew acknowledged, 'Aye, we were. I hoped that it might help me to make sense of Jacob's death, if I could understand the workings of his mind. The windmill had been close to him. I took the miller with me, to show me how it worked.'

'I see,' said Andrew Wood. 'And on whose authority, did you cut the rope?'

'On yours,' admitted Hew. He thought he saw the quiver of a smile, but perhaps he had imagined it, for when he looked again, the ghost had disappeared, and Andrew stood implacable as stone. 'Who holds the key' he questioned, 'that opens up the granary?'

'I do,' whispered Henry Cairns. 'For I am the keeper of it. The baxters have another, and have access to their stores.'

The baxter Bailie Honeyman interrupted hotly, 'The baxters is it, Henry? You may take that plainly, for a miller's tale!'

Henry Cairns said sulkily, 'What is a miller's tale, if I may dare to ask?'

'You scarcely can need to,' Honeyman retorted, 'For awbody kens, that millers are dishonest, as the day is long.' There came another rumble and low murmur from the crowd.

'Though it is true enough,' James Edie said judiciously, 'the baxters have a key, that key is safe sequestered inside the baxters' box. For any man to open it, he must turn four locks; that no one man may master, for four men hold the keys. If you accuse a baxter, you must accuse all four.'

'But I do not accuse ye,' Henry Cairns said miserably, 'For though I said the baxters held the other key – and that was not a lie,' he appealed to Andrew Wood. 'I did not say the key was used to turn the lock. The grainstore lock is broken, sir, and anyone might broach her.'

'Then anyone might broach her, aye,' repeated Patrick Honeyman. 'And whose fault is that?'

Cairns let out a groan. 'What madman,' he returned, 'would drop a body in the corn? I ask you, sirs? What profit, that? What *profit*, sirs?' His voice rose to a shriek, and dropped again. 'What profit, sirs?' he whispered.

'I see no answers to be had,' Sir Andrew sighed impatiently, 'from this wretched little man, who has told us what he knows. Then you had better purge him, and pack him off to bed.'

'Is that not what I told you, an hour ago?' asked Giles.

'*Do* it, then,' the coroner commanded. 'Let the crowd be cleared. And you and I,' he turned to Hew, 'will speak of this again.'

'Though I am loath to mention it, there is a little truth in what the baxter said,' said Hew to Giles, as they departed from the green. 'Two millers dead; both drowned.'

'It it a sad coincidence,' insisted Giles. 'Sandy Kintor's death was not an accident; and truly, I do now regret suggesting that he drowned. Yet let us rather say, he was smothered in the grain. No matter how he died, he was killed unlawfully. The same cannot be said for Gavan Lang.'

'And yet,' reflected Hew, 'this second miller's death provokes a second glance at the death of Gavan Lang. For how can we be sure that Gavan drowned by accident?'

'There was no mark upon the corpus that suggested otherwise. He went into the pond in an attempt to catch the fish. And everybody knew he meant to catch the fish,' objected Giles.

'That is my point,' said Hew. 'That everybody knew.'

'Even so,' said Giles, 'he could not have been persuaded to go deep into the water. Unless it were by witchcraft,' he concluded.

'Unless it were by witchcraft,' Hew agreed. 'Two millers drowned, and three, if you count Jacob; that cannot be coincidence.'

Giles corrected patiently, 'One miller drowned; one hit upon the head and buried in the corn; and one that died of sickness, known as holy fire. One died of natural causes in a tavern bed; one was killed unlawfully; the other died by accident. Death is random, Hew. It does not fall in patterns, as you seem to think. It comes as soon to millers, as to all the rest.'

'Everybody knew, he meant to catch the fish,' Hew had wandered off, on another train of thought. 'And everybody knew that Henry Cairns was sick. What made Henry sick?'

'Sickness,' Giles declared, a little tetchily, Hew thought. His capacity for diagnosing close had been exhausted, he supposed, upon the corpse. Giles preferred, at best, to be equivocal.

'Then what caused the sickness?' Hew went on relentlessly.

'As I am persuaded, something that he ate.'

'Could he have been poisoned?'

Giles answered with a frown. 'What is it you suggest?' he asked reluctantly.

'That whoever lured the miller to his death made sure that Henry Cairns was indisposed. And since the sickness clears him from the crime, perhaps he did inflict it on himself.'

'Henry was not well enough to lift his head, much less hit a man, and drive him to his death,' asserted Giles.

'Then someone may have had in mind to kill him too. These matters are not random, Giles, there is a purpose to them, that I cannot think divine.'

'You may be right,' Giles sighed. 'Though I can see no purpose, in the death of Gavan Lang. As for Henry Cairns, I had the sense he knew what was the matter, and would not confess it.'

'That gives weight to the suggestion, that he brought it on himself,' suggested Hew.

'I think it likely that he did, though he had no intent to cause himself such harm. He ingested some foul substance, and found it disagreed with him. His wife and children all keep well, and none of them has been affected. His wife is cruel and cross to him, yet she is not a shrew, and so I am inclined to think, he brought it on himself. If he will not confide it, we may never know. For though I treat his body, yet I cannot cure his soul. These matters are perplexing, I admit,' said Giles. 'Now let us to the Swallow Gait, to break this news to Meg. She loved your miller well, and she will find it vexing, as I think.'

They found Meg in the nether hall, with Lilias and Maude, 'Come to see the babbie,' as Lilias explained to them, with a seraphic smile.

'The bairn would not rest, till I brocht her to see him,' said Maude apologetically. 'I have left Mary in charge and cannot be gone away long.'

'Let her stay awhile,' suggested Meg. 'And Hew will see her home. You will, Hew, will you not?'

'Beyond a doubt,' her brother sighed.

Maude accepted gratefully. 'You are right kind. The lass is close confined, and feels it, desperately.'

Maude looked strained, thought Hew, as though the task of keeping Lilias confined began to take its toll. Her grey eyes settled briefly on Matthew in his crib. 'You have been well blessed, with a fine fair boy,' she said, almost inaudibly.

'Hold him, if you will,' offered Meg.

Maude put out her hand to touch the baby's cheek. 'I will not disturb him at his rest.'

'I will hold him,' Lilias said, reaching eager arms towards the sleeping babe.

'You mauma, pet,' said Maude.

'Let her, Maude,' protested Meg. 'Show her how to hold him. It can do no harm.'

Maude Benet shook her head. 'You cannot conceive of the harm that it can do. For she will want her own bairn, for herself. He is not a poppet,' she explained to Lilias. 'And he is not a pet. You cannot plague and play with him, as you do Gib Hunter.'

'He is not Gib Hunter,' Lilias returned, with an open clarity both fierce and unexpected. 'Gib Hunter is a *cat*. And if you put a bonnet on him, he will bite and scratch.' She sucked her thumb reproachfully.

'So much she has learned,' Maude sighed. ''Twere better, after all, to take her home.'

'Ah, let her stay,' insisted Meg. 'There is no harm.'

Maude hesitated. 'You will see her safe, sir?' she inquired of Hew.

'I shall indeed,' he promised her.

'Then I thank you all. Lilias, be good. And do as you are telt.'

'She is troubled, I think,' Hew said, as she left.

'It must vex her,' Giles reflected, 'to see her daughter with the little child; that brings to mind what cannot, and what must not be, for Lilias.'

'It is partly that,' accepted Meg. 'She daily frets and fears for what the future holds; what hope is there for Lilias, what vestige of a life for her. And partly that . . .'

Lilias came tugging at Meg's sleeve. 'I want to hold the babbie in my arms.'

'And so you shall,' Meg promised her. She sat the girl down in a low-backed chair and settled Matthew in her lap. 'Hold him *there*, and *there*.' Lilias gazed down at him, poking out her tongue

136

in a frown of concentration. 'And will I sing my song to him?' she posed.

'Aye, sing your song,' said Meg. 'For he will like that very much.'

Lilias began to sing, clasping tight the swaddling bands. 'Mixter maxter maks guid baxter.'

Matthew murmured in his sleep. 'He likes your singing,' Meg approved.

'What song is it you sing?' Hew wondered curiously. Lilias looked up at him. 'It is a song of the baxters. We do not like the baxters, though. For that they are a trial to us. They break my Minnie's bread.'

'Why would they do that?'

'Maude's inn makes little profit, and tis hard to make ends meet,' Meg explained. 'She falls fouls of the baxters, for baking her own bread, and fouler of her landlord, for grinding her own corn, what little she can scratch from her own bare patch of land. She does not break the rule from greed, but from necessity, when she cannot well afford to pay the baxters' price.'

'I saw that,' Hew remembered. 'Yet it seemed to me James Edie was indulgent of her crime.'

'Tis no loss to him. James Edie sells white wheaten bread, and Maude is baking bannocks, that the law says she should buy from men like Patrick Honeyman. The baxters' gild, in short, is made of many men, and each man puts his interests first above the rest.'

Lilias, it seemed, grew bored, and thrust the baby back at Meg. 'He does not speak or sport,' she complained.

'He does not,' Meg agreed. She settled Matthew back into the safety of his crib. 'Wait, and I will show you something you will like.' She disappeared into another room, returning with a wooden box, from which she took a small array of toys. They made a tiny village, carved in wood, with horses, cows and sheep, a farmer and his wife, with painted clothes and faces, a windmill and a watermill, with a wheel that turned. The figures and the mills had moving parts. Lilias clapped her hands. 'A whirligig!' she cried out in delight.

137

'A whirligig,' Meg promised, 'of your very own.' Without hint or warning, she broke into tears.

'Winds and waters,' whispered Giles, in confidence, to Hew. 'It is the little miniature, that moves maternal instinct in the woman's womb. For so a mother's milk precipitates the floods, and turns her wits to wetness. It is not to be discouraged.'

Hew had some doubts on the wisdom of this, and Meg, when she heard it, cried hotly, 'It is not the miniature, that moves my mother's milk!' She was stung by indignation into breaking off her tears. 'It is Sandy Kintor!'

Hew exchanged glances with Giles. 'What is it you have heard?'

'Sandy is dead,' Meg replied desolate. 'Sandy is dead. I heard the news from Maude, who heard it from the baxters at the inn. And he it was who made these little toys, when I first arrived at Kenly Green. Our father took me there, for solitude and rest, when I was sore afflicted with the falling fits. For it was months, in truth, before we found the medicines to keep the fits at bay, and I was frail and sick. And our father protected me, shut me up close and cloistered from the world.'

'I did not know,' her brother answered awkwardly.

'You were at the school, and at the college, then. And father did not want for you to know. Our coming caused a stir among the tenants of the land, until they were right used to it, and some did spurn and fear this rare, strange, haunted girl, and the nurse who healed her, Annie Law.'

Giles said, 'Stuff!' indignantly, still loyal to Meg in retrospect. She smiled at him. 'I do not blame them for it; they are country folk, and we met ignorance enough back in the town. I did not see it like that then, and was a sad and lonely bairn. But Sandy Kintor working at the mill had heard of my sad plight, for the mill is a fine gossip shop, where people pass the time whilst waiting for their turn. "I heard it at the mill," is what the midwives say when they bring me the news. So doubtless it was broadcast at the mill that Matthew Cullan had a queer wee bairn, who best was to be pitied, and at worst to be reviled. I was like poor Lilias, then. I know what it is like.'

'You never were like Lilias,' insisted Giles. I will not hear you talk like that.'

'Not in my heart, then understand me. But like her enough, in the eyes of the world,' replied Meg. 'The miller soon did settle that, coming to the house with a basketful of toys, and his son and daughters that were closest to my age – Janet and Elspet and Sandy his boy, that no one but his mother ever knew as Alasdair. You must remember them, Hew!'

But Hew did not. They were part of Meg's childhood, not his.

'And father, when he saw how much it pleased me, let me run and play with them, and paddle in the burn, and they became my friends. Sandy, most of all. He was the dearest boy. Subtle, and a dreamer. You would have liked him, as I think.'

'I think that she was sweet on him,' her brother winked at Giles. He was trying to subdue the aching in his heart.

'When I was six years old, I loved him, unequivocally,' Meg conceded openly. 'But we were not long friends, for millers' bairns are not weans long, and he was put to work. He did not have the knack for it. He longed to go to sea.'

'Childhood sweethearts!' smiled her husband. 'This is news to me!'

'In truth, I had forgotten it myself,' admitted Meg. 'This whirligig,' she said to Lilias, who clutched it tightly in her hand, 'will spin round in the wind.'

'I confess I am astonished,' muttered Hew, 'how quick the baxters were to spread the news.'

'Rumour travels fast,' reflected Giles, 'both good and bad.'

'We do not like the baxters,' Lilias said complacently, spinning round the sails upon the wooden mill. 'And they do not like him.' She pointed up at Hew.

'What do you mean?' asked Meg. 'They do not like Hew?'

'He meddles in their gild. It is a thing they keep locked in a box.'

139

'They are a gild. They do not keep the gild locked up in a box,' smiled Hew.

'They do,' insisted Lilias. 'It is a secret box.'

'What does she mean, that you meddle?' pressed Meg.

Hew pulled a face. 'I gave them some advice,' he admitted. 'Legal advice. In short, they demanded it. It turned out awry, and was not well received.'

Lilias shook her head. 'You meddled with the windmill. Now your miller's dead. And that should be a warning to you, so the baxters said.'

'Who was it said that?' demanded Giles.

Lilias shook her head. 'The baxters said it. Mixter maxter maks guid baxters. But we do not like the baxters, for they take our bread.'

'It is the foolish chatter of a child,' concluded Hew.

'She hears things; you should heed her, Hew,' his sister countered anxiously.

'She has told us nothing we did not already know. Tam Brooke said the same thing at the green this afternoon. The baxters are unsettled, and they want the mill; the rumours start to spread, and that is what she heard.'

'Even so,' muttered Giles, 'you should take better care.'

'What say you, that it was because of me that Sandy Kintor died?' demanded Hew.

'We do not say that. You know that we do not say that.'

'His was not the first suspicious death,' said Hew. 'Then there is Henry Cairns.'

'What of Henry Cairns?' asked Meg.

'There, at least,' said Hew, 'we steal a march on you. The miller Henry Cairns is taken sore and sick. Most likely poisoned, as I think.'

'Poisoned, aye,' conceded Meg, 'though by no human hand.'

Her brother stared at her. 'What do you say?'

'His wife came by this morning, Giles – I forgot to mention it – for vomiter and purgative, and told to me the tale. Henry has been eating mussels,' she replied.

'Mussels?' echoed Hew.

'Mussels would account for it,' Giles accepted sagely. 'Trust a woman's tale.'

'He bought them from a fishwife,' Meg explained, 'on his way to kirk, a little pot of mussels, steaming in their broth. Effie told him not to, for Henry broke the Sabbath rule, in buying them that day. But he could not resist them, and drank them at a gulp. It was God's judgement, Effie said, that he defiled the sacrament. She did not care if Henry went to Hell, but she would not be dragged there in his wake. She is sour and cross, and Henry Cairns is mortally ashamed.'

'Dear, dear, poor man,' said Giles. 'Together with the horrors he has seen, he must think himself upon the brink of Hell. You see, Hew,' he went on, 'there is no malice there, but foolish misfortune.'

'I see,' Hew exclaimed, 'that there are no secrets to be kept from Meg, while she is close confined; and I must marvel at it. How is it that you hear things, Meg? All things come to you!'

His sister smiled. 'As Lilias, in her confinement, hears the baxters' secrets, and writes them in her song. She hears their secrets closest, for they take no note of her. Men do things; women know things. And that is the way of the world.'

Chapter 12

Kenly Mill

The mill at Kenly Green was working still, for Sandy had resumed where his father had left off. Hew continued past it to the little cottage where the miller had lived with his wife, further up the burn. The cottage was clean swept and neat; the widow had contrived to keep everything in place. She welcomed him, with a deferential patience that he felt he did not deserve, bidding him to sit close by her at the fire, and feeding him with biscuit bread left over from the wake. The baxters had provided it, from kindness, free of charge.

'Was that no' a'fy guid of them?'

Hew agreed it was. The sugary confection turned to powder in his mouth. The miller's eldest daughter had been married in the spring, and he had sent a hogshead from his cellars for the feast; he worried now it had not been enough. The mill house, he remembered, had been dressed with yellow flowers.

'It is kind of you to come and see us,' said the miller's wife. Ellen was her name. And he had been afraid that he would not remember it. *Sandy, Ellen, Janet, John*, he whispered in his mind.

'Your faither ay was kind to us,' she said.

'Mistress . . . Ellen, I am sorry for your loss. If there is aught you need . . .' There would not be, of course. 'The papers are drawn up today; the mill and cottage are secured, in Sandy's name and yours. My nephew is your landlord now, though that is but in name, for nothing else has changed.'

He cursed himself, for want of tact: *for nothing else has changed.*

142

Yet Ellen did not seem to notice it. 'That is your sister's wean. How do they now?' she asked.

'Well . . . they do well. They both are . . . quite well. Matthew will be christened, at the Holy Trinity.'

'Aye? Then that is braw,' she approved. 'Is he a bonny bairn?'

'He is,' he answered desperately. 'A fine and bonny bairn.'

'And is it then his mammie, he looks after? Or has he mair a likeness o' his dad?'

'Of both of them, I think.'

'His mammie is a bonnie lass,' she said.

He found the small talk stifling, and could think of no way out. 'I thought that I might have a word with Sandy at the mill.'

'With Sandy?' Ellen echoed, baffled for a moment. 'Oh, you mean with Alasdair.'

'With Alasdair. Of course.'

'Now that is a kindness, sir, and he will be pleased. That will please your brother, will it not?' She turned to her daughter Janet, who was standing by the fire, as though she wanted confirmation of the fact. Janet stirred a pan of pottage on the flame.

'He will like it well enough,' she answered, Hew sensed disapprovingly.

'He will like it more than that,' her mother said. 'He liked your sister, too,' she turned again to Hew. He sensed that she was drifting now; he did not know if it was Sandy that she meant, or Alasdair.

Janet murmured, '*Maw* . . .'

'Whisht. He does not mind an auld wife's tale. You dinna mind it, dae ye, son?'

Hew promised he did not. 'They played thegither at the burn when they were bairns. A miller's boys are not bairns long. She likely has forgotten it.'

'He does not want to hear it, maw,' the daughter sighed.

'She has not forgotten it,' said Hew.

'He never meant to have the mill. He never wanted it.'

'Is it Sandy that you mean?'

143

The miller's wife meant Alasdair. 'He does not want the windmill. And I am glad for that. They say there is a curse upon it. It brings death by drowning.'

'I do not believe that, Ellen. Nor should you,' insisted Hew. 'Your husband did not drown.'

'Did he not, though?' she looked at him curiously. 'His breath was stopped with corn. And is that not a drowning, after all?' Ellen dropped her eyes, and stared into the fire, as if she did not see him there. She did not say another word, and so at last her daughter answered for her with a sigh. 'I think, sir, you should go, and see my brother at the mill.'

Ellen had been right, that her son was pleased to see him. It was for a reason Hew had not supposed. Alasdair was by the dam that ran into the mill. 'There is something I must show you, sir.' He closed the sluice, that acted as a brake to stop the wheel. 'Will you come into the mill?'

Inside, his younger brother looked up from the stones. 'The wheel has stopped.'

'I stopped it. Go and tell your mammie you are come hame for your supper.'

The small boy gawped at him. 'But it isna suppertime.'

'*Do it*, John.'

John lingered at the door. 'Since Master Hew is come, will you not say about the pig?' he asked.

'Whisht.' His brother frowned. 'He has not come about the pig.'

'What about the pig?' asked Hew.

'We want to have a pig,' said John. 'Tis common for a mill to have a pig, to eat the bran and husks.'

'I do not see why not,' said Hew. 'I will send you one.'

'You mauma dae that! Or my mither will think, that I asked you for one.'

'But you did,' Hew answered with a smile.

144

'My mither disna like pigs. Her faither was a fisherman,' the boy explained. 'She will not eat the pork.'

'Many folk will not eat pork. Shut up about the pig,' his brother said.

'Do you think that pigs can see the wind?' said John.

'What do you mean?' asked Hew.

'My faither said that pigs could see the wind. They see it coloured red,' the boy replied.

His brother said, 'Tis you that will see red, if you will not be gone.'

The small boy turned and fled.

'It killed my faither,' said the miller's son – he was the miller, now, thought Hew – 'and it will not kill them.'

'What did?'

'What I am to show you. Wait, and I will close the hoppers at the top.' The miller stopped the flow of grain and blew away the dust of flour that had gathered on the stones. 'The bottom is the bedrock,' he explained to Hew, 'and it is firmly fixed. The top stone is the runner, and that is where she turns.'

'I see it,' answered Hew.

'Yet what you do not see, is that the runner has been dressed with a hundred little grooves, these furrows that are cut in it; they shear the grain like scissors, so it is not crushed. The sharpness of the cutting is what turns the corn to flour.'

Hew saw, and understood.

'These little cuts grow blunt, and the stone must be resurfaced, once or twice a month. It is a skilled and careful task. My faither had the art, as I myself have not, so I must use a stone dresser, a pickman, as we call them, for picking out the grooves. The millstones are expensive, and are carefully preserved. They are bought in from abroad. The best are Cullin stones.'

'Cullan?' queried Hew.

'It is a place that they come from, on the river Rhine.'

'Cologne, possibly?'

'I do not ken it, sir. But they come from across the sea, and are worth a lot. Now it is essential, that the stones do not grind dry, that is to say, they must not be set too close, or without a grain between them. For one thing, it might strike a spark, and set the mill on fire. But more than that, it hurts the stone. A moment's rubbing dry shows more wear on the millstone than several weeks of grinding. And for that reason every miller has a bell tied to the hoppers with a rope, that will ring to warn him if the grain is running low, that he can keep them filled, when he cannot spare a boy to watch them all the while. My youngest brother has the task of heeding to the bell, and checking that the corn runs free, and in a steady stream. It is a tedious thing, and yet it is a vital one, that I have done myself, and God help the bairn who chanced to fall asleep at it, and had a rude awakening from his dreams. No matter that; it comes to John, as once it came to me. A miller kens his millstones. He knows them by their hum, the sweetness of their song when they are running true. And no one knew them better than my faither did. Well, sir, when my faither went to speak with Robert Wood, they went together to his mill. My faither looked over the stones. He told me they were badly worn, and that there was a deal of damage to the grooves, as though they had been badly set, and left to grind to dust. He said the same to Robert Wood. And Robert Wood the landlord swore the stones were freshly dressed, the day before the miller died, and were not turned since.'

'Is that so?' Hew's interest was awakened. 'Then what might that mean?'

'It might mean that the landlord did not tell the truth,' Alasdair explained, 'and sought to pass off poor stones, in the place of good. Tis possible he swapped the stones. For I have used the pickman, that worked for Gavan Lang, and he has confirmed, the stones were freshly dressed. Tis possible that Robert thought to keep them for the windmill, and replaced them with another set. But why would he deny it, then? My faither put to Robert Wood, that the stone could not be used, and Robert Wood was not best pleased. My faither thought it like to sour the place he had with him, and so he was resolved to keep his peace with Robert, and to dress the stone himself. My faither had the knack for it,' he added wistfully, 'as I do not.'

'I understand you,' answered Hew. 'For so I felt about my father and the law. As fathers often are dissatisfied in sons, I disappointed him.'

He was not sure what made him say it; a sadness in the miller's voice somehow invited confidence. The miller looked surprised. 'Oh, no, sir, you are wrong. Your faither was right proud of you. And you are very like him, stubborn, in your way. I hope you will not mind it, if I speak my heart to you?'

'I do not mind at all,' said Hew.

'Well, sir, I began to think, suppose that Robert Wood had told the truth.'

'Suppose he had? What then?'

'The damage that my father saw, could happen in a moment, sir, if someone opened up the sluice while the stones were dry. Suppose that someone opened it when Gavan Lang was in the pond?'

'The sluice was closed,' Hew pointed out, 'when Gavan Lang was found.'

'A moment, sir, was all that it would take, for Gavan to be swept below, and pinned down by a gate, that afterwards was closed. And a moment is all that it takes, to do the damage that my father saw, on stones that are ground dry. So once it happened here, that when the mill was stopped, a horse that came to water at the burn by accident let loose the gate and set our wheel to turn. It took my father several days to repair the damage to the stone.'

An awkward thought occurred to Hew. 'The horse was not Dun Scottis, I suppose?'

'My father, sir, did not report the horse's name,' the miller's son said tactfully.

'But surely, then,' objected Hew, 'the hopper bell would ring?'

'It did, and should. Yet it is very likely that the hopper bell was

147

stilled, or that it was not heard outside the mill. Since Gavan's family have moved on, we cannot now find out.'

'Then did your father know the death was not an accident?' asked Hew.

'I do not think he reasoned so far. Why would he, sir? It is his own departure makes it seem more strange, and throws it a light, that seems more dark and sinister. Though he may not have known it then, yet he saw the clue to it, the means to find it out. We know not who he may have told, apart from Robert Wood.'

'And so you think this knowledge led him to his death?'

'I suspect it, sir.'

'Yet Gavan went into the water of his own free will,' Hew considered. 'Do you ever trap fish?''

'John does, sometimes, with hooks and lines. He throws them back, of course, he kens the fish are yours,' Alasdair said guardedly.

'That is not my point. Gavan Lang set traps to catch the eel, that were wrought from willow. Do you know how they work?'

'I have seen them, sir. They are long and thin sleeves, and the fish swims inside. And when he is in, he sets off a catch, that closes the trap, and keeps him inside.'

'Then a fish could not have closed the trap, unless he were inside it?'

'Unless he were inside it, or a very clever fish,' Alasdair agreed. 'A fish with human hands.'

'That,' said Hew, 'is what I thought. Then I think that you are right, and Gavan's death was not an accident. And whether he suspected it, your father may have known of it, and it is more than possible, that for it he was killed. Have you told this to the coroner?'

'I have been afraid,' the miller's son admitted, 'even to tell him. Because he is the brother, too, of Robert Wood.'

'I think that you are wise. I counsel you, tell no one else, but keep this matter close.'

'Then will you find the killer, sir?'

'Alasdair, I promise you, that I will find him out.'

'I thank you. But my name is Sandy, sir,' Sandy Kintor smiled. 'No one but my mother ever calls me Alasdair.'

Returning to the turret tower, Hew found Giles in consultation with Sir Andrew Wood. 'Gavan Lang was murdered,' he interrupted breathlessly, 'I know how it was done.'

The doctor shot a warning look, as Andrew Wood said tersely, 'Well, go on.'

'The string that tied the trap was cut, and the trap was closed. The trap was left to float into the centre of the pond. The killer knew that Gavan Lang would see the trap, and seeing it was closed, would know the eel was caught inside.'

'It was not caught inside,' Andrew Wood objected.

'Precisely,' answered Hew. 'The trap was closed by human hands. It was a trap for Gavan Lang, to lure him into the pond.'

'Ingenious,' said Andrew Wood. 'Once Gavan Lang was lured into the pond, then how was he persuaded he should drown?'

'Once Gavan Lang was in the pond, the killer opened up the sluice, and Gavan was sucked under it. Before he was swept further, the sluice was closed again, and Gavan Lang was held fast by the gate. He had not, as we supposed, fallen through the broken rung, but was in fact, trapped under it. For why would he approach the damaged rung, unless it were the force of water that had swept him there?'

'This is speculation, Hew,' Giles interrupted wearily. His eyes to Hew looked dark and bruised. 'You cannot know that someone opened up the sluice.'

'The opening of the sluice is what provides the clue. It did damage to the millstones that were inside the mill. Sandy Kintor saw it.'

'Who told you this?' asked Andrew Wood.

'It matters not who told me,' Hew retorted. 'Ask your brother Robert for the proof.'

'Be quiet, Hew,' groaned Giles.

Andrew Wood said coldly, 'What has Robert Wood to do with this?'

'Two murdered millers, and both were at his mill,' Hew replied succinctly.

'What is it you imply? That Robert dislikes millers, or that someone else dislikes his mill? Consider very carefully, before you make reply,' suggested Andrew Wood.

'Neither,' Hew faltered, a little too late. 'In truth, I do not know.'

'You can name no suspect?'

'None, as yet,' admitted Hew.

'I see.' The coroner turned again to Giles, who was sitting, head in hands, with a look of blank despair. 'Two murdered millers, then, as we must suppose,' Sir Andrew noted dryly. 'Perhaps you can tell me, Doctor Locke, whether this is better, or yet worse?'

Giles answered with a groan.

'But what has happened here?' demanded Hew. 'Has there been another death?'

'Worse than that,' said Giles, 'it is Bartie Groat!'

'Bartie Groat has died?'

'Now *that,*' the coroner declared, 'might yet prove our solution. Yet sadly, Bartie Groat has not died. Bartie Groat has blabbed the contents of the letters round the town.'

'Oh Giles, I am so sorry,' Hew exclaimed. 'But why did Bartie do it?'

'It was the death of Sandy Kintor, in the end that proved too much for him,' said Giles. 'His wits were turned to water, and he was afraid. You cannot blame an old man for his fears.'

'I do not blame him,' answered Andrew Wood, 'I blame you.' He turned to look at Hew. 'I gave you no authority, to look into the windmill, with the miller Sandy Kintor, who afterwards was killed. And I gave you no authority to have the letters read, by a jabbering, blabbering old fool of a Dutchman, who blabbed them round the town. Wherefore I hold the two of you responsible, for the clamour and confusion we now have in our midst. The people are in terror and despair. *He told me that red gillyflowers had blossomed in his heart*: what sort of sense or solace are they meant to take from that? Half of them are sick, and the rest of them are crazed, and at each others' throats, and all of them are raging, and stark staring mad.'

'They are not mad; they only think they are,' asserted Giles.

'They are not mad; they only think they are,' repeated Andrew Wood. 'If you can tell the difference, Doctor Locke, and make it plain to me, then you must be a wiser man than I will ever be. You told me, sir, you promised me, there was no infection, no magic, plague, or trick, no possible contagion, that could come from that ship.'

'There is none,' Giles protested.

'Then what, sir, is *this*?'

'The fear of it,' said Giles.

'Aye, sir? Then mend it!' Andrew Wood said sharply. 'Since the college here has caused it, the college must mend it.'

'How shall we do that?'

'Explain to them,' Sir Andrew challenged, 'why they need not fear. Else I may have unleashed a fury on the town, because I did believe you, when you said that it was safe.'

'It is safe,' Giles insisted. 'It is not the sickness, but the fear of it infects. The sailors on the ship, and Jacob in the port, died from a sickness that is known as holy fire. It is not a contagion, that can pass from man to man. It died out on the ship. And I am now quite convinced that I have found the cause. As for the millers in the town, none of them contracted it, and they were not bewitched. They died at human hands.'

'Can you prove this?' asked Andrew Wood.

'I can explain my theory. But a theory is not proof.'

'Then that must suffice,' the sheriff sighed. 'Since the rumour started in your college, then let the college put it right. You, sir, are respected, in the town. Therefore, put your case, and put it plain. I will call a meeting in the college hall, and you will give a public lecture, to allay their fears.'

151

'In the college hall?' Giles echoed, startled.

'In your college hall. For since the rumour started here, it is only right and proper you should set it straight. These walls are cloistered, and the crowd are bound to come, from common curiosity. And you will still their fears. You will tell them – tell us all – how these people died. And *you*, God willing,' he said bitterly to Hew, 'will rout out our murderer, and find a man to hang. I will make a proclamation in the marketplace, and you shall hold your lecture tomorrow afternoon.'

'Bartie Groat be damned!' swore Hew, once Andrew Wood had gone. 'May all his sleeves and handkerchiefs fall into streams and puddles.'

'We never should have asked him,' Giles concluded. 'This is all my fault.'

'Not so. But is it true, that you have found the cause of the sickness on the ship?' demanded Hew.

'I am convicted of it . . . yet . . . I did not think to test it in the common field,' Giles admitted. 'I know not how the world will take it. I have not yet told Meg, whose common sense remains my arbiter, in all essential things. I hoped to write of it to Adam Lonicer.'

'Will you not tell me what it is?'

The doctor shook his head. 'The theory wants refinement, Hew, it is not ready yet. In truth, I am not sure . . . I know not how to put it to them.'

'In plain words,' Hew suggested, 'that are not convolute. As though you meant to spell it out, before the smallest wean. Their thoughts are crooked, Giles, and you must do your best to put them straight.'

Chapter 13

Ignis Sacer

'Are you well prepared,' asked Hew, 'to put your case?'

Giles answered doubtfully, 'In part. I have concluded my report into the cause of that same sickness, which afflicted Jacob and the others on the ship.'

'What was the cause?' interrupted Hew, who hoped to bring the doctor swiftly to his point. His hopes were dashed, as Giles said enigmatically, 'For that, you will have to wait. My fear is, that the matter is untested and unproved, and may sound with hollow resonance, on dull, unpractised ears. What did you mean, *plain words*?' he demanded suddenly. 'Do I not always speak plain?'

'Not always,' Hew admitted, with a grin. 'There is a certain risk, that if the argument is too abstruse and convolute, that you may baffle and perplex, and make more opaque, what you hope to elucidate. I would counsel, choose words for their ripeness and simplicity. Speak clear and true, and, to be short, do not equivocate.'

'You call equivocation, what is proper balance,' argued Giles. 'It cannot be a flaw, to weigh upon both sides.'

'Yet there are times,' said Hew, 'in which it is essential to take sides, and commit to argument. This is a case that you must strip of paradox, laying bare the facts. For you must quell the tempests that are turning in their minds, and still the winds and waters in their hearts. They want a clear direction, that you must provide, and not take them round in circles. You must prove it plainly, to rid them of their fears.'

Giles nodded. 'You are right. I shall make it plain. And I shall use what players call their *properties*, to help me put the case.'

'What properties?' asked Hew suspiciously.

The doctor winked at him. 'That you must wait and see. It occurs to me,' he changed the subject, 'that since we come to talk about the millers' deaths, it is more than likely that the killer will be present in the room.'

'I have thought that too,' said Hew. 'It seems to me a certainty, for how could he resist? And I intend to closely watch the crowd, for any sign of guilt.'

Giles hurried off to read his notes and collect his props. The whole of the baxters' gild, the bailies of the council, and many other freemen of the burgh had gathered at the college gate. Among them, Hew saw Robert Wood, the miller, Henry Cairns, the Reverends Auld and Bruce and Traill, together with the elders of the kirk of Holy Trinity, the master from the grammar school, and the fruitman, Wullie Clegg, who sold pears that never ripened from a bucket at the cross. The students too attended, turning out in force, and Wullie Clegg had brought with him his dog.

James Edie and Patrick Honeyman appeared in dual capacity, among a little cohort of the local magistrates. They were tuned for discord as soon as they arrived. Honeyman took issue with a student at the gate, appointed as an usher to escort them to the hall. The offender, noted Hew, was the tertian, William Wishart. As the hour approached, Hew began to sense a restless curiosity, a close demanding scrutiny that might not prove benign.

The crowd had grown too large to fit into the hall. Some were squeezed, like schoolboys, onto forms, placed in ordered ranks the full length of the room. Others stood behind, or clustered round the sides. The students jostled noisily, crammed in at the back, and spilling out through doors and windows to the night beyond. Giles stood on a platform on the far end of the hall, behind a small lettroun. Hew stood at his side, looking at the crowd. The candles in their sconces round the room were lit, and threw a random scattering of light. Hew called out to Paul, stationed at the door, 'We want more lanterns here. Illuminate the crowd! Let no one rest in darkness, for I want to see them all.'

Giles produced two objects, which he set out on the board: a loaf of bread, and a piece of corn. Hew surveyed them curiously. 'Have you brought your dinner?'

'They are the properties. Or what you might call evidence.'

'Evidence of what?'

'That will soon emerge. I do not like this crowd,' Giles muttered nervously. 'I was not expecting quite so many. I had not understood ill feeling ran so rife between the college and the town. I should perhaps have sent the students to their rooms. The bailie, Patrick Honeyman, has made complaint of William Wishart, whom he accuses now of insolence, compounding some offence he has committed in the town. He demands apology, which Wishart has refused. I do not suppose you witnessed these events?'

Hew shook his head, 'I was not party to it.'

'That is to the pity, for I cannot find a witness that can be impartial here. The student and his friends deny it, as they might. Honeyman is adamant, and since he is chief magistrate, I feel duty bound to take him at his word. He demands that I punish the boy, or else deliver him for sanction to the burgh court. And I am quite perplexed, as to how to try the case,' confided Giles. 'Do I take the student's part, for he is one of ours, and likely is the victim of a grudge against us all; or do I take the bailie's word, and make him an example, the better to repair our damaged standing in the town?'

Hew gave this some thought. 'I know the student who is here in question, and I know the baxter who has brought the charge,' he replied judiciously, 'and it would not surprise me, if both were found at fault.'

'No doubt,' Giles agreed. 'Yet you are the one who told me so emphatically, there is no place for compromise, in laying down the law. So pray advise me plainly, which do I defend?'

'In this case, I must answer, both,' insisted Hew. 'Though I will

155

acknowledge that that does depart from rule. That is, advise Patrick Honeyman that the matter will be dealt with in the college, according to our laws; and advise the student he must make apology. Then make him write it out in Latin verse. This has the twofold effect, of proving irksome to the student, who will find it onerous, and infuriating to the bailie, who will not understand it, and will interpret it – correctly – as being condescending, without having any cause to make complaint. It will be an exercise of William Wishart's Latin, and that, in itself, can only do him good.'

'That is the justice of Solomon,' Giles said admiringly, 'for which I am most grateful.'

'If you will,' Hew offered, 'I will oversee the task. And I will tell young William Wishart that since the bailie has no Latin, he may write whate'er he likes. so long as it is perfect in the grammar and the verse.'

'Now that,' reflected Giles, 'is simply wickedness.'

'It is a small revenge. A sop, to add sweetness to the student's task, in case he is most bitterly aggrieved. It is entirely possible that he is innocent,' said Hew. 'Nonetheless, he and the bailies were better kept apart. I shall keep my eye on William Wishart.'

The coroner stepped forward. 'Are you ready to begin? The mood is dark and fretful, and I would not have them wait.'

'Aye, ready,' Giles agreed.

'I will make them still.' Andrew Wood possessed a grim authority that lulled the restless audience into a sullen peace. 'You are come to listen, not to speak; be still,' he told them bluntly, 'and this man will tell you how the sailors died on the wreck, and how the two millers here died in the town, and he will put your minds at rest, that ye need not be afeared of some black magic or the plague, which rumour I ken has beset you, that ye are all riddled with fears.'

There was a troubled silence, and then an answer rang out sceptically. 'Oh aye, what man is that, then?'

Andrew Wood glared back into the crowd. And for all the score

156

of swinging lanterns placed around the hall, the voice came from a hidden darkness. Hew could not tell whose it was.

'He is Giles Locke, the doctor and professor of medicine, and besides that, the principal of this fine college, in whose hallowed hall you are now privileged to sit,' affirmed Sir Andrew Wood.

'Oh aye?' the voice replied, in tones that answered all.

'He is, besides, our visitor,' Andrew Wood returned, 'which is to say, he is appointed to visit and report on all suspicious deaths, whether by poison, or murder, or any other person taken away extraordinarily.'

'Which you could say, right enough, is what has happened here,' the heckler stirred.

Sir Andrew grew exasperated. 'Will you stand, and show yourself?'

'Oh *aye*,' the voice returned, thick with scorn and irony, safe within the confines of the crowd. It was an ominous refrain, which returned to haunt Hew after in his dreams.

'If not, then haud your tongue,' demanded Andrew Wood. 'This man is our visitor, as all of you must ken, and those that did not ken it, ken it now. And he is here to tell you, that there is no magic here.'

'May I put a question?' came another voice. The speaker rose up from his bench, and continued languidly, 'As you may see, I am not afeard to show my face. The better I might say, sir, I am not cowed by you.'

It was Sir Andrew's brother, Robert Wood, and Hew felt the coroner bristle at his side. He faced his brother square across the room. 'Questions at the end.'

'Yet some things are better to be set out at the start,' Robert answered calmly, 'the better to allow for perfect understanding. I question Doctor Locke, on his credentials, since he is disposed to speak with such authority, upon these strange events.'

'What can you mean, sir?' his brother charged indignantly. 'His credentials are right here, as I have made most plain to you.'

'There is a question you do not address, that causes some concern,' continued Robert Wood. 'I wonder if the principal would care to answer it. For it concerns a matter that I think must be made clear.'

'Put your question,' interjected Giles, 'and I will do my best to set your mind at rest. Do you wish to know, where I obtained my degrees?'

'Not at all,' smiled Robert Wood. 'Your education is not open to dispute. I merely thought to ask, whether you yourself have ever practised magic.'

The whole hall seemed to hold its breath. All eyes, save for Hew's, were turned now to Giles. The doctor answered, 'Not at all, in any sense. Why is it that you ask?'

'I thank you, sir, in turning to the question,' Robert Wood replied. 'I have heard that you keep human body parts in your room, for purpose of experiment. Can you now confirm for us, whether this is true?'

The whole hall fell to shuddering, in horror and in fear. 'What body parts?' a nervous baxter asked.

'As I understand,' said Robert Wood, 'it was a human foot. Is it true, sir?'

His brother interrupted. 'Giles Locke is an anatomist. The parts of which you speak are vital in his work.'

'*Vital*,' Robert stressed the word, as though to point the irony. 'Professor Locke, do you teach medicine in the schools?'

'No, not as such,' admitted Giles.

'There is no course in anatomy? And if your students at the college wish to train in physic, they must go abroad? Is that correct?'

'That is correct. And yet,' Giles rallied, 'that may not always be the case. The new foundation of the university provided that a mediciner should be principal of St Salvator's, and a lawyer his depute, and both to go about researches, to the enhancement of the college, and its higher faculties. The parts of which you speak

158

belong to my experiments, into the way the body works; they serve no hidden purpose, magical or otherwise.'

'Then you are not a witch?'

'I can well assure you, I am not a witch.'

'What is your purpose, Robert?' demanded Andrew Wood.

'In seeking out the truth. Is that different from yours?' his brother retorted.

'Your question has been answered. Hold your peace.'

'It has,' Robert bowed and took his seat. 'And I am grateful for it, Doctor Locke.'

Whatever his intention, he had achieved success in stirring up the crowd. Hew felt the tension rise as Giles began to speak.

'You come here today on account of the Dutch ship the *Dolfin*, to hear me explain to you how its crew died. Now most of you know that letters have been found, that describe the fatal symptoms that were suffered on that ship, and many of you feared the ship had been bewitched, or else it was a plague, that has since unleashed its torment on the town. I am here to tell you that it was not magic, and it was not plague, but a sickness known as *ignis sacer*, that is, holy fire. The symptoms of this sickness are twofold: on the one hand, it is manifest in burning of the limbs, which begins with a creeping and an itching of the flesh, and ends in a dry gangrene, whence the flesh will rot; the limbs affected blacken, and drop off. And the other set of symptoms – which may coincide, though rarely, in one and the same man, and which I am assured are due to the same cause – is a delusionary madness. Both sets of symptoms were observed in letters taken from the boat, both led to death, and both were visible in Jacob, who died at Benet's inn.'

'Who brought the sickness with him to the town,' a voice moaned from the void.

'Who did *not* bring the sickness with him to the town,' corrected Giles. 'The sickness died with Jacob. What happened to the millers was another sort of perfidy, and I will come to that. But for the moment, I mean to explain to you what I think caused this holy fire, and how, by that cause, it cannot spread to you.'

'How can you say that?' cried the voice. 'It has already spread. My wife has had the itching in her hands. My daughters, too, complain of creeping of the flesh. Help them, doctor!'

'Aye, mine too!' another called.

'And I!' A wave of panic flowed around the room. 'Is there no physic we can take?'

'You have no need for physic,' Giles assured them patiently. 'Because you are not sick. The symptoms you report are in your mind.'

'We are come for medicines, why won't you give them to us?' the crowd persisted fretfully.

'Aye, then, very well,' sighed Giles. 'Come to me at the end of the lecture, if you remain still unconvinced. Yet answer this now; you complain of itching and a creeping of the flesh. Does any one of you have blackness, or decay of the extremities?'

This was followed by a short and earnest pause, a puzzled, close self-searching, in the secrecy of candlelight, broken by a scream from Giles Locke's servant, Paul.

'God help me, sir, I have! My thumb is black!'

He waved his hurt hand frantically, coming close to tears, while the crowd around him parted in a curve.

Professor Locke confirmed, his patience now a sliver, 'And that is because, as you may recall, you hit it with a hammer, putting up a pothook by the kitchen fire. Your accident this morning turned the ether blue; it took a little longer to happen to your thumb.'

The ensuing laughter helped to ease the mood. 'But why, sir,' someone asked more reasonably, 'should we suffer from these symptoms, if the windmill is not cursed?'

'The symptoms are delusional. They are not real,' said Giles.

'And yet,' said Robert Wood, 'and yet, you say that delusions are a symptom of this fire.'

Giles admitted, 'Aye, and that is also true. And yet, this is a different sort of thing. The mind is skewed by fear. In fact, I am persuaded that this was the type of delusion under which Jacob was labouring, when he died, and that the two sorts of symptoms – madness and dry gangrene – though they coincide, do not concur – that is to say – did not concur, in him.'

Hew shook his head and murmured, 'Too abstruse.'

'I mean,' Giles replied to him quietly, 'that the sickness does not have the same effect on each man it infects. Some have gangrene, some go mad. Rarely, they do both. Jacob's madness, coming late, was conscience, as I think.'

'So much I understand. Yet how can you be sure, that the delusions of the town are not the selfsame sickness?' Hew whispered.

'The truth is, I cannot, for there must always be that one small seed of doubt. But if my theory is correct, then they are not the same. Stay with me, Hew, for if I lose you now, there is no hope,' Giles whispered in reply.

Sir Andrew turned to scowl at them. 'I pray you, speak no whispers. Make your answers plain before the crowd.'

Giles nodded, and spoke out, 'You have heard about a letter in the Flemish,' he began, 'that describes the sickness on the ship. I have seen the like before, in a small village in France, while I was at the university in Paris. It was known there, as I said to you, as ignis sacer, holy fire, on account of the burning and the blackening of the limbs, which has the appearance of charring.'

Hew wished that Giles would not dwell on the blackened limbs, which did little, as it seemed, to reassure the crowd.

'This sickness, then,' continued Giles, 'is called the holy fire. Which is the name that we have given to that febrile sickness called the rose, for this other was unknown here.'

'Until now,' said Robert Wood.

'Until now,' acknowledged Giles. 'It was also known of old as St Antony's fire, because the monks of that order had some skill in curing it. And why was that?'

161

'Because it was the devil caused it,' someone else suggested. 'And it is the devil brings it to us now.'

'Tsk. We cannot count the monks a force against the devil,' put in the man from Holy Trinity. 'Or we might cure it now, by our own more honest prayer.'

'There is no cause to cure it, for the risk is passed,' insisted Giles. 'Yet I am interested to know what led to their success, for as far as I can tell it was no art or medicine they employed, but rather . . .'

'A more potent form of magic,' came a murmur from the baxters, which Giles chose to ignore. 'They took the afflicted into their monasteries, and there they were themselves immune to the affliction, which leads me to suppose that it was not infectious. Indeed, I am persuaded it was not what they did, but something they did not do there, that brought about the cure.'

'You are too diffuse, and too mysterious,' Hew whispered. 'Take them to the point.'

'I come to it. I am persuaded, it was something that their patients ate or drank, that was different from the matter that the monks ate or drank, that brought about recovery. The monastery was self-sufficient, and had its own supplies. Well then, what? I asked myself. The notion that the sickness came in food or drink is there in Jacob's letters, and I sense that he suspected it. For here he says, *We sailed up coast to Rotterdam, for casks of Rhenish wine. The schippar and his friends ate well that night. The meat and bread were fresh . . . I made my small supper of biscuit and salt . . .* and here, *It began with Frans Hanssen, the wine merchant, who suffered flux and creeping of the flesh, and burning in his limbs.* Something, I would hazard, that they ate or drank, and that the whole crew did not eat or drink, at least at first. The cabin boy, Joachim, was last to be afflicted. What was it that they ate, they did not give to him?'

'Wine?' suggested Hew. The doctor shook his head. 'Tainted wine is foul. And likewise, when we feast on tainted flesh, though we sweeten it with spices, yet we know tis rotten by the taste and scent. We know our food is rank, when we see the little worms. Whatever it was that they ate, they had not suspected it. What was it then, in common use, that did not taste amiss, and yet was not consumed in common on a ship? Something that was plain, and yet was somehow fresh. Jacob told us, he ate biscuit bread and salt, and he was not afflicted, not at first. I asked myself, what was it, they ate on that ship, that nothing has remained of it, no single scrap or crumb. And then I came to thinking of the *Kreuterbuch*.'

'And what is that?' demanded Andrew Wood, impatient for an ending to the tale.

'It is a book of herbs by Adam Lonicer, who is the chief physician in the town of Frankfurt – I spoke of him before, when you paid little heed,' Giles said aside to Hew. 'As some of you may know, my wife just recently has had a child; a few may be aware she suffers from the falling sickness.'

Hew wondered why on earth his friend would mention that, at such an awkward time, and frowned at him. Giles continued, unperturbed. 'In the months that led to the confinement, I was greatly exercised, in finding any physic that might help her in her pains. And to this end, I wrote to Adam Lonicer, and he was kind enough to write to me. I have a copy of his latest *Kreuterbuch*, in which he talks of Kornzapfen – that is a little cone, that grows inside the grain – a grain of corn like this –' he held up the sheaf, 'save that this is barley, and no doubt his was rye, which is not quite so common in these parts. This little corn of grain he says the midwives use, to ease a woman's childbirth and make strong the womb. I wrote to Adam Lonicer, to ask him where and how this grain core might be used, to which he gave a caution, that using in excess provokes the symptoms that I have described to you, as holy fire. And he sent me the case notes of a poor woman who had died most painfully in childbed in this way, on which account I set aside his book, and did discount the grain, as any use to Meg. But the symptoms he describes were the self same symptoms Jacob has described in his letter from the ship. And so I ask, again, what is such a common food that no one would suspect it, and yet is scarce upon a ship, so that they kept it from the cabin boy? The answer is *fresh bread.*' Giles held up his loaf. 'My theory is, the blight that killed the sailors was present in the corn, that they baked into their bread.'

There was a moment's heavy pause, before Patrick Honeyman rose roaring to his feet. '*Bread?*'

'It looks like one of yours,' James Edie put in dryly. 'For at least, for certain, it is not one of mine.'

It was a peculiar irony, reflected Hew, and a particular misfortune, that the loaf that Giles had brought up from the kitchen as his prop had chanced to bear the stamp of Patrick Honeyman.

'You misunderstand me,' Giles responded hurriedly. 'I do not mean to say it was *your* bread . . .'

He offered too little too late, for the cry had already rung out, 'He says it is the baxters, the baxters who have poisoned us!'

Giles protested faintly, 'I do not say that at all.'

But the room was in an uproar. He had lost control.

Chapter 14

A Wrong Foot

As Honeyman loomed dangerously, Hew's eyes were drawn to the far side of the room, where a group of students passed from hand to hand some object they kept hidden underneath their cloaks. Hew could not tell what it was. It came to rest at last with George Buchanan, who accepted it reluctantly. He stood a moment, wretchedly, and held the object close, until his friends propelled him forwards and he opened up his hand. Hew watched the drama build, a series of small incidents impressed upon his mind, like the vague reflections of a dim and distant dream, which bore no sense or meaning for the present place or time. George Buchanan lifted up his arm, and launched his missile – later, it transpired, a Honeyman bread roll – in a perfect arc, before the words of warning could settle on Hew's lips. And for a second, as he threw, the boy's glance crossed with Hew's, an actor's comic mimicry of horror, guilt and fear. The bread roll rose and soared. It struck the bailie Honeyman, even as he glowered, his grim and heavy menace coming close to Giles. Honeyman fell forward with a little grunt. He staggered to his feet, and turning with a roar, felled the man behind him with the full force of his fist. A second man rose up to answer for his friend, and knocked the fleshy baxter whimpering to the ground. And in a heartbeat, all the baxters fell to pummelling, as fierce and heavy battle broke out in the hall. George stood pale and gawping at the carnage he had caused. Benches were upturned, and someone seized the lectern from the stage to hurl the whole thing bodily, clean across the room. Andrew Wood

165

withdrew his sword, and blustered ineffectually. He was not heard above the din. A rain of bread and buttons showered above the hall, collected from the lining in the students' coats. The students and the baxters fell out into the night, and spilled onto the cloisters beneath the gaping moon, where the battle ranks split up and gathered strength. Close combat had commenced, between the college and the town.

'Make fast the gate and keep them here, and I will fetch the guard,' panted Andrew Wood. The students stormed the dormitories, and from the upper windows scattered ink and books, pouring out the water pots onto the green below. From the kitchens, they emerged with sacks of flour and eggs, and the baxters were anointed with the raw tools of their trade, baffled and bewildered by the cloud of wheaten dust, lashing out and thundering, thrashing left and right. They were a steady match for the sheer, delighted fury of the boys. The fight was stilled at last, by the return of Andrew Wood with soldiers from the garrison, and a single, bitter pistol shot, blasted at the moon, that blew away the clouds that hung above the square. The students and the baxters stopped and stood aghast, their floured and bloody faces ashen in the gloom.

Andrew Wood said brusquely, 'I will rout these people out into the street, if you round up your students.' The baxters were dispersed, and the college gates were closed once more upon the night.

It took a little time to gather in the students, and settle them again into their former groups. Beneath the dirt and bruising, restless faces shone, exhausted and exhilarated in their battle lines. Hew sent Bartie Groat for cloths and bandages; the mathematician fluttered round the close, like an agitated moth trapped inside a lamp, and as little use, thought Hew. 'Dear, dear,' said Bartie weakly, 'it cannot do us good to be standing in this air.'

'We shall stand here,' answered Hew, 'until all are accounted for.' He saw no sign of Giles.

Gradually, the roar died down. The students clustered meekly as the scale of their delinquency began to dawn on them. A hundred watchful eyes were turned to Hew. The regents reported, 'All found, except for George Buchanan and Professor Locke.'

Hew suppressed his fear, calling through the ranks – impossible, it still seemed, not to think of them as troops – 'Has anyone seen George Buchanan? George?'

A student answered meekly, 'I do not think, sir, that he left the hall.' He spoke it in the Latin, anxious now to please. The words seemed strangely comical against his flour-stained face. They were boys, not savages, thought Hew. 'Take them to their rooms,' he ordered his regents, and see them safely settled for the night. Our inquest on this matter will keep until the morn.'

As the students trooped to bed, quiet and subdued, Hew went back to the hall. All the lamps but one had been extinguished in the fray. The one remaining light was set upon on the floor, to cast a gloomy commentary upon the doctor's face. Giles knelt there in the dust, like a penitent at prayer, before the lifeless form of George Buchanan.

'Dear God,' Hew whispered. 'Is he dead?'

'He was not breathing when I found him. He draws breath again, though he is not yet sensible,' Giles spoke, dull with weariness.

'Then you have restored him to life.'

'I have restored him,' Giles agreed, as though he found no comfort in the fact.

He placed his right hand tenderly beneath the student's head and raised him from the ground.

'I cannot see a mark on him,' said Hew.

'His hurts are deep within. He fell here by the door, and was trampled upon by the crowd. This arm is broken, as I think.' Giles was on his feet now, with the student in his arms. The boy lolled back upon the doctor's shoulder, yet he did not stir, as if he was the smallest bairn, or Matthew, in his swaddling bands.

Giles said, 'I will take him to my house.'

'Giles . . .' Hew began.

'Do not say it, Hew,' his friend pleaded earnestly. 'I pray you, do *not* say, that this was not my fault. I will take him to my house, where Meg will nurse and care for him. Can I leave you, to see to things here?'

'For sure. The students are dispersed, and sent off to their beds. The house is quiet now.'

'And no one else is hurt?'

'Cuts and bruises, nothing more,' said Hew. 'Sir Andrew Wood has gone to vent his wrath upon the town. I heard him vow to make examples in the marketplace. Yet he will find it difficult to put to good effect. The bailies were complicit in the fray. I saw the minister himself lash out and floor a college macer who had trodden on his gown. It will occupy the sheriff for a while, before his close attentions are directed back at us.'

'As no doubt they will be, in due course. This poor boy! I did not apprehend the whole place was a tinderbox. God help me, Hew! To think that I held out a loaf of bread before a room of baxters, and told them that was what had made the sailors sick.' Giles groaned.

'To be fair,' reasoned Hew, 'that was not what you said.'

'It was what they understood. And what else, after all, should they understand, by such wanton showmanship? It was pride, pride, Hew! I thought it was so clever, and so subtle, and ingenious! God help me, I did it with *bread*. And the outcome of my vanity is grave for this poor little boy.'

George indeed looked like a child, nestled in the doctor's arms.

'Yet George was not blameless in this,' noted Hew.

Giles stared at him. 'Not blameless? Of course he is blameless! He is in my care, and under my authority.' He turned away, trudging from the hall and down towards the Swallow Gait, without another word. Hew stood to watch him go, each anguished step made heavy with the burden of the boy.

A calm had fallen on the college, rooted in despair, as the students lay awake, and wondered what the dawn would bring. The cloisters were littered with debris: eggshells and bread crumbs, sharp shards of pottery, the remnants of a chamber pot, its contents still intact.

168

The servants were alert and watchful at the gate. One of them undid the locks to let Hew pass. 'All quiet, sir?'

'All quiet now. I will be in the tower, if I am wanted here. Wake me, at the slightest sound.'

'Do you expect more trouble, then?'

'It would surprise me, to hear more of it tonight. Nonetheless, do call me, if you have concerns.'

'The kitchens are concerned that there is no flour, and likely no more bread for the students' desjones, sir. We cannot hope our order will be filled,' the porter pointed out.

'Then they must go without. The fast may concentrate their minds on the rigours we have doubtless yet to come. If you hear complaints, refer them back to me,' instructed Hew. He hardly noticed that he had assumed command. Yet the college mustered gladly, and bowed to his authority.

The garrison had done its work, and applied its sanctions through the town, with a ruthless, clear efficiency that left a solemn silence in its wake. The North Street was deserted, but for a solitary sentry, by the turret tower. To Hew's astonishment, he saw that it was Maude. 'What are you doing here, and at this hour?' he confronted her.

'I came to hear how Jacob died. They would not let me in. They said it was for men,' said Maude. For four hours she had waited there, and kept her quiet vigil on the threshold of the college, while battle raged within.

'Aye. I'm sorry for it, Maude. It is our rule,' Hew explained to her. 'Yet you were well away, for there has been a fray tonight, a tumult and a brawl you would not care to see. You would have been ashamed of us.' And to see her there, sad, concerned and vexed, for Jacob, who had died a stranger in her house, he felt ashamed himself that it had come to this. Maude was worth the lot of them, he thought.

'I heard,' admitted Maude. 'There was a wee bit stirring in the street. The garrison have had their hands fu', for the baxters are a force that do not grumble quietly. James Edie said it was the bread,' she ventured suddenly.

169

'Aye, it was,' admitted Hew. It was the bread, in every sense, that started the affray.

'Then I am to blame, sir,' she blurted out.

'Why are you to blame?' asked Hew.

'I gave him bannock I had baked. It was not baxter's bread. It was the same bread, sir, you ate yourself, when you came for your dinner with the fish. And you did not turn sick, sir . . . yet, James Edie said . . .'

'No, no,' he reassured her. 'James Edie has lied to you, or you misunderstood. The bread you gave to Jacob can have done no harm. Whatever ill befell him, happened on the ship.'

'You mean I did not kill him, sir?'

'Of course you did not kill him! Put it from your mind!'

Hew slept fitfully, and was awoken shortly after five by the rumble of a handcart in the street. As soon as it grew light, he rose and dressed, returning to the gate. 'All peaceful here?'

'No news. The cloisters have been cleared and swept. The regents called the students from their beds at five, and set them on their knees for an hour of prayer. They went to it like lambs.'

'Good work. Then bid them watch them close, and keep them to their task. We shall have no tumult in the hall today. I shall spend the morning with Professor Locke.'

'Then are we to feed them? Or make them go without?'

'Do you have the wherewithal?' asked Hew.

'It seems, sir, that we do. The bread arrived this morning. Seven steaming baskets, full of good, hot wholesome bread.'

'It is not poisoned, I suppose?' Hew considered sceptically. The porter grinned. 'That did cross our minds, too. The bread comes freshly baked, and free of charge.'

'Surely, not from Honeyman?'

The porter shook his head. 'It comes from James Edie, sir, and with the baxter's compliments. A gesture of good will.'

It was evident to Hew, arriving at the Swallow Gait, that Giles Locke had not slept. However, he attempted a weak smile. 'The boy is out of danger. The bonesetter has been, poor bairn; that was an ordeal for him. His sister Clare has come to sit with him. She has asked for you.'

'Why would she do that?' Hew was conscious of the flutter in his heart. He felt that Giles must sense it too.

'As it seems, she trusts you.' Giles ran his fingers through his hair, a gesture of defeat, and utter weariness. 'God knows, that there can be no reason why she should trust me.'

'She has every reason,' contradicted Hew. 'You saved her brother's life.'

Giles did not reply to this. 'She sat with him all night.'

'How could she have known to come?' Hew asked.

'Her husband told her. He was at the meeting. It is safe to say, that he is not best pleased.'

'The college and the town are both at peace,' said Hew. 'The winds blow fresh, and light again. Perhaps it was required, to clear the heavy air.'

Giles answered hopelessly, 'This storm brings devastation in its wake. And now I must resign my post, as principal and visitor.'

Hew exclaimed, 'Do not do that!' Before he could say more, the door behind them opened, and Clare Buchanan came into the room. 'Professor Locke, my brother is asleep. And your good wife is kind enough to sit with him, while I go home to rest, and change my clothes. Your pardon, Master Cullan,' she said quietly to Hew. 'I thought . . . I hoped . . . that I had heard your voice. I wonder if you would consent to walk with me a while? I feel a little raw, and bruised, to step alone into the sun, at the close of such a dark and melancholy night. Do you think that strange?'

'Not at all,' insisted Hew, touched to have her confidence.

'You are so very kind to me. As you, Professor Locke, are kind to George. To bring him to your house, and treat him with such care. I know not how I can repay the debt, for if I give you all I have, it could not mean as much to you, as this has meant to me. With all my heart, I thank you for it.'

171

'There is no debt,' Giles answered hoarsely. 'For I am at fault.'

'You are not at fault,' said Clare. 'In truth, you are more blameless than you know, and we are more to blame. And as I understand it, it was Andrew Wood, who stirred this melting pot. Whoever brought the baxters through the college gates must surely be to blame, for some worlds set apart are never meant to meet.'

Hew felt astonishment at what she seemed to know. He thought of Meg, in her confinement, and Henry Cairns' wife, and Maude, left standing patiently outside the college gate, and wondered by what secret art, such women came to know the world.

'I will return,' Clare promised Giles, 'this afternoon.'

'Aye, mistress, do,' the doctor answered listlessly. 'I will keep George at my house until his bones have healed. He shall not risk the tumult of a horde of boisterous boys.'

'You are too kind. I pray you, walk with me,' she said again to Hew.

'Gladly,' Hew said awkwardly, and followed to the door. 'Where is it you are going?'

'Nowhere,' Clare confided. She was lovely in the light; the sun began to dapple in her hair, and though she had not slept, her face was fair and fresh. Her eyes were dark and watchful, and he found he could not look at her. 'How does your brother now?' he asked.

'I thank you, he is well . . . at least, not well,' she answered truthfully, 'but the better for your sister and the good Professor Locke. Your sister is quite lovely, is she not? I dare to hope I might become a friend to her.'

He dared to hope it too. 'I think it very likely you are almost the same age.'

'A woman does not like to speak about her age,' she chided him. 'How old is your sister?'

'Meg is one and twenty.'

'Then almost the same age,' Clare confided with a smile, 'for I am twenty two. Poor George,' her thoughts grew darker. 'He has had to endure the visit of the bonesetter, and that, I confess, was a hard thing for him. As it was for me.' Clare fell silent for a while, before she ventured, 'I think that you must know, sir, what I want to say to you.'

It took him by surprise, so that for a moment he was not sure at all, although he knew, had always known, at heart.

'And what is that?'

'My brother, sir, is in such dreadful pain. As he lay weeping through the night, he confessed the truth. He told me what he did.'

Hew stilled her, with a look. 'Then do not speak it, Clare. For if you tell me what he did, then I may have to act upon it.'

'He knows you saw him do it, sir. You do not need to lie for him,' said Clare. 'And though it can be no excuse, he did not know the trouble it would cause.'

'I know that he did not.'

'He does not ask for pity, for he knows that he did wrong. I have no right to ask it. Yet I do implore you, if there is a way, to keep this matter close within the college walls; then do not tell the coroner; do not tell Andrew Wood, that it was George who started the affray.'

'As to that, you have my word,' said Hew.

'Your kindness, then, is more than we deserve,' Clare answered quietly. 'I thank you, sir, with all my heart, and bid you make the matter known to Doctor Locke, for he has been so good to us I could not bear to break my brother's confidence. It is a want of courage on my part. I understand of course, that George must be expelled.'

'I will put this matter to Giles Locke, and since I know the workings of his heart, as I do know my own, I can tell you now, what he will say,' said Hew.

Clare answered fearfully, 'And what is that?'

'He will say your brother George was sadly led astray, that he has been misused, and was another's instrument, that he was gravely hurt by it, and had no understanding of the harm he caused. He will say that he has suffered, more than he deserves. And he will say it, not for kindness, but because it's true. George will remain in college, and he will not be expelled.'

Clare's eyes were bright with tears. 'You cannot know how much this means to us. But suppose that someone else saw George?'

'I am persuaded, no one saw him but the students at his back, who since they were complicit are unlikely to confess. Giles Locke will amend it,' Hew assured her.

'Then I am content. For Robert says, all eyes were on the baxter, and Professor Locke, and he himself could not discern the cause of the affray. He was most vexed at it.'

'Robert?' Hew repeated with a frown.

'Aye, my husband, Robert Wood. He was at the meeting there last night. We must not tell him, sir,' Clare iterated anxiously.

Hew brushed this aside. 'You are the wife of Robert Wood? The brother of the coroner?'

'Aye. But does it matter, sir? I thought you must have known.'

'I did not know.' Hew shook his head. Why should it matter, after all? And yet he minded bitterly. No husband in the world could leave him more dismayed than Robert Wood. A dreadful thought occurred to him. 'Did you tell your husband Giles Locke kept a foot?'

Clare said, 'What? A *foot*?'

'A human foot,' persisted Hew. 'You saw it in his rooms.'

'Oh! I might have done. I do believe I did, for I had thought it strange. I do not understand you, sir. Did I do wrong?'

Chapter 15

In the Body of the Kirk

Hew walked back to the house, where he told Giles about the boy. And Giles responded as his friend had known he would. 'Poor, benighted bairn! We will not hand our students to the council or the coroner. Such faults as we must mend, let us amend ourselves, within our own high walls, and according to our laws. No student of St Salvator shall suffer at the market cross, so long as I am principal.' To Hew's relief, the doctor gave no further hint of resignation.

'I shall go, now,' Giles resolved, 'and see if George lies waking, for the heavy load of conscience may keep a boy from rest, and hamper his recovery, that with judicious counsel, I may hope to ease. Stay, and make your breakfast here. Paul tells me that James Edie sent a loaf of bread. I know not if he meant to mock, or to appease.'

Hew commented, 'He sent some to the college, too. I wonder if he hopes to steal a march on Patrick Honeyman. He is a shrewd contestant if he does.' He settled in a chair beside the fire, and presently a girl appeared with bread upon a tray, followed by the servant Paul, with a cup of ale.

'Will you broach the bread, now, sir?' Paul wondered dubiously.

'Aye,' said Hew, 'why not?'

'We dinna like to try it, till the master tastes it,' Paul admitted.

Hew broke off a piece. 'It is unlike you,' he remarked, 'to stand on such a ceremony. If you require your master's sanction, before you will break bread, then you have far less to you than I had supposed. I took you for a man, with a sharp mind of your own.'

'As I am, sir,' answered Paul, uncertain what was meant, and whether he should take it as a compliment or not. 'You ken sir, that I mind my mind – my *ain* mind, as it is – as closely as I mind Professor Locke.'

'You mind it much more closely, as I think,' said Hew. 'And if you listened to the doctor more, then you would eat the bread, and you would not be troubled by these fears.' To prove his point, he buttered it.

'It wants the doctor's sanction,' Paul persisted stubbornly. 'And it is for that, that James Edie sends it here this morning to the house. He fears ill rumour will affect his trade.'

It seemed to Hew it had already done so, for the girl declared emphatically, 'I care not if he gies it free, or if he gies a shilling wi' it, I wadna taste a crumb of it, nor let it near my mouth.'

'Nor I, sir,' muttered Paul.

'Oh, for pity's sake!' said Hew, and took a bite. 'The baxters have mistaken,' he assured them through the crumbs, 'what the doctor said. The tainted grain was rye, and in the bread from Rotterdam, and all of it was eaten on the Flemish ship. No scrap of it remains here in the town.'

'So I have advised the town,' Paul protested loftily, 'yet they will not be told. Their minds may not be settled, till they see the doctor standing public in the marketplace, to taste and give his blessing to every baxter's bread. There are some sixty in the gild.'

'But this is plain madness,' cried Hew.

''Tis madness, sir, plainly, they fear.'

Hew turned with a groan towards Meg, who had come at that moment for breakfast, with Matthew asleep in her arms. 'Your servants will not eat the bread!' he reported scornfully.

'Though they may not, I will,' she answered with a smile. She set the infant rocking in his crib, and cut herself a piece. 'Do you still suffer from the burning in your hands?' she asked the serving lass.

'Aye, tis hot and sair, I doubt it is the fire,' the servant whimpered.

'Then you can rest in peace, for I have made a salve for it, and you will find a vat of it behind the kitchen door. Rub it twice a day into your hands, and in a week your fire will be quite cured,' instructed Meg.

The girl snatched up the tray. 'Then may I go right now for it?' she pleaded eagerly.

'For certain,' promised Meg. 'And you may go as well, Paul, and rub it on your foot, or any other secret place, where you may have the itch, as cure and prophylactic for this present plague. If anyone should come here, complaining of the same, then give them each a cup of it, and tell them that their symptoms will be gone within the hour.'

'Aye, madam,' answered Paul. 'I will make a stall of it, and set it in the street. Tis likely we will do a roaring trade. What think you, we should ask for it?'

'You will not ask a penny, Paul,' Meg replied severely. 'Or you will bear the full force of the doctor's wrath. That will keep them busy for the while,' she said aside to Hew.

'But why do you indulge them, Meg? Why did you not tell them, that there is no fire?' he whispered in reply.

'So that they may be cured,' his sister answered simply, 'of their sickness and their fears. Canny's hands are red and raw from scrubbing Matthew's sheets in hard yellow soap, to which she seems to have a peculiar antipathy. Yet if I were to tell her that, then she would not believe me, for in her heart she *knows*, it is the holy fire. The only way to cure her is to make a salve. The remedy is lavender, camomile and goose fat. It will soothe their skin, and do it no great harm.'

'Your perspective on the matter is quite different from your husband's,' Hew remarked.

'Aye,' admitted Meg. 'Giles seeks to tell the truth, yet truth itself at times is not the most efficient strategy, for it is often not what people wish to hear.'

'What make you of his theory, that the source of this strange sickness was a blight upon the grain?' Hew asked her bluntly.

Meg took pause for thought. 'I wonder that you ask me,' she

177

replied at last, 'who have no proper learning, in medicine or the arts.'

'You have knowledge of the world that takes you far beyond it,' answered Hew. 'And when it comes to nature, no one understands it more than you. I trust you for your wisdom, as much as I do Giles. I have lived long enough, and in those years have learned enough, to know that there is much more in the world, than all our art and learning can ever hope to show. So tell me what you think.'

'I think,' conceded Meg, 'that Giles may well be right, and that the holy fire is caused by blight upon the grain. And yet, I do believe, that the world is not prepared for it, and will not hear or heed the value of his words. His theory is too absolute, too radical and strange; it challenges the stuff, the staff of life itself, and he was ill-advised to put it to the town. He is resolved to let the matter rest; he will not press the case, nor write to Adam Lonicer. I fear that he has come before his time. His song is out of tune, and it will not be heard.'

'Poor Giles! At least,' reflected Hew, 'he has no cause to blame himself, for what occurred to George.'

'Aye, poor bairn. He has made contrition, in a flood of tears, and Giles had not the heart to speak severely to him, in his present state of health. He rather is inclined to blame the other boys. How is it that you saw the students urge him on, when no one else appears to know what started the affray?'

'Because,' said Hew, 'all other eyes were fixed on Giles and Patrick Honeyman, while I had come to look among the crowd. I thought to find the killer, hidden in the gloom, that I would read his secrets written in his face, and see his guilt shown darkly, in the flare of candlelight. A vain and foolish hope.'

'But do you think it likely still that he was in their midst?' considered Meg.

'I think it very likely that he was.' In his mind, Hew saw Maude, standing on the North Street, and wondered why the thought had not occurred to him before: 'But only,' he gave voice to it, 'if the killer was a man.'

Meg echoed his confusion, 'Oh! I had not thought of that.'

'What did you make of Clare?' Hew changed the subject, though it followed closely from the self-same train of thought. 'She looked pale and anxious, as I think.'

Meg was not deceived, and fixed him with a look that might cause a man to blush, had he not been accustomed to a younger sister's scrutiny. 'Clare appeared composed, as a loving sister should, in such grave and fearful circumstance.' She added disapprovingly, 'She is married, Hew.'

'So I have been told, to the dreadful Robert Wood, who must be twice her age.'

It was as well, perhaps, that Meg's answer was eclipsed by the return of Paul, who came in with the minister, the Reverend Geoffrey Traill, from the kirk of Holy Trinity. The minister came sporting a large bruise on his cheek, and sought for ministrations, of a more worldly kind. 'I hoped you might have an ointment to diminish it,' he appealed to Meg.

'I hope, sir, yon contusion, is no' the haly fire,' Paul objected wickedly.

The minister glowered back at him. 'It is not the holy fire, lad, as ye do well ken. I cannot let the guid folk think I have been brangling,' he excused himself.

'They ken you have been brangling, for they saw it for themselves,' Paul pointed out. 'They will not think the worse of you, to see it in your face.'

'I may amend the swelling, but I cannot help the stain,' Meg said apologetically.

'Ah, well,' the minister accepted with a sigh, 'I doubted it was vanity. I will write it in my sermon, and make a bitter point of it, for so it may be better, to confront these things head on. How does Matthew Locke?' He addressed the infant in his crib, with a sternness that suggested that he put the bairn to test. 'Is he well and hale, and ready for his baptism?'

'He is, all those,' answered Meg. 'I think you know my brother, who is to be his gossop?'

'For certain, we have met.' The Reverend Geoffrey Traill looked suspiciously at Hew. 'Hew Cullan as his gossop?' he blustered, sotte voce, 'Do you think that's wise?'

'Why not?' queried Meg. 'My brother is most proper and devout.'

'I do not question his devotion, yet,' the minister gave up the act of closer confidence, glaring straight at Hew, 'I think you will allow, that whenever there is trouble in the town, your brother is to be discovered lurking at its heart.'

'I do not allow that,' Meg replied indignantly. 'My brother is a man of law, and he has never lurked. If he is at the heart of it, then he is not its cause.'

'Yet what example is he to a bairn?' posed the Reverend Traill.

'I cannot find a better one,' said Meg.

'I pray you both,' smiled Hew, 'do not argue over me.'

'I weel ken you are clever,' sneered the Reverend Traill. 'And yet with all your cleverness ye cannot yet amend this sick and heavy pestilence that penetrates our town. In truth, if I may say so, with deference, after all, to the good Professor Locke,' he gave a nod to Meg, 'it seems to me your learning only makes it worse; your law is ineffectual.'

'It is ineffectual,' Hew admitted, 'when we cannot find the man who breaks it, and when his deadly sins are hidden in a crowd.'

'No man can be hidden in a crowd,' said Geoffrey Traill. 'His sins are known, and seen, always, by God.'

'Then so I hope you will advise him,' answered Hew, 'since he must be a member of your kirk.'

'How can you know that?'

'It is more than likely, since your congregation is more than half the town.'

'Aye, like as not,' the minister accepted. 'Then I must point my mind to it and take the sixth commandment as my present theme.'

'I wish to God you would,' said Hew.

'I do not like the tone in which you speak His name,' observed the Reverend Traill.

'It is heartfelt, I assure you,' Hew returned.

'In that, I do believe you,' the minister replied, with unexpected grace. 'For once you made me look into my heart, not liking what you saw, and when I looked inside, I found it grieved me too. And so I know your stubbornness is founded in good faith, and that for all your faults, you do not want for courage. And as I hope, you will approve my plan, to settle the dissension in the town. For though it is not subtle, it may do its work, and it will embrace the pure clear truth of God.'

'In truth,' admitted Hew, 'any attempt to still the conflict in the town is to be commended.'

'My plan,' explained the Reverend Traill, 'is to call for a holy communion. For the sharing of the Supper, as has always proved most popular, is our most special Sunday in the kirk. And since it is, with baptism, our only other sacrament, the people thrang and flock to it, and beg for it like bairns. And they enjoy it more than the whipping of the whore, or to see the scolding fisher wifies silenced with the branks, because it is a common thing in which they can all share. Though it may be observed,' he reflected sadly, 'that they reserve a certain pleasure, for thae other things as well. Now in our kirk of Holy Trinity, we celebrate Lord's Supper maybe once or twice a year, to which they all look forward, with glad and quickened hearts. So let us have a special one, to bring them all together.'

'That,' Hew exclaimed, 'is a pure stroke of genius!'

'Though it were pride to say so,' admitted Geoffrey Traill, 'I take some satisfaction in the plan. Since no one may take supper while in conflict with his neighbour, it often has the force of settling small disputes. It concentrates the mind, on attending to the catechism. And I need hardly tell you, for I ken you see the point, that the body of the Lord, in which they come to share, is signified in *bread*.'

'Genius, as I said,' asserted Hew.

The Reverend Traill looked gratified. 'The inspiration, ye must ken, comes straight from God. And since the Holy Communion

181

will take a wee while to arrange,' he turned once more to Meg, 'I hope you may be clean by then, and come to take the sacrament, for you will miss the baptism.'

'How, then,' Hew demanded, 'will you miss the baptism?'

'Because it is too soon,' his sister answered sadly. 'I have not been kirked.'

'Not kirked? Tis stuff and superstition, for certain, you must come.'

'It is not advised,' the minister assured him, 'though there is no service for it, in our book of prayer, that a woman pass abroad, before she has been kirked. And as your sister intimated, it is yet too soon.'

'Then let the christening wait,' suggested Hew.

'That too, is not advised,' the minister said tactfully. 'An infant's life is fine and frail, and like the fragile frigate, that sets out in the storm, is often overcome.'

'I do not mind it, Hew,' protested Meg. 'It will make me happiest, if you will go with Giles.'

'If that is what you wish,' her brother answered sceptically. Another thought occurred, and he turned to Geoffrey Traill. 'Your congregation, sir,' he pointed out, 'is made up from the centre of the town, while the farmlands on the south side are sequestered to St Leonard's.'

'Aye, that is so. Though some of them defer to us,' the minister explained, 'because the hours of service suit. And when we hold communion, people come for miles, to take their turn at supper with the Lord.'

'So I have inferred. But what of Henry Cairns?' asked Hew. 'He seems to be a member of your kirk, although his house and mills are on the south side of the town, and on land belonging to the priory.'

'Ah, yes, Henry Cairns,' the minister grinned ruefully. 'He comes to us, as I have heard, because he likes the *crack*. The crack has cost him dear, for he will have to pay out for a new communion cup.

Though we have washed it out with vinegar, it proved to no avail. *Mussels*, if you please!'

On Sunday, Giles took Hew and Matthew to the Holy Trinity, where Matthew was baptised into the body of the kirk. The Reverend Traill announced the new communion day, and a tremor of excitement shuddered through the crowd. Hew was impressed by the minister's command, the tenor of his thundering, that kept the restless people captured and enthralled. And yet there was a man among them, shadowed and unmoved, a man who was a murderer, and hid his face from God; and though God saw and knew the blackness of his sins, he had still succeeded in keeping them from Hew.

The coroner, Sir Andrew Wood, was waiting at the door. Hew had been surprised to see him in the church. He wondered how he came to worship far from home, and if he searched the upturned faces with the same intent as Hew. He did not join his brother on his family pew, but stood quiet at the back. His presence cast a shadow on the infant's sacrament.

'A happy day!' he greeted them. 'And a fine son, too,' he mentioned cheerfully to Giles.

Giles accepted cautiously, 'Indeed.' He had not seen Sir Andrew since the meeting in the hall.

'And a master stroke,' said Andrew Wood, 'by Geoffrey Traill. I do not think the tumult proved a bad thing,' he confided. 'For it released an energy, that like the whirlwind pent would leave more damage in its wake, were it not given scope to run its course. Now it has been diminished, as I think. Therefore,' he said graciously to Giles, 'I cannot hold you very much to blame. The fault was partly mine, for insisting on this course, and the outcome was restorative; nothing lifts the mood, like a good and bloody fight.'

'And yet the poor boy, George Buchanan,' Giles reminded him, 'was gravely hurt.'

'Collateral winds blow cross. We must expect some casualties,'

Andrew Wood said callously. Hew exchanged a sober glance with Giles.

'The baxters, too, have called a truce,' the coroner went on.

Giles nodded. 'Honeyman is most contrite. He does not wish to lose the contract for the college bread, and he accepts he was hot-headed, and intemperate in the hall. He understands that I had meant no slur upon his bakehouse.'

'The truth is,' Hew pointed out, 'that if we are no longer seen to buy his bread, the rumour that his flour is tainted can be thought to gather strength.'

'Precisely so. And he knows well that James Edie will be quick to take advantage of it. Therefore are the baxters' grumblings turned amongst themselves, and away from us. He is pleased to accept William Wishart's apologia,' Giles observed to Hew, 'for whatever slight he felt was done to him.'

'I will oversee it,' promised Hew.

'Honeyman is shamed, as a bailie of the peace, that he should take such part in disorder and affray. His reputation and his business were on brink of ruin,' reported Andrew Wood. 'Therefore, he must swallow down his pride, however sour the taste. I must confess, to a small prick of sympathy. He claims – would you credit it – that someone threw a bit of bread at him. He thought his life in danger, and so he did strike out. For that reason, I excused him his part in the affray. If you give up the culprit, I should be obliged to you. For while I have concluded that the battle was a useful one, still this public riot must be seen to be condemned. Else we will have a plague of civil disobedience.'

'Yet why do you suppose,' asked Hew, 'that we must have the culprit in our hands?'

'For he must be a student,' Andrew Wood explained. 'The baxters had brought with them no bread. If you have not discovered him, any name with do.'

'I think, sir, that it will not do!' Giles was plainly shocked by this.

'Is this your justice?' Hew demanded.

'It is my example,' answered Andrew Wood.

'I have no name to give you,' Giles informed him quietly. 'If you would seek to have one, then you must take mine.'

'I see.' Sir Andrew let the words hang heavy in the air. 'Then I shall expect you to observe a closer discipline, and keep your students cloistered from the town.'

'We have forbidden them the town, on the most stringent penalties, until the end of the term,' Professor Locke confirmed.

'Then that must be enough.'

Hew dared to hope the coroner had let the matter drop. Sir Andrew turned to speak to him. 'The matter of the windmill is still to be resolved. You have assured me that the millers' deaths were not an accident. And yet you have no evidence. And, as it would seem, no way of finding evidence, that might point out the killer.'

'The killer, sir, is hiding in the crowd,' asserted Hew, 'that congregates in kirk, and round the mills. He is like a corn seed, in a sack of grain.'

'Or perhaps like the blight, of which the doctor spoke,' Andrew Wood said dryly. ''Tis plain enough to me, that you will not thresh him out. Therefore I am resolved, to take another tack. And I have a notion, how we must proceed.'

'What do you propose?' asked Hew.

'I will tell you that tomorrow, at your house at Kenly Green, where I shall come to dine with you, at two o'clock.'

'But I am not at home,' objected Hew. He had remained in college, in support of Giles.

'You will be there tomorrow,' the coroner informed him, as he took his leave.

'What do you make of him?' Giles inquired of Hew.

Hew answered thoughtfully, 'He is not Michael Balfour, to be sure.'

Chapter 16

A Gift Horse

The arrival of the coroner caused consternation in the kitchens of the house at Kenly Green, for there had been no guests since Matthew Cullan's funeral.

'What will the sheriff eat, sir?' the cook demanded nervously.

'What he is given,' answered Hew. 'Bannocks and salt fish.'

'We canna gie him that, sir!' The cook was scandalised.

Hew took pity on her. 'Aye then, very well. Bake a pie of rabbits, to my sister Meg's receipt, and serve it with a flagon of the gascon claret wine. To follow it, a pottage of pippins, pears and plums. We will take it in the great hall. Set a place for Nicholas.'

Since Hew had moved to town, the great hall had been closed and its furnishings kept free from dust in linen drapes and sheets. The chimneys had been swept, and the fires had not been lit for several days. The room was cold and desolate. 'The place will soon warm up,' the servant said.

The place had not warmed up since Matthew Cullan's death, when the great hall had been filled with the feast that marked his funeral, where cushions, rugs and tapestries around the great oak bed, and the flare of beeswax candlelight, had mellowed the stone walls. And a bleak enough winter that was.

'It need not be so warm,' Hew said. *Not for Andrew Wood.*

'When a man comes to another's house, with intent of threat, then that is hamesucken,' he remarked to Nicholas.

'Do you think,' his friend replied, 'that he intends to threaten you?'

'I have no earthly notion what he may intend. I wish that you would watch him, and comment on his character.'

Nicholas demurred. 'I am a poor judge of men.'

'You are pure in heart. Then look into his heart, and tell me if you see a soul.'

'You seem to speak,' said Nicholas, 'as though you had invited the devil to the hearth.'

'Though he comes uninvited, so I feel I have,' admitted Hew.

By the striking of the clock at the kirk tower of St Salvator's, Sir Andrew Wood arrived upon the quarter hour, that followed after two. At Kenly Green, the time was measured loosely by the sun, the turning of the tide and the browning of the pie, which, by two o'clock, was slightly overdone, its sweetly pungent liquor bursting from the seams. It lay upon the board, in a fragrant pool of stickiness. It was, thought Hew, too good for Andrew Wood.

The coroner had left his servant waiting by the door.

'Will your servant sit with us, or in the kitchens down below?' Hew inquired politely.

'He will not,' said Andrew Wood. He had taken off his gloves, yet had not removed his sword. The servant at the door was fully armed. 'He will remain until I leave, and what he may do then, will depend on you. Who is this?' he demanded, glancing at Nicholas.

'Nicholas Colp, my secretary,' said Hew.

'*Nicholas Colp.* I know the name.' The coroner allowed his eyes to rest on Nicholas, who did not flinch, but met his scrutiny with quiet, measured gaze.

'You came into the king's will. Indicted for a felony,' the coroner remarked.

Hew replied for Nicholas. 'You are well informed.'

'Quite so. He may leave us,' answered Andrew Wood. Nicholas flushed, glancing at Hew. Hew said, 'Nicholas may stay, for he is in my confidence. He always dines with me.'

'Though he may have your confidence, yet he does not have mine,' said Andrew Wood.

'This, sir, is my house,' objected Hew. 'And Nicholas remains. For if the matter here is secret, I shall want a secretar. And if is not secret, then there is no cause for my secretar to go.'

Sir Andrew Wood said coldly, 'I advise you, sir, do not chop logic with me.' He turned to speak to Nicholas. 'I think you will not mind to take your dinner in the kitchens, among the other servants in the house?'

'I do not mind it,' Nicholas replied. 'By your leave,' he said quietly to Hew, 'I will go back to the library.'

Hew sighed, 'As you will.' The servant at the door stepped aside to let him pass.

'You have a done a great discourtesy,' Hew accused the coroner, 'to my dearest friend.'

Sir Andrew was amused. 'Was that your dearest friend? I thought your dearest friend was Doctor Locke.'

'My other dearest friend,' said Hew, blushing at the foolishness.

'You have an open heart, my friend, that you should guard more closely.'

'I am not your friend,' Hew blurted out, before he could restrain himself. He felt that he was drawing closer to the precipice, about to plunge headlong into the abyss with his horse. He dearly wished that Nicholas had stayed.

'So I do infer,' Sir Andrew smiled. 'Yet I am glad to note your evident hostility does not extend so far as to blight your hospitality. I see you have a banquet set out on the board. What is in the pie?'

'Conies,' Hew confessed, 'from our warrens in the wood, baked in their own blood, with a wine and sorrel sauce.'

The coroner approved, 'A ripe autumnal feast.' He took up a serving spoon, and cut into the pie.

'I will call the serving lass,' said Hew.

'No servants, I implore. Let us manage by ourselves.' Sir Andrew ladled steaming flesh and juices to a plate and handled it to Hew, who took his seat reluctantly. It struck him as absurd that he was served his dinner at his own house and great hall, unwilling and ungrateful, by the coroner of Fife.

'It is better,' said Sir Andrew, 'if we are not overheard; as you have learned from the example of your colleague, Bartie Groat.' He wiped his mouth fastidiously, though Hew had seen no trace of liquor pass his lips. The coroner poured out the wine and gave a cup to Hew, as if he were the master in someone else's house. He followed Hew's quick glance towards the servant at the door. 'He remains there till I leave.' Sir Andrew read Hew's mind. 'At which time, you may serve him as you will, for he is to remain with you until you go to Ghent.'

'Am I to go to Ghent?' demanded Hew, in mingled indignation, excitement and surprise. 'To *Ghent!*'

'As I dare to hope; that you may find the answer to the riddle of the mill. Take Jacob's book and letters to the beguinage.'

'What makes you think the answer lies in Ghent?' asked Hew.

'For it is plain enough we have not found it here. And Jacob had a secret purpose when he put that windmill on the ship. So much is implicit in the words that he has written to his wife: *I feared he had suspected me, and found out my intent.* It seems that only she can tell us what he meant by it. I have a feeling that our friend was sent by someone else. He said as much to Maude, for as you will infer, I too did take the time to question her.'

'He said,' remembered Hew, 'that he was not himself, as he wrote also in the closing of his letter, in the rigour of his sickness, *And how then should you know me, when I do not know myself?*' The pattern of the words stayed pressed upon his mind, the dark and hopeless franking of a last despair.

'So he may seem,' Sir Andrew said, 'a man bewitched, transfigured in his sickness from his own true form.'

'As he was, from conscience, as I think,' said Hew.

'Perhaps. And yet,' reflected Andrew Wood, 'I think that Maude mistook the words that Jacob said to her. My man that kens the

189

Flemish has informed me *Ik niet mijn eigen ben* means not, as Maude supposed, *I am not myself,* but rather *I am not my own.'*

'*I am not my own?*' repeated Hew.

'Aye. Tis plain enough. He told her he was someone else's man. And so I bid you find whose man he was, and with what dark purpose he came here to these shores. The windmill has a force in her that seems to be malevolent. For even now her dizzy sickness turns us upside down, while honest men have died for her. I fear her for a Trojan horse, sent to bring us tumbling to our graves.'

'Then you should take her down,' suggested Hew, taken by surprise at the frankness of this confidence.

'I wish to God I could,' the coroner said fervently, 'and yet, I fear, by doing so I might unleash more horrors in her wake. For all, I cannot quite disperse the deeper dread of witchcraft. Supposing she were cursed?'

'You do not believe that,' Hew assured him, 'For you are strong-reasoned, and an honest, doubting man.'

'Ah, but do I not?' the coroner demurred. 'What *is* a curse? Is it a real, and a palpable truth, or a sick man's terror, that starts us from our sleep? I do not understand what these forces are, or by what means they are sent here to unsettle us, but I know that they do unsettle us. You have witnessed their effect upon the town. I see no other way that this chaos will be stilled, unless we trace the whirl-wind to the place from where it came.'

'But why do you send me?' questioned Hew.

'Have I not said?' Sir Andrew answered wearily. 'So that we might know the nature of the threat, in finding out its source, and better understanding it, were better able to defend ourselves. Find why Jacob put that windmill on the ship, and at whose request.'

'That is not my question,' Hew repeated, 'Why would you send *me?*'

'Because you have a knack in finding secrets, that has not gone unnoticed,' the coroner explained.

'It seems you have been watching me,' Hew reflected wryly.

'Many men are watching you,' answered Andrew Wood. 'And it were well, that you were made aware of it. You have come into the notice of the king. The king thought well of you – the king *thinks* well of you,' he corrected quickly. 'Where the king takes notice, other eyes will turn. You saved a man, and you condemned a man, that some did count as curious.'

'Not curious at all,' Hew disagreed, 'when I am trained up as an advocate.'

'And yet you do not practise as one,' Andrew Wood observed. 'I wonder, why is that?'

'Because I would not be a man for hire,' owned Hew.

'Ah, is that so? I had a notion,' Wood allowed a smile, 'that it might be something of that sort. Nonetheless, it is my hope, that you will accept this small commission.'

'And suppose that I do not?'

'That is ill-advised. Yet it must remain as your prerogative.'

Hew sat thoughtful for a moment, before he pointed out, 'The millers in the town were killed by human agency.'

'So I understand,' the coroner agreed.

'And if I am removed to Ghent, then I will have no chance of finding out the killers.'

'I have considered that. And yet it seems to me, in spite of your best efforts, that the trail goes cold. The faces of the killers have been hidden in the crowd.'

'That is the case,' admitted Hew.

'Then so it seems to me that there is little purpose in your staying here in town. It is rather to be hoped that a distant, measured gaze may turn a sharper angle on the people in the crowd, where from a close perspective, your vision may be skewed. And I shall set the garrison to closely guard the mill, and make it known that no decision will be made upon her fate, until we have the news that you report from Ghent. And that, I think, will stay the killer's hand, that by the grace of God, we may see no more deaths. And meanwhile, no petitions shall be heard.'

'Nor that of your own brother?' Hew inferred.

The coroner replied, 'I do not understand you, sir.'

'Your brother, Robert Wood, who has been most assiduous in his claims to the windmill.'

'Ah, now, I see!' Sir Andrew Wood acknowledged, for the first time, smiling openly. 'You have fallen for the common misconception that I favour my own brother, Robert Wood. Aye, you do think that – and yet there's more!' The coroner began to laugh. 'You must learn to dissemble, Hew! You think that I am sending you to Ghent, to protect my brother from suspicion of these crimes. Yet, I can assure you, that is not the case.'

He was serious again. 'Do you have any reason to suspect my brother?'

Hew admitted he had not. 'Yet both the men who died were engaged to work his mill.'

'That is true enough,' conceded Andrew Wood. 'Yet since the deaths were plainly to his disadvantage, he can hardly be indicted on that count. You should know, sir, that my brother is no different in my eyes from any other man. And if you bring me evidence that Robert is a murderer, then I will take him to the gibbet and hang him there myself. And I will do it without passion or pity, or conscience, or grief. So you must understand me, if you are to be my man.'

'God help me, for I do,' said Hew. 'And though I will go to Ghent for you, I will not be your man.'

'Then I doubt that must suffice,' the coroner said cheerfully. 'In truth though,' he concluded, 'there may be a reason yet to keep you far from Robert, for his silly young wife Clare has lost her heart to you.'

'But we have scarcely met!' Hew protested with a start.

'Yet you have impressed her. For it was at their house I heard your praises sung, not, as I misremembered it, by Robert, but by Clare. Clare is weak and vulnerable, and women of her sort are more treacherous and deadly than the villain with his sword, for they twine their grasping fingers in the sinews of your heart. Beware her, Hew, and all her kind,' Andrew Wood advised.

'I fear that you have lost me, sir,' Hew shook his head in bafflement. 'For I have not the slightest notion what you mean.'

'Then see you keep it so. As to the matter, now,' the coroner returned, 'I have brought with me the letters and book, that I wish you to take with you to the beguinage in Ghent, to the woman, Beatrix, to whom they are addressed. Take also Jacob's ring, which you will recover in the morning from Professor Locke. You may spend a moment in your sister's house, making your farewells, yet your visit must be brief. There is a ship sailing from Dundee to Campvere. God willing, it will sail in four days' time; since winter now draws close, boats are few and far between. Once you are in the nether lands, you will have four or five weeks, at the most, before the last ship sails, or you may find yourself stranded until spring. Michael here will go with you, and take you to the ship.'

'There is no need for that,' objected Hew. The coroner ignored him. 'Michael,' he repeated, 'will take you to the ship. I have letters here prepared for the shipman, Master Beck, and for George Hacket, who is our Conservator at the staple of Campvere. They will furnish you with everything you need. From Campvere, you must make your way to Ghent, by whatever means you can. You will understand, the countries are at war, and our influence does not extend beyond the port of Vlissingen. I do not know if the roads or waterways are passable. Hacket will be better placed to tell you more.

'I will furnish you with all the papers you will need. As you are aware, you will require a passport when you leave Campvere; the staple is itself a special case and you may assume you are on Scottish soil, such privilege as you will find there extended to you. Consider it safe haven, and Hacket as your friend. Trust those he trusts, and I would advise you, no one else. Always expect the worse, until you know the better of a man. Yet that lesson as I know, you have learned from your experience.'

Hew flinched at this, as Andrew Wood went on, 'Four sets of papers are required, together with the wherewithal for bribes, as you are to pass from place to place. And Hacket will provide a man, that kens the Flemish tongue.'

'I do not want a man, for I prefer to go alone,' Hew retorted quickly.

Sir Andrew sighed. 'But that is rank stupidity, as you must surely know,' he pointed out. 'Since you do not know the politics, or lying of the land, and you do not ken the Dutch, and the country is at war, then tis plain enough to see that you cannot go alone. Hacket will provide a man, and that will be an end to it.'

Hew had to concede there was some sense in this, yet privately determined he would hire a man, and not of Hacket's choice, who was no doubt in the pocket of Sir Andrew Wood.

'And the man that he provides,' Sir Andrew Wood concluded, 'will go with you to Ghent. Are we then agreed?'

'We are agreed,' said Hew. 'Yet may I ask you something?'

'Aye, you may.'

'You are Lord Comptroller to the royal court. The man that is the pocket to the king.'

'For my sins, I am.'

'And yet the king no longer has control.'

The coroner corrected him. 'The king is safe and well, and we have stable government, under the Earl of Gowrie.'

'And what of Monsieur d'Aubigny, the so-called Duke of Lennox?'

'The so-called Duke of Lennox,' Andrew Wood repeated, 'is no longer in the close sphere of King James' influence. He is expected, very shortly, to depart for France. It is a state of affairs that sits well in London, with the Queen Elizabeth. And I myself cannot be sorry his excesses have been curbed, for as you have observed, I hold the purse strings to the pockets of the king. Does that answer your question?'

'It does not, sir,' Hew challenged boldly. 'For I would wish to know whence your commission comes.'

'As I think you do know,' answered Andrew Wood, 'I have it from the Crown.'

'Ah, the Crown!' smiled Hew. 'And what is that? Is that King James, or Gowrie? Is it Arran, or Lennox, or the lord enterprisers? You say that I am watched; then tell me who is watching me. Tell me, if you will, whose man are you?'

'I think you understand, I cannot answer that,' the coroner returned.

The next day, Hew set out, with Sir Andrew's servant Michael at his side. The coroner had also left behind a horse, which Michael would return to him once Hew was on the ship. He was glad enough to leave Dun Scottis safely banked, where a quiet winter pasture kept him safe from risk, for Dun Scottis was a horse who seldom travelled well. He wrapped the documents carefully, mindful of past accidents. Yet the presence of the escort, and the unfamiliar mare, felt faintly disconcerting, as though he were a renegade and taken under guard. Hew himself was armed with dagger and a sword, and in command of both, in case of dire necessity. He made the man stand patient while he broke his fast, more to prove a point than from a wish to cause delay, for the thought of an excursion, on this bright October day, had wakened up an impetus he realised that he had not felt for several sluggish months. In his inner heart, he was anxious to be off. He forced himself to stay awhile, and sit through the formalities of breaking bread with Nicholas. And at his friend's request, he knelt awhile to pray with him, that he should not depart without the blessing of the house.

The gift horse was nimble and slight, taking to the track with a lightness, ease and grace that cast a poor reflection on the dull trudge of Dun Scottis. Hew resolved to enjoy the ride, in the cool fresh sunlight, and ignore the brooding presence of the servant by his side. He gathered momentum, flying on the wind at a speed Dun Scottis had not thought of in his dreams.

'You must pace the horse, else you will tire him out afore we reach the ferry port,' the man advised repressively. He spoke no other word for the whole of the four miles.

Hew dismounted at the abbey wall, and gave the man his horse to hold, walking to the Swallow Gait. Since it was early still, he found both Giles and Meg at home. They were sharing breakfast in the nether hall, with Matthew settled in Meg's lap. Hew noticed that his upper bands were loose, and his fists waved free. 'The fury is unbound.'

'It is only for a moment,' Meg explained. She caught the infant's hands. 'He is about to have his bath. Would you like to see it, Hew?'

'I do not think so,' answered Hew. He supposed that infants, since they must be swaddled, also must be washed. He could not for a moment think why he might want to see it.

'For certain,' Giles said dotingly, 'Hew must see him bathed.'

'Another time,' said Hew, 'for I am going to Ghent.' He took a childish pleasure in their faces as they gawped at him, which later he remembered with regret.

'I do not like it, Hew,' concluded Meg, once Hew had told his tale. 'I do not like it well at all. Why would he send you far away, at this unhappy time? Surely, he can use you better here?'

'There is some little sense in it,' reflected Giles. 'And yet I think the profit there may not be worth the risk. The countries are at war.'

Meg set Matthew back into his crib and began to rock him gently with her foot.

'Do not eat the damsons,' cautioned Giles, 'or they will give him colic.'

'So you have informed me, several times. I do not think that he should go,' said Meg. 'For it will prove too dangerous.'

'You ken your brother well enough by now, to know that you have put the devil's argument. Tis danger that attracts him, beyond doubt,' Giles returned.

'Then tell him,' pleaded Meg, 'he must not go.'

'I cannot, for you know that he will do what he will.'

'Your pardon, I am here and party to your argument,' grinned Hew. 'Your husband is correct, I am resolved to go, though not through any urge to risk my life.'

'You see, Meg, it is hopeless!' answered Giles.

'I promise you, I do not look for danger,' Hew replied more seriously. 'Yet when I see the two of you, with Matthew so content, then I am the more convinced of it, that I should take the letters back to Beatrix and her child.'

'That is a kind commission, and a cruel one, too,' said Meg.

'So I understood it when I undertook the charge.'

'What are less clear to me,' Giles considered thoughtfully, 'are the deeper motives of Sir Andrew Wood.'

'I have the sense,' said Hew, 'It is some kind of test.'

'A test of what?' asked Meg.

'I do not know. The coroner has intimated I am being watched.'

'How, watched? By whom?' asked Giles.

'He declines to say. And yet, tis plain enough to put me on my guard.'

'Then you must take great care.'

'I see and apprehend it,' Hew agreed.

'But you know that he does not,' Meg observed, despairing, as her brother left. 'For though he apprehends the danger, he will blunder into it.'

Giles broke off a piece of bannock and began to butter it. 'For sure, he is your brother, Meg. He knows no other way.'

Chapter 17

Mal de Mer

The journey to the ferry port passed with little incident, and still less conversation, as the coroner's man Michael refused stubbornly to talk. His patter was restricted to 'Ah dinna ken,' with a rare and grudging 'Mebbe' where the question had been forced. Hew was glad enough to see an end in sight, as they crossed the river Tay to Broughty Ferry. From there they rode the few miles to Dundee, to settle for the night at the tavern on the shore, where the *Yellow Caravel* was moored beyond the dock. Hew was shaken from his sleep at the first faint trace of dawn, and delivered to the shipman, captain Beck, while Michael took the horses and his leave. Hew felt no regret to see him go.

The master of the *Caravel* was genial and garrulous, and promised Hew a tranquil passage on his ship. The journey, he advised, would last a mere five days, and Hew would have the comfort of the captain's cabin.

'I cannot take your quarter,' Hew objected.

'Nay, sir, so you shall,' the shipman puffed out generously. 'The *Caravel* is light, and no so well equipped for gracing special guests. The great, or captain's, cabin is the only one we have. The merchants here make do wi' pallets under deck.'

'Then so shall I,' said Hew.

The shipman would not hear of it. 'Nay, sir, not at all. You shall have it, sir, and gladly, by order of the coroner of Fife.'

He furnished Hew with bedding, cups and plate, which were tied up in a roll and strapped up to his saddle bags, ready to be shipped out to the *Yellow Caravel*.

Having nothing else to do, Hew wandered to the shore, and stood to watch the loading of the ship, the to and fro of little boats with baskets, creels and crates. Among the milling crowds, he heard the rustle of a woman's shot silk dress. It took him for a moment to another time and place; another ship set sailing from the port of Leith, where the light had faltered in a pink-streaked sky. He saw her grey eyes mocking, in the turning of the crowd, the shiver of a ghost in the dark flame of her hair and in the flawless whiteness of her skin. For a heartbeat, as he stood, he whispered to the wind. The woman stirred and smiled, holding fast his gaze. Hew coloured. 'Ah, forgive me. I mistook you for a friend.'

'Is that so?' She came close. 'Who was your friend?'

'It was a mistake. It does not matter now.'

'It was *Catherine*, that you said.'

She was teasing and inquisitive, and he was conscious that he had to shake her off. For of course, he was aware that she could not be Catherine, that the half-light of the harbour and the bobbing of the boats had thrown up ancient ghosts, that caught him unawares.

'Another lass, another quay,' he said regretfully.

'Your pardon, sir.' She would not let him go. Though she spoke low and softly, she was very young, and another, quite another, sort of lass. The brightness of her hair and the pallor of her skin were coloured by her art, and her softly ruffled silks were the loose appropriation of another woman's gown. In common parlance, she was called a common drab, though nothing, as it seemed, could be less appropriate. 'Your pardon, sir, but are you going to travel on that ship?'

She had a strange way of talking, open and precise, as if she had been schooled. Hew thought it very likely that she had been schooled. He ought to shake her off. Instead, he answered, 'Aye. Why do you ask?'

'It is only that . . .' she started and broke off. 'I have no right to ask it, sir. I'm sorry I have troubled you.'

'But you have not.'

199

It was money that she wanted, he supposed. And she had given him the chance to turn his back, and fend her off, and he had failed to take it.

'I wondered, sir, if you might vouch for me?'

Hew was astonished. 'Vouch for you? As what?' He wondered if she wanted letters of testimonial for working at the mill. The whole thing had the tenor of a curious dream, in the fragile morning light. He had the sense that he had met with her before.

'My husband is a captain in the Scots Brigade, under Colonel Balfour. He is presently in barracks at the port of Vlissingen. He sends for me to join him,' she explained. 'I have money for my passage on that ship.'

'Truly?' Hew said sceptically.

'Aye, sir, truly. Would you like to see it?'

'Thank you, not at all. What is your name?'

'Elizabeth. But Colonel Balfour calls me Bella.'

'Colonel Balfour does?' he asked, incredulous.

'Did I say Colonel Balfour?' she answered with a smile. 'I meant my husband, George. George is very anxious I should join him at the barracks. He is lonely there. And he will send a man to meet me at Campvere. And I am afeared to travel on that ship. There are no other women, and the sailors here are rough and wild. I wonder, might I travel under your protection? I want nothing from you, sir, and I shall not impose on you.'

'But since you do not know me,' Hew observed, 'how can you be sure of my protection?'

'I cannot, sir, of course,' Elizabeth agreed. 'And yet I feel that, strangely, we were meant to meet. And I know you felt it too, when you called that name. There is a bond between us.'

'Ah, no, no, no, no!' Hew shook his head. 'I will not have that! When I called out to you, it was a mistake. Forgive me, mistress, but I cannot travel with a woman that I do not know. Pray make yourself known to the shipmaster. He will ensure that your journey is safe.'

Elizabeth said meekly, 'Aye, sir, you are right, and it was foolish to expect it. I am sorry that I have disturbed your peace.'

She quickly moved away, and Hew had all but forgotten her, when he came to board the small boat that would take him to his cabin in the *Yellow Caravel*, to find her in the grip of one of the sailors, while another struck her hard across the face. Hew stepped in at once. 'I do not like to see you strike a woman,' he said coldly.

The sailor asked, 'Why not?'

'That is not a woman, sir,' his colleague echoed reasonably. 'She is a common whore.'

'She is under my protection.'

'She is what? Oh Jesus Mother Christ,' the second sailor swore, and spat into the sand. 'Ye will have to take it up with Master Beck.'

The genial captain soon appeared, and Hew demanded of him, 'Has this woman not paid passage for the ship?'

'She has paid it, aye,' admitted Master Beck, 'but there was a mistake. She shall be reimbursed.'

'There is no mistake. She will come aboard, under my protection.'

'Under your protection?' The shipmaster was startled. 'Oh, no, son – sir – I dinna think that a guid idea. The law forbids us to transport a woman to Campvere, unless she is of proven character, someone's daughter, or his wife.'

'Elizabeth is someone's wife. Her husband is Captain George . . .?' Hew looked to Elizabeth. 'Captain,' she confirmed.

'Captain George *Captain* of the Scots Brigade, stationed now at Vlissingen, under Colonel Balfour,' Hew reported smoothly.

'Colonel Balfour? Ah, I do not think so, sir.'

'You do not think there is a Colonel Balfour?'

'Of course there is a Colonel Balfour,' Elizabeth said huffily. 'He calls me Bella.'

'I have no doubts of Colonel Balfour,' Beck concluded with a sigh. 'Take her wi' ye, if you will. But keep her out of trouble on the ship.'

Hew saw her next on the *Yellow Caravel*, shortly after they set sail. Already, he was feeling queasy, and it did not help that he had gone on deck to see the Dundee windmill circling in the distance, turning its white sails against a darkening sky.

'Where we are going, there are a good many of those,' Elizabeth remarked.

'Aye,' he said shortly. He had no wish to encourage her.

'I heard that the captain had given you his cabin,' she tried next, like a bairn that came fishing through his pockets to find sweets. Sucket candies, in a box. Marmalades and sugar plums. He closed his eyes in horror, at the last thing he should think of now, but found it did not still the giddy motion of the ship. 'Do not say a word. Do not even think it,' he replied.

She pouted. 'Why are you so cross? You never used to be so cross.'

'What?'

'You never used to be so cross. You liked me, then.'

Hew demanded, '*When*?'

Elizabeth seemed not to hear. 'I forgot to thank you. Colonel Balfour will be pleased.'

'I pray you, now, do not pretend. There is no husband,' Hew informed her, 'in the Scots Brigade.'

'You, sir, are quite wrong,' Elizabeth replied, 'for there are a good many husbands in the Scots Brigade. And all of them are pleased to see me. Especially Colonel Balfour. He calls me . . .'

'*Bella*, aye, I know,' Hew groaned. 'Please go away.'

'But I have not thanked you yet,' she said.

Hew lost his balance as a wave of sickness struck him. Elizabeth, distracted for a moment, turned. '*He* likes me too,' she pointed to a merchant walking on the deck. His name is Archie Chandler, and he likes me very much.'

'Then perhaps you should attach yourself to him, instead of me.' Hew fought against the dizziness, feeling his gorge rise. He tried to close his eyes again, but still the windmill turned.

'But I,' replied Elizabeth, 'do not like *him*. Archie Chandler is a brute. I saw him strike his servant full across the face, and burst his poor nose open like a plum. That was uncalled for, I think. Why do you not have a servant?'

'Elizabeth, desist!' Hew could hold to decorum no longer; he fled to the ship side and vomited into the spray. Elizabeth came after him, 'You are sick!'

'Clever lass! Well done!' Shakily, he wiped his mouth.

'Yet the waves here are not very fierce.'

'Aye, I confess, I have no stomach for the sea. It is a weakness, of which I have two. I am a poor sailor, and a poorer judge of character, else you would not be standing by me on this ship.'

Elizabeth ignored the slight. 'In truth, you don't look very well. You should ask your sister for some physic.'

Hew, about to spew again, stared at her instead. 'What do you know of my sister?' he quizzed.

'That she is kind, and not as cross as you.'

'Who are you?' Hew demanded.

'You knew me once. You liked me, then,' she answered wistfully.

'But I could not have known you, unless you were a child . . . You are Jennie Dyer!' he exclaimed.

'I was, once. Not now.'

'What are you doing here? I thought you went to France?'

'I did. I met a fine man there. Fine and brave and *old*. I lived with him until he died, and then his family turned me out, and I went up to Vlissingen with Colonel Balfour. But I was hamesick, then,' she sighed, and spoke in the vernacular, 'and thought I would come back, to see my brithers and the bairns. You would think that after a' that time they might be pleased to see me. And yet it seemed that they were not. I bided for a while at the haven at Dundee, but the menfolk there are miserly and cruel, and now I'm growing old, my looks are all but gone,' she finished plaintively.

'What age are you now, then? Sixteen?' She was flawless, beneath her thick paint.

'All but,' she agreed.

'You dyed your hair.'

'Of course I did. For was I not the dyer's child? Now I go back to join the soldiers at the camp. It is a rough and ready trade.'

'And it must be a dangerous one,' Hew reflected soberly.

'Sometimes. But it is a *life*. I suppose you do not want to take a turn?' She grinned at him. 'For free?'

'You suppose quite rightly.'

'Tis pity, then. But whisht, for here comes Archie Chandler!'

The merchant sidled up and cleared his throat, 'Good sir, may I know your terms?'

Hew stared at him. 'Your pardon, sir?'

'The young lass there. What terms?'

'I do not understand you,' answered Hew.

'Come now, sir, do not pretend. For I am discreet, and we are both of us men of the world. I beg you, name your price.'

'If you do allude to what I must suppose,' Hew replied coldly, 'then you impugn this lady's honour, and do hurt to mine. Do I understand, you take me for a pandar?' He drew back his cloak to place a hand upon his sword. Chandler stepped back, startled and confused. 'Beg pardon,' he stammered. 'As I do assure you, I meant you no offence. I had not understood the lady was . . . reserved.'

'She is under my protection,' Hew declared.

'Aye, for sure,' the merchant muttered, backing off.

Elizabeth burst out laughing, and threw her arms around Hew's neck. 'Oh, you poor dear fool! How sweet you are!' She hurried after Chandler, calling, 'Master Archie, wait!'

'Jennie! Don't!' cried Hew. But Jennie paid no heed, and another wave of sickness sent him heaving from the deck.

He spent the next four days and nights inside the captain's cabin, where he sometimes stirred, and sometimes slept, and sometimes spewed and sometimes groaned, until upon the morning of the fifth day he turned blearily to find the morning light had filtered through the slats and that Jennie twitched the curtains that were closed around his bunk.

'Jennie, you cannot come here,' he groaned.

'I came to tell you,' she said sweetly, 'that the ship is come to dock, for we are at Campvere, and you must now get up. And what a sight you are! Still sick, for all these days. You want a proper lassie looking after you. Braw, it is, in here,' she looked round appraisingly. 'All that Archie Chandler wis a bed roll fu' of straw.' She veered between the fine talk of the court and the brash and breezy banter of the common whore.

Hew tried to sit up shakily. 'You have no sea legs, right enough.' Jennie pursed her lips. 'Has it always been like that?'

'It has grown much worse,' he told her, 'in the last few months.'

'And what has made it worse, I wonder?'

Hew resisted stubbornly, 'I do not know.'

'You dinna ken? I doubt you do. What happened to you, in the last few months, that made you sick at sailing?' she persisted.

'I suppose it was that . . . my horse capsized a ferry boat, and I almost drowned,' admitted Hew.

'You see? You do ken what it was. It is your fear of drowning, not the rocking of the boat, that makes your stomach sick,' she concluded shrewdly. 'It's all in your mind. Like a man I once kent, who couldna keep his end up.'

'I am much obliged to you,' he answered wryly, retching in the chamber pot.

'Not much use in that when your belly's dry as dust. Suddenly, and unexpectedly, she kissed him on the cheek. 'I'm no that proud mysel'', she added as an afterthought, 'but you might want to have a wash.'

Unconsciously, Hew touched the place where she had kissed 'What was that for?'

'It was to say goodbye. For I must slip away, when we are off the boat. I cannot let them catch me. And it is to say that I am sorry.'

'What are you sorry for?' he asked.

She answered, wickedly, 'The trouble you are in.'

The boat had come to rest at the Scots quay in Campvere, where the captain and his crew now bustled back and forth, unloading hides and wool into the stores and warehouses that lined the busy pier. Across the narrow strip of water, Hew could see the bright facade and fine Dutch gables of the factors' houses, high windows flanked with wooden shutters, glazed and crossed with lead. One bore a small carved lamb set into the stonework – the mark of the wool merchant, surely? 'I made my wealth from wool,' it spoke, 'and from my wealth, I made this house, which will stand living testament long after I have gone.' It reminded Hew a little of James Edie, who bore the baxters' stamp in the golden sheaf of wheat he wore pinned onto his cap, both badge of his profession, and mark of his success. The lamb house had a twin, with a carving of a round-beaked, bulbous bird, which Hew could not identify, and the significance of which was lost on him. A family name, perhaps? And beyond these fair proud houses ran a row of streets, through town hall and marketplace, towards a gothic church, whose grandeur and great size appeared to dwarf the little town, surrounded on all sides by the river and the sea.

Struggling still to stand, Hew was the last to disembark from the *Yellow Caravel*, tripping weak and shakily along the narrow plank. Since he had not yet found his sea legs, he might well have hoped that the grip of terra firma would hold him in her grasp. Yet this proved not the case, for no sooner had his land legs made contact with the earth than they gave way and crumpled. Hew fell tumbling to the ground.

'Ah, no you don't, young master, up ye come!' He heard a harsh voice ringing in his ear, as he was roughly seized and pulled back on his feet. 'Ye are wanted in the Scots house, and will come precipitate.' This was not the gracious welcome Hew might have expected, from the courtesy and deference he had met with on the ship. He looked round for the shipman, Master Beck, who was watching the unloading of his cargo in the dock. The crates, sacks and tuns were winched from the ship and trundled off in carts. Beck gestured reassuringly. 'I will be there, by and by. Give my best respects to the Conservator.'

Hew was taken from the harbour up towards the marketplace, where the Scottish nation had their lodgings, close to the town hall. Here the merchants ate and slept, and enjoyed the privilege of tax free meat and drink, while in the stadhuis they held court, according to Scot's law. Inside, he found the office of the Scots Conservator, occupied already by the merchant, Archie Chandler. George Hacket sat before them at a writing desk. Chandler cried at once, leaving Hew in no doubt who had called for his arrest, 'This is the ruffian I have accused!'

Baffled, Hew answered, 'Of what?'

'Of perfidy and infamy of a most pernicious kind.'

'Your pardon, sir,' Hew turned to appeal to the Conservator, 'but may I know the nature of this charge?'

'You speak, sir, as and when you are addressed,' the Conservator retorted, which did not seem the most auspicious start. 'The nature of the charge, of which you stand accused, is one of theft.'

'Aye,' said the merchant, 'Can you deny, you robbed me?'

'I can, and do,' Hew answered in astonishment. 'Yet what is it that you suppose you have lost?'

'My purse, sir, while I slept, was taken from my pocket by your little whore,' Chandler swore indignantly.

Unconsciously, Hew smiled. 'Ah, Jennie, you minx,' he applauded her, under his breath.

'You see, sir,' cried the merchant, 'how the villain smiles? I think that we have caught a viper in our midst, that flees from darker waters he has stirred at home, supposing his iniquities are hidden from our courts.'

'In truth,' admitted Hew, 'I had not realised that on coming to Campvere, I left such devastation in my wake, or that I should be taken for a brigand.'

'It seems to me, sir, that you think this is a jest; yet I assure you, you will not be laughing when the noose is at your neck,' the merchant sneered. 'Is that not so, now, Master Hacket?'

'No court of law, that patterns on the Scots, will hang a man without he has defence, or fails to let him make his answer to the charge,' objected Hew. 'Is that not so, now, Master Hacket?'

'That is so. And yet this is no matter, sir, that you should take so lightly, for you will find,' said George Hacket, 'that we have no patience here with thieves.'

'Indeed, I do not laugh at it,' protested Hew. 'But if this merchant has been cozened by a whore, then he should take the moral, not to lie with whores, or else make honest payment to them for their pains, for surely such as lie with him are sorely put upon. I do not see at all what it has to do with me.'

'It is plain what it has to do with you,' the merchant roared, 'she is your punk.'

Hew scowled at him. 'My *what*?'

'Your harlot, sir, your hussy, drab, your kittock, pink. Is that not plain enough for you? Tis plain enough to see you were her pimp.'

'So this madman did address me on the *Yellow Caravel*,' said Hew to the Conservator, 'when as I said as plain to him, as I do to you, that I had no connection with the woman that he bought, at whatever price. Indeed, I was astonished, that he asked me to sell her to him, for, as I made quite clear, she was not mine to sell.'

'You sent her to my bed!' the merchant roared.

'Indeed, sir, I did not.'

Hacket gave a snort of irritation. He was aptly named, thought Hew, for a justice of the peace, like a humph of disapproval, or the clearing of a throat. 'Do we have this woman in our grasp?'

The guard replied, 'It seems, sir, that she slipped away.'

'Well, go and look for her! We cannot have her loose about the town. Have her stripped and whipped, and put back on the ship.'

'But she has robbed me, sir!' the merchant whined.

'True, I had forgotten that,' Hacket said judiciously, 'Then have her hanged. Will that appease you, Archie?' he demanded of the merchant.

'I suppose, sir, that it must,' Archie answered grudgingly, 'as lang as I have reparation, too, fae *him*,' he jerked a thumb at Hew.

'It seems to me,' said Hew, 'that you have been well served, and with the ready justice you deserve.'

'It seems to *me*,' returned George Hacket, 'you were best advised to hold your tongue. What creature are you, sir?'

At that moment, captain Beck appeared, announcing cheerfully, 'Good morrow, masters. All unloaded, and, I hope, all well?'

'All is not well,' Hacket said bluntly, 'since you have brought us a shipload of whores.'

'Ah,' said captain Beck, 'that was a mistake. You showed to him the letter, did you no?' he asked aside to Hew.

Hew replied, 'Not yet.'

The captain looked dismayed. 'Well, why the devil not?' he hissed.

'He has not asked for it,' admitted Hew.

'Well gie it him, now, you loun!' demanded Beck. To Hacket he explained, 'He kens nothing of this woman, for he hasnae been too well. And he has left the cabin in an awfy state. He is what ye might call an innocent abroad.'

Hew had a letter in his bag addressed to George Hacket, which bore the sheriff's seal. Though the words inside were brief, the letter seemed to take the Conservator a long while to read. At last he closed it thoughtfully, and slipped it in his coat. 'There has been a mistake here,' he informed the merchant. 'This man is here on business of the Scottish Crown, and he is not involved in a dispute with you. Therefore, I bid you beg his pardon for the slur. And further, I would counsel you, not to lie with whores. Your indiscretion shall be made known to the minister at our kirk. We have our own kirk, here,' he explained to Hew, 'according to our morals and our faith, that takes a dim view of these matters.'

'Quite properly,' said Hew.

'What!' the merchant roared. 'Am I not to have satisfaction?'

'You will beg this good man's pardon, and be satisfied with that. On your knees,' suggested Hacket.

Hew thought, in all conscience, he could not consent to that. He began to feel uncomfortable. 'No, sir, I implore you, let us part as friends,' he offered to the merchant.

Chandler thundered past him, snarling, 'I will see you damned!'

Chapter 18

A Man for Hire

George Hacket glowered at Hew. 'You are here on business of the Crown, and I have been enjoined to extend every courtesy. Yet I must warn you that I do not stand for discord here. We are accepted by the people in this town with privilege and kindness, and in return, it is our duty to respect their peace, and be sure not to offend them. We do not, sir, bring whores to their clean sheets. We do not cheat and rob from them, or pay them less than we do rightly owe. We do not sneer at their manners or their food, and while we may observe that they are fond of cabbage, and that their pottage tastes like barrels full of dust, we keep it to ourselves, and do not deign to mention it. We treat their woman civilly, and do not spit and curse when we are walking through their streets. We treat them, sir, as they treat us, as friends. And most of all, we do not shame ourselves, to squabble and to bicker with our fellow Scots, that they might think us rude, uncivil or unlearned. We not flyt or brangle, or bring riot to their streets. Do you understand, me, sir?' he iterated coldly.

'Clearly,' answered Hew.

'That I am pleased to hear. This letter states that you must go to Ghent, and asks that I provide you with a guide. The writer is presumptuous, in assuming that I have a man to spare, for that is inconvenient at this time. There are, however, several Scottish soldiers idle in the town, one of whom will no doubt serve your turn, and I will put a notice in the barracks, and have a man sent to you tonight. I suggest you leave for Ghent first thing tomorrow morning.'

211

'That is the plan,' admitted Hew.

'In which case,' Hacket said, 'you must find somewhere to stay the night. It is usual for our countrymen to stay here at the Scots house, where they may sleep and eat at the preferential rate, yet I fear your presence here has not been well received, and you must pay the penalty, of staying at the inn. Master Beck will see you to your rest, and presently you may expect a man to come to you.'

The Conservator dismissed him with a brief wave of his hand. 'I trust, sir, and hope, that we shall not meet again.'

'He does not seem to like me much,' Hew remarked to Master Beck.

'You do not need to mind him, sir, for he will see you right,' the genial captain said. 'He is a good man, in his way. He has the keeping of the Scots part of the town, and he keeps it well, but there is enough for him to oversee the commerce and the court, without he has to mind our manners too. The Dutch folk are right guid tae us, and he wad not offend them for the world.'

'No more should I,' said Hew.

'It is the matter of the whore, sir, that has vexed him,' Beck explained. 'It is a point of present law, that no wench might be brought here on a ship, unless she is a married wife of good repute, to prevent those woman whoring after soldiers, which in this time of war is now a nuisance and a scourge. The wee lass running loose is an embarrassment to Hacket, that he and I will both be called to answer for back home, if the lassie is not found.'

'Then I am right sorry,' Hew replied contritely, 'that I have caused you trouble. I had not understood the lass's full intent.'

'Aye, sir. But what is trouble, but the bared excitement of a tedious time? The world were dull without it,' answered Beck. 'Though it might have been better,' he admitted nonetheless, 'had you kept her to your cabin, and not thought to share her out.'

'But I did not . . . you mistake me, sir . . .' Hew stammered, with a blush.

The shipman winked at him. 'Whisht, son, dinna fret, for we

have all been young. Look, here we are at the inn in the tower – the Campveerse toren, they cry her; and she stands as sentry here over the town, at the end of the haven, a gate to the sea. Is she not a bonny sight? She is part of the town's old fortifications, though she has been an inn now for some eighty years.'

'She looks brave, indeed,' admitted Hew.

'And you will have a room that overlooks the wattir, and the sweetest, freshest linen anywhere in town. And the cooking is beyond compare. They do a roasted pig, where the skin is cracked black, and the fat is sweet and melted, soft into the flesh, the like of which you will not find at George Hacket's house.'

'Then it cannot be a penalty to stay here,' answered Hew.

'The penalty is in your purse, for you will pay full duty on your wine, forfeiting the privilege. Though it may hurt your pocket, tis a small price to pay. God speed, you, sir,' said Beck.

A young girl showed Hew to his room. Her name was Annet. 'The sheets are fresh for every guest,' she told him.

'Thank you, that is good to know.'

'Will you stay here long?'

'Tomorrow I must go to Ghent.'

She nodded. 'One night, then.' The girl was tall and fair, with pink scrubbed cheeks and a white linen apron and cap over her blue-striped dress. 'You speak English well,' he complimented her.

'Thank you. My father wished for me to learn. He thought it would be good for trade. You will not find it spoken so much, when you go further south.'

'Do many Scots come here?'

'Only the rich ones.' She smiled at him. 'Why do you not stay at the Scots house, sir?'

'Because I quarrelled,' he confided, 'with a merchant on the boat. A man called Archie Chandler.'

'*Ach!*' She exclaimed, with a word he did not understand.

'What did you say?'

'Your pardon. It is a bad word in the Dutch,' she admitted. 'It is the name of a disease, and I do not know the English for it. In our language, we use sickness, sometimes body parts, as expressions of disgust. My father would not like to hear me say it. But I do not like that man.'

'Nor do I,' answered Hew. 'Is your father the innkeeper here?'

'No, sir, but his friend,' the girl said enigmatically. 'The innkeeper has many friends. He is – what would you call it? – a man of diverse parts. He will find you horses to take you down to Vlissingen, once you have crossed the ferry. What will you have to eat, sir?' she changed the subject suddenly.

'What you think is best.'

Annet considered this. 'I do not know,' she said at last. 'The lobsters and the waterfowl are best, but it is now too late in the year. The roasted pork is good. But the Scots do not like to eat pork, or salad roots, or greens, or any of the things that might be good for them.'

'I will have the pork,' said Hew.

'Then I will tell the cook. We have a very good cook here. It is the cook, who cooked the fowl for Prince Willem's wedding feast. There were peacocks, and herons, and bittern, and quail.'

'That must have been a grand occasion.'

'It was, sir,' she agreed. 'But I was then a small child, and I do not remember it well. The linens and glass were brought from Middelburg. My father said a great deal of it was lost or broken. Perhaps he will marry again,' she said, a little wistfully, 'and have another feast here.'

'Why should he marry again?'

'Because a prince must have a wife, must he not? And his wife died shortly after he was shot. That was his third wife, that escaped the nunnery, the one he loved the best. Everybody loved her, and I do not think that he could love a fourth wife more.'

'You say that he was *shot*?'

'Yes, sir. Did you not know? I supposed that everyone knew,' said Annet. 'The Spanish king has put a price upon his head, of 25,000 guilders. That is more money than I have ever dreamt of. He was shot at his house in Antwerp, several months ago, and though he did not die, the shock of it has killed his wife. It is a tragic tale.'

'How did it happen?' asked Hew.

'It happened because the Prince of Orange is a good and proper prince, who always gives close counsel to those who wish to speak with him, and so he is exposed. He was shot at close range, in the face, and the force of the blast was so fierce that it blew off his assailant's hand, though it must be said that that he did not live long enough to notice it, before the prince's men had cut him down. And it were well for him he did not live long after, for the people are devoted to the prince. Well, sir,' Annet went on, 'the first that the prince was aware he had been shot was when he noticed by the smell of singeing that his ruff was on fire.'

'Good God!' Hew exclaimed. 'But had the gunshot missed him, then?'

'Indeed, sir, not! It went in *here*,' the girl gestured to her jaw, 'and came out here,' she brushed against her cheek, 'and the powder burned so hot that it closed up the wound.'

'It cauterized it?'

'I expect so,' she agreed. 'But the wound did stay not closed. And when it opened up again, his doctors could find no way to stop the flow of blood, until one found the place inside his mouth from where the issue came, and stopped with his finger, which they did, in turns, until the blood was stemmed, as I heard, after seventeen days.'

'A finger in the dyke!' smiled Hew. 'Then he has not been in command, these past few months?'

'Oh, no, sir! He has never lost command. He gave orders from his bed, and when he could not speak, for all the doctors in his mouth, he wrote the message down. He asked that his attacker should be spared. It was, of course, too late for that.'

'Annet, that is a wondrous tale.'

'He is a wondrous prince, and much loved, especially here in the

Walcheren. He seeks to free his people from the Spanish tyranny, allowing us to choose how we may say our prayers. But perhaps you also have a prince like that, in Scotland?'

'We have a young king, James,' answered Hew.

'And is he also patient, resolute and brave?'

Hew struggled with the answer. 'He is very . . . *young*,' he said at last. 'How old are you, Annet?'

'I am fourteen,' Annet said proudly.

'Then he is a little – but only a little bit – older than you,' he told her.

'Ah,' Annet allowed. 'Then perhaps he is yet to grow into it. The pork is roasting on the spit, and will take another hour or so to cook. You may come below to have a drink, and watch the boats.'

'I should like that,' answered Hew. 'I look forward to the pork. Did you know, Annet, that pigs can see the wind? They see it coloured red.'

Annet screwed up her nose. 'Who told you that?' she asked.

'A little Scottish boy.'

'And who would ask the Scots? What do they know about pigs, or about the wind?' she answered critically. 'If you want to know of wind, then you should ask the Dutch. And as to the pig, then no one but the pig knows what it sees.'

Hew did as Annet had advised, and was sitting in the window with a cup of claret wine, admiring the sunset and looking at the boats, when a gruff voice addressed him, 'You are Hew Cullan, as I must suppose?'

'I am,' admitted Hew.

'I heard that you were looking for a man.'

This stranger had the rough and ready manner of the Scottish soldier, dressed in dark brown breeks and jacket of thick wool, with a battered leather jerkin on the top. He was solid and thick set, above the middle height, with plain dark looks and thoughtful eyes that marked a clear intelligence; a force, thought Hew, to reckon with.

'I might be,' Hew said cautiously. 'Did George Hacket send you?'

216

'He might have done,' the man agreed. He lacked the air of deference that was usual in a servant, which was no disadvantage, in Hew's books. 'What's your name?' he asked.

The man said, 'Robert Lachlan.'

'Then sit down, Robert Lachlan, and tell me what you do. I want a man that kens the Flemish tongue, and knows the way to Ghent.'

'A little more than that, by all accounts,' Lachlan answered cryptically.

'What do you mean?' asked Hew.

'I saw your wee bit street lass, tumbling by the barracks.'

'She is not my . . .' Hew gave up the protest, asking, 'What has become of her? Is she safe from harm?'

'I left her on a lancer's horse, on her way to Flushing. She's *free lancing*, you might say. She telt me that you wanted looking after.' Robert Lachlan grinned.

'You are presumptuous, both of you,' Hew scowled at him. 'For I require no nurse.'

'She meant you no offence.' The soldier met his gaze. 'Hussy that she is, she took a shine to you.'

'For a servant, you are bold in your assertions,' Hew objected, less indignant than amused.

'For that I beg your pardon, sir; I am a soldier, used to speaking plain.'

'So I understand. Your manners matter less, to me, in truth, than if you know the way to Ghent,' said Hew. 'If you can take me there, I'll pay you well.'

'If you can pay me well,' said Robert with a smile, 'then I can take you there. I came from there but lately, sir. We stood in battle for her, only this last month.'

'Dear God!' answered Hew. 'Then what was the outcome?'

'The outcome, sir, for Ghent, is that the Calvinists did hold her; the Spanish retreated, and are somewhere further north. It is to be hoped that you do not meet them on your travels.'

'Yet if you are a soldier, are you not presently engaged?'

'I am at present idle, sir. In truth, I am resolved to now retire from soldiering, for I have fought here for ten years. And I thought of going home, which is why I fetched up here. If I am honest, sir, I hoped to work my passage, for I cannot pay the fare,' Lachlan answered frankly.

'Ten years in the Scots brigade! Is there no recall?' asked Hew.

'Doubtless, if I had spent ten years in the Scots brigade. I am a soldier, sir. I fought first with the Spanish, and after, with the Dutch. And lately, I have been engaged among the Scots brigade.'

'You mean you are a mercenary!' Hew exclaimed.

'I am a man for hire, sir.' Robert Lachlan answered. 'Was it not a man for hire that you required?'

Hew shook his head. 'I thought that men were dying here, for conscience, and their faith.'

'Then you know very little, sir, how wars are fought and won. Doubtless, there are some,' the soldier answered thoughtfully, 'who fight for honour, or for faith. Some for duty, some for love. Myself, I fight for money, because it is my trade.' He yawned and stretched. 'And I confess, I weary of it, grening to retire.'

Though it was plain to Hew that Lachlan saw no fault in this, he could not reconcile it with his own view of the world. 'Then you have taken arms against your fellow Scots?' he pointed out.

Robert Lachlan sighed. 'Who do you think is fighting, here?' he answered patiently.

'The Spanish,' Hew retorted, 'and the Dutch.'

'And do you then suppose the Spanish side is full of Spanish men? They're few and far between. There are Flemish, Spanish, English, Scots, Welshman and Walloons, fighting on both sides. And I have lately come from Ghent, standing with the Welsh and Scots, to save that town from falling into Spanish hands. And do you think the Flemings there were pleased to have our help?' Robert Lachlan spat onto the fire. 'They'd see us damned to hell.'

'Aye, and so they might,' Hew suggested grimly, 'when it is for fortune that you fight.'

218

'You dinnae get it, do you?' Robert said exasperated. 'Do you have your ain profession, sir? Or are you but, a *gentleman*?'

'I trained up in the law,' admitted Hew.

'As what, an advocate?' Robert Lachlan asked. It now seemed he was interviewing Hew. 'Then can you claim you do not do precisely what I do, when you stand in court? Are you not yourself, no better and no worse, than a man for hire?'

'I thank you for your trouble,' Hew replied abruptly, 'but I do not want your service. I will find another man.'

Lachlan sighed. 'Pray pardon, I speak bluntly, I do not know right well how to parley with a gentleman. I am a soldier's soldier, and a soldier's man. By your good grace, sir, I may learn my place,' he capitulated humbly.

Hew grimaced. 'Understand, I have no quarrel with the way you speak to me; I am not your master, thus you have no place. I have no doubt that what you say about the law is true, and it is why I do not practise it. Your pardon, and I mean no offence, but I cannot share my quarters, my thought and my goodnights, with a man who is a mercenary, fighting on both sides.'

'Strewth,' said Robert Lachlan. 'For a man that means no offence, you're good enough at giving it. Tis little wonder you have enemies already in the town.'

'I have no wish at all to make an enemy of you,' Hew replied sincerely. 'The truth is, Robert, you and I could not get on. We do not, and we cannot ever, understand each other. Yet since you came here in good faith, and had hoped to find a place, I gladly give you money so that you may have a drink.'

'That you will not share with me. I thank you, but I do not want your money, and I do not want your drink,' Robert said abruptly, 'if I can give you nothing in return.'

To Hew's dismay, he did not leave the inn, but joined a group of Flemish merchants drinking at the bar, whose raucous laughter soon ensuing proved him expert in their tongue, and must have cost him dearly on a common soldier's pay. The soldier's pride was hurt, as Hew supposed. In due course, Annet brought the pork, which was just as crisp and succulent as promised. He was finishing the dish, and a second cup of wine, when a messenger appeared, with a note from George Hacket. He was wanted at the Groote Kerk, straight away.

'Where, and why, and what?' he asked the boy.

'It is the great kirk on the square, the Dutch and Scottish church, for they have caught the hussy, that was brought here on the ship, and the minister is holding her for questioning,' the young boy told him breathlessly.

'Aye, then, very well,' Hew answered anxiously. 'Will you come to show the way?'

'I cannot, for I'm wanted, now, elsewhere; I am a messenger. And yet you cannot miss it, sir. It is not far.'

Robert Lachlan looked up from his stool, drinking down his cup. Once Hew had left the room, he paid his bill and went.

In the darkness, several lamps were lit, and Hew made his way from doorway to doorway, following the lights towards the market square, beyond which he could see the church. Once or twice, he felt a shadow stir, as though something followed, but turning back, saw nothing but the moon. He kept the harbour on his right, afraid of falling in the darkness, conscious of the lapping of the water on the wall. The path narrowed slightly at the entrance to the square, and there he saw a figure stepping from the shadows, and a calm voice spoke in Scots, 'Master Cullan, is it not?'

'It is, sir,' Hew confirmed it. He thought at first that the Conservator had sent out a guide, until he caught the glint of steel.

'Your purse, Master Hew,' the voice continued pleasantly, 'may purchase you your life.'

Hew had met cut throats before, and held fast his nerve. 'Aye, for certain,' he said softly. 'Take my money, spare my life. Let me find my pocket.'

He opened out his cloak, shadowing his purse, but as the stranger lunged to cut the strings, Hew drew his sword and struck. He heard a curse, the clatter of a dagger on the ground, as his assailant clutched his wrist. Hew stepped forward, 'Ah, I do not think so, friend.' This triumph proved short-lived, for a blow from behind set him thudding to the ground. Instinctively, he closed his eyes, unable to defend himself, and felt his eyelids sticking, thick with blood.

And for a while, it did not end. He knew it would not cease till he was sick and senseless, every sense distorted, heightened, stretched and flooded with the stream of blows. He heard a far off roaring, like the rush of blood, a distant curse and cry, the sound of running feet. And then, to his surprise, the onslaught stopped. Someone was sitting him upright, easing his hands from his head. 'Sit up, now, peace, you are not killed.' He saw Robert Lachlan somewhere up above.

'Chandler's men,' said Lachlan.

'How did you know?' groaned Hew.

'I followed you.'

'And why would you do that?' Hew returned suspiciously.

Lachlan looked affronted. 'I have saved your life,' he pointed out.

'So it would seem,' agreed Hew. 'But how am I to know that you are not in Chandler's pay?'

'Because, if I had been, you would be dead,' Lachlan said simply.

From the corner of his eye, Hew was looking for his sword. 'Is this what you were searching for?' Lachlan inquired. 'Better not to leave it on the ground.'

'Thank you,' Hew conceded. 'The Conservator . . .'

'Must not see you have been brawling,' Lachlan interrupted. 'For all he is a patient man, you wear his patience thin. And he is another man, that hasna taken much to you. Let us get you off the street.'

'How, brawling?' Hew objected. 'Clearly, this was a trap.'

'As I understand it, you made the first cut,' Lachlan grinned. 'And a pretty stroke it was. I had not hoped to see you fight so well.'

'Much good did it do me,' Hew acknowledged sourly. 'I missed the oldest trick, and did not watch my back.'

'Aye, well, there were three of them,' Lachlan conceded graciously. 'You had little chance. Whisht, I hear the watch. Let's get you home.'

'What about him?' As he struggled to his feet, Hew caught sight of a body, slumped in the shadows. 'Jesu, is he dead?'

'Good point.' Lachlan turned the body over with a kick, leaving Hew to wince as the figure stirred and groaned. 'Not killed,' he called out cheerfully. He kicked the man again, and pulled him to his knees. 'Open up your coat.' Robert Lachlan lifted up Hew's sword, and the man screamed in terror, as Hew shouted, 'No!'

'Dinna be a fool!' Robert snorted. He wiped Hew's bloody blade across his victim's shirt and sent him sprawling back into the dust. 'Clean and tidy,' he approved, as he returned the sword to Hew. 'Now we shall see you home. And you may thank your stars that you have not offended Annet.'

They returned to the inn, where Annet helped to smuggle them in through the back, bringing fresh towels and water to the room. Lachlan sat Hew on the bed. 'Take off your shirt!'

'I thank you, but I do not think . . .' said Hew.

'Whisht, you silly beggar, and do what you're telt,' instructed Robert Lachlan. Robert stripped the shirt from Hew's back, using it to wipe the blood from his head and face.

'That's a good shirt!' Hew complained.

'Not so good now.' Lachlan peered at the cut on his head. 'You will feel it in the morning.'

'I feel it now,' said Hew. 'And I should like to go to sleep.'

'I do not doubt it,' Robert answered grimly. 'Nonetheless, we must go to the bar. You must not appear to have been fighting. For do not doubt that Hacket's men will come.' Lachlan pressed a towel against Hew's head. 'Hold hard, and stop the bleeding. Else I will have to stitch it, and I have no wish to hear you whimper like a girl.'

'You are so very sure,' objected Hew, 'I cannot take a stitch.'

'True enough,' Lachlan said, 'that though you speak like a lass, you fight like a man. No offence.'

'Though you fight like a man, you talk like a limmar,' snorted Hew. 'None taken.'

'You have a fair few bruises there.' Lachlan examined Hew. 'And a low hit to the back. Next time you pass water, look for blood.'

'And if there is blood?' pursued Hew.

Lachlan shrugged. 'Mebbe, you might die,' he guessed.

'Jesu, thank you. Is it too much, to hope for a surgeon?' grumbled Hew.

'For certain, it is too much. Did I not tell you? We must cover up the fight.' He rummaged through Hew's saddle bags. 'Clean clothes! Then what it is to be a gentleman! Put on another shirt and coat, and come downstairs. Annet will swear blind we were not out tonight. Pull your cap well down, to hide the bandages.'

'I thank you,' Hew said awkwardly, holding out his purse.

Lachlan shook his head. 'I do not want your money.'

'I thought it was for money that you fought,' objected Hew.

'You mock me, sir. And I have saved your life; that does not mark a gentleman,' Lachlan answered quietly.

'In truth, I know that, Robert, and it is not meant,' said Hew. ''Tis simply that I do not understand. Why should you save my life? For as you said yourself, it is for money that you fight.'

'That's true enough. And yet there is another cause – not yet faith or honour, that you rate so high – why a man might fight,' Lachlan mused.

'Aye? Then what is that?'

'Pleasure!'

Lachlan burst out laughing at the horror on Hew's face, leaning forward to take up the purse. 'No, you are right. Money is the main cause. Money's good. We shall spend this spoil together, on French wine.'

Hew protested, 'Be my guest, but only, let me sleep!'

'Jesu, you are slow. Did I not tell you, that you must be seen?'

Lachlan helped to dress him in another suit of clothes and rammed the clean cap smartly on Hew's aching head.

'We shall get you drunk, or at best, seeming drunk, that will explain why you are somewhat worse for wear. Do not wriggle like a bairn,' he scolded as Hew winced. 'Remember that you are not hurt.'

'Tis hard enough that, with every part hurting,' scowled Hew.

'Come then, let us drown the pain,' Lachlan said more kindly.

His strategy proved sound, for no sooner were they seated at the bar when the Conservator appeared, flanked by the town guard. 'There has been a brangling in the street, and the perpetrators fled. I wondered what you knew of it,' he inquired abruptly. Hew felt hot and dizzy, and the sticky patch of blood was sticking to his hat. He wondered if it had begun to seep through.

Lachlan answered for him. 'My master is a little worse for wear. He has drunk a good deal of the claret wine. Is that not true, Annet?'

Annet nodded. 'He has been at it all night.'

'What happened?' Hew questioned weakly, finding his voice through the fog.

'Two of Archie Chandler's men were set on in the street. One cut through his hand, almost to the bone.'

'That sounds,' said Hew, 'like a defensive wound.'

Hacket glared at him. 'Understand, it will not do,' he answered heavily. 'We allow no fighting here.' Suddenly, he softened. 'Aye, you do look rough. Tis foolishness to drink so much; your belly will be raw still from the sea.'

'So I have warned him,' Lachlan mentioned dryly. 'He is raw through and through, and he will not be told.'

Hacket started. 'Do you let your servant speak so? Do you let him drink with you?' he asked Hew in astonishment.

'He is not . . .' Hew checked himself. 'He is not accustomed to the service of a gentleman. I have yet to break him in.'

'Aye? Well do it, soon,' the Conservator advised him. 'And God speed you on your way.'

'Am I then your servant?' Lachlan demanded once Hacket had left.

'So it would seem. God help us both,' muttered Hew. 'Tell me though, why should I trust you?'

'Why should you not?'

'Because you are a man for hire.'

'You are a rare lawyer, sir,' Lachlan retorted, 'that won't stand for hire. And yet you take your pleasure in the fight.'

'You mistake me,' Hew said softly. His bones ached, he felt dizzy, and a little sick. 'For I swear, I take no pleasure in the fight.'

'No? I saw you draw your sword without a qualm. You would rather have cut off his hand, than relinquish your purse.'

'That was instinct,' Hew protested. 'I had no desire to hurt the man.'

'Aye? A soldier's instinct. You have fought before. I saw the scars. Someone cut you with a knife. The wounds were stitched.'

'Aye, it's true, that someone tried to kill me once.'

'I'll warrant, then,' said Lachlan shrewdly, '*someone* died.'

'As it happens, someone did,' Hew stood up and sighed. 'Though not in the way you suppose. Robert, you misjudge me. And I am prepared to admit, that I have misjudged you. You are not in any way what I expected of a servant. As servitude goes, you are not very good at it. I, for my part, dislike playing master. Nonetheless, you saved my life, and if you want it still, the place is yours. Tomorrow I shall leave for Ghent. Here is money; hire fresh horses. I will pay you by the day. Now, though, I am going to bed. And, for all the world, I would not be disturbed before the morrow. You are right about one thing.'

'What is that, sir?' Lachlan asked grinning.

'I am raw to the quick,' his new master groaned.

Chapter 19

De Windmolen

There were four or five inns in Ter Neuzen, each of them marked with its own painted sign – the *Bittern*, the *Heron*, the *Hart*, the *Blue Boar* – that gave hope of comfort and welcome to all. In Scotland, the taverns were shuttered and closed, and marked after dark by a few grudging lamps, where naming and signs were unknown. And yet the promise of a warmth and welcome free to all had soon worn thin, as they were turned away from every door.

'They cannot all be full,' Hew grumbled, in the cobbled courtyard of the *Golden Orb*. It had seemed to him in any case a place of last resort, of dubious repute on the seedy side of town.

Robert Lachlan grinned. 'I think it more than likely they are not. They dinna like the English much.'

'We are not English,' Hew pointed out. He felt hungry, tired and cross, vexed by the charade that passed for hospitality among the lowland Dutch.

'Or, indeed, the Scots. They may have had some trouble,' Robert said evasively, 'with soldiers passing through the town.'

'What sort of trouble?' Hew inquired.

The soldier shrugged. 'The common sort. They brangle in the bar, and do not pay the bill, and such. I will try a little harder, at the next, to plead your case.'

And at the next, the *Rose*, he made a brave attempt, to win through shameless flirting with the lass behind the bar, who put up a fine-spirited defence. At last he left her, laughing, and reported back to Hew, 'No luck.'

226

'Why not?' demanded Hew. The sky was growing dark, and he felt the pull of suppertime.

'Her mistress will not hear of it. The last Scottish soldiers who lodged here riddled her cheese with lead shot.'

Hew gaped at him. 'Why, in pity's name, would the soldiers shoot the cheese?'

'They didna shoot it,' Robert explained patiently. 'They filled it up with shot. It is a common trick. The cheese is brought out to the table whole, on little carts. They weigh it first and after, and the customer is charged by weight for what he takes. The soldiers strive to limit the discrepancy, by making little riddles with their knives, that they fill up again with stones or musket shot. This last lot overreached themselves, and sent the cheese back heavier than when it came. Her mistress, says the lass, was not best pleased.'

Hew began to wonder whether Robert was a hindrance, rather than a help.

'Perhaps it might help more, if I spoke to them in French,' he sighed. 'Let us try the next one, here, the *Swan*.'

'Or mebbe not the *Swan*,' Robert answered quickly.

'And why not the *Swan*? Have you brangled in the bar, or made riddles in the cheese?' demanded Hew.

'Neither, I do promise you. Yet there is a matter of the lass behind the bar. It is remotely possible that she has borne my child,' the soldier answered sheepishly.

'Of which you gave no warning when I took you as a guide,' Hew said with a groan. 'Have you any other secrets up your sleeve?'

Robert did not answer this. 'I think, in view of all, we must venture out of town. According to the most obliging lassie in the *Swan*, there is another tavern on the Antwerp road, that is clean and comfortable. It is along a country track, and takes us from our way. I fear I cannot vouch for it.'

'If you are not known there, then that is for the good,' Hew replied severely. 'Since it is growing dark, then let us set our course for it, and once we have arrived there, see that you behave yourself.'

Robert fell in behind him, with a meek and quiet countenance Hew doubted would last long, and they took the low road west. The inn was four or five miles out, in deep flat swathes of countryside, with little else in sight. It stood beside an old, dilapidated barn, upon a piece of land that once had been a farm, where now a clutch of lonely chickens scratched. Beyond were fields of cabbages and rye, with a single wooden windmill on the other side, from which the inn, predictably, had taken both its name, and the picture etched crudely on its painted sign, *De Windmolen*. Hew suppressed a smile. How many inns and taverns bore that weary name, that bordered on canals and looked on quiet streets? Hundreds, he supposed. Robert stopped. 'I dinna like it,' he said bluntly. 'It is too remote.'

Hew felt a wave of irritation. 'What matters if it is remote? We shall be peaceful here.'

'Too peaceful,' murmured Robert. 'You forget, there is a war. And when there is a war, people never are at rest. We are too far from the town.'

'Then what do you suggest? We have exhausted Ter Neuzen and Sluis. And it is now too dark to go much further on.'

'Aye, very well,' Robert said reluctantly, 'but do not drop your guard.'

In contrast to the inns in town, they were welcomed by the keeper and his wife, and their daughter of sixteen, a comely girl who wore a broad-brimmed hat, as though she had been working on the farm. They were shown a whitewashed room, which overlooked the fields. Since the outlines of the windmill sails were shadowed on the walls, the inn was aptly named. The room was plainly furnished, in a simple, country style, with two small lits de camps, two stools, and blankets of bright blue. An earthen jug and candlestick were set out on the window ledge, beneath the wooden shutters open to the moon. The evening air was chill. Hew nodded at the girl. 'It's very clean.'

'The Dutch are always clean,' Robert said dismissively, as though it were an irritant, that ought to be excused. 'There is no lock here, just a bolt. Do not leave anything of value in the room.'

'There are no strangers here but us,' Hew pointed out. He unpacked his bag, and hung up his cloak, yet kept his purse and letters close inside his shirt. The soldier nodded, 'Well and good. Do not take off your sword.'

'You are too suspicious,' Hew complained. 'I see nothing wrong.'

'It is not always to be seen,' said Robert enigmatically. ''Tis more a whisper, hint or scent, that puts you on your guard.'

Hew did not take him seriously. A man who spent his life upon the other side must find it hard to trust. The welcome of the place was plain enough to see, and no other hope of shelter was on offer for some miles. The bruises he had suffered at Campvere still throbbed, and he felt tired and cold. He closed the wooden shutters upon the chill night air. The room, for all its cleanliness, still lacked a decent fire. There had been a bright warmth in the lower hall, and the smell of baking meat, that lured him like a lapdog to the hearth. 'Tell the lass, the room is fine, and we are pleased to take it. Let us go and eat.'

The bar below began to fill, and the lass was serving supper in a corner by the hearth, shuttered from the drinkers who were gathered round the bar. The men were Flemish farmers, of broad and brawny stock, oddly grim and taciturn. One of them, perhaps, was the miller from the mill, the others hands and labourers, from the fields and farms. None glanced up as Hew and Robert settled by the fire. Robert shifted restlessly. 'I do not like it, for it is too quiet here.'

'Because there are no roaring boys? The clamour and the squalor you are used to in the town? Be grateful, we have found a sober, decent place,' argued Hew.

'Mebbe,' Robert pondered. Suddenly, he grinned. 'There is a saying in the Dutch, Voor herberg, achter bordeel, that means inn at the front, whorehouse behind.'

'You think there is a brothel here?'

'I very much fear that there is not,' the soldier confessed. 'It means that things may not always be quite as they seem.'

Hew looked around, but saw little to alarm him. He wondered if the drinkers had returned here from a funeral, or else they were a much more sober breed of Dutchmen, that were not given over to rash merriment or mirth. Yet they caused him no offence, and accepted none from him, and it was far from clear what Robert's worry was. He suspected lack of sport, for Robert Lachlan's weakness was to be spoiling for a fight; he would not be content with a gentler pace of life.

'I fear you must resign yourself to have a quiet night. What do they have to eat?'

Robert called the girl, whose smile made welcome contrast to the drinkers at the bar, and spoke with her at length.

'The ordinair is eel,' he reported briefly, 'stewed in a green sauce.'

'So little,' teased Hew, 'in so many words.' Robert did not rise to this. 'Or else there is rabbit, with prunes. That costs a guilder more.'

'The rabbit, then. And you?'

'The rabbit, if you're paying.'

'Two rabbits, then, and white Rhenish wine,' suggested Hew, who did not feel like red.

Robert relayed this message, to which the girl replied. He reported with a frown. 'They have no wine but Spanish.'

'The Spanish then. Yet does it signify?' asked Hew.

Robert answered thoughtfully. 'Possibly, though likely not. It need not mark allegiance. For here, as a rule, an inn may not sell both, for fear they are tainted and mixed. Excepting that, they may serve Rhenish white and Spanish red, that cannot well be mixed, yet according to the girl, the red is Spanish too. And since they sell the Spanish, they do not sell French. Yet if you do not mind the Spanish then it does not signify.'

'I do not mind it,' answered Hew. 'Two rabbits, and a jug of *Spanish* white, will see us well enough.'

'I will stick to ale, sir, if you will. I have no wish to drink tonight, for we may want our wits.'

'For what might we want them?'

'I never drink, sir, while I work. A sober wit will see you safe to Ghent, and that is my intention. Once we are in Ghent, I will drink the taverns dry.'

'Fair enough,' sighed Hew. Robert's watchfulness was beginning to unsettle him, and he began to start at the creaking of the door. It was true that the ambience was oddly dull and dour, and that the drinkers at the bar seemed as mirthless as the grave. Hew sensed this was a place where no one would get drunk. In contrast, though, the serving lass came bustling to and fro, with a warm and bright good nature that brought the room some cheer, and the rabbit from the kitchen came steaming in its broth, with its hind legs split and roasted and a dish of buttered greens.

'These people,' muttered Robert, 'are curiously fond of eating buttered kale.' He pushed aside the cabbage in disgust. Nonetheless, the meal seemed to relax him, even as it failed to have the same effect on Hew. The wine was thin and reedy, and had a bitter taste, and as he ate and drank, he had the feeling he was watched by a figure at the bar. Robert, for his part, gave no sign he had noticed, until Hew chose to remark upon it.

'Oh aye?' the soldier turned his head. The man at the bar returned his stare, steady and belligerent.

'Well, now, so we are.' Robert wiped his mouth, stretching lazily. 'I will go and have a word with him.'

For the first time that evening, he seemed properly at ease. Hew realised he was warming to a prospect of a fight. What turned out to be a blessing in the alley at Campvere no longer seemed so welcome on the journey down to Ghent. 'If you are come to fight,' he warned, 'then you will want for work.'

'You do mistake me, sir,' Robert Lachlan said, 'if you think I look for trouble. The truth is that I know that man. I fought with him at Ghent.'

'With him, or against him?' Hew inquired astutely.

'As it happens,' Robert answered, 'both. He speaks our tongue, in a fashion, for the man is Welsh.'

'Then let us go together,' Hew proposed, 'and ask him why he stares at us.'

'Best not to, sir, for that you are a gentleman. He will not talk to you. In truth, he is an ill-bred cur. His morals are elastic, like the Welshman's hose.'

'What do you mean?' laughed Hew.

'The Welshman's hose is stretched, to any size or shape.'

'It seems you have a proverb and a prejudice,' said Hew, 'for every foreign race. Go, then, and talk to him. Yet know, that if you threaten him, then you will lose your place.'

'I understand,' said Robert, with a rare show of humility, that Hew did not believe.

He watched the soldier make his way towards the bar, and move towards the Welshman, drawing up a stool. The other man did not resist, and Hew observed him calling for a second stoup of ale, which he passed to Robert Lachlan. Presently the pair were thick enclosed in long and heavy talk. Hew left them to it for a while, feeling dull and dizzy from the close heat of the fire, before he decided to retire to bed. He made his way towards the bar.

'I am going to the room. Will you ask the girl to send another cup?' he instructed Robert Lachlan. The Welshman turned upon him with a sneer. 'So this is your new posting, Robert, nursemaid to the gentlefolk.'

In view of his instructions, Hew could hardly rise to this. Robert answered placidly. 'Aye, and I will follow you. I will not be long.'

Hew went back to the room, to find the maid had lit a fire and set fresh linen towels upon the folding beds. He sat down on the blanket, pulling off his boots. Robert came in after with a cup of wine. 'The girl says she will bring you water, if you want to wash.'

Hew agreed, 'I do.' The room was warm and pleasant in the

crackling of the fire. He stripped down to his shirt, lying on the bed.

'What was the talk with your friend?'

Robert shrugged. 'Talk.' It seemed his mood had changed again. He opened both the shutters, letting in the moon. 'Do you have the sense that someone has been here?'

'Of course they have been here,' Hew pointed out. 'Someone lit the fire.'

'And someone else,' said Robert, 'has been going through your things.'

'What things?' murmured Hew. 'Close the shutters, light the lamps.'

'In a moment,' Robert said. He lit a candle from the fire and placed it on the window ledge, looking out across the fields. 'It is too quiet here.'

'How can it be too quiet, when we wish to sleep?' objected Hew.

'The other rooms look out upon the yard. Why are we in this one?' Robert mused.

'Because,' Hew answered patiently, 'it has the better view. What is it, Robert? You are like a cat, that prowls upon a roof. We go to Ghent tomorrow, let us now be still.'

Robert paced the room again, and buckled on his sword. 'By your leave, sir, I will go outside, and look around the yard. I need to take a piss.'

'Granted,' Hew said sleepily. The servant eyed him sharply. 'How much have you had to drink?'

'The Spanish wine is potent.' The world seemed well when his eyes were kept opened, but when they were closed the room seemed to spin.

'Bolt the door behind me,' Robert said.

Hew was startled back to life by a light knock on the door. 'Hot water, sir,' the girl called out, or something of the sort, in Dutch.

'One moment!' It was surely but a moment since Robert Lachlan

233

left, and yet the candle on the window ledge had burned down to a stub and the fire lay out in ashes, smouldering in the hearth. Where was Robert, then? And how could it be possible that Hew had slept the night? Heaviness oppressed him. He felt confused and dazed. He pulled back the bolt. The girl who brought the water jug had somehow disappeared, and in her place were five or six black–bearded men. Hew saw a grinning flash of teeth and steel, and two men held him fast while the others turned to strip and search the room. Hew asked them in bewilderment, in Latin, Scots and French, what was it they were looking for. They answered with a sneer. And then they lit upon the catechism, tucked inside his bag. The book was seized, and brandished, thrust into Hew's face. 'I do not understand,' he whispered. 'What it is that you want?' They answered him in Spanish then, with dark and mocking grins. He understood the meaning though he did not know the words.

They took him by the arms and marched him from his room, and through the tavern drinking hall out into the yard. At this early hour, the house was already awake, and breakfasting. Two or three guests looked up at curiously, but none of them ventured to help. The innkeeper's daughter fetched water from the well, and passing, Hew called out to her, yet she would not look up. He saw Robert with the Welshman in a corner of the yard, crying out his name in clear and frank relief, turning to despair as Robert turned his back. In the bitter Flemish morning and the coldness of its light, he knew that Robert Lachlan was someone's else's man. Hew felt himself enclosed by rough and heavy hands, gagged and bound and blanketed, and thrown upon a horse, before the last dregs of the wine again took their effect, and he slipped once more from consciousness. Which may have been a blessing, after all.

He awoke, he presumed, in a cell of sorts. He knew that he was there because of Robert Lachlan. Robert had betrayed him at the Molen inn; perhaps he had betrayed him from the very start, staging the attack in the alley at Campvere. Hew had little doubt he was a spy for Andrew Wood, and that Andrew Wood had wanted Hew to disappear. Yet he could not think why. Surely, not to save a brother, for whom he had no love? Then family honour, Hew supposed, or some grave secret of the state. It seemed unlikely he would ever come to know. Whose man was Andrew Wood? The question turned relentlessly, and yet he could not answer it. He fretted most of all, for the fate of Meg and Giles. He had no way of guessing what had happened since he left.

His own fate, too, gave cause for some concern. His prison was the cellar of some great stone country house, where a heap of woollen blankets served him as a bed, and kept him from the comfort of an early grave. The penetrating cold reduced him once to tears, grateful for their warmth upon his frozen cheeks. He was fed and watered once or twice a day, and allowed a little light, from a candle at the wall. They sometimes came at night, to wake and question him, though their questions were haphazard, and showed very little art, and as torturers, they struck him as peculiarly inept. He had no misconception that they were the Inquisition, and yet they made it plain to him, that horror was to come, and he would come in time into more practised hands. The matter, as he understood, was Jacob's catechism, which they had brought with them from the inn. The charge against him, he assumed, was one of heresy. And though they tricked and toyed with him, and kept him there for sport, they had a deeper, darker purpose, which he began to dread.

To dilute the fear, which at times seemed overwhelming, he made use of the candlelight in learning to speak Dutch, by reading Jacob's creed. It helped to pass the time, and took his mind from what was yet to come. He found some words were closer to the Scots than to the English tongue, and that if he spoke them aloud, they gave up their sense to him. It reminded Hew of learning Latin when he was a boy, teasing out the meaning from his Seneca or Cicero. He had been quick and good at it; the puzzle pleased him well. It was a code, a secret to unlock, a hidden store of wisdom to while a winter's night.

'Wat is uw enige troost, beinde in het leven en sterven?' 'What is your only . . . *troost* was trust perhaps, the thing of which you were assured . . . both in life and . . . *sterven* he assumed was death, aye, what else but death? What is your only trust – or solace, he supposed – both in life and in death?

'Dak ik met lichaam en ziel, beinde in het leven en sterven, niet mijn, maar mijns getrouwen Zaligmakers Jezus Christus eigen ben.' 'That I with . . . something and . . . body and . . . soul, both in life and in death, not mine . . . but belong to my . . .

'That I with body and soul, both in life and in death, am not my own, but belong to my saviour the Lord Jesus Christ.'

And then he saw at once what Jacob meant, and understood the words that he had said to Maude:

'Niet mijn . . . eigen ben.' 'I am not my own.'

'What is my only comfort, both in life and death?'

'That I am not my own, but belong to Jesus Christ.'

For Jacob had been no one's man, yet he belonged to Christ, and whispered his last prayer to comfort him in death. That brought to Hew no comfort now, at all.

Chapter 20

Soldiers of Fortune

In the dawning light of the late October morning it was already cold; an early frost instilled a stillness that was absolute. The soldier tied the letters and the creed into a sack, which he hung around Hew's neck, so close that Hew could feel the hot breath on his cheek. This sack, as he supposed, was to be his San Benito, or penitential garb. The soldier grinned, and showed a mouth of broken teeth. A pity, Hew thought ruefully, if this turned out to be the last face that he saw.

The soldier stood behind and drew his sword. Hew felt the blade tickle the back of his neck. The soldier urged him, 'Walk.'

Hew answered, 'Where?' Calmly, and evenly. He would not let them see that he was afraid. 'Where would you like me to walk?'

The soldier said, 'You, walk,' pleased with his few words of English. He slapped Hew on the back, hard enough to push him forward, without him falling to the ground. It was the sort of slap that Hew had sometimes given to Dun Scottis, encouraging, exasperated, rather than unkind.

It was a long, cold walk. So long that in the course of it, Hew became detached, immune to bitter sunshine and the yawns of sleepy labourers, to windmills and canals and woods and far off fields, and to the dull, insistent pricking of his bared and bruising feet. He did not want the walk to end. But end, it did, in a quiet copse of trees where the birds were mute and desolate.

'Kneel,' the soldier said. And Hew could not resist. His hands and feet were bound, and a strip of riband placed around his eyes. And there he knew at last, that there were no inquisitors, that there was only death. He gave up his last prayer, in cursing Andrew Wood for sending him to die so far away from home, and in a pile of leaves. Like Jacob, he was lost.

Hew heard a twig crack behind him and the whistle of a sword. He knew that it was time. And while he had imagined he was ready for the moment, he now realised that it came too soon, too late for him to make his peace with God. The birds around were silent as the man approached. He felt the cool draught of the sword; as the bonds that tied his feet were cut, and he fell sideways from the sudden force. In retrospect, he realised that his own voice had cried out, a shrill, involuntary sound that he felt ashamed of, though it did not come from any conscious sense of fear. He lay face down in the leaves, and felt their soft damp muddiness, before strong hands took hold of him, and dragged him to his feet. He realised it began again; the game was not yet done, with a sense of terror, resignation and relief. His heart clung still to life. The men who held him now spoke Dutch, as he inferred from their few grunting murmurs of command. He knew that that meant little in itself, that there was no one in this place that he could trust. They did not speak to him, or give credence to his cries, his trying, inarticulate, to connect with them. They did not seem to notice him at all, but swept him from the surface of the forest, as though he were a sack of gathered leaves, or a corpus they had found, littering the land, that they must now clear up. He thought, perhaps, he was; and in this last strange trail of time had somehow failed to hear the scythe that stripped and cut him down, and had become a ghost. The stiffness in his knees and the rawness of his wrists where the rope began to chafe suggested he lay open still, to fresh and deeper pain. The men were Dutch, he told himself, and yet it brought small comfort; he was cut off from their pity by the strangeness of his tongue, and from common understanding by the bandage round his eyes. And the Dutch, as he had heard, had exquisite forms of torture, that were too explicit even for the Scots. And so he found no solace in the sudden change of hands, for fear that there might be no sweeter course than death.

He was taken to the edge of the wood, and lifted, still blindfold and bound, onto the back of a horse. He could feel its broad flanks, a great Flemish beast, several hands higher than his slow Dun Scottis, and broader in the beam. The swerve from the ground took him dizzyingly high, and Hew entwined his fingers in the horse's mane, for fear he would fall. He was comforted to feel his captor climb behind, to steady and to settle him before him like a child. Though he had not ridden double on a horse since he was six, yet he was thankful for the rider's skill and expertise, as he held him to his place, spurring the horse on. He felt a desperate fondness for this man, who held him through the darkness, the giddy bump and sway, and in whom he was obliged to place his trust.

Hew judged from the sounds there were four or five men on horses around them; the man at his back was heavy and tall, and had his hands and eyes been free, and even with his sword, he could not have overpowered him. They had ridden on perhaps for half-an-hour – Hew had long ago lost any sense of time – when the ribands round his eyes were cut, and he cried out in pain. He thought it was a trick to hurt him, before he realised that it was the noonday sun; they had travelled on for several hours. He saw that he was riding with a troop of Flemish soldiers, roughly dressed and fiercely armed, and that they brought him to the threshold of a Flemish town. Emboldened by the sight, he asked aloud, in Dutch, 'Antwerpen?'

There was a moment's hesitation, before one of the soldiers confirmed, 'Antwerpen.' Though nothing more was said, Hew took a scrap of comfort in the word, spoken without rancour or evidence of threat. At Antwerp, at the least, he felt no fear of Inquisition, with Jacob's catechism hanging round his neck. It was, as he assumed, a safe, Reformers' hold. There was a marked lift in spirit in the soldiers at the gate, where they stopped to joke and jostle with the Antwerp city guards. Hew hoped that he himself had not occasioned it, for he had still the sense that they were bringing home a prize. He was aware of curious eyes as he was taken down the street, handfast on the horse, with the soldier braced behind him, careless and unkind, as though he were a runaway, taken to be whipped. And whipping, as he knew, was the least that they might do to him. The people watched him pass, with frank and curious gaze, and pity for the consequences he must have in store. Hew had heard it said that the Flemish were inclined to sympathy for others who had fallen foul of laws, in part because they were resistant to authority, in part as a revolt against the cruel and stringent penalties that often were attendant on the smallest crimes. They had the reputation of a fiercely stubborn race, who scorned to bear the yoke, and shared a common grudge, the wicked and the good, against the force of law. In that respect, he judged, they were quite different from the Scots, who were keen on retribution, and saw justice done with relish. Both approaches filled him with a sickening squeamishness, and a gnawing apprehension of what was soon to come.

They came into a courtyard under heavy guard, where after some exchange of words, Hew was lifted bodily and set beside his horse. He saw the locks and gratings of another prison gate. And as it closed behind him he felt his hopes give way. His long, blind ride on horseback and cold trek through the woods had robbed of him his wits, like a melancholy sleepwalker, falling in a dream. The dream became more vivid as he was brought in through an entrance port into a central hall, where a woman waited, fine and fair of face. She spoke to him in French, 'Come, monsieur, he waits.'

In the centre of the room was a large oak standing bed, with thickly woven drapes of ochre, red and black. The curtains opened back had the look of a campaign tent, for a heap of scrolls and documents was strewn across the coverlet. Around it were four or five soldiers, who came to and fro with papers and packages, brought to the man in the bed. A young boy by his side stood with pen and ink. A little further down a chessboard was set out, where a second man sat thoughtfully considering a rook. The room was large and light, and bright with coloured tapestries, while the marble floor was chequered like the chess set it contained. The player on the bed loomed up to look at Hew, and spoke to him in French. 'Come into the light, that we may see what hope our intervention bought.'

The voice was low and kind. As Hew approached the bed he saw light, reflective eyes, intelligent and searching, and a neatly sculptured beard, lightly flecked with grey. The beard was thin and straggled on one side, where the hair refused to grow. Above it was the horror of a sunk and, blasted cheek, a mass of thick confusion, taut across his face. The cheek was turned again, returning to the chess, considering his queen. The second player looked at Hew and grinned. 'Will you not bow your head, to the prince of Orange-Nassau?' It was Robert Lachlan. And Hew dropped to his knees, as his head began to spin. He saw the chessboard mirrored in the marble of the floor, and strong hands came to catch him as he fell into a faint.

Hew was not surprised to wake up in a warm soft bed, to find Robert Lachlan sitting at his side. 'I had the strangest dream,' he told him. 'I dreamt that you were playing chess with Prince William of Orange. He had a hole in the side of his face.'

'It was not a dream,' Robert Lachlan said, 'You are in his house. And when he comes to speak with you, as he is like to, presently, I'll thank you if ye dinna make a show of me, by gawping at his face the way you did before. Though he is not a vain man . . . Pfah!' he finished with a gesture of disgust.

'I did not think that it was real,' whispered Hew.

'It's real enough,' said Robert grimly.

'And then I thought you had betrayed me,' Hew admitted.

'And why would I do that?'

'I thought you were in league with Andrew Wood, and had sold me to the Spanish Inquisition.'

'Who is Andrew Wood?'

'The coroner of Fife,' Hew closed his eyes again.

'And why would the coroner of Fife want to sell you to the Spanish Inquisition?'

'I do not know.'

And Hew told Robert Lachlan, as he had not done before, of

Andrew, and of Robert Wood, and of the college and the baxters, and of Jacob and his windmill, and why he went to Ghent.

'Strewth!' said Robert Lachlan. 'The company you keep. I ken not how you come to think that I would take my orders from a man like that. Some of us,' he mentioned pointedly, 'are more particular. You do know, I suppose, that band of renegades who held you in their grasp was not the Inquisition?'

'So I had supposed. Who were they, then?' asked Hew.

'Fly by nights, free lancers, looking for a chance; they hoped to turn a profit from your sins. They never meant you harm. For though,' he added cheerfully, 'they would have slit your throat, and left you in a ditch, as soon as they grew tired of you, there would have been no malice in it.'

'That,' said Hew, 'is good to know. And yet I do not understand what happened at the inn.'

'I warned you,' Robert said, 'that something wisna right. Papists there, the lot of them. You'd think,' he snorted in disgust, 'that with all their chaff and chanting they wad be a bit more cheerful, would ye no'? It was the wee bit lassie that betrayed you.'

'I thought it was the Welshman,' whispered Hew. 'Surely, not the girl.'

'The lass,' insisted Robert, 'who went looking through your things, and saw Jacob's question book, and kent it for a creed. And did the silly hussy not then take it in her head, that you were one of they preachers, who go about the countryside stirring up the crowd and are a nagging thorn in our Spanish masters' side. So she goes running to those men, who were camping in her barn, and they imagine there is profit to be had. And she it was, of course, who slipped the potion in your drink.'

'But Robert,' Hew objected, 'You were gone all night.'

'And so I was, and more the fool, in telling you to bolt the door,' the soldier answered with a smile. 'I went out for my piss, and look around the yard, and nothing did I see. Then coming back, I found I couldna wake you from your snores, and so I spent the whole night sleeping in the stables with my horse. And no more did I know of it, until I saw you taken by the Spaniards through the yard.'

'When you turned your back on me,' Hew reminded him.

'You cannot doubt I turned my back. For there were six of them and one of me, and even with the Welshman, I did not like the odds. I gathered up our things, and slipped away, precipitate, for want of better help. The Welshman, for his part, I sent to follow after, to find out where you went. Few men are more useful, than one who knows both sides. He it was who brokered the exchange.'

'Your pardon, Robert, for I have misjudged you,' whispered Hew. 'I thought you were a man for hire.'

'You do not see it, do you, sir,' the soldier sighed. 'For that is what I am. There is a difference, plain and clear, between a man for hire, and a man who lies about the side that he is fighting for. I think you do not follow it. Suppose that in your court, you act for the defence; you do not hope to damn the man, and see that he is hanged. Yet in another case, where you will prosecute, you find yourself upon the hanging side, and no one says that you have turned your coat. You paid me, sir, to see you safe to Ghent, and that is what I mean to do. And if another man should offer me another sum, to stop your passage there, then I should turn it down, just as the lawman in your court will not accept a bribe, to prejudice his case. That does not mean that in another case, he will not fight upon another side. And so it is with soldiering. Each battle is a separate case that I will fight, according to the task, and if I do accept a task, then I will see it through. If I hold your colours, then I work for you. And so, when you were taken hostage at the inn, I rode here to Antwerp for audience with the prince, for he, I knew, would gladly hear your case.'

'But why,' asked Hew, 'the secrecy, the walk, the wood, the horse . . .'

'With the help of my Welsh friend, we set up an exchange, for a captured Spanish captain and a purse of Spanish gold. You were brought to, and recovered from, a secret, neutral ground.'

'Then my rescue,' said Hew, 'has cost the prince dear.'

243

Robert Lachlan shrugged. 'The captain, in the scale of things, had proved of little worth. And yet it was enough, to persuade the band of renegades they took a bigger prize. As to the rest, then you shall hear it from the prince himself, for here he comes.'

The prince had entered with a smile, and Hew attempted to sit up, as Robert Lachlan left the room. 'I pray you,' Willem said, in French, 'do not get up. You see, that now our roles have been reversed, and I find you in bed. You must excuse my deshabille, when first we met; my people have grown used to it, and I forget it must perplex a stranger, to see me holding court like a grande dame in her salon. My physicians have forbidden me to rise before the noon, and yet I find that much can be accomplished still in bed. I have seventeen physicians,' he concluded with a smile, 'and I cannot help but think that the time of my recovery, has been protracted by the sum of seventeen.

'They serve to tell me, nonetheless, that you have not been hurt, which I am pleased to hear.'

'Your grace,' said Hew, 'I thank you, sir, with all my heart, for my safe delivery.'

'For that,' the prince replied, 'you have to thank your servant, Robert Lachlan. Robert is a good man. Once, he saved my life.'

'You do not mean . . .' Hew could not help but glance at William's face. The Prince of Orange touched his cheek with a regretful smile. 'Alas, it was some other time. I fear my life is held in great account, and is worth far more to others, now, than it can be to me. Then what am I do? Do I turn my people from the gate, when they desire to speak with me, for fear that they will take my life? What sort of man does that, cannot be called their prince.

'But you are come from Scotland, as I understand. That place is dear to us, and helps us in our cause. Your king is green and young. How does he bear up, in these heavy times?'

'He is young, sir, as you say,' admitted Hew. 'At present he is under thrall, and struggles to hold power. He is susceptible to influence.'

'God help him, then,' Prince Willem said, 'for it is hard to be a prince, and harder still to be a boy. He has not, I think, been blessed with that close loving childhood, which I once enjoyed.'

The comparison placed James in harsh, unflattering light; strutting and hysterical, fearful of attack from strangers and from friends. William's selfless sacrifice could not be more remote. The thought appeared disloyal, and Hew pushed it from his mind. 'I cost you a captive, for which I am right sorry, sir,' he changed the subject quickly.

'The Spanish captain? He was not worth much,' the prince conceded generously. 'It cost us more to feed him than the benefit it brought us to keep him in our care. I understand that you are going to Ghent, on business of the Scottish Crown?'

'To the begijnhof, there, your grace, if it still stands,' said Hew.

A shadow crossed the prince's face. 'It does, though it is much diminished, and is damaged by these wars. Ghent has a Calvinist republic, of some fierce intensity. It was never my intent, to suppress the Catholic faith; it was never my intent, to persecute and purge. The inhabitants of Ghent are a proud and stubborn band, that fear and fight oppression, and have always suffered for it. They are in danger now, of giving up their town, for the sake of a regime which is too extreme and cruel. Yet one can only do so much,' he spread his hands. 'If you will go to Ghent, I cannot promise what you'll find, but I will do my best to help you on your way. You could, if you wish, ride back towards Sluis, and take the canal from the Sas van Gent; that is the quickest route. But more safe and less conspicuous perhaps, is to take a barge along the river Scheldt, starting here in Antwerp. The river route is longer, and more intricate, yet it will take you there with little fuss. There is a boatman has a barge that sails this afternoon. He lives aboard the lighter with his family, and the quarters may be cramped, yet he will get you there by dawn.'

The prince held out his hand for Hew to kiss, that Hew received in awe, to brush before his lips, and later on that day, he went with Robert Lachlan to a mooring on the Scheldt, and from the quiet river bank set off at last for Ghent.

245

Chapter 21

The Spinsters of Ghent

The Scheldt wound its slow and peaceful way to Ghent, through soft flattened marshlands and flax fields lined with windmills, where Hew and Robert Lachlan followed in a Flemish boatman's barge. Beyond the city walls they glimpsed the high tower of the belfry, the churches and cathedral; the Gravensteen and citadel stood harsh and sober garrisons, a grim reminder of the forced suppression of the town. The walls did not enclose the city as a whole, for the confluence of rivers formed a part of its defence, and Hew saw a bewildering array of locks and ports and gatehouses, where the level of the water flow controlled the passage of the boats. A hundred bridges opened up and closed, and the crisscross of the rivers and remains of the canals divided up the city into scores of islands, circled by waters of deep brackish green. The honey strands of flax left retting in the dew had mellowed to the palest grey, that gave the land the look of sheets of water, and the scent of clover, wheat and liniment. Down river, where the retting sheaves had choked the river bed, the flax had ripened to an acrid pungency, distempered in the waters of the sluggish Leie.

As the boat came in to dock, Robert Lachlan said, 'The begijnhof is on the north-west outreach of the city, near the road to Bruges. I will walk with you as far as the gate, and ask after Beatrix. Tis likely they will have a sister there who will interpret for you, if it turns out Beatrix kens no French. There was a time when all the nuns spoke French, and Latin too. Those days are past, I doubt; the convent is much smaller now.'

'But are you not to come with me?' asked Hew.

Robert swore. 'Not I. I lack the softness and the manners that can converse with them, as I confess, the sisters in their veils and hoods unnerve me; I cannot think it natural to see so many women draped and gathered in black cowls. I have had a horror of it since I was a bairn, for then I had a soul. Their habit of the veil sore plagues and vexes me.'

'What? Afeared of nuns? When you would face the Spanish in the field and fall into a bar room brawl without a qualm?' teased Hew. 'Afeared of nuns!'

'What sane man would not be?' argued Robert. 'With their bobbins and their pillows and their pricking and their pins, their spinning and their stitching, they make any man's flesh creep. And when you gasp your last in the infirmary they flutter round like devils dressed in black, like spinsters, like spiders. Is it not so much a fear, as an antipathy. It is part of it, the sense that they want to save my soul. Tis fearsome as a clutch of lassies wanting you to marry them. But worse than that,' he shuddered, 'is when they do not want to marry you, for most of them are married yet to God, though there's ay but one or two of them that slip away.'

'Like Beatrix,' Hew reflected.

'Aye, like Beatrix,' agreed Robert. 'And, God knows, I do not have the words to speak to her, in Flemish or in Scots. That wants a light touch, a lass', or *yours*.'

'I am obliged to you for the comparison.'

'Ye ken fine well enough,' said Robert, 'what it is I mean. The lassie will greet, and I can't abide that.'

'You are as soft as butter,' Hew said sternly, 'for all your swagger and your roar. A soldier, feared of nuns!'

'And you are green as kale,' Robert Lachlan scowled. 'There is no man alive that does not tremble at the sisterhood. Now, to the gate, and there my part is done.'

They had come upon the gatehouse, across a wooden bridge, for the convent was itself a little island, enclosed within its own high walls and moat, a closed and private enclave, in a city full of citadels. Robert stood for what seemed an age in conversation with the portress, before he stood aside at last and motioned Hew to pass.

'There is a old nun, Sister Agnietje, will take you to the house of the grande dame – the groot juffer, as they cry her,' he explained.

'Is that, then, the mother superior?' queried Hew.

'Something of the sort, though they do not call her that. She is elected from the sisters of their own accord, and not imposed upon them by their church – by what little they have left now, of their church. Go with Sister Agnietje, and she will sort the rest. I telt her that you come from Scotland, and have news for Beatrix, nothing more.'

'That was a long time in the telling,' noticed Hew.

'Aye? The sisters lead a sheltered life here,' Robert Lachlan grinned. 'So it is only mannerly, to spend some time in courtesies. When she is close enclosed, she is bound to miss the crack.'

'It seems,' said Hew, 'that you have overcome your fear of nuns.'

''Tis the aulder ones that fright me,' Robert answered cheerfully. 'For no doubt I was flyted by one, when I was a bairn. But yon's a braw wee lassie – Marthe, is her name. The plain one, as I doubt? She disna suit the name. And so I was for telling her, for it is good with nuns, to quote the gospels to them. Tis a thing they like. And like it she did, and a bonny wee thing in her blush. She's used to working in the gardens, but she hurt her hand, and the infirmer telt her to rest. This is her first day on the gate.'

'And Beatrix?' Hew reminded him.

'Oh, aye. She is here, too, right enough.'

'And you are quite sure, Robert, that you will not come?'

'Not for the world. By your leave, sir, I have done what you did ask, and brought you to the nunnery. Nothing would persuade me to go further in. I will go to an inn, sir, and find us a room. The best are in the corn market.'

The portress left them at the gate, returning in a moment with an aged nun, whose eyes were bright within her withered cheeks, dry and creased like paper. 'Sister Agnietje,' Robert's conquest beamed, her cheeks still faintly flushed.

'That's Agnes,' Robert grinned, 'to you and me.' Agnes looked as if she could have been a hundred years of age, shrunk inside her habit to the stature of a child. She did not speak, but took Hew by the hand. Robert grinned. 'Good luck!'

Hew had thought that the begijnhof would be something like the college of St Salvator, austere and silent cloisters, shuttered from the world. It was not as he expected, for instead he found a labyrinth of whitewashed walls and houses built of red and yellow stone that sheltered in the autumn sunlight; there were gates within gates, and walls within walls, each one opening out onto quiet paths and gardens, knots of herbs and willow trees, here a fountain or a hedge, and there a bench or arbour planted in the shade. Beyond the high brick walls were vines and orchards, wintering plums and cherry trees, rows of figs and pears. The stripping of their fruit and leaves did not disguise the beauty of the trees, that stretched and bared their branches high behind the safety of the walls, protected from the wind. In summer, Hew imagined, they hung ripe and flush with fruit, and light with blossom in the spring. Between the orchard and the square there was a drying green, and a dozen nuns were pegging out clean sheets, soaped and scrubbed and rinsed out in the grey, still moat. The air was scented warm and singed, with hops and flax, and honeyed bread and spices baked upon a fire. And in spite of the industry Hew saw around him – the washing and the drying and the rooting of the pig, the scattering of barleycorn among the scrabbling hens – the begijnhof had a stillness and tranquillity that struck him with new force at every twist and turn; the painted doors and windows netted with white lace, the neatly tended gardens and rows of knotted herbs, a world at peace, in miniature, sheltered from the crowd. It was seclusion, not confinement, and less a shunning or a shying from the world, than a simple, pure integrity, which set the place apart, as of itself, alone. It was quite unlike any other place where Hew had been. He did not feel unsettled there, as

249

Robert Lachlan feared, but restful and at peace, though whether it was yet the quiet, yellow stone of the little town and gardens set round the square, or by grace of those who lived in them, he could not have told. Sister Agnietje held him by the hand, her own hand dry and fragile, like a leaf in his, and warmed him with her smile.

He followed through a maze of walls and wooden doors, through lintels and stone archways engraved with names of saints, until they came to a fine house in the centre of a close, lined with rows of trees. This he supposed was the huis van de grootjuffer, the house of the mother superior. Agnietje led him through the courtyard to a sunlit room, simply furnished, in the plainest style. The nun sat on a high-backed chair, surrounded by a circle of small girls, one of whom stood at the grande dame's shoulder, reading from a book. The child stopped and stared as Sister Agnietje approached. She spoke a few words in Flemish, beckoning to Hew. The grande dame clapped her hands. 'Allez, vite, mes enfants!' The small girls scrambled to their feet, and formed a solemn line by Sister Agnietje. Hew replied in French, 'Ma dame, I have disturbed the lesson, je vous en prie, I pray you, do go on.'

'Not at all,' the grande dame said. 'The reading hour is now complete. And they will go with Agnietje, who teaches them to spin.'

Hew turned towards the little nun Agnietje, and thanked her as he bowed. She did not respond.

'She does not understand you,' said the grand dame with a smile, 'for sister Agnietje, for all the years that she has spent here, has never learned to speak French. And she does not see you, for she is almost blind.'

Hew exclaimed, 'I could not tell!'

'Agnietje has lived here for sixty years. And she knows every turn and path, for here in the beguinage, there is little change. She does not venture out beyond these walls.'

'But how, then, can she teach these little girls to spin?'

'It is a long time,' the nun acknowledged, 'since Agnietje has made lace. Yet she can spin the finest thread, of any sister in the beguinage. She spins the thread by touch. The flax is all the better spun in rooms of darkness, for the graze of sunlight glancing off the fibres breaks the brittle thread. The flax is spun like gossamer, a fineness and a lightness that makes the threads invisible on all except the blackest cloth. Her blindness is no hindrance in her craft; it is, perhaps, a gift.

'*Walk*, Katheline,' she admonished a small child, too anxious to be out among her friends. The girl dropped a curtsey, 'Pardon, ma dame Ursula.'

'Which of these children is Lotte?' Hew asked impulsively.

The grande dame looked puzzled, 'What do you mean?'

'Lotte, the daughter of Beatrix van Straeten.'

The grande dame fixed him with a look, and waited till the children had trooped out with sister Agnietje, before she offered her reply.

'Lotte is an infant, and too young to learn her letters; or, indeed, to spin, that we teach our little daughters from the age of six. Who are you, monsieur?' She spoke to him in the same calm tones of caution, with which she had admonished Katheline, and Hew had the sense he was being rebuked; he felt like a child in the schoolroom.

'Ma chère grande dame . . .'

'My name is Ursula.'

She was implacable, composed, and in a way, magnificent, and Hew had no conception how he might begin with her. He felt that he should fall before her on his knees, and began to understand why Robert had refused to come into the nunnery, for Ursula, he had no doubt, could see into his soul.

He did the simplest thing, and told the truth. 'I have come from St Andrews in Scotland, to see Beatrix van der Straeten and Lotte. I bring her sad news of her husband. He came upon a ship into St Andrews Bay. The ship was wrecked, and all the crew were lost.'

Ursula said quietly, 'Jacob Molenaar is dead?'

251

'I fear it, ma dame.'

And he could see that Ursula had been affected by his tale, though she did not allow her mask to slip – and yet, he thought, the inference was false, for it was not a mask, but a seam of self assurance that ran through to the heart, like diamond through a rock.

'Your pardon, sir,' she said at last, 'but how am I to know you speak the truth?'

'He left behind him letters,' answered Hew. 'And he left this.' He took the ring out of his pocket and handed it to Ursula. He did not think it sensible to offer her the creed.

'Albrecht's ring,' said Ursula. And for a moment, Hew thought he saw a tear form in the corner of her eye.

'Who is Albrecht, ma dame?'

'Albrecht is my brother,' she replied, her fingers closing tight around the ring.

'Jacob took your brother's ring?' asked Hew.

'He did not take it,' Ursula replied. 'My brother Albrecht is the father of Beatrix, and was a diamond merchant in Antwerp. He gave this ring to Beatrix. And Beatrix gave it to Jacob, on the day that he left Ghent. Jacob would not have removed it.'

'He did not, ma dame.'

'Then I must believe that what you say is true. This is sad news.'

'May I ask you, ma dame, how Beatrix came to be here at the beguinage? Since she is your niece?'

'You may. It is a sad tale, though not, in these times, such an uncommon one. She came as a girl of thirteen. Her father had a shop in Antwerp. When the Spanish soldiers came, and sacked the town, his business was destroyed, and he sent Beatrix here to me, to keep her safe. That was in the winter of 1576,' she sighed, 'and followed from the treaty that they call the pacification of Ghent – when we were promised we may worship as we pleased, though little peace we had from it. The diamond ring was all that Beatrix had of Albrecht, to link her to her former life, and all that my poor brother had left to give to her. He died in abject poverty, broken in his heart.'

252

'Then how,' said Hew, 'did Beatrix meet her husband, Jacob Molenaar?'

'She met him here,' Ursula acknowledged with a smile, 'at the begijnhof. I see that startles you. Yet it is not so strange, though we do not encourage it. Our sisters take no vows that bind them to be brides of Christ; they make no pledge of poverty, that forces them to give up all their wealth, and relinquish diamond rings. And those who can afford to, keep servants in their house, and so they do support and serve the rest. Though for the most part, we live simply, for our needs are not extravagant. And our younger sisters wander daily through the town, to tend the dead and teach in schools and bring nurture to the sick, so they are not cloistered as you may suppose. It is a brave man, nonetheless, who sets his heart and cap against the beguinage, and many of our sisters come here to escape unhappy marriages. And yet it does occur, from time to time, that a man and woman fall in love, and the beguine seeks to leave, and when that happens, of her own free will and choice, then we will not hinder her, but wish her on her way, with God's good love and grace. And so it was with Beatrix and her husband, Jacob. They met here in the beguinage, where Jacob was employed in some simple works of carpentry, in passing on his skills to the sisters in our care.'

'You teach them woodwork, too?' Hew inquired, amused.

'We would be self-sufficient in all things,' Ursula said simply, 'and sad to say, the Calvinists had done some damage to our church, that we lacked the skills to repair. Since it was never Albrecht's wish to have left his daughter to a lifetime of retreat, we gave her gladly up to Jacob Molenaar.'

'And why, then, did he leave her here, and go off to sea?'

'He left her when his father died; and Jacob Molenaar found out,' Ursula said sadly, 'that he was not the man he thought he was.'

'What do you mean?' Hew asked in astonishment. 'That he was *not himself*?'

'In truth, you might say, he was not himself,' Ursula agreed. 'For it was when he found out that he was not the man he thought he was, that Jacob Molenaar changed. He thought that he could have a better life, than the one that he had here in Ghent. And to be fair to him, it was never his intention to have left his wife and child. He always meant to send for them. What did not change was Jacob's love.'

'Ma dame,' said Hew, 'I do not understand. 'What brought about this change?'

'As I think I said to you, Jacob's father died. His father was Clays Hansen, the timmerman.'

'And Jacob's name was Molenaar? Then he was not his son?'

'Though he was not his son,' Ursula agreed, 'the name does not signify. A man may take as byname whatever he may choose, for unlike our own given names our surnames are not fixed, and need not pass from father down to son. So if a man be timmerman, whose father is a cook, there need be no connection in their style of name, but one is Jan the timmerman, the son of Jan the cook. Molenaar was what we called him here. It means simply, Jacob the miller, though that did not encompass him; for he was more than that, a skilful engineer. He knew how to work the wind, as well as any man. His father – for, for want of better word we ought to call him that, and Jacob knew no other – Clays Hansen, had been a ship's carpenter, before he settled here as millwright in the town, and it was from him that Jacob learned his art, and earned the name of miller. Clays Hansen had a Scottish wife.'

'His mother was a Scot!' said Hew.

'His mother was, beyond a doubt, a Scot,' Ursula said oddly. 'Though not Clays Hansen's wife. But setting that aside, Clays Hansen's wife, that Jacob knew as mother, died when Jacob was a child; he had not known her long. She was a woman, I recall, called Ruth – Ruth Adams as I think. Clays Hansen met her at a place called Dondie.'

'I know that place,' said Hew. 'Indeed, I did set sail from there.'

'Indeed? Well, he met her there, and married her, and brought her back to live in Ghent, and with them came their little child, and that was Jacob Molenaar. Though they were old, indeed, to have a little child, and shortly after, Ruth Adams died. Clays Hansen, for his part, lived on for twenty years, and he brought little Jacob up to follow in his trade, and no man could have loved his son as dearly as did he. And then, three months ago, Clays Hansen died. And on his deathbed, he told Jacob Molenaar that he was not his father, but his uncle, for Ruth Adams had been Jacob's aunt. His father was her brother.'

'Who then, was his mother?' wondered Hew.

'Clays Hansen did not say. But as Jacob understood, the girl had died in childbirth. And she and Jacob's father were not wed. Since Ruth had a husband, and no child, and her brother had a child, and no wife, the simple thing was for Ruth and her husband to bring back the child to Ghent, and keep him as their own. And Jacob, when he found this out, became persuaded he might find another, and a better, life, for Beatrix and for Lotte, far away from Ghent, where the Spanish were not knocking with their daggers on the door. And he became, in truth, a different sort of man, than the boy who had been son to the timmerman Clays Hansen. And that was sad to see. For I never saw a boy more wanted or more loved, or a prouder father, in the whole of Ghent.'

Chapter 22

A Changed Man

'Why have you come?' asked Ursula to Hew. 'It is a long way to come.'

'I brought Beatrix a letter,' Hew replied.

'But even so,' said Ursula, 'it is a long way to come, to bring a letter.'

'I think, perhaps,' said Hew, 'that you should see it. There are questions I must ask, if not of Beatrix, then to you.'

'Why do men,' sighed Ursula, 'always have to ask so many questions?'

'I do not know, ma dame. But if you read the letter, you will understand.'

She read it silently. 'These are terrible words,' she acknowledged.

'He writes about a sickness that is known as holy fire,' said Hew. 'It infected the crew of the *Dolfin*, driving them mad.'

'I have heard of it,' said Ursula, 'though I have never witnessed its effects. It is not so holy, as I think.'

'The provost of our college is a fine physician. It is his belief the sickness stemmed from tainted grain, that was taken on the ship in flour or bread, poisoning the crew.'

'If that is so,' said Ursula, 'it did not come from here. For we have had no sickness in the town. Ghent is the central marketplace for grain, for many miles around.'

'We think the bread was purchased further north, at Rotterdam, perhaps,' suggested Hew.

'That is always possible,' Ursula agreed. She looked back at the letter in her hand. 'This is a dreadful letter, and it will break her heart.'

'I place it in your hands, and trust upon your judgement, whether we should give to her, her dying husband's words. You know her fortitude and strength. And yet I am assured, he wrote the words for her. We have to make her understand, in spite of what he says, that Jacob was not lost. He did not die alone, but in the house of a good woman, who held him in her arms, and laid him to his rest,' said Hew. And for the rest, the questions he must put to her, he thought that that could wait.

'And was she a good Christian, this woman?' Ursula asked.

Hew hesitated, 'I do well believe, ma dame, that you would think her one,' he answered her at last, 'though she keeps a sailors' tavern, that some call a low place. She is a good-hearted soul and a widow. Her married life was not a happy one.'

'There are many women here,' said Ursula, 'who have not had happy marriages.'

'She has a daughter too, who is sore afflicted, wanting wit and grace.' It was a cruel depiction, he reflected guiltily, of the lithesome Lilias, who wanted none of grace, for all she lacked of wit.

But Ursula replied, 'We are all God's children, and afflicted in our way. This woman's part in Jacob's death must bring my niece some comfort, and we must give our thanks to God, that in her care and kindness she was there, and not think to reproach her for the sort of house she keeps. Well,' she folded up the paper with a sigh. 'Will you come, mon fils? We can defer no longer. Let the deed be done.'

'I will come, ma mère.'

She led him through the courtyard to the little close of houses built of red and yellow bricks, stopping at the third one from the end. Beatrix sat before the window, where the light fell through the slats onto the pale blue cushion nestled in her lap, and a dozen wooden bobbins spun and turned, bent in concentration as her fingers worked the lace. In the centre of the floor a little child sat

257

playing pat-a-cake, with an older novice from the beguinage. The girl took up the infant's chubby hands and clapped them, while the infant gazed on stolidly, through solemn, sleepy eyes in rosy-tinted cheeks. Fair threads of flaxen hair escaped the small lace cap, too fine to braid or pin. Beatrix, looking up at last, let out a startled cry. Her hand flew to her mouth. And whether it was Ursula, her sad and sombre countenance, or perhaps the stranger coming in their midst, it seemed she knew at once, without the need for words. The cushion slipped unnoticed from her lap, the bobbins clattered on the floor, and Lotte learned the clapping trick at last, delighted with the bobbins and their scatter of bright beads. Ursula spoke softly to her niece, reverting to the Flemish as she took her in her arms. Presently, she whispered, 'will you wait outside, monsieur? And I will come and find you, when the time is right.'

The novice scooped up Lotte and followed Hew outside. 'What has happened here, monsieur, to make the mother weep?' she asked him anxiously. He found he could not answer her, for he did not know the words.

Beyond the high walls of the convent still, a dozen windmills turned. Hew heard no other sound from the little house. He walked a little further, coming to the church, stripped bare of its idolatry and artefacts of Christ, where doubtless, God would hear him, sending up a prayer. He felt a deeper quiet in that place. Outside upon the green, the sheets and linens flapped and furled, like sails of bobbing boats. The children were released from morning school, and flexing their taut fingers, squinted at the sun, where for a while, at least, they knew no other cares. Hew knelt upon the stone and was kneeling still, when the voice of Sister Ursula awoke him from his prayers.

'There you are, mon fils; now what has brought you here?' she asked, so full of warmth and sadness that he longed to have her blessing. He rose quickly to his feet.

'You are not a Catholic, as I think,' she went on shrewdly, 'yet you have found God here, in our broken church. Or, am I wrong?'

'I found something here,' admitted Hew, 'and if not God, then something deeper.'

'Foolishness, my child. What can be deeper, after all, than God?'

'*Patience,*' Hew said, simply.

'Patience? Ah, we have that here. I fear that it was something Jacob lacked.'

'Beatrix will talk to you now,' she brushed past him, without touching, and he felt her calm composure, the cool swish of her skirts. 'She has many questions. And the worst has past. She will be looked after here.'

'And Lotte?' questioned Hew.

Ursula nodded. 'Lotte is in the garden, with Paulina and Sister Agnietje. Agnietje, bless her heart, is not good at looking after little ones. She does not see them if they eat laburnum seeds, or fall into the well. But Paulina is watchful, and quick on her feet, and Agnietje is careful and kind, and has a soft lap, and a low crooning song, that will lull a cross child to her sleep. Together, they make up a careful nurse, and so it is in the begijnhof, for what we lack in parts, we make up as a whole. A child can play at will, yet never go unwatched. There are many places worse to bring up a little girl. Still, Lotte knows her mother, and her mother wants her child. It is how things should be. I shall take her home. Go on to Beatrix, talk to her, and tell her I shall come again, with Lotte, in a little while.'

Hew was startled. 'Am I to go alone?'

'Go, and have courage, my child. For is that not why you have come here?' She took him by the hands, 'God sees your heart, and knows your will is good. Know that she will hear you, now the worst is done.'

Beatrix was composed, though pale as linen flax. Her eyes were deep and wet with unshed tears. She did not wear the habit or the white hood of the faith, but a simple linen cap and light blue linen dress, and Hew supposed that she was not a true begijnte, perhaps she never had been one, for it did not seem to matter to the nuns.

259

'You may not wish to have it now, but Jacob left you this,' he told her, bringing out the creed. 'For fear of it offending her, I did not wish to offer it before the holy mother. But I thought that you might wish to have it, since it brought your husband comfort in the hours before he died.'

Beatrix forced a smile, reaching out her hand to take the book. 'His faith was not the same as mine, and yet it did not come between us. And I would wish to have it, for it is a part of him. And you are right in thinking that it would not please my aunt. We call her the grande dame – the groot juffer, and not la mère, though you are correct if you suppose that she is mother to us all, and most of all, to me. I have been thinking,' she said suddenly, 'about the little boy Joachim, and whether someone ought to tell his mother.'

Hew's spirits sank. The thought had not occurred to him, and now he saw at once that he must seek her out, and break the dreadful news.

'I see her every week,' said Beatrix, 'in the Friday market, selling herbs and flowers. She is so very proud of him, and tells the world that he has gone abroad, to seek his fortune overseas.'

Hew nodded miserably.

'She has no expectation,' Beatrix went on quietly, 'of his ever coming back. Then do you think it is so very wrong, to leave her with her dreams?'

Hew swallowed. 'I do not think it is so very wrong,' he answered hoarsely.

'Nor do I,' said Beatrix. 'But I must ask my aunt. She tells me Jacob did not die alone. Was that the truth, monsieur? Or was it meant as kindness? For I do not count it kindness, if I am not told the truth.'

'I think that you must know,' said Hew, 'that she would not tell lies to you.'

'I know that she would not. That is not what I ask.'

'It is the truth,' said Hew.'

'Then it is a comfort, and I thank you for it. Where did Jacob die?'

'In a clean, warm feather bed, in the comfort of the inn.'

'Though that is good to know, it is not what I meant. I mean, what was the place? What city, street or town?'

'He died in St Andrews. It is a town in Scotland, on the coast of Fife,' said Hew.

'I know it,' Beatrix smiled. 'Then I must be content, for Jacob died at home. He found the place that he was looking for. Then he was not a stranger at the last,' and she was smiling through the tears, for the tears had overflowed.

'I do not understand,' Hew told her, when the tears were quelled at last. 'According to the grande dame, his aunt came from Dundee.'

'His aunt,' Beatrix explained, 'was living at that place when Clays Hansen first met her. But her brother came from Sint Andreas, and that was the place where Jacob had been born. Or so Clays Hansen said.'

'Then what,' asked Hew, 'was Jacob's father's name?'

'He was Jacob, too. Jacob Adams. And Jacob said, that he would change his name, once he had come to Scotland, to Jacob Jacobsen. I do not know, monsieur, what my aunt has said to you,' she put in suddenly, 'But I should not like to think you thought that Jacob was a bad man. For he was not a bad man, I assure you.'

'Why,' Hew asked her cautiously, 'should your aunt have told me that he was a bad man?'

'She should not. It was only that she did not think that he should go from Ghent. She thought he should be satisfied with what he had. Yet it cannot be wrong, I think, to hope to have a better life, and who can blame him, if the life he had was wrong, for he could not have known, he was not who he thought he was.'

'Beatrix,' Hew said gently, 'though I do not believe that Jacob was a bad man, there is something that I do not understand, and have to ask. He wrote in his letter that he thought the sea-captain suspected his intent, had somehow found him out. Do you know what Jacob meant?'

Beatrix sighed. 'I do, monsieur, for he wrote to me from Vlissingen.

He had lied to the sea-captain, and that deception had weighed heavy on his mind, for Jacob is – was – an honest man, at heart. It was the only way he could persuade the sea-captain to take him up to St Andrews, and let him build his windmill on his ship. He met the man at Vlissingen, where he was looking for a carpenter, to take aboard his boat, and Jacob was the right man for the task. And so he had free passage, well assured, but the ship was going to Hull. So Jacob struck a bargain with the man; he had a venture to build windmills in the port of Vlissingen, importing them to Scotland, where such mills are scarce.

'He would build a windmill, aboard the captain's ship, and take it to St Andrews as a sample of the wares, and then the two of them would start in business, all along the coast. Of course, it was a trick, for Jacob meant to keep his mill, and never to return, there were to be no profits, from the business back in Vlissingen.'

'We have the mill,' said Hew. 'It was salvaged from the ship. And if you wish to sell it, then the town will gladly pay.'

Beatrix shook her head. 'I will not sell it, for he meant it as a gift.'

'A gift?' repeated Hew.

'A present to the town. For he was not quite sure how he would be received, or whether they would welcome back a long-forgotten son. And so he thought that he would bring a gift that they could not refuse. That when they saw the windmill, and understood its art, then they would welcome him with open arms. My aunt did not approve of it. She said that it was pride.'

Then the whole town had fought, for possession of a gift, and had tried to take by force, what was already theirs. And in the quiet convent, in the war-torn town of Ghent, Hew felt bitterly ashamed of the place that he called home.

'You must keep it,' Beatrix said, 'for it was meant for you.'

Before Hew left the beguinage, Beatrix brought two packages and pressed them in his hand. 'This is Flemish lace. One is for the keeper of the haven inn, who took care of Jacob when he died, and the other is for you, to give to your wife.'

He smiled at her. 'I thank you. These are exquisite, and Maude will be delighted with her gift. I do not have a wife. But if I may, I will give it to my sister, who has just had a child.'

Beatrix answered, 'Wait,' returning to her press. 'This is for your sister.' She brought out another piece. 'For if you do not have a wife, then you will have one very soon. And all of us are sisters, are we not?'

'This is too much,' protested Hew.

Beatrix answered through the tears. 'I promise, you, monsieur, that it is not.'

She walked him through the square and past the green, where the daughters of the nunnery were playing on the grass, wild as little birds, and sheltered from the gaze of prying eyes. And as she left him at the gate, she took his hand and said, 'My aunt will tell you Jacob changed, yet I do not believe that, monsieur. For in his heart, he stayed the same, and he was always true to me; it matters not to me, if he was Jacob Molenaar, or Hansen, or Jacobsen, or Adams; he was, and he will always be, my Copin.'

Hew discovered Robert Lachlan sprawled upon a bed in the best room of the house of the finest inn in Ghent, with an empty flagon at his side. 'Had to start without you,' he explained. 'You were gone too long. A' gone. Fetch another . . .'

'You have had enough.'

'Nor yet begun,' Robert contradicted him. 'Lay down for a nap.'

'How much have you had?'

The soldier shrugged. 'It is on your reckoning, when you come to pay for it.'

'Then far more than enough.'

'What is that?' Robert sat up, and pointed to the package in Hew's hand.

'Lace, from the begijnhof.'

'Nun's lace?' the soldier whistled. 'That's worth the finest whore in town.' He stretched out a hand.

263

'Touch, and I will cut you to the bone,' Hew assured him icily, his hand already placed upon his sword.

Robert pulled back in astonishment. 'Jesu, you are ticklish and pepper-nosed tonight. What devil has got into you?'

'Desist from your profanities!' snapped Hew.

'Jesus Christ!' swore Robert. ''Tis the nun's curse has snared you, just as I predicted it, for so the evil spinsters weave their wicked webs!'

Hew abandoned Robert in disgust, retreating to the street outside for air. The inn was sited near the corn wharf, where the boatman's barge had docked, and walking further on, he found the marketplace, the wide, three-cornered square between the guild church of St Nicholas and the finest city houses of the guilds and trades. As the staple town in Flanders for French imported wheat, Ghent was home to the most furious and frank transactions Hew had ever seen, where a raging stream of wagons, carts and trucks rumbled past incessantly, and bartering went on, aggressively and noisily, in Flemish and in French. This commerce was reserved exclusively for men, and Hew felt dazed in the ferocity of masculine exchange. The heady chink of coin and loud and forceful bargaining pressed in on every side, and the speed and force with which the trade took place was frantic and bewildering. Dockers, bakers, packmen, shipmen battled forth at every turn, haggling over bolls of wheat and sacks of yellow corn. The furiousness reminded Hew of Patrick Honeyman, whom he imagined dwarfed and swept away, in this fierce flux of grain. And in his mind's eye, he saw once again the corpse of Sandy Kintor, lying by the granary, his last breath choked and stoppered by the flood of corn, overwhelmed and drowning, at the baxters' hands. For in his heart, he knew that it must be the baxters. For who would leave a corpse to rot inside a granary, and risk the precious grain supply, increasing the reliance on imported flour and forcing up the price of bread? And who, indeed, had access to the granary, and, since they held the key to it, had surely known about the broken lock? 'Who profits now?' he heard the miller bleat, the fearful form of Henry Cairns, brought weeping to his knees. It had been a baxter, beyond doubt. The baxters made their profit from the staff of life itself. They kept their secrets close behind the banner of their gild.

Overwhelmed by the noise and the thrang, Hew fled from the market to the narrow band of streets that intersected Ghent and lay between its waterways. In the lanes around the square were rows of little stalls, with bread and books and candles, liquor and hot pies, smoked and salted fish and slabs of roasted pork. Among them he noticed a spectacle shop, whose keeper called out in thick Flemish French, 'Opticks, monsieur; perspectives, illusions, toys of all kinds.' Hew was enchanted. 'Aye, why not?' The cabinets within would have captivated Giles, with prisms of rock crystals and pyramids of glass, each promising a new perspective on the world. Their maker wore a long grey beard and velvet doctor's cap, a magus from a magic book, philosopher and conjurer, combining art with trickery. 'Come see, sir,' he beseeched, uncovering a snowstorm in the smallest speck of dust, discovering God's pattern in the torn wing of a fly. There were glasses and lenses of all sorts and shapes, hollowed and bevelled and convex and curved, pyramids, cylinders, coloured and clear. He showed to Hew a multiplying glass, that threw the object back upon the baffled eye, making one of many, fashioning a crowd. By geometric alchemy, he mingled mathematical and magic, mystic arts. And he had pictures, too, that tricked and teased the mind, that through a glass obliquely, showed secrets or told lies. Some were pleated, set in strips, to show a split perspective – wisdom, folly, health or sickness, human virtue, human fault – when viewed from left or right. One picture had a mirror that reflected back a death's head, from the painted canvas hidden underneath. It was the optick, realised Hew, that Giles must have alluded to, 'in which a man might see an image not his own'. No art or magic in the glass, but the reflection of another angled picture, intended to alarm, to baffle or amuse.

Hew saw glasses that distorted what was in plain sight, and glasses that made sense of images distorted, glasses that made one of many, others, like the multiplier, that made many out of one. A dozen small figures, arranged in a circle, viewed through a cylinder, fused into a whole. He bought the multiplier as a gift for Giles, and turned to leave the shop. And there he stopped aghast, to catch his face reflected in a common looking glass, plain and undistorted, hung above the door. In the midst of these illusions, it took him by surprise.

'What is it that you see?' the shopkeeper asked shrewdly, his last and finest trick. Hew was lost for words. What was it that he saw? A young, fair scholar's face, a little thin and thoughtful, growing grave and pensive, showing signs of age. Who was he, after all? What was it he was doing there? He saw his own life plainly in a glass, his family, hope and friends, his training in the law, and saw it scatter in confusion, no more closely centred than he had ever been. What compulsion drove him? He was, as he assured himself, his own man to the last. And yet he had no notion what that really meant.

Hew hurried to the inn, and finding Robert Lachlan in a stupor on the floor, he woke him with a kick. 'Do you want to stay with me, and see this matter out?' he demanded bluntly.

Robert answered cautiously, 'I might.'

'Get up, then,' Hew instructed. 'We are going home.'

Chapter 23

The Flemish Miller's Gift

On a grey November evening as the light began to fail, Hew and Robert Lachlan came riding from the west to the clock tower of St Salvator's, inscribed in darkening skies. St Andrews never looked so fair, thought Hew, as on arrival and departure, where wild winds swept and scattered waters from the bay and drizzled soft white spray on walls of yellow sand. Robert Lachlan, for his part, was less impressed. 'Is this it, then? The great metropolis? Three streets?'

Three streets, in which a world converged and bowed before the hollow, windswept arches of its old cathedral church: the broad and leafy South Street, the townhouses and colleges, the kirk of Holy Trinity and mercat with its cross; and deeper lined within, its criss-cross of baxters, thieves and whores, philosophers and fisher wives, clergymen and cooks; their cloisters and courtyards, their dinner bells and boats. 'What did you expect?' asked Hew.

'Well,' said Robert with a sniff, 'for sure, it isna Ghent.'

'But Ghent is a huge city. You forget that this is Scotland. I think you were away too long,' Hew smiled.

'Or mebbe,' Robert countered, 'not long enough.'

'Where is it you are from?' his master asked.

The soldier shrugged. 'A wee place in the west. You would not have heard of it. I will not go back there.'

'Have you no other friends?'

'I had a sister once. She would not know me now.' Robert said dismissively. 'I will stay here for a while. Perhaps I will find work.

Your man Robert Wood may want a miller still to work his mill. I could be a miller. It cannot be hard.'

'I do not recommend it,' answered Hew. 'If you will, I could let you have land.'

'And what would I dae with that? Grow neaps, and cabbage kale?' The soldier shook his head. 'I thank you, but I do not think so.'

Robert proved ill-fitted for a servant in the town, for his manners at St Salvator's were awkward and restrained; he could not wait at table, and he would not help the cook. Nor did he fare much better with the doctor on the Swallow Gait, for Meg received him sceptically, and he fell out with Paul. 'What sort of man is that?' asked Meg, 'you bring home as a friend?'

'An honest one,' insisted Hew.

'I fear,' whispered Giles, 'that your brother has acquired a new friend for Dun Scottis. Yet we must be thankful, he is back at all.'

Robert lodged for two nights with Maude Benet at the haven inn, but on the third she told him that the house was full. 'I do not want him here,' she said to Hew, 'he drinks too much,' which seemed an odd objection, from the keeper of a tavern.

'He has shown no sign of violence, as I hope?' asked Hew.

'He has not. Yet he is melancholy in his cups. He is the sort of man who drinks when he has nothing else to do, from idleness. And I have seen too many guid men thrawn by drink, to want to see another one,' she answered enigmatically.

And so, for want of better plan, Hew took Robert home to Kenly Green and left him there with Nicholas, who took to him with quiet grace, and did not seek to judge. Hew returned alone, to report to Andrew Wood. He found the coroner at home in the tolbuith in the mercat place, where he fulfilled his offices when he was in town.

'I heard,' Sir Andrew greeted him, 'that you have brought a man with you from Ghent.'

'Good news travels fast,' noticed Hew.

'Do you intend to keep him?' Andrew Wood inquired.

'He will go where he will, for he is not a lapdog to be kept.'

Sir Andrew answered tetchily, 'When are you to learn? The man is your servant, and a servant is to keep, or dismiss, as you decide. I advise you to dismiss him.'

'I had a notion, once, that he might work for you,' Hew confided.

'And why should you think that?'

'I thought that you had set him, to spy on me.'

Sir Andrew gave a narrow smile. 'Regrettably, you overstate my power. I would I had such influence,' he said.

'Do you mean overseas?' asked Hew.

'I mean, over *you*,' the coroner replied. 'The man I set to spy on you was beaten to a pulp, by your servant, Robert Lachlan, at the Groote Kerk in Campvere. He wiped your bloody sword upon my servant's coat.'

Hew exclaimed, 'Sweet heaven! Then he meant to kill me!'

'Not at all,' the coroner demurred. 'His orders were to watch, and keep you safe. His error was to let things go so far. For he was on the boat with you, and saw your indiscretion with the little whore; your weakness for such women, as I feared, distracts you. My man thought you deserved your lesson; which was not a judgement he was free to make. Yet you may be assured he would not have let them kill you. What he had not foreseen was that you were so supple with your sword, or should be so savage in your own response.'

'It was instinct,' Hew excused himself, 'and nothing more. I do regret the hurt I did the man.'

'Your instinct, then, is sound and quick, and should not be a matter for regret, for it has served you well. My own man fared more badly in this matter. George Hacket found him wounded in the street, and had him hanged, precipitate, for the blood that Robert Lachlan had smeared upon his coat.'

'Oh, my dear God,' murmured Hew. 'Then the poor wretch was hanged for my sword?'

'You need not waste your tears on him. For he had failed his task.'

'Aye, but to be hanged for it . . .!' Hew said, ashen-faced. 'And yet,' he countered suddenly, 'If Hacket hanged him for it, how is it that he lived to tell the tale?'

Sir Andrew laughed. 'There you have caught me out. Aye, very well, Hacket did not hang the man. He kicked him up the arse and sent him home to me. And for all the use he is to me, now banished from Campvere, he may as well have hanged.'

Hew groaned. 'I cannot tell the falsehood from the truth!'

'Indeed,' the coroner remarked, 'As I may sometimes think the same of you, without corroboration of a close intelligence. All such reports were thin, since you went south from Vlissingen. I heard you were in Antwerp, with the Prince of Orange; the devil only knows what you did there.'

'It is the devil's tale,' smiled Hew, 'that takes us somewhat crooked from our proper path.'

'Then we shall hear it presently, and move on first to Ghent. Yet tell me, if you will, how you did find the prince? In spirit and in health?'

'I found him quite remarkable. You know he has been shot?'

'So we have lately heard,' the coroner acknowledged. 'So close a violation of the person of the prince has sent a tremor that reverberates throughout the crowns of Christendom, except, of course,' he ended with a smile, 'that of our own King James, who has not been told of it, for fear that he would piss himself.'

Hew felt a prick of sympathy for James. 'Yet as I understand it,' he mentioned in defence, 'he saw his own grandfather blasted by pistol shot, when he was a mere bairn of five, and watched the old man, in the throes of his agonies, give up his life through his bowels. Then it is less remarkable to find these terrors now awakened, in a young man of sixteen.'

'Though there is truth in what you say, it is the counsel of a sad, reflective heart,' Andrew Wood returned, 'and such soft indulgences do not assist the king. For now the time is ripe for him to cease to be a bairn, and set aside his night terrors, and wild and frantic fears, that he may take control, and take a firmer grasp upon his crown. You are mistaken, I assure you, if you consider that I do not know his worth, or that, for all his weaknesses, I do not take his part,' he concluded quietly. 'No more of that; the whole town holds its breath, and waits for your report upon the windmill. Then what have you to say to us?'

Hew told him the story of the Flemish miller's gift. 'Maude Benet spoke the truth,' he verified at last, 'when she reported he was *not himself*. For though she saw it slanted, though a dark perspective glass, she saw into his heart, reflecting back, distorted, the words of Jacob's prayer. For he was Jacob Adams, a Scot, St Andrews born. His circle ended just, and as the windmill turns, it brought him to his close, where he had first begun.'

'And so,' the coroner summed up, 'the windmill, all along, was meant for us?'

'It was,' acknowledged Hew. 'Nor was there ever ill intent. For those attendant horrors we have witnessed through the town we brought upon ourselves, by force of our own greed.

'The baxters and the millers, and your brother, Robert Wood, are locked into a chain of close and common bondage that circumscribes the town, where every link is fragile, taut and strained. The balance of their power became so delicately strung, one puff of wind unsettled it. Whoever had the windmill, had power over the land, power over the elements, and power over the town. He could turn the town itself, in the blowing of the wind. Which promise was enough to persuade a man to kill for it.'

'The question is,' said Andrew Wood, 'which man?'

'As I suspect, the baxters. Who else should profit quite so much from power over the mill? Who else would force famine, sullying the grain, forcing up the prices of the bread? Who knew the grain store lock was broken, and that Gavan Lang had planned to catch the fish?'

'There are no secrets at a mill,' reflected Andrew Wood. 'And what is known to one is known to all. The baxters hide behind the banner of their gild, and keep their knowledge hidden in a multitude of locks. I cannot hang them all, else we shall have no bread. No matter, as I hope, you will flush them out, and they will start to feel the close

271

heat of their fires. Nor shall they hope to profit from their sins. The windmill will be put to common good, and held in common interest for the town, and known as Jacob's windmill, the Flemish miller's gift. The millers of the town shall work it each in turn, and no man shall make profit, more than his own share. Though I suppose there is a chance that Jacob's father, Jacob Adams, will appear to press his claim, his kinship to the miller will be hard to prove.'

'I do not count that likely,' answered Hew. 'For I can find no trace of Jacob, or James, or of any man called Adams, who is living in the town, who is of an age to have been Jacob's father. I have spoken with the man from the kirk of Holy Trinity, and he thinks it most likely that the family moved away, avoiding the scandal of a bastard birth. His parish records do not stretch so far, and he himself has only been here for the past six years.'

'You are forward, sir, in making these inquiries,' the coroner observed, 'before you came to put the case to me.'

'I wanted to be able to submit a full report,' Hew acknowledged quickly.

'Indeed. Then may I trust, that you hold nothing back?'

'You have my word,' said Hew, 'that you have seen into my heart, as I, I do believe, have seen a glimpse of yours.'

'Perhaps,' allowed the coroner. 'Yet no more than a glimpse.' He allowed himself to smile, briefly and elusively. 'Our paths will cross again. And you will know me better, as I think.'

The news spread quickly through the town that the windmill had been promised for the common good. And so it had appeared to Hew, until a few days later, he bumped into Bartie Groat. The old professor greeted him, expressing his delight, effusively and fluidly, through his pocket handkerchiefs. 'Hew! My dearest man! How very glad I am to see you safe restored from Ghent. I hope you will please me, by stepping in at suppertime, for I have long been longing to listen to your tales.'

'You do not mean tonight? The pity is . . .' Hew floundered, while he thought up an excuse, but Bartie Groat outwitted him. 'I know you do not care to take your dinners in the hall, and so I have arranged for something in my rooms, and you can have no notion, Hew, how much I have looked forward to it, for I was born in Flanders, as you know, and I have not been back there since I was a boy. According to Giles Locke, you met the Prince of Orange. The *Prince of Orange*, no less! Then will you not indulge an old man's whim?'

'Aye, very well,' sighed Hew.

'Splendid! Come at nine, when the students are in bed, and we shall have canary sack, and we shall have a pudding, and a trotter pie,' Bartie Groat enthused.

Bartie's quarters were above the dinner hall, and smelled of old mens' undershirts, cough syrups and kale. The pie was cold and heavy, and the wine was thin. The evening drew on, inch by inch, in mournful reminiscences, as Bartie wondered whether such and such a street or house or tree stood still there in its place, each hint of deviation moving him to tears. When Hew could stand no more, he said, 'The hour is late. I cannot keep you longer from your bed.'

Bartie blew his nose. 'Dear, dear. I have been so immersed in these reflections on the past that I lose sight of my interest in the present news. Do I infer correctly, that the baxters are to have their windmill after all?'

'You have not inferred correctly,' Hew answered with a groan. 'I hoped your taste for rumour and false gossip had been curbed. The windmill is sequestered to the common good, and whoever takes her turn, it will *not* be the baxters.'

'Then I am misinformed,' reported Bartie Groat, 'for I heard it spoken in the mercat and the close, that the miller's father was a man called Jacob Adams.'

'And so he was,' admitted Hew. 'And yet there is no Jacob Adams living in the town, nor any man called Adams in the baxters' gild.'

'Except, of course, James Edie,' Bartie Groat replied.

Hew gaped at him. 'Whatever do you mean?'

'My dear, it is self-evident. For Jacob is the same as James, as I am

273

sure you know. And Edie is Adie, and Adie is Adamson, and Adamson is Adams, in the Dutch. The names are cognate, Hew. As any dull boy knows, who knows his roots,' Bartie said complacently.

'James Edie!' Hew exclaimed. 'And I had no idea!'

'As I recall,' reflected Bartie Groat, 'he had a sister, Ruth, who went to live in Ghent. He told me of her once, in reverence for my fondness for the place; it was not common knowledge, as I think. He said he had not heard from her for many years, and he supposed her dead, yet he did sometimes wonder how she did. I think it more than likely that she changed her name, as is the common usage when we move abroad – as I have done myself – and Edie became Adams. When Jacob learned his father's name, he learned it in the Dutch.'

'Bartie!' Hew declared, 'you are beyond compare! Do you think James Edie is aware of this?'

Bartie blinked at him 'I think he must be, do not you? For if he had a child, and gave it to his sister, he cannot have failed to notice it. Where are you going?' he protested, as Hew made for the door.

'To speak to Jacob Adams.'

'But surely, at this hour . . . !'

'That is the beauty of the baxters,' Hew returned. 'They bake their bread by night.'

But though the ovens were ablaze in Baxters' Wynd, and the warmth of baking bread began to filter through the streets, Hew found no trace of Edie in the baxter's shop. He had gone to take his supper at Maude Benet's inn, in curious good humour, the prentice gave report, and had left no hope or promise of a quick return. Hew wandered to the shore, to find the tavern closed, and all the drinkers gone, the lantern in the doorway blown out for the night. The door was open, and Maude was still awake, sweeping out the rushes from the bar, the air behind her thick with soot and smoke.

Hew asked, 'Have you seen James Edie?"

'He is in the windmill,' answered Maude. Before Hew could reply, she had closed the door, and disappeared into the room beyond.

But then, of course, reflected Hew, for where else, after all, would

274

the baxter choose to come, to gloat upon his fortune, but to Jacob's mill? And as he looked across the gloom, he could see a trail of light, reflected in the water in the harbour by the boats, coming from the windmill on the shore. He made his way by moonlight, feeling for the door. It opened to his touch. 'James Edie?' he said softly, but James did not reply, and the sound resounded hollow through the timbers of the mill. The lantern dipped and flickered on the wooden floor, and shone its gentle light upon the baxter's face, curious, and intimate. James Edie's right hand rested on the handle of a knife, which had somehow slipped inside him, buried in his coat, as though he had that moment meant to pull it out, when he was called away. Hew lifted up his hand, sliding out the blade, and found it came quite easily, in a sticky, viscous trail. A narrow stream of blood began to bubble in its wake, welled behind the blade like the water in a dam. It was the little knife that Maude had used to slit and gut Hew's fish, when she cut out its beating heart and held it in her palm. Hew wiped the wet blade on the dead baxter's sleeve.

Though the inn was in darkness, the door was unlocked. Hew felt his way inside, and back towards the kitchen, where he replaced the fish knife in its pocket on the wall. He made, and heard, no sound. The door to Jacob's closet was ajar, and through it he observed a prick of light. Cautiously, he opened it. The shutters were half open to the moon, and Maude had left a candle burning by the bed, that cast a thoughtful shadow on her face. She sat silent by its side, with a pillow in her lap, and for a moment, Hew expected busy hands to twitch and throttle back and forth, like Beatrix at her pillow making lace, until he saw what Maude was looking at, and why she held the pillow softly in her lap, so still that not a single feather stirred. She was looking down at Lilias, in the shadow of the moon, where the moonlight spun to silk each separate, silvered strand of her daughter's flaxen hair. And Lilias, sleeping, made no breath or sound. Gib Hunter lay beside her, curled into a ball.

Maude turned to look at Hew. 'God help me, but I could not do it,' she said.

Hew made still his voice, calming the flutter he felt in his heart. 'It was because you loved her too much.'

'You are wrong,' she told him. 'It is because I did not love her enough.'

He did not know, then, whether it was Lilias or whether it was Maude, who had slid the little knife into the baxter's heart, as softly and as deftly as the scaling of a fish, and who had held the life force ebbing through her hands, and yet he knew that they must be apart. He took the pillow from Maude's lap and placed it on the bed beside the sleeping cat. 'Will you not come, now, and let the lass sleep?' he murmured.

Maude nodded, 'Aye, I will come.'

He took her by the hand, and she came meekly, like a child. They went into the bar. 'What happened here tonight?' he asked.

'He showed to me the colour of his heart,' said Maude. 'And it was black, inside. And so I took my knife, and cut into his heart, into the place the blackness was, and cut the blackness out.'

'Then do you understand that you have killed him, Maude?' Hew asked her quietly.

'I understand it, sir,' said Maude, 'And I am not ashamed of it.' And for the reason and calm with which she spoke, he did not for a moment doubt her word.

'Will you not call the watch, sir? I pray you, call the watch,' Maude pleaded.

'Will you not tell me why you did it?' answered Hew.

'Why did I kill James?' She seemed to have withdrawn into a dream, and he wondered if she really understood it. 'I killed him for he did not grieve. He did not grieve for Jacob,' Maude explained, 'for in his joy to have the windmill he forgot that he had lost as well as found a son, and he forgot to mourn for Jacob's death.'

'For Jacob was James Edie's son?' asked Hew.

'For Jacob was his son,' acknowledged Maude, 'as much as he was mine.'

Chapter 24

A Beating Heart

Maude sat with her small hands folded in her lap. Her voice was light and low. He could not have imagined her, slipping in the knife that slid between the bones into Jacob Adams' heart.

'You do not understand,' she said.

'Then tell me,' he encouraged her, 'and I will speak for you.'

'There is no purpose to it,' she demurred. 'For why would you do that?'

'Because I am a lawyer, Maude. It is what I do.' As he spoke he recognised the truth of it. Because he was an advocate, and there was no escaping it. The prospects were not good for Maude, and yet he would defend her, if he could.

'But you cannot defend me, sir,' she countered patiently. 'You cannot speak for me before the court, and if you could, you could not plead my case to God. James Edie did not hurt me; he never was unkind to me, or used me with without gentleness, and for that I loved him. I love him still,' she added poignantly.

'You and he were lovers?'

'Once,' Maude confessed. 'We never stooped to sin again, once I was wed to Ranald Begg. And yet the spark did not die out. But it was flint that was his heart. I took my knife to cut it out, and I would do the same again, for I am not afeared of it. My heart is heavy only, that I could not see to Lilias. I should have seen to Lilias. God help me, but I could not do it.

'Have pity, sir, and call the watch, before my Lilias wakes. I know that I must suffer for my sins. And yet the hours that pass must weaken my resolve, and I begin to fear for it. Have pity, sir, and send me to my fate.'

'Aye, but in a while. Will you not tell me, Maude, what was it made you do it?' Hew persisted. If he could defend her, make a case . . . for Maude did not deserve to die, he thought. For surely, there was more, and Maude did not deserve to die. Yet in his heart, he knew the rigours of the law.

'It is a wretched tale,' said Maude. 'And you must judge me for it; do not look so kindly, sir, I beg you. I cannot thole the kindness, for it cuts me to the quick, when I deserve your scorn. The truth is, that I fell with child, when I was but a lass.'

'And the child was James Edie's?' Hew questioned. The child was Jacob Molenaar, as he supposed. The windmill turned full circle, brought the miller back to the place where he begin. He shivered. Was there not a magic after all, a dark and deeper providence, in this?

Maude admitted, 'Aye, it was. And James Edie set his mind to do the best for me, for all he could not marry me, for that he was not free.'

'He had a wife already,' Hew supposed.

'His wife is Ann Honeyman.' She lingered in the present tense, as though she took some comfort in the telling of his tale, that kept him close to life. 'Ann is cousin to the present Patrick, deacon of the gild, and a plain and shrewish woman, like him in her way. James did not marry her for love, nor for her looks, but for her father, George.'

'He married her for money, then?' asked Hew.

'For money, aye,' acknowledged Maude. 'He married her, though he loved me. And I was steeped in sin so deep I did not let his marriage bar the way.'

'And neither, I infer, did he,' Hew commented.

'He was ensnared,' Maude answered simply. 'I was seventeen, and he was twenty three, and when I fell with his child. James did what he could. He had a cousin, Ranald Begg, who was in his debt, and

James discharged the debt, in asking him to marry me. The world would ken the bairn as Ranald Begg's, and Ranald Begg and I would have the haven inn, as recompense, he said. But Ranald was a sleutcher and a sot; to gie a drunk a tavern was the worst thing he could do. Twas on our wedding night that he first raised his fists to me, and cursed the day that he was bound to raise a bastard child. James Edie saw me black and bruised, and he was vexed and shamed, and sent his sister Ruth when I was close confined, and she was fine and kind with me, that I did not deserve.'

'His sister, Ruth,' repeated Hew.

'Aye, sir. And the word means pity, does it not?' Maude reflected sadly. 'She was kind to me. She married late, and had no babbies of her own, and yet she held my hand, and nursed me through those desperate hours, when I came close to God. And when my James was born, I held him in my arms but once, and fell into a sickness so intense I did not know myself for days. And when I came to life again, she told me that my little boy had died.'

'Dear God!' said Hew. 'They told you that your child was dead!'

'They telt me that, and worse, for the minister colluded in it – that was not the Reverend Traill, that we have now, but the man that came before him. For when I first fell with child, James Edie went to him, and wept, and he made bitter penance on the cauld flair of the kirk, and bought the Lord's forgiveness wi' the baxter's purse. He repented privately, and was spared from public shame. My punishment was Ranald Begg. The minister told me that he had cast my infant in the common pit, without name or sacrament, as did befit the bastard, of a common whore. He telt me that God knew me, and all those women like me, that the devil sent them to lead good men astray. My boy had gone to Hell. And that was all the comfort that I had.'

She showed him no emotion in the telling of the tale. The devil and his kirk had wrung the tears from Maude.

'He told you a lie; a most terrible wickedness, Maude,' whispered Hew.

'I doubt it broke my heart,' she answered simply. 'For I knew not what kind of God would send a child to Hell. But that was the minister's ain wee special twist, and not James Edie's fault, that I cannot blame him for. And I will not reproach him that he took the bairn away, for what sort of a life would it have had with Ranald Begg? He took him as a kindness to us all, or so he said, and very likely that was true.'

'Yet it does not excuse the cruelty of the lie.'

'The strange thing is,' said Maude, 'that all these years, I have blamed Ranald Begg. For I thought that it was his bitterness to me that made my body weak, and that it was his cruelness caused my bairn to die. And I hated him after, and pushed him away, and mebbe if I had been kinder to him, he would not have been so cruel to me.'

'You must not think like that, Maude, for you were ill-used,' Hew objected fiercely.

'Aye. And yet I think that Ranald Begg was blameless of that hurt to me, whatever he did after. I think he thought, with me, that my wee boy was dead. For it was only then he showed a moment's kindness – putting out his great thick clumsy clummock of a hand, to stroke my hair, and I blamed him, in my grief, for our common helplessness, and pushed his hand away. Then he was wraith and ragit, and stamped and stormed and roared, and yet he did not vent his wrath on me, but turned instead on Ruth. He ordered her to go, and quit his house. And so she did. And neither I nor James Edie ever saw her again, for shortly after she left Scotland with her man, and they went to Ghent.'

'I do not know if it can bring you comfort, now,' said Hew, 'yet I can tell you, truly, that they loved that child.'

'It does,' admitted Maude. 'And James was right. I do not know what might have happened to him, had the bairn remained. For Ranald Begg and I were never friends thereafter; he was cold and cruel.'

'Then what of Lilias?' wondered Hew.

'Lilias was forced upon me,' Maude concluded quietly. 'She is the bairn of Ranald Begg, and Lilias had the worst of him. And yet, you will allow, I did not love her less for that.'

'And all this you found out, tonight?'

'Tonight,' accepted Maude.

'And so it was for that, you took your knife and stilled the baxter's heart?'

'No, sir, as I telt you, it was not for that,' insisted Maude. 'It was not because he took my bairn, and told me he had died. And it was not because of Ranald Begg. It was because . . . James was in the room with me when Jacob Miller died.' She did not call him Edie, noticed Hew. 'He watched me take him in my arms, where I felt still the flutter of his heart and whisper of his breath. And he and I together saw our lost son die, not knowing he was ours, that God had brought back home to us. He came here mad with joy tonight, with avarice, and greed, to have his heart's desire, and in his joy forgot, that he had lost a son.

'James Edie let glimpse to me the colour of his soul, and that was something he had never done. His soul was blackened, through and through, like Jacob Miller's hands. All I had to do was swear before the coroner that Jacob was our son, and the windmill would be his. He did not care for Jacob, or for the men that died, for all that he had done, to have it in his grasp, he did not need to do it for it was his, all along.'

'Did he confess to you, the things that he had done,' Hew urged, 'to have it in his grasp. Did he tell you, Maude?'

'He said no more than that. "Imagine, Maude! For all that I have done, she always had been mine." I was mad with grief, and James was mad with joy. He bid me come out to the mill, to see what he had won. And so I brought my knife and stopped his wicked heart. And he saw what I had done, for he said *Maude!* reproachful, soft, and vexed – for he was never cruel to me – as if to say, *you silly wench, I cannot help you now*, and then he died.

'And so you see, sir, what they said was true, for Jacob did die twice. I lost him as a bairn, and God returned him home to me, that I might see him die again.'

'He died here, in his mother's arms,' Hew concluded fiercely. 'And in his heart, he knew it, Maude.'

He walked towards the window looking out, towards the moonlit shadows of the mill.

'I think, sir, it is time,' said Maude. 'I pray you, do not let the sun break on this fear. Be quick, and kind, I beg you, call the watch.'

'In a moment.' He was thinking. 'Suppose there were another way to put the matter right? Suppose we did not have to call the watch?'

'There is no other way, for I have sinned, and so I must atone for it. Yet do not pity me, for I am not afraid to die. My fear is but for Lilias, that she will be alone,' considered Maude.

'She will not be alone,' insisted Hew. 'Do you have guests tonight?'

'Aye, sir. They are all asleep. The harbour is awake before the dawn, and men do not sit drinking through the night, but save their spirits for the waking hours.'

'And Elspet, too?'

'Sleeping, in the lassies' sleeping loft. She works hard, and she is glad enough to find her rest at night. But why, sir, do you ask?'

He took her by the hand. 'If you will trust me, Maude, then I will find a way to put this matter right. And I will find a way for you to make your peace with God.'

She looked at him, wide-eyed. 'And how will you do that?'

'As it began with water, let it end with fire.'

Hew took with him spirit and light; a lantern of glass and aquavitae in a little flask, tapped from the keg at the inn. The spirit he sprinkled on James Edie's clothes, the slit in his jacket now stiffened and black, and let the drops follow the course of his blood. The residue he poured onto the wooden floor, diluting the spots where the dark blood had pooled. Hew broke the baxter's grip, and twined the fingers close around the empty flask. It must look as though James Edie had passed out from the drink, for he could not shape the corpse to mimic self-defence, as though the baxter had attempted to escape the creeping flame. Outside the windmill, not a breath of air stirred, to ripple the reflection of the clear light of the moon. The flame would catch the spirit that had laced the baxter's clothes, and catch the wooden windmill like the flaring of a match; the baxter's heart of flint would set alight the tinderbox and burn away the trace of Maude's small fillet knife, that found its way so easily, into that blackened heart, that turned out after all to be but flesh and blood. As Hew held out the flame it caught the wink of gold, the small sheaf of wheat pinned to James Edie's hat. It was, considered Hew, the one small mark of vanity that showed the baxter's soul, that lifted him above the commonplace, and likely would survive the fierce heat of the fire. And at the last, or so he hoped, the little pin of gold was all that would be left, to notify the coroner how its owner died. He watched the flame ignite the baxter's cloak, and lap around the trail of spirit, seeping deep and pale into the baxter's heart. He let the lantern drop, and kicked it on its side, and watched it lap and smoulder, taking hold. The baxter's eyes were open, like the smooth eye of the fish. Hew did not allow himself to look upon the face, but he thought instead of Maude, of Lilias, asleep, and turning like the whirligig; and Gavan Lang, his blue cheek punctured by the eel; of Henry Cairns the miller weeping on his knees; of Sandy Kintor's smile, carved with Henry's spade. He heard again James Edie asking, 'What has happened to his face?' All pity for the baxter fled, as Hew made fast the door. He stood a little back, to watch the blaze take hold, and let the flames engrave its outline on the sky. The wind itself rose up, and wrought its last revenge upon the wooden mill.

Chapter 25

A Welshman's Hose

'So,' said Andrew Wood, 'this conflagration brings an end to all our hopes of a windmill for the town.'

'I fear it does,' acknowledged Hew. 'Yet as I understand, the burgh council has resolved to purchase one, to serve the common good. It may take some while to raise the funds.'

'Then if it concentrates the common mind upon the common good, it may not be a bad thing after all,' the coroner reflected.

'As I think too, if it is to be come by honestly.'

'Then to come back to your report,' Andrew Wood said critically. 'You say that you met James Edie on the night that he died, and that you saw him go into the windmill, with a bottle and a lamp, and that you found him in a wild and frantic state of mind?'

'I did,' accepted Hew. 'And had I understood the meaning of it then, I should have stopped him. Yet I did not understand it, which were a dereliction that I do regret.'

'We cannot be called to account, for what we do not understand,' observed the coroner.

'I suppose not,' answered Hew. 'And I thank you, for that is some comfort.'

'Is it?' said the coroner. 'It is not meant as one. And James Edie told you that he laid claim to the windmill, for he was Jacob Adams. What did you think to this?'

'I thought he was delusional, through overuse of drink. For there was no doubt, in my eyes, that he was both excessively drunk, and in a high state of excitement.'

'Indeed. And so you gave no credence to his claim that Jacob was his son?'

'I thought, sir, that it was something that James Edie had made up, in the hopes of securing the windmill, either to himself or to the baxters' gild. I did not then understand the full force of his delusions, or the lengths that he had gone to, to fulfil them.'

'A second matter, that you did not understand.'

'As I do fear,' said Hew apologetically.

'And there exists no evidence that Edie ever was the father of a bastard child?'

'None at all,' said Hew. And this was very true, for James Edie had taken great care to cover up his tracks. The evidence that he had had, the only hope to prove his claim, was Maude.

'And I suppose he gave no intimation who the mother was?'

'How could he, sir?' said Hew. 'When he was not the father of the child?'

The coroner considered this. 'Yet whatever had persuaded him, in midst of his delusions, that he could press his claim to be Jacob Adams?'

'I am very much afraid,' said Hew, 'that it was Bartie Groat, who pointed out that to him that Adams and Edie are cognate. Coincidence, perhaps, but scarcely an uncommon one. It seems I share my surname with the millstone at the mill, yet I do not suppose myself the miller's son. Yet it was enough, in his madness, to persuade James Edie of his right to have the mill.'

'Bartie Groat, again! Tis time a bit was put under his tongue, and he went out to to pasture,' Andrew Wood declared. 'Then I suppose, James Edie had no sister, Ruth?'

'Not as I have heard.' As Hew had heard from Maude, Ruth Edie was a half-sister, and older than her brother by some twenty years, and since another twenty years had passed since she had died, her life had passed unmarked. Except, of course, by Bartie Groat.

'And he made some wild intimations to you, in passing to the mill, that had he known all this before, then he need not have acted as he did – is that correct?'

'Something of the sort,' conceded Hew. 'Yet his words were slurred, and far less carefully expressed.'

'Which after, you did take to be confession of his guilt, that he was at the least, complicit in these crimes, yet at the time, you say again, you had not understood?'

'That is correct. For he was very drunk, and swaggering, I took small notice of him in his cups, other to suggest he should go home.'

'Which now, of course, you do regret?'

Hew conceded with a smile.

'And then – if I have understood you well, you went to see Maude Benet in her inn, and stayed to talk with her – how long, would you say?'

'An hour, perhaps? No more,' suggested Hew.

'And coming out, you saw the windmill was on fire, whereupon you called the watch, and tried to put it out?'

'I did. I had no notion, then, that he was still inside.'

'And how do you suppose this conflagration came about?'

'A dry mill wrought of wood, a drunk man drinking spirits, and an uncovered lamp,' said Hew. 'It is not so very hard to see, how it might come about.'

'Quite so,' said Andrew Wood. 'Then may I ask, why you had come so late, to speak to Maude.'

'In truth,' said Hew, 'it was never my intent to stay late to speak with Maude. I came down to the shore, looking for James Edie, for so I had been told that I might find him there.' The closer to the truth, he thought, the easier the lie, and the less the risk that he would be found out.

'And why to speak to him?'

'For I had learned from Bartie Groat the silly stuff that turned James Edie's head, and so I had resolved to offer some advice. But finding him so deep in drink, that he knew little sense, I left him in his cups. I saw the inn was open still, and since I had a gift for Maude, I stayed to give it to her.'

'Aye? What was this gift?'

'It was a gift of Flemish lace, that Jacob's wife had sent her, for the comfort she had given when her husband died. And Maude, as women do, had many questions, and she would hear about the beguinage, and Lotte, and the Flemish nuns; and so an hour did pass, before I could depart from her.'

'When you did see the windmill up in flames?'

'Aye, sir, as I said.'

The coroner stood thoughtful for a moment. At length he said, 'You give a clear account.'

'That is my intent,' acknowledged Hew.

'Quite so.' Sir Andrew smiled. 'And yet I have another version of events. I think you will not like it, Hew.'

'Pray tell me, what it is?' Hew asked, afraid that he would not like it at all.

'I think there was a magic in the windmill after all, and that when James Edie crossed it, it did wreak revenge. For I care little for your nuns, your beguinage in Ghent. The windmill brought dissension from its first day in the town, when first it was discovered, miraculously unharmed, it blighted and destroyed. The mill was evil, through and through, and never meant for us, Sickness, madness, slaughter, fire, death by drowning, pestilence! What others horrors were in store? Thank God that she is gone!'

'I . . . I had not thought of that,' admitted Hew. He felt a little weak about the knees.

'I know that you had not. For you are philosophical, and neither you nor Doctor Locke will ever willingly admit that you were wrong. The windmill is no longer, and there the matter ends.'

'Though I cannot agree with you, I cannot help but think you may be right,' said Hew, who found himself equivocal from sheer force of relief.

'I know that I am right,' the coroner replied. 'And to conclude the case, there is but one thing to be done. The corpus must be given to Giles Locke, to ascertain the cause of death.'

'Oh!' Hew stammered, with a jolt. 'It was so badly burned. Do you think that necessary?'

Sir Andrew answered shrewdly, 'Oh, I do think so. Don't you?'

There was now no time to waste, and Hew returned to Kenly Green at once, where he found Robert Lachlan playing chess with Nicholas, a curiously incongruous sight, that brought a brief distraction from the trouble that they faced. He took Nicholas aside.

'What do you think?'

'I think that he plays well.'

'He has a chequered past.'

'Have not we all? He has seen horrors, Hew,' Nicholas said quietly.

'He does not speak of them,' said Hew.

'Nonetheless, he has seen them. He will not settle here.'

Hew called Robert out, and took him privately to walk in Meg's walled garden, where the branches now were bare. 'Has the factor offered you a piece of land?'

The soldier nodded, 'Aye.'

'And a house?'

'He has offered me a house,' Robert answered glumly.

'And yet, it seems, they do not suit?'

'The land and house are fine. Tis only that . . . it is the wintertime, and there is nothing left to do upon the land. And it is that . . . you do not need me here. I had not thought the life would be . . . bare fields and books, and playing chess.'

'That is your retirement, Robert,' Hew said with a smile. 'I think, perhaps, you are not ready for it yet.'

'I have made a mistake, sir. I am not ready quite, for giving up the soldiering. Will you not release me from my bonds?' Robert asked.

'What bonds? You are a free man, Robert, to go where you will. This land I give you as a gift. Tis not meant as a prison. Tis possible that one day still you may be glad of it, and it will then be here for you; go then, where you will. Yet I would have you do a service for me, one last thing, before you go. It is a lot to ask. I wish you to return to Ghent.'

'To Ghent!' Robert groaned. 'From where we have just come!'

In spite of his objections, he did not seem too displeased.

'I beg you, do not question it. I want you to take Maude.'

'Maude Benet, from the inn?'

Hew nodded, 'And her little lass. I cannot tell you why. But I will give you letters for the beguinage. Tis there that you must take them, and leave them with the nuns.'

Robert shook his head, 'I beg you, not the nuns, for now you ask too much!'

'Patience, there is more,' warned Hew. 'I fear you will not like it.'

'I do not like it now,' the soldier grumbled.

'It is a lot to ask. But if Maude is to travel with you, she must be your wife.'

Robert stared at Hew. 'You're asking me to marry her?'

'I trust you do not have a wife already?' queried Hew.

'I am forty-four, and have never had a wife.'

'Then that is fortunate.'

'Is it? There are reasons for it.'

'Keep them to yourself,' said Hew. 'And think it, as a marriage of convenience.'

'And supposing it is not convenient?'

'I will make it so.'

'Fair enough,' said Robert. 'In truth, she is a comely wench. And I could well be settled in an inn.'

'That is *not* the plan. They will go with you to Ghent. And you will see them settled at the beguinage.'

'A pity. It is just my luck, that I must be married to a nun!' said Robert gloomily. 'Still, I doubt that it might not work out. The daughter, too, is skeich. Suppose that I should want to settle down, and take another wife,' he suddenly objected.

'It would prove no impediment. The marriage will be null, for want of consummation; and you may be assured, that it will *not* be consummated,' answered Hew.

'I somehow feared as much,' said Robert. 'And when the deed is done, what do I next?'

'Then you are your own man, and that is up to you.'

'Is that so? And suppose that I fetch up one night, and come to Kenly Green, to chance my arm with Nicholas at chess, that offer of a place would stand?'

'When you are ready, aye.'

'Should you find you want a man, to drag you from the mire, and rescue you from bandits or the Inquisition?'

'I cannot rule out that possibility,' admitted Hew.

'Then I will consider it, and let you know my answer in due course. Meanwhile, I will want some wedding clothes,' said Robert.

A few days after, coming to see Meg, Hew saw Clare Buchanan turning from the house, seemingly in tears. He hurried in to Meg. 'Why has Clare been crying?' he demanded.

'I cannot tell you that, Hew! How can you think to ask?' Meg answered in astonishment.

'I thought it might be George,' said Hew, by way of an excuse.

'It is not George. George is whole and well, and safe returned to college. Clare came to see me on a personal matter,' Meg replied oppressively.

'How so, as a patient?'

'A *personal* matter, Hew!'

'Aye, then, wait a moment!' Hew broke off. He ran out to the street. Clare stood listlessly, looking out to sea, by the old kirk of St Mary on the rock. She was no longer weeping, but her eyes were bright with tears.

'Mistress, I am thankful to have caught you. My sister Meg forgot to give you this this.' He handed her a packet of nun's lace, which he had brought for Meg. 'How beautiful!' she cried, 'but why would Meg have thought to give me this?'

'I brought it back from Flanders, and Meg has far too much of it, and thought that it would bring you better cheer.'

'Oh!' said Clare. 'Did she say that? But why should she say that?'

''In truth, she broke no confidence,' Hew assured her hurriedly, 'But are you of out of cheer?'

Clare smiled at him. 'Not now. It is a lovely thought. And yet I am afraid that I cannot accept it, for while it is most gracious, her gift is undeserved,' she answered carefully.

'I pray that you will not offend, in turning down her gift,' said Hew.

'Oh! Then I see I must not. In truth, I do not mean to cause offence. Tis only that the gift was . . . unexpected. This simple act of kindness brings me close to tears,' Clare replied inaudibly.

'The best gifts are the unexpected ones, for they come from the heart,' insisted Hew. 'I saw this lace where it was made by sisters in the convents; this one small corner takes a day to make, that would not make a corner for a pocket handkerchief.'

'It is exquisite fine,' accepted Clare. 'And you may tell your sister I will treasure it, and wear it next my heart. I thank you, Hew, for you have cheered me up.'

'Then I have done my task.' He bowed to her. 'My sister will be pleased.'

He was whistling as he went back to the house.

'Whatever is the matter, Hew?' Meg demanded. 'Do you come or stay?'

'That is a fine way to talk, when I have brought you news, and presents, too, from Ghent,' Hew flopped down carelessly into the gossip chair. 'And how is Matthew Locke,' he quizzed the sleeping bairn, 'still pent in swathes of cloth?'

'He is asleep, and well content, that you do not disturb him or rouse him to your boisterousness,' said Meg. 'What news?'

'How like you! You must wait for it, for first we have the presents. Here, for Giles, an optic glass, and here for you, some lace. And Matthew has a linen cap, and yet I see that he is wearing three of them already, and a little knitted jougs to lock him to his crib. Perhaps he should have the optic, and Giles the linen cap, to keep for his old age.'

'What piffle you talk,' Meg answered fondly, opening out the packet. 'This is beautiful, Hew.'

'It comes from the begijnhof. And you have given some to Clare,' Hew mentioned.

Meg let the parcel drop. 'What have you done?'

'I have cheered her up.'

'What were you thinking of? You cannot give her gifts. For she is married, Hew!'

'Which is why,' he told her, 'the gift comes from you. Hush then, and let it rest. The thing is done, forgotten in the corner of a hand-kerchief. You make a woman's fuss, over a scrap of lace. I had not thought you were the jealous kind. Enough of these trifles,' Hew moved smoothly. 'To the news. Now this is like to please you. The harbour inn is to be sold, and Maude to marry Robert Lachlan, and travel with him overseas.'

'Maude is going to marry *Robert Lachlan*,' echoed Meg.

'Aye,' Hew smiled glibly, 'isn't it marvellous!'

'Yes . . . no! She hardly knows the man. And he is a mercenary, Hew.'

'Retired,' corrected Hew.

'And he is taking them to *Ghent*? Isn't there a war on?'

'It will be an adventure for them. Be happy for her, Meg. It is what she wants.'

As soon as Giles appeared, Meg assailed him crossly, 'Hew is quite impossible. I wish that you would talk to him, or else prescribe a purgative, for he has lost his wits.'

The doctor did not break into his usual smile. 'Indeed, I wish to talk to him,' he mentioned ominously.

'Then talk,' Hew suggested. 'I am here.'

'Not here, but in private, at the college.'

'That sounds very serious,' said Hew.

'It is serious.'

'Then I am summoned, like one of your students. Am I in trouble?' asked Hew.

'Sincerely, I do hope not. Later, at the college.' Giles turned his back, and abruptly left the room.

Meg stared at Hew. 'That is quite unlike him. What is it you have done?'

'He has not told you?' murmured Hew.

'He has not said a word.'

'I think that it is likely he has found something out, that I hoped to have kept from him,' Hew responded thoughtfully.

'But why would you keep secrets from him? He is your friend.'

'He is far more,' Hew leant down, and kissed her. 'And that, in truth, is why. I best had go and find out what he wants.'

The doctor's presence, as ever, seemed to fill the turret tower. Hew knocked and entered, with more sense of sadness than of apprehension. 'I am here, as summoned. What is the matter, Giles?'

Giles set down his pen. 'I have sent my report to the coroner, on James Edie's death,' he said bluntly.

'Ah,' said Hew.

'I have said that he died in the fire. It is a lie.'

'Is it?' asked Hew, with a look of surprise. 'What cause had you to lie?'

'It is a lie, because James Edie died from a puncture to the heart, that was small but deep. The fire was set to mask the tracks. It almost did.'

'If that is the truth,' Hew answered evenly, 'then why should you not tell it?'

'I do not care a jot that you lied before the coroner,' insisted Giles. 'But you have lied to me. To *me*.'

293

The words hung heavy in the air. Giles asked, 'Did you kill James Edie, Hew?'

Hew answered. 'I did not.'

'And yet you covered up the crime.'

'I am afraid I did,' admitted Hew. 'It was for Maude.'

Giles listened, head in hands, as his friend explained. 'You trusted Robert Lachlan,' he replied at last, 'yet you could not trust me?'

'It was not a question of trust,' answered Hew. 'I could not implicate you in my crime. You have Matthew, and Meg, to consider.'

'But do you not see, I am implicated, Hew? I have made a false report,' objected Giles.

'I did not ask you to,' insisted Hew. 'I hoped and prayed you would not see the flaw. And if you saw it, then I wanted to be sure that you were free, to make an honest record of your finds.'

'And how could I do that, when I saw through your deception, Hew? When it was *you*?'

'You should have done it, Giles. You should do it, still.'

'And what would happen then?'

'I would take my stand in court, and defend the charge against her; or, if so required, against myself,' said Hew.

'You were prepared to stand against me in court, and to perjure yourself?' Giles asked.

'It did not come to that.'

'You covered up a crime.'

'What good would it serve,' Hew argued, 'to have let Maude hang? What would have become of Lilias?'

The doctor shook his head. 'I do not know what to say to you, Hew. What happens to them now? Maude is to be married, as you say, to Robert Lachlan.'

'That is a subterfuge, to allow them passage out of Scotland and overseas, and to ensure their safety. Robert will take them to the begijnhof in Ghent, where Maude will atone for the murder she has done, by living out her days in Christian piety. It will be her penance. Yet it will be much more than that. For Lilias will be safe, and loved, and free to roam inside the walls without the fear or threat of men, and Maude will have the solace of her grandchild, Jacob's child, and may bring a little comfort to his wife. Would you rather see her hang?'

'Of course, I would not. But to take the law in your hands . . .'

'Nor law, but justice, Giles, for law would little serve her in this case.'

'Be careful, Hew,' Giles warned. 'For law belongs to man, and justice comes from God.'

'To whom Maude will devote herself. I know it was not right,' defended Hew. 'But I could think of nothing else. No matter what James Edie did, the law does not excuse the fact that Maude deprived him of his life. Nor could she hope for mercy from Sir Andrew Wood, for he would hang his brother, if he could. And what compassion then for Maude? The law for him is black or white; the case is clear against her. James Edie was a murderer, and yet there are no proofs to indict him, saving Maude's own word. And who gives heed to that? Then nothing were more certain, than that Maude would hang. And what would profit then, or become of Lilias? God help me, Giles, I know that it was wrong, but I could see no other way.'

'You could have come to me,' Giles informed him quietly. 'As you have always come to me, your brother and your friend.'

'But do you not see? I went to Robert Lachlan, because he is a man for hire. He follows the way of the wind. You have Meg and Matthew. It is too much to lose. Oh, do not turn away from me! I cannot bear it, Giles!'

The wedding was a quiet one. There were no flowers or banquets at the inn, no bitterns, quails or peacock legs to make a wedding feast. Robert wore his new wool coat, and Maude had edged her cap with Flemish lace. Lilias wore winter pansies, and a ribbon sent by Meg. Hew had not seen his sister since his talk with Giles. He had moved out of college and returned to Kenly Green. Though

295

Nicholas was calm and kind, Hew could not confide in him. He felt an aching loneliness. Early one morning in the first week of December he saw the couple off, on the last ship from St Andrews before the winter dearth. The air was crisp and clear, and already brought a frost, that shimmered cool and fragile in the morning light. Robert, Maude and Lilias were waiting by the shore. Robert held a basket that swayed and mewed pathetically, and struggled to retain it in his grasp.

'So Gib is going too,' Hew smiled.

'The lass would not be parted from it,' Robert murmured grimly. 'God knows, you owe me for this!'

'Quite right,' answered Hew. 'For what could be more useful than a cat, both aboard the ship and at the beguinage? Gib Hunter will like it in Ghent. He will be a Flemish cat, and chase the Flemish mice,' he said to Lilias.

Lilias said, '*Ghent*. Will I like it there too?'

'You will like it best of all,' he promised her, 'because within the walls, you can go where you please, and you can make your whirli-gigs, with no one to make eyes at you. And as I have a nephew, you will have a niece. Lotte is her name, and she has flaxen hair, and pale blue eyes like you.'

Gib Hunter gave a melancholy yowl. ''Tis likely he will settle on the ship,' said Maude.

Robert snorted. 'Aye, well, we had best be off. Come then, little lass . . . and wife,' he added awkwardly.

'This marriage is annulled, you say, as soon as we arrive in Ghent?' he repeated anxiously to Hew.

'As soon as they are settled in the convent,' Hew agreed. 'For no man can be forced to stay married to a nun.'

'I will take them to the gate, and that is all,' Robert Lachlan warned. 'I shall not step a foot inside the nunnery.'

'Your fear of nuns, I see, is absolute,' said Hew. 'Ask for Mother Ursula. She will see to all. I have no doubt they will be loved, and welcomed there. Though it will take a while to learn the Dutch, the nuns are keen to teach, and Maude is quick to learn. And Lilias will have a freedom she has never known.'

Maude said, 'I am afeared, sir. You send me to a land of windmills. Always, I will think of him, and what it was I did to him. What sort of life is that?'

'I hope that you may find your peace. I know no other way to save you, Maude. Forgive me, for I saw no other way,' the plea was half to her, and half to God.

'Well, sir,' Robert said, ''tis time.'

Hew held out his hand. 'God speed you, Robert. Do not fear the nuns. For it is a brave thing that you do.'

'Brave?' Robert gazed at him through narrow, searching eyes. 'It would take more than a trip to the nunnery to clear my conscience of its sins – and before you ask it, I do have a conscience.'

'That I have never doubted,' answered Hew.

Robert offered Lilias his hand and helped her climb into the little lighter craft, laying down the basket with Gib Hunter in her lap. Gib seemed to settle at the murmur of her voice; she crooned a little song to him. Hew knew not what the wind would bring them, but he hoped it would be peace. Robert had returned for Maude, who bowed down her head, and stepped into the boat, without once looking back. Hew watched them till the little craft had landed by the ship and three small figures climbed upon the deck. The wind was light and cold, the day was fair to sail, as the first pale trails of sunlight rose across the bay. Hew shivered. Maybe, in an hour or two, he would call on Meg.

Giles had woken early, and was standing by the crib, looking at the infant in the moon's faint fading light.

'Do you think he has my eyes?'

'He has your eyes,' Meg humoured him. 'Now let him close them. Leave him to his rest.'

'He has your brother's chin,' persisted Giles, 'I hope he will not prove as stubborn.'

'Are you angry with Hew still?' asked Meg.

'You know that I am not.'

'Giles, come back to bed.'

He lay down on the counterpane, and allowed her head to settle on his shoulder. Absently, he stroked her hair. 'Would you kill for Matthew?' he inquired.

'In a heartbeat, if I had to.'

'So would I.'

They were a moment silent. Then Meg asked, 'What are we to do with Hew?'

'Hhm? Should we be doing something?'

'He means to fall in love again.'

'Then that is to the good. Though I had not remarked it.'

'He means to fall in love with Clare Buchanan.'

'Ah. Then not so good.' conceded Giles. 'But there is nothing we can do. You know as well as I, that your brother will not listen to the counsel of his friends. He has a head for danger, and must see it out.'

'Then you are both alike.'

'Do you think so?' Giles considered. 'I suppose there's truth in that. Do you mind it, Meg? You never did before. But things are different now. We have a child.'

'It makes a difference, aye. But I do not mind it much. So long as you come home to us,' Meg murmured sleepily. 'You make our world complete.'

Giles gazed at her, and at the sleeping bairn. 'Then I am well content. For in my eyes, you make the world.'